DECIDE to HOPE

JUNE A. CONVERSE

Printed in the United States of America

First Printing, 2018

ISBN-13: 978-1983706431
ISBN-10: 1983706434

June A. Converse
Sandy Springs, Georgia

www.JuneConverse.com

*To my husband
because you are in my corner, I find the strength to face each day*

CONTENTS

Hope is being able to see that there is light
despite all the darkness.
~ Desmond TuTu

COURTNEY

Kathleen stepped on the top step, shook the sand from her sandals and forced herself to walk the few feet to her front door. Placing her forehead against it, she fumbled for the keys buried in her pocket and breathed in the salty humid air. With the moon obscured behind storm clouds, she had to use her index finger to guide the key into the first lock. The first click helped slow her heart rate. "Almost safe," she breathed into the wind. Click. Click. Every time a lock slid open, her heart rate decreased.

A loud clap of thunder shook the boards underneath her feet. Startled, her fingers opened and the keys thunked to the deck. She spun around in time to see the lightning streak above the ocean. "Lighting," she whispered at the evidence of nature's power. "Lighting," she said again before she crushed the smile that threatened to form. Another boom vibrated through her body. Another flash brightened the sky.

Forgetting for just a minute her need to get inside and hide, she allowed one of the doors in her mind to slide open. The Before Door. Against the increasing wind, she gripped the headscarf she always wore and moved toward the lounger nestled in the corner of her deck. After settling back in the cushion, she tipped her face to the storm moving in her direction. While she slowly unwound the scarf, a memory seeped into her consciousness.

"Mommy, please come inside," her four-year-old pleaded. "Daddy, the lighting is gonna struck her. Make her come in." The round face squished against the glass door. All ten fingers created sweaty evidence of the girl's fear.

"It's light*ning*, not lighting," she corrected for the hundredth time. "I'm fine, Honey. I like the lightning. I'll come in before the rain hits. Go cuddle with Daddy. I'll be there in a few minutes."

Courtney stuck out her tongue and danced it across the glass until the next blast of thunder sent her scurrying to Seth's lap. Even from a distance of twenty years, Kathleen heard the frustration as her daughter settled into her father's lap.

Kathleen traced the rough edges of skin normally hidden by the scarf. "I'm sorry I made you stop saying 'lighting' and 'struck'," she said, turning to the empty lounger beside her. In her mind's eye Kathleen saw the gorgeous young lady tighten her ponytail and harrumph. She imagined the words her daughter would say. "Mom, please, you're worrying about stupid stuff again. I can't be twenty-four years old and still saying 'lighting' and 'struck'. I already get made fun of for this southern accent you saddled me with."

Kathleen closed her eyes and reached over the space between the two chairs. Her fingers traced the iron armrest, pretending it was Courtney's arm. She made believe she could touch her daughter. She acted out a conversation that could never occur.

"It smells here," the mirage said.

"That's the storm stirring up the sea life. You smell the ocean." Holding the image behind closed eyes, Kathleen pulled the scent into her nostrils. Salt. Sand. Marine life.

"Why did you choose this beach?"

Keeping her eyes closed and the picture intact, Kathleen said, "Because I hoped you'd visit."

"I'll come anytime you want. We all will. You just have to let us in."

The person and the dream sat in silence as Kathleen continued to stroke the armrest.

"Did you do it today?"

The sad sigh emerged all the way from Kathleen's stomach. "No."

In Kathleen's imagination, she listened as Courtney shuffled to sit upright. Courtney crossed her legs and settled her arms over her chest. "Mom, do I have to make you pinkie swear?" An imaginary arm pushed out with a pinkie extended.

"Pinkie swear," Kathleen whispered into the wind. She lifted her arm and her pinkie. "I swear I'll plant one plant before the end of the week." She wiggled her small finger, continuing to pretend her daughter's skin touched hers.

"Remember, Mom. Pinkie swears are sacred. I've had to do a lot of crap because of this."

With her finger still moving in the empty air, she answered, "I know. This week. One plant. Do you have one in mind?"

"That's your area of expertise." The sweet voice paused and added, "Things are going to get better. The days will get easier."

Kathleen dropped her hand, letting her fingers trail on the deck. "I don't think so."

"You used to tell me I had to do my share. Well, back at ya. You have to try harder."

A new boom of thunder catapulted Kathleen into the present moment. Jerking her hand back, she watched one more stripe of lightning play across the darkness. With the same pinkie, she traced the path of the lightning. "I don't want to try."

Swiping the single tear that trickled down her face, she laced the scarf through her fingers and moved back to the door. In the utter darkness of the porch she groped on the deck until she found the keys. Three more clicks, and she entered her version of safety.

Once inside, she stood in the darkness, not needing to look at the pictures to know where one of Courtney hung. Top row. Third from the left. A black-haired pixie-sized toddler popped out of the water with a huge snaggletooth grin. "I hoped you'd visit, but I can't let you in," she repeated to the empty room. She slid all the locks back into place. Dragging the scarf behind her, she moved to her bedroom.

As she went through her bedtime routine, she slammed the door on the past. She climbed into bed, burrowed into her pillow, and waited for sleep to relieve her.

Bolting awake, she clamped her knuckles in her mouth to stop the scream for help. Dropping to her knees, she began her nightly crawl across the cement floor. Tucking herself deep into the corner of her closet, she rested her head on her shoes, forcing her breathing to slow. Phantom pain began at the left side of her head and moved in tiny increments, stopping just below her hip. The pain she liked. The pain she deserved.

She huddled in the closet, listening as the powerful storm pounded the surf. She imagined the scattered debris and the wave-ravaged dunes. As she tried to find sleep, she was unaware that tomorrow her own life would also be reshaped.

VACATION AMBUSH

"This is why I prefer to just do it myself." Matt Nelson slammed the phone into its cradle. "I don't need this shit anymore." He threw his pen across the room. "Jessica?" he snapped to his secretary. He tossed a third folder across the expanse of his desk, watching as it skidded across the polished surface and landed on the floor, haphazardly scattering its contents across the Persian rug. "Where the fuck is the folder on Jeff's case?" A fourth folder flew to join the clutter.

Jessica appeared in the door, stooping to retrieve the Montblanc pen. Leaning against the doorjamb, she tapped a folder with the pen and stared at him.

He grabbed both sides of his head, pulled at his hair and met her glare with one of his own. "Is that it?" He pointed towards her hands, narrowing his eyes on the binder.

No response. With raised eyebrows and pursed lips, she continued to tap-tap-tap.

After a long moment, Matt collapsed into his chair, laid his head back on the leather, and dug his fingers into tired eyes. "Please stop that tapping. This is the first silence I've had all day." For now, at least, Matt's phones were quiet. Silence descended as his chest collapsed on a long exhale.

The guest chair crackled, but he didn't raise his head or open his eyes. "Sorry I yelled." When thick stillness greeted him, he raised his head and looked at Jessica.

The woman who had been with the firm longer than he had, the woman who had helped his father create a successful business, the woman who had been his mother's best friend and who had been in his life from birth sat rigid across from him. Her lips pinched, she clasped the folder against her chest. She raised an eyebrow and started the tap-tap-tapping again.

"You didn't yell," she said with a voice that matched the staccato tap-tap-tap. "Two weeks ago you yelled. Last week you yelled and added some colorful language." Tap-tap-tap. "Today it seems you have progressed to even more colorful language, *bellowing*, and my all-time favorite…" She tossed the pen across the desk where it slid to the floor and landed with a thud "… throwing things."

Gripping the armrests, he lowered his forehead to the desk and fixed his gaze on the pen at his feet. "God, Jess, I am so sorry. I don't know what to say." He paused, hoping for a response, a sign of forgiveness.

Jessica said nothing.

"Jeff's driving me f—" He caught himself, blushed, then finished his thought, "crazy. He didn't listen when Andrew told him not to claim those deductions. Now it's our fault he's being dragged into negotiations with the IRS."

Matt lifted his head, rubbed at both temples. With teeth clenched, his attempt at a smile failed.

Jessica still said nothing. Instead, she lowered the file, laced her fingers on her lap, and closed her eyes. After a long sigh, she finally looked at him. Her expression was filled with a palpable sadness.

"He chose not to take our advice. Jeff's just a jackass. You need to trust Andrew to do his job," Jessica said.

Matt shook his head. "If *I* had told him, he would have listened."

"Really?" she said. "Oh yeah, I forgot. You're the great and powerful Oz."

"Jess?" At her tone and sarcasm, his anger morphed to confusion.

Jessica huffed out a breath and placed her palms on the walnut desk. "Look at me, and then I want you to hear me. Don't just listen, but *hear* me."

Feeling his heart rate rise, he squeezed the armrests until his knuckles turned white. Matt closed his eyes for a long moment before lowering them to hers. "I'm not a teenager anymore. I don't have time—"

"Have you noticed how miserable you are?" She looked at the family photo taken almost ten years ago—the only personal item he kept in his office.

"Jes—"

She held up her palm. "Let me finish," she said, reaching across the desk to hold the picture. "I know you'll say it's because you lost your mom recently and your dad's sudden retirement added to your workload." She put the picture back. "But this started a long time ago. Your mother wanted so badly to talk to you. She needed you to look af—" She broke off, shook her head. "But the cancer prevented that."

Matt sucked his bottom lip between his teeth, ran his right hand over his face. He looked over at his mother's smiling face. Burying his face in his palms, he spoke through his fingers. "I truly don't have time for this. Can't it wait?"

"No, I don't think it can. I'm not sure we haven't already waited too long," she whispered just loudly enough for Matt to hear.

Matt again rested his chin in his palms and raised his eyebrows.

"I promised her, Matt. I promised her I'd get you to—" She stopped mid-thought, placing the file on his desk but not pushing it towards him.

The file was thin, too thin to be Jeff's records. Curiosity warred with annoyance. He'd loved and respected his mother above all others, but he didn't have time or the inclination for some cheesy self-analysis. "Jessica, I need to get Jeff's file. Once I have that situation resolved, I'll try to find the time to do whatever it is."

She maintained eye contact but again said nothing.

"Why can't this wait?"

"The answer is a bit complicated. But for now, I'll just tell you that your mom felt some urgency. And she said the timing would be obvious." Jessica gestured to the mess on the floor. "I think it's obvious."

Matt stood, cracking his neck left and right. His lips tightened as he pushed his shoulders back. "I need you to get me Jeff's file. I need to get that handled and then—"

"I can't do that. I made a promise to your mom and I intend to keep it."

Matt ground his teeth together, closed his eyes, searching for patience. Before he reopened his eyes, he took several deep breaths. When he opened them, he walked around to sit in the chair next to her. "If I let you say whatever it is you need to say, will you let me get back to work?"

Holding the file close to her chest, she, too, pulled her shoulders back, rose to her full height, and held his gaze. "You're going on vacation."

He blinked, jerked up, and stalked across the room, stepping around documents littered on the floor.

"I've already moved your appointments. I let the assistants working on the cases know, and I talked to Patti and Dave about the more complex cases. All the arrangements are made. You'll be—"

Matt stopped her with his raised right hand. He strode to the panoramic windows. Placing his palms on the marble ledge, he gazed at the bright blue sky of Minneapolis. With his face to the cityscape, he said, "I don't appreciate being railroaded and treated like a child. I simply cannot leave the firm right now." Before Jess could respond, his cell phone vibrated. Without turning to the room, he hit the green 'accept' button. "Matt Nelson."

"Matt. Your secretary called mine and that will not work…"

Matt pulled the phone away from his ear. Glaring at it, he listened from a distance while the Jackass yelled at him.

"It's your job to get me out of these taxes and fees. I will not accept—"

Slowly Matt's thumb slid across the screen where he punched the red 'disconnect' button. He tossed the phone onto the ledge and let his focus return to his city. "See why I can't go right now? I'll plan a few weeks after…" He turned back to his office, finding it empty except for his mess and the thin file resting in the center of his desk. "Shit." His left foot connected with the chair, spinning it wildly across the floor. "Shit." He rubbed his face, yanked the chair back over and situated himself in front of the file. As if the file might burn him, Matt kept his hands fastened on his thighs. Just looking at it made his gut tighten in a unique combination of anger, anxiety, and anticipation. "Shit."

"She was right." The deep voice of his father made Matt look up toward the door.

"Dad? What are you…Are you…Is everything all right?"

"Yeah, yeah," his father said as he walked deeper into the office, closing the door behind him. "Didn't mean to startle you. I'm good. Getting better every day, actually." He walked to the conference table and rested his back against it with his palms behind him.

Matt drew his eyebrows together and rose. "It's great to see you, but why are you here? In the city? At the office?"

"Jess called me yesterday. She told me it was time."

Matt bunched his shoulders around his ears while his teeth worked his top lip.

"She didn't tell me about this." His dad indicated the papers scattered at his feet. "She said nothing at all about the firm. She told me she was starting the vacation ambush." He shrugged, giving Matt a half-smile.

Reddening, Matt said, "I'm not going on vacation. She's being—"

"They're right. Your mother and Jess. You are a great tax attorney. I couldn't have left my firm in better hands. But…" Joe shrugged again. "But there's something you need to do.

12

Something else. Something so much more important."

Matt pinched the bridge of his nose, wiping the sweat from his face and glaring at the man who had taught him everything, the one man who should understand why he couldn't leave right now. "You look better," was all Matt could think to say.

"The garden is keeping me busy, and it's more exercise than I realized." He paused, mirroring the lip chew. "She's right about this. You'll see. You'll understand once you take the time." His smile turned sad. "I never let you do that. I never taught you to do that. I waited until it was almost too late." He took the seat Jessica had vacated. "I taught you to take control. *To be in control.* I was raised to be a man's man—we aren't supposed to feel or analyze emotions. We set a goal, we pursue the goal. Simple. My goal was to put you in that chair." Joe pointed at the executive chair he used to occupy. "I think—"

"You never pressured me to be an attorney or even work here." Matt sat with his elbows on the desk. "I—"

"I didn't do it on purpose. I don't think I put words around it. But now…" Joe looked over Matt's shoulder to the window.

"Dad, I'm fifty. I don't need to make a change. We're busy. I'm stressed. But—"

"No," his father barked before softening his voice. "That's just it. You don't know what you need. And maybe it's not all about you. Go on this vacation. These people…" He looked at the stacks of files all around the room. "These people are not important. Something so much more important is waiting for you."

Matt rubbed his eyes and sighed. Shaking his head, he reflected the same sad smile back to his father. "I'm not sure what's going on with you and Jessica, but I can't go right now. After the holidays. I'll go after that. How's that sound?"

His father stood. Walking around to Matt, he said, "Just think about it. Your mom gave me the garden. She's giving you something, too." He squeezed Matt's shoulders. As he walked away he added, "Go figure it out. There might be a better path. The chair will be waiting for you when you're ready." The door clicked closed.

Matt looked around his space at shelves of law books and tax codes. His desk phone blinked furiously with messages. Even as he watched his computer screen, email messages poured in. Lastly, he looked at the files littering the oriental carpet. He massaged his temples. Swiveling the chair to face the windows, he watched as white clouds danced through the blue sky.

His cell phone rang. His desk phone rang. Matt watched the sun move upward. Someone knocked on his door. His phone rang again. He ignored it all. "I'm needed here," he said to the window. In his mind, he reviewed all the clients who needed attention. "Mom, I can't go right now. I promise, I'll go after Christmas." Determined to get to work, he ran his hands through his hair and over his lips one more time before facing his desk.

A box sat on the ink blotter atop a thin file. Matt cocked his head, staring at the mysterious orange Nike shoebox. He pulled it closer and read the note Jessica had taped to the top.

Matt ~

You leave today. A car will pick you up at the condo at two. Go home. Pack. The plane tickets, rental car confirmation, and all the other travel information you need are in the file. I won't bother asking you not to take work to do. I __am__ going to ask you to take some real time to relax.

The box is not to be opened until you arrive. You're going to a beach, so pack for sand and sun. I know you'll be tempted to open it. Don't. Open it tomorrow.

I love you like you're my own…trust me ~

Jess

He pulled the box into his lap, turned it over and around. He shook it. Not heavy. Not light. The contents made a soft thud on the sides. Not shoes. Not a puzzle. A generous amount of tape closed all four sides. Chewing the inside of his cheek, he considered his dad's and Jessica's words as they rattled around in his mind.

Matt put the box on his lap and turned back to the Minnesota sky. *Vacation? Vacation.* He let the words roll in his mind as he shook the box some more. Just before he could toss the box on the floor and get back to his job, both his cell phone and desk phone rang. His shoulders tightened more with each ring. *Vacation. Something so much more important is waiting for you.*

Matt lifted the phone. Then he dropped it back in its cradle. He smiled, picturing Jeff's angry face. The smile broadened as he turned the cell phone off. He stuffed the cell phone into his pocket, nabbed his briefcase, and loaded it with his laptop, Jessica's file, yellow legal pads, and, of course, his Montblanc pen. Snatching his tie off, he tossed it in the mess on the floor.

The desk phone started again. *Vacation.* Tucking the orange box under his arm, Matt stepped on the scattered papers and walked away from Nelson, Nelson and Johnson.

Okay, ladies, let's see what you're up to.

ORANGE BOX

N ow that he was here he fought the urge to turn around and get on the next plane back to his own world. Leaning against the counter, Matt catalogued the location of his exile. A tiny kitchen. A tiny living room. A tiny bedroom and bath. A tiny Keurig. He sniffed and looked at the coffee cup. *Even it's tiny*. It was because of the box. The orange box loomed so large, felt so threatening, that Matt could not properly evaluate his surroundings. The box and whatever it contained overshadowed everything.

Scowling into the cold coffee, he tightened his grip on his mug. The box seemed to incriminate him. He could not grasp what the allegations might be. Feeling stupid but also wary, Matt shoved the box to the far corner, retrieved his laptop, his yellow notepad, and his personal pen. With precision only a tax attorney could master, he lined up his tools from left to right.

Before his phone finished powering up, it vibrated. *Jeff calling*. Squeezing the phone in one hand and rubbing his eyes with the other, he waited for the phone to quiet. He glared at the phone and then at the box, considering the options. Before he could decide, the phone started again. "You really are a jackass." Frustrated that a stupid shoebox intimidated him but also glad to have an excuse to avoid it, he pulled out the information on Jeff's case.

While he tried to focus on his work, the orange box maintained a dominance in his peripheral vision. He planted both elbows on the counter, running his palm over his neck and into his hair. "Fuck it," he said to the room. Reaching over, he yanked the box toward him.

Before he lifted the lid, his gut tightened and sweat sprouted on his lip. *Just do it*. He laughed at his unintentional pun and his irrational fear. *It's just a box*. Matt punctured the tape. Lifting the lid, he frowned. Inside he found a collection of standard size white envelopes. With his fingertips, he counted ten envelopes. His eyebrows drew together and his lips disappeared beneath his teeth as he plucked one at random. A plain white envelope. No return address, no company logo, no label. In blue ink, someone had written a nondescript "7" where a mailing address would be. That was it. Perplexed, disappointed, and annoyed, Matt pulled another—4. Another—8.

He upended the box and dumped all the contents onto the counter before sorting the envelopes numerically. He flipped each one over. *Sealed*. No more clues. He mashed each envelope with his index finger. A few were thick. One by one he shook them, then he re-created his numerical train of envelopes. Even though it was ridiculous, he bent forward and sniffed. Nothing. As he tapped his teeth with his fingers, the buzzing phone drew his attention, and he watched it skitter across the counter and clatter to the floor.

Matt looked from the phone to the envelopes, from the envelopes to the phone. *Something so much more important is waiting for you*. Matt reached for the phone and found the off switch. Wariness gave way to curiosity. For the first time since his encounter with Jessica yesterday, and for the first time in years, Matt Nelson's laughter boomed so loudly it startled him. *Afraid of envelopes? Ridiculous. Whatever you've got up your sleeve, Jessica, bring it on*. Along with the first envelope, he gathered his notepad and pen before heading to his tiny deck.

Blinking at the bright sun reflecting off the sand and blue water, he wiggled his nose at the salty air and lowered himself into a chair. He watched the ocean crash into the shore and listened to the voices echoing up the three floors. With his upper lip between his teeth, he gathered the courage to break the seal.

A picture tumbled into his lap. "Mini," he whispered as his fingers traced the picture of himself with his childhood dog. He turned the picture over and faced his mother's handwriting: *Matt, age 11*. A thirty-nine-year-old picture. Even more curious now, he balanced the photo on his left knee, picked up the envelope, and pulled out the paper within.

The handwriting and stationery pulled him out of his reverie. He bolted upright, sending the chair flying backwards and crashing into the sliding glass door. His chest seized and his breath stuck as his body registered the wrongness of what he held. Heat rose into his face as cold sweat sailed down his back. "What the hell?" He kicked the rickety furniture out of his way, sending the notepad and pen to join the picture lying on the ground. The paper crumpled in his tight fist as he paced the small area.

He took a few deep breaths, closed his eyes, and reminded himself that he trusted Jessica, that there had to be some reasonable explanation. Pulling the chair upright, he sat and tried to straighten the wrinkles from the paper. He picked up the picture and stared into those big, doleful eyes.

The familiar stationery caused Matt's chest to tighten again. His fingers trailed across his mother's embossed initials. "Mom," he breathed.

My darling Mattie-boy,

I can just picture your surprise. Have you finished your pacing? And don't be angry with Jess—this is my show, not hers.

I can see you in my mind's eye. On the left is your yellow legal pad, your laptop will be in the center, and on the right will be your pen. My notes are in numerical order in one long line. You hold this letter with your left hand so that your right hand can pull your hair. Although you might not be aware of it, your upper lip has a small sheen of what your dad and I always called "Matt's fear sweat". Am I right?

Today we found out my cancer has returned and treatment will only detract from my quality of life. It's okay, Mattie. I promise you, it's okay.

I'm leaving this earth with only one regret. I had one more thing I needed to do, but—

That's not quite right. I had one thing I needed you to do. A precious gift I need to give you. But you aren't ready yet. And you need to be ready. I realize it's not fair I'm doing this via letters. That was never my plan. I wanted to talk, to help, to encourage. If I'm totally honest, I wanted to watch. I wanted to be with you when your heart bursts open.

Pay attention. To yourself. To others. To what your heart says. You must focus like you've never had to before. Leave behind NNJ for a while. Follow the path I've put before you.

You're rolling your eyes—stop it!

You've never been afraid of hard work. And this will be hard work—different work. The payoff can be amazing. I understand you're impatient to know more, to understand. Slow down. I'll explain as we go. For today, here's what I need you to do:

Turn off that phone. You only need you.

Take a deep breath and wipe your lip.

Let me ask a question that requires your complete attention and honesty—What in your life is interesting, intriguing, exciting, <u>worthwhile</u>?

Now, go to the beach. Experience the wonder around you. Be honest with yourself. Talk to me. I promise I'll be listening.

Just promise me you will try. I <u>need</u> you to do this, Mattie. This may be the most important thing I've ever done. You'll see—you need it, too. Do not read the next letter until tomorrow.

Trust me—I love you—Mom

PS—For now, don't mention these letters to your sister. This is your journey—not Patti's.

On his second reading Matt laughed at the accurate picture of his work area. He frowned when he wiped the fear sweat. On his third reading his eyes filled. On his fourth reading his agitation rose. "Mom, you're right, I don't understand what's happening, and I'm already hating this."

After retrieving his yellow notepad and pen, on top he wrote four words: *interesting, intriguing, exciting, worthwhile.* He sat watching the waves and the people as the words scurried through his mind. For maybe the only time in his life, he sat still enough to hear his heart speak. His frown deepened when his heart remained silent. *This is stupid.* He chucked the pad down and fought a desire to hurl his favorite pen down to the sand.

With shaking fingers, Matt folded the letter and placed it back into the envelope. He went inside, positioned the first letter at the head of the envelope train, and situated Mini's picture on the top. "What do you have to do with anything?" he asked the picture. Disgusted at his mother, at himself, and at four little words that migrated from entertaining to accusing, he tossed the pad onto the counter and stalked to his bedroom.

All right, Mom. My lip is dry. Just get on with it so I can get back to my life.

As he dressed he revisited all that his dad and Jessica had said. Before he stepped out of the condo, he snagged his mother's first note, folded it neatly, and placed it into his pocket. As he stroked the envelope his heart gave him a clue. *You can't come up with an answer because there is no answer. Because your life's empty. That might be her point.*

He grunted, rolling his eyes. *Vacation? Who was Jessica kidding? This is woo-woo, manipulative torture.* "It's time for more than one beer," he said to the wind as he ignored the truth that envelope number two would shatter his perfectly ordered world.

A LOVELY ROBOT

Rosie's Bar and Grill sat perched only thirty yards from the white foam and only a ten-minute trudge from Matt's rental. He pulled the buzzing phone from his shorts pocket. His jaw clenched when Jeff's name flashed on the screen. "God, you are such a pain in my ass." For the second time that day he powered his phone off. *Mom, this had better be important, because I will have hell to pay when I get back. Can't I please just think about dinner, beer, and my team?*

After climbing the five steps from the beach, he shook the sand from his flip-flops before walking across the covered deck and entering the dark bar's cool interior. To his relief, several flat-screen TVs displayed game after game. Scanning the screens made Matt's relief shift to annoyance when he realized each TV played either the Atlanta Braves, Tampa Bay Rays, or Miami Marlins. He scanned the beer taps. *Ahh, something's looking up.* He licked his lips as he stared at the Sierra Nevada Pale Ale logo. After he chose a stool where he could see several screens, a cardboard coaster sailed his direction.

"What can I—" The waitress cocked her head and furrowed her brow. "You look familiar. Have you been here before?"

"Nope. I'd never even heard of this beach until today." He

tipped his head toward the taps. "But I'd give anything for a Sierra Nevada."

She shrugged as she filled a frosted mug. "Welcome to Rosamunda Beach. We don't get a lot of tourists this time of year. What brings you here?"

Matt rolled his eyes then smiled. "My mother made me." He paused, touching the pocket where her letter sat before adding, "And, yes, I know that sounds absurd. It feels absurd."

The woman eyed him as the head of his beer settled enough for her to top off the beverage. "You're a bit old for that, aren't you? Do I need to check your ID?" she teased as she put the mug in front of him.

Matt lifted the brew to his mouth and took one long gulp. "I think the gray speaks for itself," he said as he ran his hand through his more salt than pepper hair.

Touching her own brash red hair, she said, "That's the beauty of hair color. I'm Rosie Alberston."

"Rosie, as in Rosie's Bar and Grill?"

"Yep. You gonna want dinner?" She reached behind her to grab a menu.

Matt looked at the TVs above him. "You willing to change one of those TVs to the Twins?"

A man dressed in a black t-shirt and jeans marched up next to Rosie. With a remote control in his hand, he asked, "Twins fan?"

"I'll take the Twins, the Gophers, the Vikings, the Timber-wolves, the Wild. Anything Minnesota." Matt reached across the bar to clasp the man's hand. "Matt Nelson."

"Sam Crowley." Sam changed one of the TVs. "Looks like your team sucks."

Matt's face dropped at the abysmal score. "A lot of things suck lately," he said under his breath.

"You're from Minnesota?" Rosie asked nicely, but her face looked like she'd just sucked on a lemon.

Matt cocked his head at her. He looked over to find Sam's eyes narrowed at him, too. "Are Minnesotans not allowed here?" Sam and Rosie looked at each other with expressions Matt could only describe as wary. He shut his eyes, took a deep breath and an even deeper gulp of his beer. *Dinner. Beer. Game.* Picking up the menu, he asked, "What do you recommend?"

"Everything," Rosie started.

"Burgers," Sam said at the same time.

Matt laughed. "I'll have a burger with cheddar. Medium-rare. Extra pickles. No other salad stuff. Fries. Ketchup. Yellow mustard."

"Well, aren't you decisive," Rosie said as she strolled to put the order in the computer.

Sensing the insult, Matt ignored the comment and leaned back in his seat, his head tilted to watch the game. By the time he took his first greasy bite, his team was already in the hole 6 to 0. *Come on, guys. Give me this.* Three more strikes. "Shit," he said with a full mouth. "Simmons, it's up to you." Strike. Strike. Pop-up. Annoyed, he twirled around in his seat just in time for her feet to hit the top step.

Every detail registered in Matt's mind. Slender. Too slender. Pale blue short-sleeve dress, form-fitted to the waist then flaring to the knee. White flip-flops. A multi-colored straw bag. White earphones stretched from the bag into her ears. Large, dark sunglasses. A dark emerald and pink scarf wrapped around her head. Her shoulders were erect and stiff. Instead of entering the restaurant, she pivoted and moved toward a table tucked in the deck's back corner.

She placed the bag on one chair and retrieved what Matt assumed was an iPhone. She walked to the chair deep in the corner. Before she sat, her hands moved over the scarf, adjusted the earphones, and pushed the sunglasses more firmly to her face. She then turned the chair to face the beach. She never smiled. She never frowned. Her face remained expressionless as if she were a mannequin incapable of emotion.

A lovely robot. He turned to find Rosie standing just behind him with her focus on the same woman. "She should just wear a sign." He pushed his empty mug in Rosie's direction.

"What did you say?" She whipped around to look at him, tipping her chin toward the woman. "What did you say about her?"

He pulled back and raised his hands in surrender. "She's a lovely woman, but she might as well wear a sign that says 'Caution: Danger Ahead' or 'Don't Come Any Closer.'"

Rosie's eyebrows pulled in tight. Her eyes flashed a potent mix of anger and distrust. "Maybe you should heed those signs." She snatched his now empty mug and stalked off to the far end of the bar.

She waved her hands around in Sam's face, forcing a chuckle from Matt at her overreaction to his innocent comment.

Sam glanced his way, narrowing his eyes and pursing his lips.

The chuckle faded. *Beer. Dinner. Team.* He touched his pocket. "Focus." Another runner crossed home plate. Down 7 to 0. Disgusted with his team and compelled by the woman's captivating strangeness and Sam and Rosie's odd reactions, Matt turned to contemplate the woman in the scarf.

She sat utterly still. Rigid. Frozen. As he watched, Sam approached her with a glass and a salad. She didn't move. At all. Although Sam's mouth moved, the woman didn't acknowledge him in any way.

As Sam walked away, the woman's shoulders rose and fell in what appeared to be three deep breaths before she began the oddest mealtime ritual Matt had ever witnessed.

She repositioned her chair so she faced her salad. She did not remove the earphones or the sunglasses. As if to confirm its position, she touched the emerald scarf.

She raised both her knife and fork to the salad. She made six straight cuts from side to side. She rotated the bowl one-quarter turn and repeated the process. Although Matt could not verify it, he was certain the salad lay before her in a perfect checkerboard pattern. With her left hand, she picked up a spoon and scooped a bite of the salad into her mouth. She turned the bowl another quarter turn and ate another bite. Six turns. Six bites. All with a spoon.

Spellbound, he refused to tear his eyes away.

She finished the sixth bite, set down the spoon, grabbed the glass of tea, and drank six small sips. She placed the glass on the table, covered the bowl with her napkin, and returned to her position overlooking the sand. As she resettled, her hands roamed over the earphones, sunglasses, and scarf.

"If you're finished with the show, you might want to finish your fries," Rosie said.

Startled, he turned, expecting to see anger to match the tone of voice. Instead he found sadness. Profound sadness. After taking a long sip of water, he asked, "Does she always do that? The cuts? The six bites?"

With her eyes towards the woman, Rosie pulled her lips into her mouth and nodded.

"The scarf, the sunglasses, the earphones?" he asked.

Rosie nodded and walked away.

Matt's lungs deflated. "Man, that is one odd woman. Beautiful." He shivered and added, "Cold." *Alone*, he amended, not understanding where the word originated. *Isolated. Afraid.*

"Not cold," Sam responded to Matt's rhetorical statement.

Matt glanced up at him.

"She's not ready for you." Sam held Matt's eyes for a few too many beats before walking away, leaving Matt to wonder what the man meant and what he was missing.

Matt wiped the sweat from his face even as a cold sensation moved down his back.

FOCUS

A beach is a unique blend of energy and calm, of agitation and tranquility. *Wonder how many people on the beach find serenity.* He, for one, did not. He identified with the waves as they broke on the shore. In the cheap beach chair, Matt squished his toes into the cool sand while the water swirled around his ankles. *Do I want an exciting life?* His eyebrows pulled in tight as he tried to remember the last time he'd been enthusiastic about anything. Popping the last bite of bagel in his mouth, he leaned his head back on the chair, closed his eyes, and tried to find one thing, just one thing, that felt worthwhile. No answer materialized. *But do I want to change? Is comfortable such a bad thing?*

The hairs on his arms rose first. Again, that chill raced up his spine and into his hair. Matt turned his neck to the left and opened his eyes. *Nothing interesting.* He gripped his thighs as the tingle forced a shudder through his body. He turned to the right. Heading toward him, dressed in black yoga pants, a black short-sleeve shirt, white shoes, and a black baseball cap, was the woman from Rosie's. Robot Woman.

Again, she wore dark sunglasses and earphones. As she got closer, he saw sweat pouring down her neck and calves as her pace remained strong and steady. Her face, what he could see of it around the large glasses, continued to have an unnerving blankness. Her head did not turn left or right. Like the night before, her actions were robotic. Mesmerized, Matt followed her movements until she disappeared from view.

He took a deep breath and settled back into his chair. "Focus on your own uninteresting life," he chastised himself. Before his eyes slid closed, his brain snagged on a detail. Underneath her black ball cap, a white scarf floated like a ponytail out the back. *A robot wearing a scarf.*

Matt's thoughts drifted to NNJ and all the work that awaited him. He pondered various strategies to attempt against the IRS for Jeff. A loophole existed, of that he had no doubt. For every tax law the government created, they created triple that number of loopholes. It was Matt's job to find the holes and exploit them. Mentally he flipped the pages of the tax code, rejecting one idea after another. *Dammit, Jeff. You did this to yourself.*

The sun rose higher. The heat melted into Matt, so when the chill arrived again, without hesitation he turned. Same pace. Same posture. Drenched with sweat. Matt glanced at his watch. By his calculation, Robot Woman had passed him over an hour ago. Without conscious choice, he rose from his chair and moved in her direction. He locked his eyes on those dark glasses, ran his hands across the sweat pooled on his neck, and stepped forward.

In three steps, they would collide. Before that could happen and without a single change of pace or obvious facial expression, the woman shifted four steps sideways and went around him.

Matt's body pivoted to track her as she moved the four steps back to her original path. The chill spilled down his back, and a sudden urge to go after her gripped him. He planted his feet in the sand, forcing himself to let her walk away. Once she was out of sight he rubbed his hands over his face and over his lip. *Focus, fool. Focus.* He collapsed into his chair, forcing open his mental tax codes.

UNTIL TODAY

Like yesterday and the day before and the day before that, her day begins at 6:35 when she crawls out of the closet. She dons yoga pants, a short-sleeve black t-shirt, white socks, and walking shoes. She brushes her teeth and covers her head with a white scarf. After placing a black ball cap over the scarf, she puts on dark sunglasses and earphones, and grabs a bottled water. She secures six deadbolts before she heads to the surf.

Heading south, she walks ninety minutes before reversing course. Her head turns neither to the left nor to the right. She speaks to no one. She does not smile or nod. Her pace remains constant. Although people frolic around her, the waves crash near her, the sun warms the surrounding air, she feels nothing, hears nothing.

Until today. Today, he stepped into her path. Today her chest pounds, her fists clench. Today she bites into her cheeks until blood fills her mouth. Today her body maintains her pace as her mind races. "He's here," she whispers when she reaches home. She closes the door behind her and slides to the floor. "He's here."

ENVELOPE #2

For the first mile of his afternoon run, four words crowded out Matt's music. *Interesting. Exciting. Intriguing. Worthwhile.* On the second mile, a new word joined his musings. *Alone.* It wasn't until the last leg of his run that his mind landed on his mother's most important and troubling accusation. *You aren't ready yet.* Hoping to outrun the rain, he increased his pace and tried to remember when, if ever, he'd not been ready for something.

With a fresh bottle of water, he leaned against the counter and looked at the letters. With his eyes focused on Mini's picture, he mused out loud, "What am I not ready for?" After a deep cleansing breath, he wiped at the moisture on his lip. "And for shit's sake, what am I afraid of?"

On his notepad, he rewrote the four damning words, repeating them over and over again. With his pen, he created an intricate pattern around each word, paying particular attention to the word *worthwhile. I think I'd be okay not having anything particularly interesting. But nothing worthwhile?*

"Mom, you said if I listened you'd talk. Well, I've been sitting here a while and you haven't said a word." He shut his eyes and searched his recent memory for anything to place on that sheet of paper. "I concede defeat. I have a boring, worthless life. Let me guess, you have a plan to fix that."

His eyes popped open and he applied his pen to the page. "Scarf Woman." Sitting back in his seat, he ran his fingers along his lips and stared at those two words. He traced the words and then added "Alone. Afraid." Keeping with his ingrained habits, Matt began a list of observations and questions. "Sunglasses, earphones, no responses, checkerboards, six bites, long walks. Who is she?"

He scrubbed his hands across his face. "That woman has nothing to do with you and whatever it is Mom wants." He ripped the paper from the notepad, tore it in half and tossed it on the counter. He shook his head and laughed at himself. *This is getting more and more ridiculous by the minute. Just open the next envelope.* He forced his back straight and plucked up envelope number two.

Mattie ~

I expect that you have an empty piece of paper. I think we need to do some work. Don't you?

I will pose a couple of questions to you. Here is what I want you to do:

1. Write the question on your notepad (yes, I know you have that nearby).

2. Write any and every answer that comes to you. Go with your gut, Matt. Don't censor. Don't judge. Just write.

3. Let your answers ruminate for the rest of the day. If anything new comes to mind, add it.

I can hear your groaning and see you rolling your eyes. Please stop. Ready?

Take a deep breath, wipe that lip, and let's get to it.

~~~

What in your life is worth fighting for? What has ever been worth fighting for? Have you ever had to fight for anything?

I should warn you—a worthwhile life is not an easy life. Maybe I should ask that first: Do you want a worthwhile life?

~~~

Forgive me if I seem short-tempered. I'm not. I'm a bit desperate. I'm worried. I wanted you there already. I wasn't expecting my cancer to return. I made a promise, and every day, every minute that ticks away I'm afraid we (you) will be too late.

I told you to slow down. Now I need to slow down, too. I trust we'll be in time—we have no choice.

I'm with you. Talk to me, Mom

Matt lowered the letter to his lap. Thoughts froze and then careened. A strange tightness settled in him. With a white-knuckled grip, Matt considered his mother's tone. Her urgency. Her cryptic words. For the first time since he'd opened that orange box, he wanted to both read and destroy every note.

With a racing pulse, Matt re-read the message before he balled up the letter and hurled it across the room. As he rose from his chair, his voice battled with the thunder. "Get to your fucking point. What is it you want me to do?" His nails dug into his palms. "Mom, if you were here—"

As he dropped into the chair his anger deflated. *Oh, Mom.*

Why didn't we talk when you were here? Why the big secret? Why don't you just tell me what you need me to do? I'm sure I can handle it.

Another boom of thunder forced Matt's head up. "I miss you, Mom. I really do." He stood, found the ball of paper, flattened it as much as possible, re-read it one more time. He pulled over the yellow notepad and began to answer his mother.

Fought for: My law degree. My position at NNJ.

Worth fighting for: My family. For NNJ's continued growth.

He closed his eyes. *That's it, Mom. That's all I got.* His eyes opened and drifted to the torn paper. He thought about the Scarf Woman as he grabbed the pieces toward him. "Haunted," he said aloud, feeling the rightness of the word. He considered the sunglasses, the earphones, her refusal to talk with Sam. *What is she afraid of?* He shoved the torn sheets aside, laughing at his own foolishness.

Beer. Dinner. Answers. Write a few questions of my own.

Satisfied with his plan, he pulled the binder sitting on the coffee table into his lap. Inside he found a listing of local restaurants, things to do in the area, condo rules, emergency numbers. Flipping back to the restaurants, he perused his choices. Steak. Seafood. Italian. Chinese. Rosie's Bar and Grill was not listed. With the rain pinging on the sliding glass doors, he revisited the odd way both Sam and Rosie had acted. Already frustrated and puzzled, Sam's final words punched him. *She's not ready for you.* His teeth clenched and a snarl gathered in his throat. He glanced over his shoulder at the ripped sheets.

"Well, if I have to get ready for my mother's mystery quest, Scarf Woman might as well get ready for me. She's intriguing. That should satisfy you, right, Mom?"

LUCAS

Kathleen's fingers dug into the sand until she reached something like soil. She created a crater, poured in fresh water. Before she pulled away, the memory of two tiny hands joined hers. Paralyzed with the memory, she held still while Lucas's fingers dipped into the soupy sand.

"Grammy—"

Kathleen's hands stopped and her eyes closed at the sound of her Lucas's sweet voice. "L-man." Her mouth formed the words, but her voice box refused to engage on a name she had not spoken in almost three years.

"Grammy—"

With her face still staring into the hole, she opened her eyes to the memory of the tiny hands that used to dig in the dirt with her.

"What we planting?"

"You aren't going to approve," she responded with a tease.

"Tell me you aren't?" he asked.

"I am." With one hand, she dug deeper, with the other she reached out to collect the plant she'd purchased just that afternoon.

"Green vegetables," he said with a definitive whine to his voice.

"Broccoli," she acknowledged as she placed the seedling between her vision of his fingers. "Hold it steady." She gripped the plant's roots and held them against the dirt floor of their new home.

"I hate broccoli."

"You never tried broccoli."

"It's green. I would hate it."

Kathleen smiled at his words, but she dared not look away from the plant, scared if she looked up she'd see his face. Equally scared she wouldn't see his face.

Together they filled the hole with the combination of dirt and sand.

"Why can't we plant something I like?"

"It's fall and about the only thing we can plant is vegetables." She didn't bother to tell him that the broccoli would not grow. She didn't tell herself that she was glad it would not grow.

"That sucks." He giggled like he did whenever he used what he considered an adult word. Kathleen—Grammy—never corrected him. His giggle was too precious to waste on a silly word correction.

"We can plant strawberries and other berries when the season is right."

"You pwomise? Stwawbewwies, bluebewwies, waspbew-wies, blackbewwies," he listed all his favorite fruits, and in his excitement, his *r*s turned to *w*s just as Courtney's had done at his age.

Reluctant to get caught in another promise, Kathleen kept scooping and patting at the dirt. As she suspected, her Lucas jumped to another topic without noticing her non-answer.

"Kiley wants to be a princess for Halloween?"

"You don't sound like you like that idea."

"She wants me to be a pea. She says that's perfect because I'm a pea-brain."

"Ahh, *The Princess and the Pea.*" She didn't respond to Kiley's taunt. Her philosophy was to let the kids settle their own problems unless blood appeared.

"I'm not a pea-brain. I don't even eat peas. I want to be Batman."

"You're always Batman."

"Batman's the best. Why change?"

"Good point. That proves you aren't a pea-brain."

He started bouncing up and down kicking sand around, excitement leaking into their space and forcing the words out of his mouth more quickly than he could control. "Oh yeah, a safety zone is coming for you. It's—" Abruptly, he stopped talking. "I didn't say that right." He paused as if maybe the right words would appear. "Grammy, are you mad at us?"

The words and the mournful tone of his voice forced her face up. Just across the small plant and within inches of her face, Lucas's sky-blue eyes implored her.

"I'm not mad," she answered, holding herself utterly still, hoping the sound waves didn't drag his image away. "Why would you think that?"

"Because you never say our names and Daddy says you have our pictures turned to face the wall."

Closing her eyes again, she pantomimed pulling him into her lap, wrapping her arms around him, and squeezing him until he wiggled in her lap and snorted. Every time he tried to hold in a laugh, he snorted. Her imagination fed her a dirty little boy scent—half baby shampoo, half sweat and grime.

"Why do you do that, Grammy? Do you want to forget us?"

Kathleen held her breath and choked on the sob as the little boy faded away. When his earthy scent disappeared, she finished planting the broccoli, grateful she did not have to explain that to remember the beauty, she'd have to remember The Event.

EYES

As he walked up the steps, Matt turned his head toward the table where Scarf Woman had sat. Four empty chairs. The tension in his shoulders dissipated. *Focus. You're here because of your mother, not her.* Disappointment and relief battled within him.

"I'm not sure if I'm surprised you're back or I was expecting it," Rosie said as Matt walked toward the same stool he'd occupied earlier. "Sierra Nevada again?"

"I can't tell if you're glad or disappointed. Either way, I'll take the beer."

Rosie stared into Matt's eyes for a long moment. "Is this is a good idea?" she asked without giving him a chance to respond. Turning toward the taps she filled his mug. "Food?"

Great, more cryptic comments. Matt reached for the brew then gulped a swallow before answering, "The burger was delicious. I'm not picky, so give me whatever you think I'd enjoy. But please be sure I have some of those fries." Looking above him, Matt crossed his fingers and hoped his precious team could pull out a win. "Rosie, pregame starts at seven, do you think we could switch the channel?"

Sam appeared to Matt's left. "Changing the station now," he

said as he pointed the remote to the TV.

The daily sports review show played while Matt munched on his fries and the quesadilla Rosie had given him. He waited for his team to take the field. With the last pull on his beer, he felt the hairs on the back of his neck rise and his shoulders tense. He shivered as a chill slid down his back.

"You okay?" Rosie asked.

Matt looked up to find Rosie's head cocked. Sam, he noted, was pouring a glass of tea. "She walked in, didn't she?"

Rosie's eyebrows rose before her head turned toward the deck. She checked her watch and a barely-there smile appeared. "Do I ask how you knew that or tell you it's none of your damn business?"

Matt gripped his empty mug and chewed on his inner lip. "Sam's pouring the tea." Unwilling to acknowledge his body's reaction, he lied as he jerked his head in Sam's direction.

Matt stood to face the deck. Same chair. Same earphones. Same body posture. A scarf with pink, green and blue swirls. Tan shorts, light pink short-sleeved shirt. White flip-flops. Since she faced the ocean again, he couldn't see her face, but he'd bet his entire year's salary she was wearing dark sunglasses. He watched Sam place the tea on the table. He spoke a few words but received no response.

Sam met Matt's eyes as he worked his way back toward the bar. A sad smile followed by a look of resignation slid across Sam's face.

Rosie's presence spread behind him. Before he faced her, Scarf Woman rose and turned to him. She lifted her sunglasses and lasered her eyes directly on his face. Frozen, Matt stared at her as she stared at him. Her eyes remained glued to his while she gathered her belongings. She lowered the glasses, used her empty hand to touch the scarf, and walked out of the restaurant.

"Holy shit," Rosie exhaled behind him. "Sam, did you see that?"

Matt jerked around to find Rosie and Sam looking from each other to the woman and over at him.

Sam leaned across the bar. "She's never done that."

"What? What do you mean?" Matt's voice stuttered as another chill ran along his frame.

"She's been coming here every day for months. Never once has she made eye contact. There has only been one person she's shown those eyes. I've gotten her to speak a couple of times, and so has Rosie. But this was the first time," Sam glanced at the empty table and then at Rosie. "Until today we've never seen her eyes."

Matt clenched his thighs and glanced over at Rosie and back to Sam. "Could you tell how blue they were?" When neither Sam nor Rosie answered, Matt continued, "What's her deal?" He had no idea what his voice conveyed, but Rosie did not approve. He could almost see her hackles rise.

"Rosie," Sam said, "we knew, and she knew, he was coming. She saw him yesterday. She came back anyway."

Matt's teeth clamped together and his eyes widened. "What the fuck are you talking about? Are you suggesting you knew I was coming here?"

Sam and Rosie looked at him with wide eyes and open mouths.

"*I* didn't even know I was coming here. I'd never heard of this beach or this restaurant. I don't know that woman."

With deep frowns, Sam and Rosie looked at each other and then back at Matt.

Matt continued his rant, "I don't want to know her. I just wanted dinner, beer and baseball. Can I do that?"

Rosie's eyes narrowed and her shoulders went rigid. "Consider it done." She walked to the taps on the far side of the bar.

Sam glared at Matt. "She shouldn't have sent you."

For the second time that evening Matt sat frozen in his seat.

"Go back home, Mr. Nelson. We'll take care of Kathleen."

This time Matt's snarl was not soft nor subtle.

ENVELOPE #3

When the door to the condo crashed open, the knob created a divot in the sheetrock. Panting and dripping, Matt halted just inside the door. With his hands on his knees, he struggled to slow his breathing and fight off the chill caused by the air conditioning blowing on his wet skin. After hearing Sam's final blow and putting some pieces together, Matt had tossed a fifty on the bar and ran as fast as wet sand and blowing rain would allow.

He straightened and looked across the small kitchen to the train of letters arranged on the bar. He forced his hands into fists. His heart throbbed in his chest, and the moisture on his upper lip was fear rather than rain. *Focus, Matt. This is a just some weird misunderstanding.*

Calmer, he walked toward the bathroom where he toweled his hair and replaced his wet clothes. Still shivering, he made a cup of coffee before facing the next letter. "I need answers, Mom. Something's going on and I'm the only one not in on it."

He snatched up the next envelope, but before he could open it, he noticed the pieces of paper where he'd written Scarf Woman and the questions he'd formed. Even though he believed it was inane, Matt talked to his mother.

"You should have seen her eyes, Mom. The same blue as a Minnesota sky. Electrified. I swear if I had been close enough, I would have been able to read words in those eyes. Why do you think she looked at me that way, huh? Sam says she's alone. I get that. But it's more than loneliness. I don't understand what that means, how or why I sense her presence. Maybe she's not haunted. Maybe she's the haunter." Matt laughed out loud. "I sound stupid. I feel stupid. I'm acting stupid." He wadded up the torn pieces of paper and completed a perfect three-point shot into the trashcan. "Enough. Let's do this."

Okay, Matt, we're going to have a hard talk. Go back to your answers. Did you put anything about passing the Bar? If you did, strike it. Do you remember the weeks leading up to the exam? You maybe studied one hour a day—maybe. It always drove Patti crazy how easily it all came to you. You succeeded, but you did not have to fight. If you put something to do with NNJ on your list, strike that, too. Not that you haven't work hard—you have. But working and fighting are not the same thing. And, let's be honest, NNJ is not "worthwhile". It's a great company. I'm proud of what your Dad and I built. Since I'm dying, I get the pleasure of being blunt—NNJ is about helping rich people keep their money out of the hands of the IRS.

What does that leave? Family? You certainly WOULD fight for us and for Patti's brood, but thankfully that's never been necessary.

You have fought for one thing. I sent you a hint in the first envelope.

Matt paused in his reading, allowing his shoulders to slump

and his head to sink to the counter. *Has my life been that easy?* His fingers drifted to the first envelope where Mini's picture sat. With his fingertips, he traced around the dog's ear, her muzzle, her fat body. He gripped the letter in one hand and the memento of his dog in the other.

<<<>>>

Mini. You fought for her. You fought your dad. You fought the vet. You fought me. Do you remember finding her? Think back, Mattie, what was it that made you willing to fight so hard? At first you'll gravitate toward all the reasons Mini needed you—and that's important. But after that, what I want you to focus on is what ABOUT YOU, what WITHIN YOU, made you willing to fight?

That precious dog was worth it. She pulled out the best in you—she pulled out the real you. When she left, so did you. Search and find yourself again.

You want more—in life and in this letter. I know you have questions. Hold on to them for a little longer. It will all make sense soon. Get ready to fight. I love you, Mom.

<<<>>>

Matt re-read the letter three more times, and with each repetition his emotion changed. Confusion moved to frustration, which moved to concern. Mini had died just after he left law school twenty-six years ago. She'd been his dog for thirteen years. He could not understand why his pet was important now. Concern morphed back to confusion. No mention of Sam or Rosie or Scarf Woman. "I obviously needed this trip. I'm going fucking nuts."

He powered up his cell phone, hoping his father could shed light and sanity onto the situation. Before he located the contact information, a memory assailed him.

With his father on a par-three golf course, young Matt heard the pup. Just on the other side of the fairway lay a small brown creature. Matt bolted over and found her. Her large brown eyes looked at Matt, and Matt fell head over heels in love. In vivid detail, he recalled how his father had helped him wrap the pup in the dirty golf towel. At the clubhouse, his father used a phone book and found a vet. Matt sat in the backseat of the car, murmuring reassurances to the dog while ignoring his father's warning they would not be keeping that dog.

He pictured his father's sadness as he explained they'd be leaving the puppy at the vet. He imagined his arm clutching that pup to his chest, preparing to fight for what he believed was sent to him. Only to him. He'd begged with tears streaming down his face. "She was on that golf course at that moment so I would find her. Don't you see, Dad, she's mine." To prove his point, he'd lowered his face near the snout and the dog rewarded him with sloppy licks and nuzzles. With chocolate eyes that matched the pup's, he'd looked up at his father. "And I'm hers." On the drive home, his father prepared him for his mother's arguments.

"I don't want a dog, Joe," his mother had said. "And before you say it—" she pointed a finger at Matt "—you'll tell me how you will take care of it, feed it, walk it, clean up after it. But that will last a week, and then I'll have something else to take care of." She wagged her finger first at his Dad and then at him. "The answer is no. The vet can find her a home."

For the first time in his eleven years Matt's little body puffed up at his mother. "She's not an it. Her name is Mini. And she's mine. She found me and I found her. I will not—I cannot abandon her." Tears leaked down his face again, even as his body shook in anger. "Please don't make me."

His mother crouched down and pulled him to her chest with the dog wiggling between them. "Why are you so adamant she's yours? She has a home somewhere. People who are looking for her."

"We can put flyers up, but no one will claim her because she's meant to be with me." He pulled out of his mother's embrace, tucked Mini under one arm and planted his other hand on his hip and rallied, "I felt her before I heard her." He wiped the snot from his reddening face and stood as tall as possible, fighting his embarrassment at admitting such a thing. "When we came up on the fifth hole I got this tingle. I can't explain it, Mom. A chill. When I saw her, her eyes looked right at me. It was as if she was calling us to be together. For me to take care of her and her to take care of me." He'd brought his eyes to his mother's. "She's alone. Her face, Mom. Her eyes."

Staring now at Mini's photo, Matt understood. That woman at the restaurant—that Scarf Woman—was his and he was hers. He'd felt her the first time she'd entered that restaurant. The same tingle. The tingle he'd sensed only one other time in his life. He understood it was absurd to compare the lovely woman to his pet. Yet he couldn't deny, wouldn't deny, his reaction to her and hers to him. It had happened again this morning on the beach. Her eyes had told him the rest.

Mom, did you feel her, too? Turning his phone off, Matt re-read all the letters again. "I'll get ready, Mom. Show me how. And you're right. I think we need to hurry."

THE CHAT

After a poor night's rest, Matt had awakened that morning feeling foolish. Foolishness was a new and unwelcome emotion. He'd made assumptions, jumped to conclusions, made an ass of himself. After breakfast at a local diner he'd marched into the small condo kitchen, packed the envelopes back into the orange box, retrieved his briefcase, and studied Jeff's situation. It took six phone calls and layers of research before he had Jeff's answer. With that resolved, a welcome sense of control returned to Matt's world.

"Jeff, it's Matt Nelson. I've spent the morning pouring over your filings and finally found the one entry that opens a door for negotiation."

"I thought you'd turned this over to Alex," Jeff responded.

"I spoke to him earlier. We agreed that the complexity requires my intervention."

"Listen, I need to know you'll take this seriously. I haven't been able to reach you for days. We're talking millions of dollars here and I can't afford to leave that on the table."

Matt took a deep, silent, breath. "I had unexpected family business to address. But that's done. I expect to be back in the office by Monday or Tuesday. Regardless, I have all your documents with me and access to everything else online. Alex and I plan to spend the afternoon filing the petition with the IRS. I should return it to you by tomorrow morning."

After a long silence Jeff answered, "Sounds good. Will you answer my calls now?" His voice didn't hide his anger.

Matt shoved his hands through his hair. "Let me remind you that this is happening because you chose not to take our advice. So, do you want me to package your documents and forward them to you? I can recommend another firm." He tapped his fingers on the counter as he waited through yet another long silence.

"If you can assure me you are on top of this, then I'd prefer not to make a change."

"Expect to get petitions for your signature first thing tomorrow. I'll call you if we hit any unforeseen problems."

He spent several more hours reviewing, recalculating, and completing the paperwork for Jeff. Lacing his fingers behind his head, Matt sat back and sucked in a deep, satisfying breath. He allowed himself a few minutes of intense satisfaction before turning to his email. "212 emails. I've been gone, what, two days?" Before he could decide the best way to organize and tackle the information, a chat window opened.

Matt—are you there?

Hey, Jess—Good news, we solved Jeff's problem. The package is being finished now. Alex will get you a copy for the master file.

Matt watched and waited as the cursor blinked, accusing him of something he did not understand.

Jess, you there?
Yes.
Do you need something? I've accumulated over 200 emails. Are there always so many?
Have you met her yet?

Matt stared at the words as his chest tightened and that chill returned. The orange box filled his peripheral vision while he waited for Jess to say more, to say something useful.

Matt, have you met her yet?
Who?

Matt's stomach churned as he waited for her response, his pulse matching the blinking cursor. In a vain attempt to relax, he straightened the papers and moved his pen to its proper position. He shifted in his seat and waited. And waited. And waited. A drop of sweat dribbled from his temple and settled on his lip.

Never mind.
What?!

Another long, painful wait.

Forget it. It was a long shot. Since you're already back at work, do you want me to make the arrangements for you to come home?
Will you tell me what's going on?
Do you want me to make arrangements for you to come home?

With narrowed eyes and sweat forming, he hammered on the keys.

No. I want you to tell me what this is all about.
Which letter are you up to?

Matt pulled the orange box closer, rifled through the contents, and pulled out Mini's picture.

I finished the first three.
Are you willing to stay at least through letter five?

He chewed on his lips as he dug out envelopes one through five. Holding the letters in his hand, with Mini's photo propped against his coffee mug, he faced his choices.

Will the next two letters explain everything?
Yes and no.

Matt closed his eyes and shook his head. Rising from the chair, he paced back and forth in front of the screen. "I'm sick of riddles." With his index fingers, he beat at the keyboard.

Can't I read these when I get back?
Do what's right for you.

"Yeah, right." He rolled his eyes then completed a few more paces in front of the counter.

I need a vacation from this vacation.

Jess did not respond.

Let me think about it. I'll call you tomorrow with my plan.
Do me a favor. Find a place called Rosie's. Go there for dinner tonight. Okay?

Matt halted and gaped at Jess's response. "Fuck." His hands jerked at the roots of his hair. When he didn't respond, Jess added one more comment.

Your mom loved you. Can you trust her for a few more days?
I'm trying, Jess. I really am. But I hate being played with.
That wasn't her intent. You know that. Call me tomorrow. I'll be sure Jeff gets everything.

Before Matt could respond, she disconnected. He stalked over to the deck and gripped the metal railing. He watched a new storm swirl over the ocean. A crash of thunder jolted Matt from his reverie. "Mom, I need answers in the next letter or I will go back to my comfortable but boring life."

ENVELOPE #4

Without acknowledging his fear, Matt plucked the fourth envelope out of the stack. Ripping it open, he paced the room as he read.

I wish I was with you. You have so many questions and I can only guess how frustrated (or should I say angry) you are. Be patient with me, Mattie. As I said earlier, this was not the way I planned to do this.

What did you remember about Mini? Let me tell you what I remember. You were a skinny little thing, but when you argued with me about keeping her, you stood ten feet tall. You told me you "felt" her—do you remember? I never told you this, but I understood what you meant. I "felt" your dad the first time he walked into the lecture hall. There were over 200 kids in class. He sat in the sixth row, three in from the right. Maybe it's wrong to compare your love of a dog with my love of your dad—but what I've learned in my seventy years is that love is love, wherever you find it.

Your devotion to her was breathtaking. Rare. Precious. That was worth fighting for—her love for you and yours for her. When she died, you closed off part of yourself or you quit listening. I so need you to reopen your heart.

Have you ever had that feeling again? You described a chill. I don't

think you have—if you had, you would have fought tooth and nail to keep
this someone in your life. I believe you broke it off with Sarah because
your heart never told you she was the one for you. Are you willing to act
if you ever find that specialness again? Are you willing to pay attention
to your heart? I guess those are your questions for today. ~ Mom
    P.S. Go to a place called Rosie's Bar and Grill. Pay attention.

Matt balled the letter in his fist and lobbed it through the living room. "God dammit, Mom. I need to know what the fuck's going on and that's what you write?" Pulling on his hair, he marched across the room. "Pay attention to what?" He pulled the fifth letter out of the box, but hesitated. "Not now. I can't face another one right now." He tossed the envelope on the counter, grabbed his umbrella, and joined the storm.

THE FEELING

Matt headed straight to Rosie, who was taking a table's order. Crowding in behind her, he forced her to turn her attention from the customers to him.

"What time does she arrive?" he asked.

Rosie took a step back from him and glared.

Matt's stare bored into hers, his muscles tightening with each second that ticked by. He waited with his hands balled into tight fists. When the wait became too long, he raised his left eyebrow.

"Who do you think you are?" Rosie's voice shook. "First, you can't interrupt me. I have a business to run and it does *not* revolve around you. Second, what my customers do and don't do is none of your business."

He didn't move, didn't even blink. He kept his face calm. In his profession, he'd faced many liars and cheaters. Rosie didn't fit those qualities, but the technique was the same. Wait, give her no option but to fill the tense emptiness.

Rosie's shoulders slumped and her face softened. She smirked and shook her head in what might have been amusement. She nudged him out of her way. "Go to the bar. Let Sam get you a beer. I'll finish doing my job," she said sarcastically, "and then we'll talk."

He dipped his chin in a half-nod, turned and settled into his seat at the bar. When Sam made eye contact, he said, "I'm lost as to what's happening here. But my gut's telling me I'm going to need you on my side." Matt sat straighter and extended his hand across the bar. "Truce?"

It took a few beats, but Sam's hand met Matt's. "I'm getting the evil eye from Rosie. What did you do?" he asked as he tossed a coaster at Matt.

"I want some information and I'm not going away without it," he replied with a shrug and a tight grin.

Sam finished pulling the beer before asking, "What information?"

"You told me she comes here every night. What time does she usually arrive? I'm betting it's the same time every night. And a name would be nice." He gulped a mouthful of beer and wiped the foam from his lip.

"Why are you interested now? Last night you were adamant you wanted nothing to do with her."

At the tone of the question, Matt's body tensed for a few seconds. Forcing himself to relax, he asked, "Did you know my mother?"

Sam pulled back at the change of direction.

"Come on, Sam. First I'm exiled to this beach by my secretary who hands me a box of letters from my mother, each one stranger than the last. You and Rosie make odd comments and give me even odder looks. My secretary and my mother told me to come here for dinner. Everyone is in on a secret. A secret about me." Matt's voice rose with each sentence.

Rosie joined Sam and looked to each man.

"He asked if we know his mother," Sam explained to Rosie but kept his eyes pinned to Matt.

Matt gripped his mug and turned to Rosie. "So, do you?"

"Her name is Betty, right? An avid gardener?"

Matt's eyes closed as the breath escaped from his lungs. He forced his fingers to loosen while he twirled the glass around. "Yeah, that's my mom," he whispered. He looked back at Rosie. "Can you clue me in?"

"We expected her to come back. She told us she'd be back in a few weeks and she would bring her son. That was several months ago. We'd both given up on her." She looked to Sam, who nodded his agreement.

"She died." Matt's voice trembled. "Six months ago. She'd had breast cancer a few years ago. It returned and spread before she had a chance." He dropped his face and swallowed, his eyes stinging.

Rosie reached across the space and clasped his forearm. "We're so sorry. She was a great person. She came here for the big garden show twenty miles away. She said she decided to stay a few towns over because she expected to need a break from gardening talk." Rosie smiled.

"Yeah." He raised his head, ran his hand up his neck, and stared at the ceiling. "Did she know Scarf Woman?"

Sam chuckled. "Scarf Woman? I suppose that's better than other terms you could have used."

Matt's face leveled to his and a small smile spread on both faces. His eyebrows rose as he waited for an answer.

"Kathleen started coming here well over a year ago. As I told you last night, she speaks to no one. Except for a few words that

Rosie and I force out of her. Until…" Sam paused and looked to Rosie.

"Until your mom," Rosie finished. "Your mom showed up here the first night of the show. The first thing she did was to ask us to change a TV so she could watch anything Minnesota. Those were her words, 'Anything Minnesota.' Sam and I laughed at her accent and a friendship was born."

No one spoke for a long time.

"On her second night your mom asked about Kathleen. Like you, she noticed her and wondered."

"Did you give her more information than you did me?"

"Well, she was nicer." Rosie smirked before turning serious. "But no, not really. When we wouldn't tell her much she shrugged, stood up, and strolled straight to the deck. She didn't ask, she didn't say a word. She pulled out a chair and sat next to Kathleen as if they were old friends."

Matt laughed and took another drink. "That's my mom. She decides she wants something and nothing gets in her way." Matt's smiled faded as he looked away from them. *She fights. My mom fights.* "Kathleen." The name rolled off his tongue on a whisper. "You said my mom was sending me. What did that mean?"

Sam swallowed, backed up a step, and leaned against the back bar. "Somehow, after a day or two, she got Kathleen to talk. Your mom was here for just over two weeks. She spent every night at Kathleen's table and talked. At one point, she leaned across the table and took the sunglasses off Kathleen's face. I froze. So did Rosie. But Kathleen smiled at her, said a few words, and put the glasses back in place." Sam's eyes drifted toward the deck.

"Any idea what they talked about?"

"Flowers. At least that's all we ever overheard. Meanings and messages in flowers." The man rolled his eyes. "I didn't get the fascination."

Matt finished his beer and tried to decide if he wanted the answer to his next question. "Where do I fit in? What does this have to do with me?"

Sam's head jerked back to him. "She didn't tell you?" When Matt shook his head, Sam continued, "On her last night here, your mom told me and Rosie that the two of you would be here soon. That you would *feel* Kathleen."

Matt's eyebrows pulled in. He flattened his palms on the bar, leaned over the space. "I need you to think about something. Did she use the word 'feel'? Did she emphasize it the way you did?"

Nodding, Sam said, "Oh, yeah, for sure. Rosie and I talked about what that could mean. She told us you weren't ready yet but she'd fix that." Sam smiled. "I believed her. I hoped you were the answer." His smile leveled into a scowl. "It seems ludicrous now. Whatever she thought you were, whatever she thought you could be, you aren't." Sam, too, leaned forward, invading Matt's space. "Your mom was a great lady. I'm sorry to hear about her passing. But you're not—"

"I'm asking you to tell me what time she gets here." Matt moved into the last few inches of space. His nose an inch from Sam's, Matt waited.

Sam backed away, smiling. "That's better. That's the man your mother sent." He glanced at his watch. "6:36. You've got twenty-four minutes. She'll put her foot on the top step at 7:00."

Rosie stood behind Matt. "That gives you twenty-four minutes to tell us what you want with her."

Matt slumped and reached into his pocket. He pulled out the picture of Mini. Extending it to Rosie, he said, "That's my dog. Mini. I found her when I was eleven. My mom used the word 'feel' because that's how I described finding Mini. I felt her before I saw her. God, I sound—" Matt ran his hands through his hair. "I haven't experienced that sensation again until Scarf Woman—" He paused and smiled at Rosie "—until *Kathleen* walked in that first night. I assumed it was the air conditioning hitting my back. Until it happened again yesterday on the beach and here last night."

Rosie handed the picture back. She looked at Sam as he walked around the bar and put his arm around her waist.

"Kathleen has reacted to only two people since we've known her. Betty and him." Sam's head tilted Matt's direction.

Rosie stretched to her full 5'4" height and took in an audible breath. "We gave you her name. You know she arrives at seven. I believe you mean her no harm—"

"Rosie, something has to change for her. It's been almost three years. She can decide for herself—"

"Can she, Sam?" Rosie snapped. "She doesn't even decide what she has for dinner. Same meal every night. I agree something needs to change. But does it start with him?" She shoved her finger in Matt's direction.

"I guess that's up to him and to her," Sam said. "Both of us are here. I feel as protective of her as you do. We both saw what happened last night. Hell, as cheesy as it sounds, we both felt what happened last night. All we can do is stand back and watch."

Rosie and Sam stared at each other with worry and sadness etched in their features.

As Matt listened to their conversation many new questions rattled in his brain. *Same meal? Every night?* Breaking the tension, he jumped in, "I have no idea if I'll try to meet her or not. Why don't I order dinner, let the clock tick to seven, and go from there? Who knows, whatever happened last night might have been an anomaly." He knew he was lying. Matt was sure of only two things in his life right now. First, his awareness of her was not an anomaly, and second, he would approach Kathleen tonight.

Rosie closed her eyes and nodded. "What can I get you?"

Sam caressed her shoulder and disappeared down the bar.

"A club sandwich and a salad. Bring the salad first. If I don't finish it, don't let me have the sandwich. I've eaten shit since I got here." Matt smiled as tension released from both their bodies.

Rosie gave him a genuine grin. "Dressing?"

"Ranch. Add a glass or two of water, too. No more beer until I drink 'em."

Rosie keyed in his order while Matt turned to the TV above his head. No Twins tonight, so he settled into the Atlanta Braves game and tried to ignore the time.

As it turned out, there was no need to monitor the time. A distinct trickle of cold sweat hit his spine. The clock read 7:00. Even as the chill seeped into his entire back, he forced himself to face the televisions. He didn't want her to run again. He had no idea what he wanted, but he didn't want her to run.

Sam came toward him with a large bowl of greens. "Did you—"

"Yeah. Seven, on the dot." He shook his head and shivered.

"She kept her gaze focused on you as she went to her table. I couldn't see her eyes, of course, but her face stayed riveted to your back. If you'd turned around she would have walked away again."

"That's why I didn't turn around. Can I assume she's in her chair, facing the ocean? Headphones, sunglasses, and scarf secure?" He kept his eyes aimed toward the game.

Sam rounded the bar and entered Matt's field of vision. "Yeah. Rosie served her tea. She'll deliver her salad at 7:10."

"Does she talk to Rosie?"

"She says 'Thank you,' and if Rosie asks a direct question, she'll answer it. The only time Rosie tried to ask something even remotely personal, Kathleen stood and walked out. No drama. She simply walked away. So Rosie sometimes mentions the weather or she'll suggest a TV show. Kathleen makes no face-to-face contact, but she will respond. That's it."

"And with you?"

"I've delivered her food or drink every now and then. Same treatment. I helped build out her bungalow, so I can always ask if everything's good there. One time she asked me to come fix something."

Matt's eyes closed and he ran his fingers through his hair. He opened his eyes, loosened his jaw. "What's her story?"

Sam looked at Matt then toward Kathleen. "Her name is

Kathleen Bridges. She lives at Rosamunda Beach. Obviously there's more. But that's all I'm willing to share." He started to walk away but turned back. "And, Matt, let her tell you. Don't find out any other way. Okay?"

Matt placed the fork on his plate and tried to read the message behind Sam's words. After a moment, he nodded in agreement and ignored the butterflies dancing in his stomach.

Out of the corner of his eye, Matt watched Rosie walk past with a salad. He turned and watched her take the salad to the table on the deck. "Kathleen," he whispered. *That name doesn't seem right.* He shook his head at such an odd idea and began his study of Scarf Woman.

A pale pink blouse over white shorts. Same sunglasses, same earphones. A wildly colored scarf.

Matt's head tilted as he observed the same eating technique. Cut six times, turn, cut six times. She placed her knife on the table, selected the spoon and ate six bites. She drank six sips and then turned back to the beach.

Matt closed his eyes and shivered. *Haunted.* The word landed like a thud in his brain.

"You need to finish your water so you can have a beer," Rosie said, startling him.

Expecting to see anger, he turned to face her. She was watching Kathleen. He took a long sip of water before speaking. "I never see her order. How does she end up with a salad every night?"

"Her first night here she ordered a salad with very specific toppings. When she left, she told me that she'd like that salad again when she came back. That's the most words she's ever spoken to me."

"So, always the exact same meal?"

Rosie nodded.

"Does she ever talk to *anybody*?" he asked.

Rosie's mouth tipped into a small grin. "Well, your mom."

Cracking his knuckles, Matt scrunched his eyes as he considered the puzzle of Kathleen. He cataloged her peculiarities. "It must mean something," he muttered under his breath. "My mom went to her table and talked. I'm curious, did my mom do all the talking or did Kathleen talk too?"

Rosie put a beer in front of him. "The first night your mom did most of the talking. But the second night, she must have found something that sparked Kathleen, because from then on they chatted like women do. I wanted to join in but they talked about gardening and I don't have a green thumb. And," she shrugged, "I was afraid to break their bubble."

"How long does she sit there?" he asked.

"She'll walk off the deck at nine. If there's a storm she'll wait it out until ten. At ten she leaves no matter the weather. On Saturday, it's a bit different."

He wanted to understand what was different about Saturday, but he asked something else instead. "Do you know why she always wears a scarf?"

Shocked, Matt watched Rosie's eyes fill with tears. When one escaped down her face she swiped it as she turned away. "Yeah," she whispered, "I know." She walked away without another word. He checked his watch. He had twenty-two minutes before Kathleen walked away.

He wiped the last of the beer from his mouth. *I feel it, Mom.*

I might be in for a fight. Are we sure about this?

Seventeen minutes. Taking a deep breath, he captured Rosie's attention and with a nod called her over.

"Ready for your check?"

Matt looked at Rosie.

"Hey, Matt, are you ready for your check?" she asked again when Matt's silent searching continued.

With a tender and encouraging smile, he said, "No, Rosie. I want a glass of whatever she's having."

Rosie's eyes filled with tears again. "I don't know. What if—" she started, blinked, and stalled. "There's so much more to this."

"Are you willing to tell me?" Matt waited. When Rosie continued to look at him with indecision and a measure of fear, he said, "I can't explain it, but I know one thing—Rosie, *I know*—she'll be safe with me. I promise." He settled his hand on Rosie's shoulders. "Get me the drink, please."

Rosie continued to consider him for a long moment. Her shoulders drooped as she turned toward the bar and poured a glass of tea.

SAFETY ZONE

Pushing thoughts of possible reactions to the background, he approached the table as he would a rabid animal. In his left hand, he displayed a fresh peach iced tea. His right arm bent to rest on his lower back. As his mother instructed, he paid careful attention, so he noted when her back stiffened and her shoulders twitched. Moisture rose on his lip, but he forced himself to continue.

She removed the earphones, placed them in her lap before she pushed the sunglasses to the top of her head. Her large blue eyes shifted to him.

Matt's entire body braced. He halted on the opposite side of the table, formed a fist to stop the shaking. "Your ice has melted. I brought you a new tea." He bent forward and set the glass in front of her.

Before he'd risen to his full height her chair flew back, slamming the railing. An ancient iPod and headphones bounced away. The sunglasses skidded to the floor behind her. Her body turned his direction. She clutched the table with both hands and a trembling began in her legs. As if a series of switches flipped over, the shuddering moved up her torso, into her shoulders, and down her arms. Without even blinking, Matt stood still and tracked her body's movement until his eyes reached hers.

Huge, round eyes dominated her face. Dilated pupils. Irises so large they almost filled the white space. The force of her look, of her fear, forced Matt to take one step back.

Even as the tableware clattered with her tremors and sweat rolled down to the bridge of her nose, he did not, would not, break eye contact. He saw the second the fear morphed into abject terror. The eyes got even larger. The sweat dripped off her nose. Mucous ran over her upper lip as her swallowing became convulsive.

The hairs on Matt's body stood at attention, his breath sucked in through his mouth and stayed there. The chill he'd experienced in her presence became arctic. His own body twitched as if firing to run.

His body sent him warnings. Warnings to run. Warnings to fight. Warnings not to look away. He whispered loudly enough to be heard over the patter of rain, the roar of the waves, and the rattling dishes, "I'm not going to hurt you. Not ever. I'm here now. Just like she told you I would be. Betty sent me. I'm someone safe."

He heard her speak, but the words were impossible to decipher. He tilted his torso a few inches closer and raised one palm. "Shh, it's all right. I can't understand what you're saying. Can you take a deep breath?"

Her voice pitched higher but slowed enough for Matt to pick out the words. "Someone safe. Safety zone. Someone safe. Safety zone."

Several things happened for Matt that he would only realize over the next few days. First, his body readied itself to run *to* her, to catch her, to hold her. Second, although his body tightened, his mind calmed. Last, a fierce protectiveness overtook him.

He understood his place. He understood the whys of this trip. He understood all his mother's words. Matt knew, with complete clarity, that this woman was his destiny. *She's mine and I'm hers.* Without his awareness, his entire being prepared to fight.

Matt took in the deepest breath his lungs would allow. He extended a hand to her. "Take my hand. Hold on to me and we'll go from there."

Her head shook. Her lips kept moving, but no sound emerged. Yet her eyes never strayed from his.

With a soft but somewhat commanding voice Matt said, "Kathleen, take my hand."

Kathleen's eyes bulged. The dishes rattled louder.

Matt's need to protect her went into overdrive. "My hand. Now."

The gibberish continued. She swallowed and reached her hand toward his. Before palm met palm, she blinked hard and spoke clearly, "What did you say?" Her hand dropped to re-grip the table.

His eyebrows rose. "I'm not sure what you mean."

"Think," she challenged. "What did you say?" She swiped at the mess on her face.

"I'm not going to hurt you. Not ever?" he said with a question in his voice.

"No," she snapped, "not that. The last part. What was the last thing you said?" Her fingers were white where she clasped the table. Her shaking threatened to topple the tea.

"I'm here now. I'm someone safe." He pushed his palm closer

and watched as her irises returned to normal size. "Is that what you mean?" He flexed his fingers in a subtle reminder of his directive.

"Safety zone." Kathleen dropped her face. "Lucas." Like a flower closing, her torso folded into itself.

Matt reacted as her legs began to crumple. Darting around the table, he placed the chair beneath her just in time to prevent her collapse. A desperation to wrap his arms around her, to pull her into his body, assailed him. Instead, he leaned closer, not close enough to touch her, but close enough that she could feel his presence. "You're safe. I won't let you fall."

Her head dropped even deeper into her chest. Her hands flew to her lap, patting and searching. When they came up empty, they jerked to her head, touching the scarf. Her hands moved to her eyes.

Matt stooped to the ground and gathered her belongings. He placed them on the table. "Shhhh," he said close to her ear. "Relax. It's all right here." He repeated the statement until her body's vibrations lessened.

As she sent her hands to find her possessions, she tilted her head back and looked at him. In his crouched position, their eyes were mere inches apart.

Matt's torso jerked backwards. The eyes. No longer pure blue like a Minnesota spring sky. Amethyst flecks littered throughout. *Holy shit*, he said to himself. "Your eyes," he said to her.

Without moving her eyes from him, she lifted the sunglasses and covered the most beautiful, most expressive pair of eyes he'd ever encountered.

"Dazzling," he said. "Please don't cover them." He drew the

sunglasses from her face, setting them in her quivering hands.

Kathleen caught both lips between her teeth and he could tell she clamped down on them. Her lower lip trembled. She turned away and tucked the iPod and earphones into her lap. "Please, don't," she said on an exhale.

"Don't what?" he asked while he inched himself around the table. "Do you mind if I sit down for a few minutes?"

She didn't answer. She clenched her lips again, pulled her belongings even closer, bowed her head, and slumped her shoulders in defeat.

He lowered himself into the chair, feeling his body shudder. Exhaustion settled in his bones as the adrenaline drained. Matt wiped the sweat from his upper lip, sat forward in his seat, crossed his forearms on the table. *Those eyes*, he thought again. He extended his palm her direction. "Take my hand," he said again.

Blue and purple eyes lifted to his brown ones. Neither blinked as her hand came to him. When her palm touched his, her body stopped shuddering and his body warmed.

Matt shut his eyes, dropped his head, and tried to catch his breath. He held Kathleen's cold fingers in his. Surrounded by the loud bar crowd, they sat in a bubble of silent dread, fear, confusion, and even hope. Side by side, palm to palm.

KILEY

She would never know how long they sat there—her hand in his, her body and mind calm.

"Everything all right?" Sam asked, interrupting the moment.

Before the words completely formed, she ripped her hand away from Matt's. With the disconnection, the trembling started in her left foot. She pushed her foot into the floor, confirmed her scarf was secure, and affixed her sunglasses and earphones in place. Rising, she turned her face toward Sam and said in a crisp tone, "Fine, thank you." Without another word, she grabbed her bag and raced off the deck.

"Why are we running?" the little girl's voice spoke over her panting breath.

Kathleen stopped. The voice came from just behind her, but Kathleen refused to turn around.

"Grams, why are we running?"

Kathleen didn't speak.

"Look how long my hair is when it's wet."

Kathleen didn't turn, didn't move.

"Grams, turn around. Look. My hair stretches all the way to the middle of my shoulder. I hate these curls."

Inch by inch, Kathleen turned around and there stood her precocious Kiley, a long strand of wet hair pulled down. "You'll love those curls when you're older."

A full moon reflected off the girl's face when she turned a bright white smile to her. The dark kept Kathleen from seeing what she knew were large, milk-chocolate eyes with sinfully long eyelashes.

"You and Moms always say that." She huffed out the words and let the hair dance back to its tight curl. "I hate it right now."

Kiley shuffled up next to Kathleen and walked toward the bungalow. Kathleen stepped in beside her.

"So why were you running? You're a power walker, not a runner. And you don't run at night, anyway."

Kathleen took a deep breath before answering. "I was frightened."

"Oh, 'have a fright, take flight or fight'. We learned about that in science. Did you know you might even freeze? Mrs. Bostwick called it the fight, flight, or freeze response. What frightened you?"

Just as she had with Lucas, Kathleen avoided the question.

Several steps later Kiley asked, "Do you remember when I told you about Tommy Bryant?"

"The boy who picked on you? Yeah, I remember."

"Remember what you told me?"

Kathleen thought back to when Kiley had come for a weekend visit. Just the girls. Seth, Brice, Lucas, and Eli had gone in to Atlanta for a football game. Court, Amanda, Kiley, and she had a girls' pampering weekend at the cabin. Kiley had cried because some boy kept calling her names and now everyone had started it. "Curly Kiley," Kathleen said now, her heart tripping on the name.

"Yeah, him. Moms told me to ignore him. Daddy told me he'd talk to the teacher. *That* would make it worse. Court told me he was flirting and that if I flirted back it would scare him off. Do you remember what you said?"

Before Kathleen could answer, Kiley provided the punch line, "You told me to face that boy, 'chest-to-chest' you said. You told me I must face and handle my problems."

Kathleen stopped at the base of her stairs and watched the nine-year-old act like she was thirteen going on thirty.

She placed her fists on her waist, cocked her head in one direction and jutted out one hip. "Grammy. I know—we all know—well, maybe the pea-brain doesn't—" She stopped long enough to roll her eyes at her little brother's lack of worldly understanding. "You're not living." She paused, pulled her drying hair straight. "Can I come in?"

Kathleen looked from the pale face to the bolted front door and back again. Memories were not allowed. The world—the past world, the current world—were not allowed inside. She was sure that if she opened that door even a crack, the existence she had carved out would crumble like a sandcastle in a hurricane. She swallowed, tried to form words, tried to explain the inexplicable.

Kiley dropped her hands, then put them up in surrender. "Oh, Grammy. When are you going to face your own problems?"

Kathleen closed her eyes. Despair filled her heart as the girl's image retreated. She dragged her legs up the steps and across her porch. Her shaking hands struggled to get the keys into the locks. Sweaty palms slipped on the doorknob. "Please, no." She clenched her fists until her fingers ached, and she rubbed her damp palms on her clothes.

Kathleen entered her dark space, closed the door, dropped to her hands and knees, and crawled to the only place she felt safe.

Inside her closet, she shivered from cold and from dread. "Please, no."

The shadows became memories.

REFOCUSED

Ignoring Sam out of basic self-preservation, Matt dragged himself off Rosie's deck.

His flip-flops filled with sand and scratched his feet. He didn't notice. Fat raindrops splattered his face and hair. He didn't notice. The waves crashed against sand as thunder boomed around him. He didn't notice. Blue and amethyst eyes filled Matt's mind. Amethyst, his mother's birthstone. *Mom, please tell me what's going on. I'm in no man's land here.*

Matt's feet took him back to the condo, through the door, and across the space to the small patio overlooking the beach. His mind raced everywhere and nowhere.

With feet propped on the railing, he sat in the wicker chair and stared into the darkness. He replayed every detail of his encounter with Kathleen. When he closed his lids, her vivid eyes, her terror, her physical reaction, his physical reaction—he saw it all, he relived it all.

Exhausted, overwhelmed, weary, Matt laid his head back on the uncomfortable wicker. He drifted to sleep with a single question captured: *Are you ready to fight?*

He slept. He did not rest.

The ringing phone woke him. He opened his eyes only to

clamp them shut when the sun pierced his retinas. "Shit." Lights flashed behind his eyelids as he listened to his phone stop ringing and Skype start pinging on his computer. "Fuck," he said when he glanced at his watch. He looked down at the beach and knew he was too late to catch Kathleen on her walk. Running his hands through his still-damp hair, he cursed himself for not setting an alarm. A wave of guilt swept through him, followed by profound relief he had more time to reconsider.

The phone started again. "Oh no. Not now," he said to his reflection in the patio door. He kicked off the sandy shoes, scratched the area between his eyebrows. "Dammit." He took a deep breath and walked to the phone.

Nine missed calls from Jeff. Three from Patti. Matt raised the screen on his computer. Two Skype attempts from Patti.

Mom, let me get a shower, some sustenance, and then you need to give me step-by-step instructions. He rebuilt his train, touched letters one through four and headed to a hot shower.

As soap drifted over Matt's body the hot water settled his nerves but also heated his anger. Anger at his mother and at himself. He brushed his teeth and stared at his face in the mirror. Grunting, he wiped the sweat from his upper lip. "Fear sweat," he said to himself. With a shake of his head and roll of his eyes, he spat, rinsed, dressed. The white envelopes, the computer and the phone ignored, he pursued the simple quest for breakfast.

With his bacon and eggs, Matt also consumed a healthy dose of doubt, frustration, and embarrassment. As he'd resolved to do while eating, he gathered all the envelopes along with Mini's photo and put them back in the orange box. Shoving the orange box across the counter, he said, "Mom, I'm not sure what you expected. I'm not sure who you thought I was but—" He shook his head and opened his computer.

"Matt, what the hell," Patti started the conversation. "What's going on and why aren't you answering your damn phone?"

As guilt warred with indignation, Matt sat back on his stool, sipped his coffee, stared at his sister, and waited.

Patti shifted in her desk chair, moved a few pens around, and glanced at Matt's stoic face, and her bluster receded. "Jessica sent me this email telling me you were going on vacation. *Immediately.* She told me to leave you be. That was three days ago. Are you all right?"

With his elbows embracing the computer, Matt got closer to the camera. "What else did Jessica tell you?"

Sneering, she replied, "That's it. Literally." She counted on her fingers. "One, you were heading off for two weeks' vacation to some beach in North Carolina. Two, Alex would handle Jeff's shit. Three, if it was an emergency she knew how to reach you. When I asked her for more information she said you'd been needing a break since Mom died and now was the best time." She shrugged and then her head drew back. "Is that all that's going on?"

He chuckled. "Yes and no. Let me just say Mom had this all planned out and Jessica's job was to pull the trigger. It's more complicated than that, but it doesn't matter. I can tell you all about it—you still coming up for the board meeting?"

Patti's fingers worked at her lips for a long moment. "That's all I'm going to get? You leave NNJ, you leave Jeff's shit, no explanation, no phone call." Her eyebrows narrowed as she pinched her lip harder. "And you mention Mom."

Folding his arms over his chest, Matt sat back again. "Mom had a letter for me. I'll show you when we get together. She asked Jess to send me away to read it. Mom came to this beach for a gardening show. Mom, Dad, and Jess ambushed me." Matt looked away from the screen and sighed. "I came, I read, I did what she asked." He looked back to the screen with his bottom lip between his teeth. "She needed me to take care of something. I did what I could." He didn't tell her that he couldn't stop fear sweat from forming. He didn't tell her how much he wanted to—even believed he should—stay on the beach, with this woman.

Her face moved closer to the screen. "Mom sent you a letter?"

"Yeah. A box of them. I'll let you read them next week. Why is Jeff—"

"Mom sent you a bunch of letters?" She sat back, tapped her fingers on her desk, muttered something under her breath.

"She met a lady down here and wanted me to follow up on something they'd discussed," Matt hedged.

Patti swiped at her eyes. "Mom sent you a bunch of letters." A statement, not a question. She turned away, giving Matt a view of the back of her chair and the California skyline.

"Patti, come on. It wasn't like that—"

She held her hand up, halting his words. After several silent seconds, she turned back around, giving him a blank face. "So rather than handle Jeff, you've been dealing with some stranger."

Patti was right. He'd thought the very same thing that morning. The woman, as lovely as she was, as intriguing as she'd become, was a stranger to him. He'd planned to leave, to run away. But Patti's words, her tone, set off a protectiveness for Kathleen that stole his breath. *Stranger, maybe. Mine, absolutely.* Matt's gut clenched and a snarl twisted his lips. His eyes narrowed as he put his face right up to the screen.

"Sorry," she jumped in before he could reply. "You can tell me all about it later." She rolled her eyes and punched at the screen one more time. "Jeff is pushing me over the edge. You were supposed to call him this morning. At least that's what he said. My phone started ringing at 4:30. A.M.!"

"Patti—"

"So about Jeff."

Matt blew out a long breath, shook his head clear and settled back on his stool. He tried to read his sister's eyes through a computer screen. He pulled his notepad closer, ready to take over. "He's just an ass. As soon as we hang up, I'll call him and take his wrath. He should be thrilled with the solution we came up with. Wanna give me a heads-up on his problem today?" He nabbed his pen and prepared to take notes.

"He wants us—*you*—to save him more money. What do any of our clients want?"

Matt's hand paused above the notepad as his mother's words worked through his consciousness. *NNJ is about helping rich people keep their money out of the hands of the IRS.* The orange box seized his attention.

He looked at his sister, his business partner, his friend. After wiping the sweat from his lip, he asked, "Patti, would you describe your life as worthwhile?"

Her face scrunched up and her nose wiggled. "Oh, god, have we hit a midlife crisis? Is that what all this is about? Didn't you finish that stage when you bought that fancy-ass Mercedes?"

Shaking his head and laughing, he said, "Never mind. I'll call

87

Jeff now. Is everything good with Dave and the guys?"

"Yep." Her short, curt answer ensured he understood she was both angry and hurt.

"I'll copy you on whatever I send him. I'll have my phone with me from now on. He shouldn't have any trouble finding me. See you late next week."

Before Matt pushed the disconnect key, Patti called out, "You said Mom wanted you to meet some lady?" Her eyebrows quirked up while she propped her chin in her palms. "Did you meet her?"

Matt bristled at her reference to Kathleen as "some lady."
"Yeah, last night. It's not a big deal." Matt looked way from Patti again, a sure sign to both of them he was lying. "Mom wanted me to tell her something."

"I'll talk to you later."

He looked back at the screen. "Hold up. I'll explain it all next week. It will make more sense if you can see what Mom sent me. It's over. I'll admit it blew me away at first. But I'm focused again."

"Did you do whatever it was Mom wanted?" Her eyes stayed focused away from him. "Who was she?"

"I did the best I could. Mom—well, I don't know what Mom was thinking, to be honest. I'm not even sure what Mom knew." He, too, looked away. "I've even considered asking Dad if she was in her right mind."

"Matt," she called. Once she had his attention, she continued, "Mom was always in her right mind."

Matt gave his sister a sad smile. "You're right. But that doesn't mean she was always *right*," he said with a wink. "Relax, big sister. All's well. I'll deal with Jeff."

"When was she ever wrong?" She shook her head and snickered. "When are you heading back to Minnesota?"

"I've got one more thing to wrap up here, and then I'll book a ticket. Love you, Patti-cakes." He disconnected and spent the next fifteen minutes wondering if he'd just lied to his sister.

AMANDA

While Matt ignored his orange box and pretended he was still a tax attorney, two miles away Kathleen sat on the steps leading to the locked door of her loft. In her hands, she clutched a different white envelope. She didn't need to open the letter. The words were imprinted on her mind.

My Dear Friend ~

I came to this beach to learn about gardening. Instead, I learned about living. I have only one way to thank you—I'll send him your way. He can make you safe again. Together, you can both live real lives.

Remember your promise. Rosie's, seven o'clock. You'll know when he arrives. He'll recognize you, too. You'll be ready. So will he.

Until we meet again,

Betty

Kathleen laid her head on her knees, still clinging to the letter. "I'm sorry, Betty. I wasn't ready."

The pitiful memorial on the wall blurred as Kathleen gulped back the emotions forcing themselves into her chest.

"Hey."

Looking up, she found a vision of her daughter-in-law sitting one step down, her legs extended, her feet tapping on the wall. Kathleen blinked and waited.

"You know what made you the best mother-in-law?" Amanda's head tilted and one eyebrow lifted as if she were lecturing Lucas on why muddy shoes were not allowed in the house.

Holding the woman's dark eyes, Kathleen wiped her nose with her arm and shrugged.

"Because you rarely gave advice. You almost never asked questions that were none of your business."

"But? I sense the but," Kathleen whispered across the cramped space.

"No, not but." She smiled and continued, "*And* the few times you believed you had to say something, you said what you needed to say and then you dropped it. The best part was that you never made me feel as if you were watching to see if we followed your advice. You truly just said it and then moved on."

Kathleen nodded. "But…"

Amanda's head gestured at the black lines marking the wall. "That's not how we want to be remembered." She smiled that crooked-toothed smile she used whenever she had the last word in a debate. "It's time for you to open that damn door. It's time you open them all." Her hand moved to Kathleen's knee and squeezed.

One tear slipped down Kathleen's face as the perfect woman for her imperfect son disappeared. She flattened Betty's note and folded it into a perfect square. She touched her marks, adding a new one.

As she stepped off the last stair, she looked over her shoulder at the locked door. She clicked off the light and shut the hallway door. "Oh, Amanda, don't you see? Sometimes my advice was wrong."

ME, NOT YOU

Satisfied with Jeff's case and that his other work projects were back on track, Matt closed his computer, then ran his hands through his hair. He collected his keys and wallet and prepared to complete the last task on his list before he returned to his life. Tapping the orange box before flattening his palm on the shoe's iconic symbol, he watched the white clouds drift past his window. "Mom, I'm sorry. I really am. Maybe if you'd only talked to me, told me something…"

Spinning on his heels, he walked toward the door. As he turned the doorknob, he glanced once more at the counter. An orange box, a notepad, a computer and a pen. Perfectly aligned. *That's all my life is.* "Dammit." He stalked back to the box, popped it open and pulled out the fifth envelope. "Dammit," he said one more time before stuffing the envelope deep into his pocket.

On his walk to Rosie's, he searched for the right words, the right approach. His feet hit the deck at 6:42. *Eighteen minutes.* Nodding at Rosie, he found his usual seat at the bar.

"You want a beer?" she asked.

"No, just soda. I'm not staying long."

She narrowed her eyes and stiffened her back. "You heading back to Minnesota?"

"Yeah, hopefully tomorrow."

She snorted, looked away, and shook her head. With a deep sigh, she said, "Why did you come here tonight?" Her eyes pierced his as she planted her knuckles on her hips.

He shrugged, dropped his eyes, and replied, "I thought it best I tell her myself that whatever my mother had planned, it can't involve me." His stomach ached as the words left his mouth. He closed his eyes and forced his body to relax. When he reopened his eyes, Rosie was walking away from him. She never returned with his drink.

Matt sat at the bar, rubbing his chin, still reaching for the best words. His body chilled, alerting him when the clock clicked to seven. He clutched the edge of his seat as the iciness raced down his back. Staring at the ceiling, he swallowed and wondered why his eyes felt so full and his throat so tight.

When Rosie appeared behind the bar and began pouring a glass of tea for Kathleen, he rose and turned that direction.

Before he moved forward Rosie whispered, "Just leave her alone, okay? Sam's on his way. He can help her from here. Your mother—and you, I guess—helped us realize we need to step up. You can leave with a clear conscience. She trusts Sam. They bonded somewhat when he was building that house. He'll catch her. Go home. Leave her alone now."

Nausea pummeled him. His hands formed tight fists as his eyes narrowed. "He'll catch her?" he fumed under his breath.

She tipped the tea glass his direction. "Your mom was an awesome lady. I hope you'll understand when I say it might be best if you didn't return to my bar." A tear tracked down her face, but she turned away without giving him a chance to respond.

Matt opened his fists and flexed his fingers. Cracking his neck left then right, he shut his eyes and took deep breaths until control returned. "He'll catch her?" *Fuck that.* He spun toward the deck and froze.

Her chair faced the table instead of the ocean. Her head hung as if it was too heavy for her shoulders to carry. Looking more carefully, he realized she wore the same clothes, the same scarf, as yesterday. Deep half-moon indentions trailed up her forearms. The earphones were not in place and her sunglasses sat askew. Even from this distance he could see the tremors racking her body. Her hands twisted into the tablecloth.

A breath stuck in Matt's lungs. As he watched Rosie try to engage Kathleen, he replayed their encounters. When her trembling hand reached toward the glass, he saw it. He saw what was missing. *Pay attention.* He understood the directive more now. *How did I miss that?* The nausea returned to his throat as he started towards her.

Three steps into his journey, a hard chest stopped him.

"Go home," Sam said.

Matt moved back one step. His fists clenched again as his control slipped. "What?" Heat rose into his face when he looked at the man.

"Matt, go home. This is not your fault. It had to happen. We've—Rosie and I—we've been watching for this. We should have intervened earlier." He put his palms up and softened his tone. "You can go home." He offered Matt a sad smile. "We will—"

Before he could finish speaking, Matt shoved him out of the way and let the snarl fly. "My mother gave her to me." The words from the first letter blinked like a neon sign. With balled fists, he glared at Sam. "A precious gift. A gift *for me*."

"Matt—" Sam started.

"I know I haven't handled this well. I'm still confused and angry with my mother. But I can't deny…" He tried to find the words to explain. "My mom was never wrong. In her first letter, she said she was giving me a gift." He swallowed, moved his eyes from Sam back to Kathleen. "A precious gift."

"Matt—" Sam tried again but Matt Nelson walked to the woman on the deck.

BIRDS

"Can I get you something—"

"Rosie, I'll take that beer now," Matt interrupted as he pulled out the chair next to Kathleen and sat. His right hand wrapped around her damaged clenched fist, protecting the skin and protecting the woman. The coil of fear in his chest released and a deep peace settled in him. *I won't miss anything else*. He ran his hand up her scratched arm, maneuvered his chair closer. "Safe. You're safe now."

Kathleen's body stopped rattling as deep breaths filled her lungs once, twice, three times. "I, I, I—"

"Rosie, can you get Kathleen's salad and bring me dinner, too?" He put his arm around Kathleen and pulled her into his body. "I've got this. Kathleen and I need a few minutes, but we'll be right here." Trying to smile at Rosie, he mouthed, "I've got her."

Rosie directed her gaze to Kathleen's forearms and back to Matt.

Matt nodded to let Rosie know he saw it, too. "Sam's here. All of us—together—we've got her." Kathleen's body twitched against him. Turning his mouth to the top of her head, he whispered into the scarf, "Shhh, relax into me for a minute or two. I won't let you fall. Remember?" He used his left hand to tuck her face into his chest. "Take the time you need." With his right hand covering her marred skin, his left hand tucked around her neck, keeping her pulled into the safety of his body.

"I'll be right back," Rosie said, more to Kathleen than to Matt. Her eyes narrowed at Matt. She glanced at Kathleen's hands now relaxed on the table. Rosie's tension released and her shoulders dropped when she mouthed, "Thank you."

"I, I, I came to tell you to tell your mom," Kathleen struggled to speak. "Tell your mom, I'm sorry. I'm not ready." She attempted to pull back, but Matt held her close.

"Don't move. Give us both a few minutes, okay? Then we'll talk." Matt's left hand flexed on her neck and he allowed his thumb to run up her jaw. He closed his eyes with his cheek planted in the scarf. *Mom, I need you right now.*

"Here's your dinner," Sam said several minutes later.

Feeling Kathleen's panic start, Matt opened his eyes, turned his entire body in her direction. With both hands on her shoulders, he said, "Look at me. Only at me." His fingers tilted her chin so that her face pointed at him. "Let me fix your sunglasses. You check your scarf. We'll eat. You *are* safe here. At Rosie's. *With me.* For the next fifteen minutes let's pretend everything is normal." Her shoulders jerked in his palms, but he felt her slight nod.

Matt moved the sunglasses so they sat correctly on her face. Collecting her hand in his again, he turned to face Sam. "Thanks, Sam." He frowned when Sam placed two salads on the table. "Salad?"

Sam's eyes flared when he noted Kathleen's arms. With an unsteady voice, he moved his focus to Matt. "Rosie's call."

Matt barked a short, nervous laugh. "Ahh, tell her I said yum and I deserve it."

Sam looked at Kathleen, who sat staring at her salad. His eyebrows raised as he looked at Matt.

"We'll be okay," he answered Sam's unspoken query.

Sam squeezed Matt's shoulder as he walked away. "We'll be inside when you're ready for refills."

Matt picked up Kathleen's knife and fork, placed them in her hands. She gripped the utensils until her knuckles turned white. "I, I—"

"I'm hungry. And if Rosie is punishing me with rabbit food, I will eat every bite." Matt poured the ranch dressing on his salad, speared a large bite and stuffed his mouth, chewing loudly and rudely.

Kathleen sat still for a few more seconds before she shifted her head and looked at him. Her lips tipped up and crinkles appeared at the edges of the sunglasses.

Matt chewed louder, prepared an even bigger bite.

Kathleen's grin got a touch bigger before she turned to create her checkerboard masterpiece. She ate six bites with the spoon, placed her napkin over the bowl, sipped her tea. With her ritual complete, she clutched at the tablecloth, put her face towards her lap and said, "Tell your mom I'm sorry. I wasn't ready." Her voice wobbled and her left foot tapped against the wood decking.

Matt tossed his napkin on the table, grabbed her hand and waited for the tapping to stop. "Not ready for what?"

"You," she said and added a whisper, "Opening doors. Living."

He inhaled a deep breath, moved his chair closer to her side. He tucked her in next to him and asked, "How did you know her?"

She forced herself back from his chest and peered at him

through the dark glasses. "What did she tell you?"

He repositioned them so they were face-to-face with his thighs surrounding hers. With his hands embracing her neck, he said, "Kathleen, my mom died six months ago. She—"

Kathleen tried to jerk away, and her feet scurried underneath them.

"Whoa. Hold on, I got you." He waited until she settled, but she would not give him her face. "Her breast cancer returned after her trip here. She didn't get the chance to get me ready. She left me letters." He reached into his pocket and pulled out the fifth envelope. "I've only read the first four." He placed the envelope on the table and put his hand back on her neck. "She hasn't told me anything. She simply directed me here. To you. But I found you without her help."

Her face lifted toward his and her hands gripped at his arms. "I'm still not ready."

"Me, either. Why don't we talk and try to understand what's happening? Can we do that?"

Her short nails dug into the skin of his arms as the pulse in her neck quickened. "She appeared one day." She swallowed, dug deeper into his arms. "Your mom pulled up a chair and started talking."

Matt's arms hurt and he fought the urge to shake her off. "That doesn't sound like my mom. She could be outgoing, but it usually took a while before she showed that side of herself."

Kathleen's grip lessened, but she still held his arms. "I didn't speak to her the first two nights except to be polite. But on the third night she pulled my sunglasses off and told me it was time. Those were her words, 'It's time'."

"Time for what?"

Her hands dropped from his arms and she pulled her neck out of his palms. "To get on with the business of living."

Matt took her hands in his and held them in her lap. "I think that's her goal for me, too."

"I'm not sure I can," she whispered as her bottom lip trembled.

He settled back in his seat, pulling their hands to his knees. After watching her for several seconds, he came to a decision. "I'm going to take your glasses off," he said as he raised his hands. Her body stiffened, but he pretended not to notice. Matt's heart clenched. Huge, bright purple irises held his gaze. With the pad of his thumb Matt touched the deep circles under her eyes. "Did you sleep at all?"

Her head shook as dampness pooled in her eyes.

He ran his thumb under the other eye and up the scratches on her arms. With his gaze on the cuts, he asked, "How did this happen?"

She tried to pull her arms away, but he held firm. "Birds," she whispered. "Birds."

Matt looked up into her sad eyes. Her eyes stayed focused on the wounds as her shoulders dropped lower and lower. "You have birds?"

"Sort of."

He raised his eyebrows and waited. "Can I meet your birds?" he asked when he understood she was not planning to explain.

"Not if I can help it," she responded. "But I may not be able to stop them now."

They sat in silence. When she looked toward the water he watched the veins in her neck pulse while he puzzled over her odd answers.

"Refills," Sam said as he presented the glasses.

Kathleen's hands jerked away and darted to her scarf and over her eyes. Not finding her sunglasses in place, panic radiated through her body.

"Here," Matt said, placing the lenses over her eyes. Before he could pull her into him, she rose and took several steps back, sending the chair crashing to the floor.

"I have to go," she stammered before bolting away.

Sam and Matt stood together and watched her run.

Without turning away from the fleeing woman, Sam said, "Please, Matt, don't start something you can't stay to finish." The man walked away without another word while Matt stared at the white envelope she'd dropped as she fled.

TWO ENVELOPES

With both letters tucked deep into his pocket, Matt hurried back to his condo. After shoving his computer and all the other paraphernalia aside, he placed the envelopes side-by-side. For a long while he stood and stared at his mother's handwriting. Somehow seeing Kathleen's name in his mother's fancy script shocked him more than anything else. *It's all real.* His head darted between each envelope as he tried to decide which to face first. Pulling the stool under him, he collapsed and pulled Kathleen's letter into his hands.

He lifted out the single page. The letter just barely held together as if it had been folded and unfolded a thousand times. Matt's chest tightened as he read.

My Dear Friend ~

I came to this beach to learn about gardening. Instead, I learned about living. I have only one way to thank you—I'll send him your way. He can make you safe again. Together, you can both live real lives.

Remember your promise. Rosie's, 7 o'clock. You'll know when he arrives. He'll recognize you, too. You'll be ready. So will he.

Until we meet again,

Betty

Although he expected his mother's name, seeing it jolted him. "Oh, Mom, what have you done?" He laid the page on the counter and faced his own.

Matt ~

It's hard doing this without knowing if you went to Rosamunda Beach. Or if you are doing what I ask. You have questions and I expect you're frightened. This letter will not make things better. I'm sorry for that.

To get the answers, you must decide if you're brave enough to ask the questions and work through the consequences. I'll tell you that I was not that brave.

I realize you're desperate to open the next envelope—to plow through for more. Don't. Please don't. Take the rest of today to think. Decide if you want to take the next step. No one can live your life, make your choices. What do you want the next 25 years to be like?

Don't laugh at me when I suggest this—try to picture a new life. Who would be in it? How would you fill your days? Who would be with you? Imagine a blank page and DECIDE how to fill it. Maybe I have this all wrong—maybe you have everything you want in life. If that's so, get on the next flight.

Regardless of your decision, you have my love—always my love.
~Mom

He stopped reading and looked through the window at the hard rain and lightning. Crushing the letter in his hand, he gnawed on his lips until the metallic taste of blood brought him back to the present. He tossed the crumpled paper to the floor, flipped off the lights and stalked to the bathroom. Patti's words followed him. *When was she ever wrong?*

In bed that night, just before sleep pulled him under, his eyes popped open. He grabbed his phone and set the alarm.

950 DAYS

A misty drizzle, gray clouds and a light wind greeted Matt when he arrived on the beach early the next morning. In one hand, he held the flip-flops Kathleen had left behind on her mad dash. In his other, protected from the rain, was the letter his mother sent her. He tried to decide where his bravery started and stopped. As he walked toward the direction he was sure she'd come, he pictured a white piece of paper.

He started with his family. Patti, Dave and their boys. His dad. Jessica and her family. He pictured golf and football, Thanksgiving and Christmas. He tried to add his office to the paper, but he couldn't force the image to stay. Closing his eyes for a few steps, he tried to picture the office's oriental carpet or the huge walnut desk. Instead, his mind filled with blue-and-purple eyes, colorful scarves, and laughter. A laughter he had yet to experience. A laughter he wasn't sure ever burst forth.

His body alerted him to her coming approach, not a chill this time. Instead, it felt as if his legs picked up speed without his making the decision. His stride lengthened, a smile spread, questions formed. Twenty yards later he saw her. Black yoga pants, black shirt, black hat, white scarf fluttering around her head. Sunglasses, headphones, and that steady stride. If she saw him, she gave no indication.

Matt slowed his pace until she moved closer. When she was within a few feet, he spun and glided in next to her. With his shoulder, he tapped her. It was several steps before she turned her face toward him. He pointed at her earphones and gestured for her to remove them.

After a heavy sigh, she tilted her head to him and removed the device. She cradled the ear buds in her right hand.

Matt's hand reached over and took her left hand in his, lacing their fingers together with her flip-flops dangling below their fingers. "What are you listening to?"

Her index finger dug into the top of his hand. "A book."

He turned his head in her direction, but she maintained her posture and pace. "A book?"

She looked at the tiny iPod attached to her pants.

"What kind of book?"

"Faye and Chace. My friends," she whispered. Her finger dug in deeper.

Using the pressure as a sign of increasing stress, he moved on to something else. "Did you get some sleep last night?"

"Yes."

After several more strides Matt waded in again, "What do you do?"

Another sigh. "Read."

"Read? Are you an editor or publisher or something?"

Her fingers loosened and she tried to pull free.

His hand tightened around hers and he tugged her body one step closer to his. "Kathleen, let's just talk. I'll tell you about me?"

As if clinging to a buoy, her hand tightened in his. "Your last name is Nelson. You turned fifty last summer. You are a tax attorney. With your father, sister and her husband, you run a very successful firm where you spend your day antagonizing the IRS. Nelson, Nelson & Johnson. Or, NNJ, as your mother liked to say. You have two nephews, Jake and Joey. Your sister and her husband run the California branch. One of your nephews, Joey, I think, will likely join the firm. The other one is more interested in doing something related to sports. You live in Minnesota. You've always lived in Minnesota. You love sports. Especially something called the Gophers. You were engaged once a long time ago but you never married." She snorted before adding, "And your mom is confident you have no children waiting in the wings."

"Okay," he stretched the word with his deep Minnesota vowels. "Did she show you my health report, too?"

Another snort, another failed attempt to pull her hand away. "You're about six foot three, your hair is more salt than pepper, you have a runner's body. Your eyes are caramel. As far as she knows you're healthy."

"Okay," he said again, a deep frown forming on his brow.

They walked another quarter mile before she turned back.

"Your turn," he said.

All four of her fingernails dug into his hand and Matt closed his eyes to the pain and the reflex to jerk away.

"I'm originally from Atlanta. Until eighteen months ago, I lived in the Western North Carolina mountains. I don't work. I read."

"Last name?"

A stumble before she answered, "Bridges."

"Family?"

After fifteen minutes of silence she said in a computer-like voice, "Two children. Brice and Courtney. Age thirty-two and twenty-four respectively. A cop and a dietician. One daughter-in-law, Amanda. Also thirty-two. Also a cop." She stopped her choreographed speech, took a deep breath, dug her nails in deeper and then continued. "Two grandchildren. Kiley and Lucas. Nine and five."

A trickle of blood oozed between Matt's fingers. His ring finger moved to trace the rough edges where her finger used to be. "Husband?" he dared.

"Gone."

Another drop of blood leaked down his hand. "How often do you see your kids?"

She tugged at her hand, wiggling until she forced him to release her. She stepped behind him and turned toward a bungalow that sat a few hundred yards away.

He followed her, shaking his deadened fingers and looking at the half-moon cuts. Identical cuts to those she had the night before.

She stopped at the bottom of her steps, turned to him, removed her sunglasses and gave him bright purple eyes. "I haven't seen any of them in 950 days." Kicking sand at him, she spun and darted up her stairs.

From the sand Matt watched her unlock six deadbolts before she slipped inside. Painted the same color as the sand, had she not walked him to the steps, he could have walked by without seeing it. Darkly tinted windows. On the left side of her porch rested two lounge chairs and a table. On the right, a swing rocked in the breeze. "950 days?" Before he walked away, he put his mother's letter and Kathleen's flip-flops on the welcome mat. With his palm against the locked door, he whispered, "I'll see you in a few hours."

PAINT OVER THIS

With her head leaning into the locked door, Kathleen sat on the top step. "Seth," she whispered into the darkness, "I said their names today." She waited for an answer that would never come. With a loud pop, she pulled the cap off the permanent marker. Extending her left arm, she added another tick mark to the wall. "Nine hundred fifty-one."

"Do you remember when Kiley drew that cartoon on the wall next to the TV?"

Kathleen stilled at the sound of her husband's voice.

"She used every single crayon in her box. How many colors? Sixty-four?"

Kathleen closed her eyes, bit on her bottom lip and held her breath.

"You wouldn't let me paint over it. You said one day it might be worth a million dollars." His voice teased her and she knew his eyes sparkled. "That girl had talent somewhere, but it was not in art." He laughed. "Or sports."

Kathleen's body started to vibrate, and her lungs burned for more air.

"Paint over this."

The air changed and he was gone.

#6

Matt~

I need to explain why I didn't talk to you about this, why I left these letters instead of sitting down with you.

It all happened so fast. I got the call from my doctor the week after I returned from North Carolina. Your Dad quit NNJ and left it in your hands. After that I faced treatments and decisions. Those are my excuses but not the reasons.

I didn't tell you because I was afraid you'd shut me down. You're like your father and talking about feelings is a slow form of torture. When I first tried to explain this to your dad—well, let's just say he thought I had lost my mind. What if you thought the same thing? What if you wouldn't listen? What if all I accomplished was getting you to defend your current life?

My original plan was to drag you to the beach with me. I even made the reservations. You and I were to go first, and then I'd have Dad, Patti, and her crew join us. A family vacation. I assumed—no, I knew—you'd recognize her. And, if you didn't—if I was wrong—I'd find another way to make her safe again.

Your dad and I go to these support group things and to start each group they ask a question. It's not a discussion question. It's a question to make us think, to help us leave our lives in the best way we can. We're supposed to ask ourselves the question over and over, using the same words, until an answer settles. I want to pose the same question to you.

What is your heart's desire? What is your heart's desire? What is your heart's desire?

The question has become so important. My answer's easy. For you and Patti to find your heart's desire. That is why I wrote you these letters.

Go for a walk, Mattie, and let that question run through your mind. The answer is your compass, your direction. Dare I say your destiny?

In the next letter, I'll tell you what I know.

Always,

Mom

PS – Ask her to tell you about what she's reading.

Sitting on his small deck, still sweaty and covered in sand, Matt digested his mother's words. Carefully he folded the letter, put it back into the envelope, and placed it under his water bottle on the table. He settled back and watched the clouds run through the blue sky.

"What is my heart's desire? What is my heart's desire? What is my heart's desire?" The more he said the words, the more the cadence matched the crashing waves. As the words continued to move from his mouth to his ears pictures formed. The family at a Gophers game, bundled in knit caps and wool scarves, cheering like crazy people. Behind him stood his sister and her family all red-cheeked and roaring. The people around him laughed and shouted.

"What is my heart's desire? What is my heart's desire?" In a new picture, he stood in the water as the sun's rays dipped and burned bronze, forming rays like the spokes on a wheel.

Her scarf fluttered in the wind, slapping him in the face as she turned in his arms. No sunglasses. A full smile.

Matt's arms gripped his chair as the picture dissolved. His imagination conjured her laughter echoing around him.

"LOVE"

With a full cooler, a book he'd pulled from the shelf in his condo, and his mother's latest letter in his pocket, Matt stood a few feet from Kathleen's steps.

She dozed in the farthest lounge chair. Her sunglasses sat on the floor. Her scarf fluttered in the breeze, and a book lay on her chest. A ray of sun crossed her calves. It dawned on Matt that even in sleep she wasn't relaxed. Her fingers curled into fists; her lips were a tight line.

"Good afternoon," he called across the space as he moved toward her.

As she had the first night, she exploded backwards. Her feet scurried underneath her, trying to find traction on the fabric. Her breath quickened and her body shuddered. Her eyes flashed open and changed from a brilliant blue to a deep purple.

"Hey, hey, it's me," he said, dropping the cooler and book. He raced to her and scooped her up in his arms. He plopped into the chair and wrapped her with his arms and legs. "I'm here, love. Shh."

Her scuttling continued, but instead of trying to get away she burrowed into him. Her hands gripped and twisted his shirt.

Her forehead landed in his chest as her head rotated left and right and left and right.

Matt kissed her head, squeezing her tighter. "Kathleen, can you tell me who's got you?" He spoke into her ear. "Who's got you?"

As if the words were an off switch, she stopped moving. Her body collapsed and molded into his.

"Who's got you?" he whispered this time.

She never responded, but her body relaxed one muscle at a time.

Matt's lips landed in her hair, his eyes closed, and he pulled in several deep breaths. "I've got you," he said. "You're safe."

With calm determination, she shook her head. "Never safe again," she slurred into his shirt.

What is your heart's desire? His mother's words moved into his consciousness. "You," he said where only he, and maybe his mother, could hear.

Matt held her close and watched the spilled ice melt across her deck and drip between the boards. He moved his hands to her neck and carefully pulled her to look at him. Blue eyes met his. Blue, he was coming to understand, translated to control. When the purple surfaced, Kathleen felt threatened.

For the first time in his life, Matt leaned in and kissed a woman on the tip of her nose. With his t-shirt sleeve he wiped the moisture from her face as her eyes tracked his every movement.

"I brought snacks and beer." He dipped his head toward the upturned cooler. "What do you say I clean this up and we settle in for a bit?" He lifted her off his body so she sat on the edge of the lounger. Rising, he picked up the cooler, then he grabbed out two beers and put them on the table. "Get comfortable. I've got ridiculously tiny salami and cheese slices."

Just as she had when he'd made a spectacle of eating salad like a child, she tipped her lips with the tiniest smile.

Matt grinned back and promised himself he'd hear her laugh. Soon.

As she moved to re-seat herself, he asked, "What are you reading?"

Her head swung to him. "What am I reading?"

He looked at the book on the ground then back at her. "You told me you read. I'm curious what you read. And"—he nodded at the book he'd left near the steps—"I'm wondering if I picked out something decent."

She popped up, took the three steps to retrieve the book. With her palms, she dusted the book, flapping the pages to get off the dirt. She clutched it to her chest before she returned to her seat.

Monitoring her movements, he wondered at her reverence for a paperback. Once she appeared comfortable he tried again. "What are you reading?"

"Do you really want to know?" she asked as she laid her head back and turned her face his direction, still clutching the book he'd brought.

"Is there a reason I wouldn't want to know?" he teased.

A slight blush moved up her cheeks as she sat up. She crossed her knees, leaned forward, and gave him a large, bright, wonderful smile.

"It's about this girl named Rachel. She has a five-year-old son and they're broke because her husband manipulated her when she was just seventeen. He ended up being one of those money-grabbing fake preachers—"

Spellbound, Matt watched as the quiet, scared, attractive creature in the corner bloomed into a beautiful, spirited, exuberant woman. His heart pounded and his gut clenched with the need to bring her back to life.

"You listening?" She shook his knee, breaking him from his thoughts.

Shaking himself back to the present, he said, "Yeah. I'll admit I got confused. I'm not a reader and that was a lot to follow."

Her smile lit the space. "It's a long book with several subplots." She shrugged. "Sorry."

He reached over and grabbed her hand. "Don't apologize. It was—*you*—were wonderful."

Purple leaked into the blue.

He pulled his hand back and pointed at his book still in her hands. "Is my book going to be that good?"

She pulled the book back and stared at the cover. "Ahh."

"That bad?"

Blue eyes sparkled at him. "It's a good book, but it's not written for men. It's about four sisters who visit Nantucket when their mother dies. I don't think there's a man in the entire book. It's what Brice would call a chick's book." When her body stiffened, the air thickened and chilled around them.

Matt jumped in, "Do you have a book I would enjoy? I have no idea what to choose."

Her shoulders relaxed and a new grin formed. She stood, tossed the book onto his lap. "I'll be right back." With a small skip in her step she disappeared into her house.

Matt ran his fingers through his hair, took a few deep breaths. "Fuck," he said. He revisited the events of the past hour. "Love?"

he choked out as he sat straighter in his seat. Before he could process his first ever use of an endearment, the door opened and she flounced out.

"Catch," she said as she threw a book his direction.

Snatching it mid-air, he turned the cover towards him. "*The Bat?*"

She resettled on her chair, crossed her ankles over knees like an excited teenager. "A detective series. Harry Hole. He's broken and he gets too involved in his cases. I've read that book three times, and even though I know who the villain is I can never find the clues."

As she talked more about Harry Hole and the other books in the series, Matt glanced at her arms. No new scratch marks. The ones from yesterday were fading. His gaze tracked past her black shorts to her red short-sleeved shirt. His eyes stopped when they reached the scarf. Red and black swirls looped around her head.

"You want to try that?" she asked.

"I'll give him a try. You going back to Rachel?"

She placed her sunglasses back on her face, stretched her short legs, flexed her toes and relaxed. She wiggled and reached for her book. When she touched it, she sighed, smiled and settled in to read.

Matt sat back, opened his book, prepared to delve into Harry Hole's world. Several pages in, Matt halted when he noted a sentence underlined. "*Not even a mother knows her child's deepest secrets.*" Matt looked over at Kathleen, who was obviously engrossed in her novel. Leafing through the pages, he discovered many other passages marked. "Kathleen," he said at the same time he extended the book her direction. When she turned, he asked, "Why are some passages marked?"

She looked at him and then at the book. She took it from his grasp and rifled through the pages. "Messages," she said as she handed over the book.

"Messages?"

"Yeah. Just words that explain things, I guess." She shrugged and turned back to her own book.

As he tried to digest the words on the page, his thoughts careened. He started to doze with a slight sweat forming on his lip, hoping he was brave enough to ask the questions, brave enough to understand the messages.

PANDORA

"Matt. Matt." The whisper-soft voice woke him from his sleep. He blinked and opened his eyes to find Kathleen's face mere inches from his own. Her eyes hid behind the sunglasses again. Licking his dry lips, he gripped the armrests and gained control over his impulse to kiss her.

"I have to go," she said.

Matt pushed himself upright, forcing her to back away. "What time is it?" He shook his head and ran his hands through his hair, trying to rid himself of the cobwebs dogging his mind.

"6:40."

He scanned her body, finding she'd changed from shorts to a pale pink dress. Her scarf swirled in a variety of pink and purple shades. "Where are we going?" he asked as he scooted his body more upright.

"I, well—" Her voice halted. "I have to head to Rosie's." She backed away. As she turned her body, she placed the headphones in her ears.

"Hold up." He rose, straddling the seat. "I'll go with you."

She stood still for a few seconds and her left foot started tapping.

Seeing her tension, Matt moved through his sleepiness, put his arms around her waist and pulled her flush against him. Instantly, her body relaxed.

"They're coming. I can't stop them anymore," she said.

"Who's coming?" he asked against her hair.

She shook her head, took a step forward, forcing his arms to drop. "I need to go." She started to the steps.

Matt caught up, linked their fingers and again massaged the rough edges.

Her fingers flexed, relaxed and then gripped his. Her forefinger tapped against his hand.

"Turn it on," he said.

Her eyebrows lifted above her sunglasses.

"Go ahead, turn on your story. I'll enjoy watching the sun lower."

Her face stayed on his for a beat before she used her right hand to turn on the device. Her stride increased to its morning pace, her face remained forward.

Matt's pocket buzzed as the lights of Rosie's deck appeared. Squeezing her hand, he motioned to the phone he'd retrieved.

With a nod, her fingers opened while she maintained her pace.

"What?" Matt answered with curtness. "And before you answer, it's Friday night and *I am supposed to be on vacation.*"

"You are supposed to be protecting my assets," Jeff returned.

Matt pulled the phone from his ear, glaring at the screen. From a distance, he heard Jeff ranting, but he saw Kathleen stopped on the sand, her left foot kicking at it. Her fists opened and closed.

With Jeff still talking, Matt stuffed the phone in his pocket, kicked off his flip-flops and ran.

Stepping in front of Kathleen, he placed his palms on her

neck. "What's happening, Kathleen? You come here every night."

A shaking hand came to his waist. "It's not quite seven."

Matt's eyebrows lifted into his hair. With his fingers, he stroked the back of her neck until she settled. "And?"

"I go in at seven. That's the promise."

"What would happen if we went in at five minutes before seven?" He held her with his fingers and his eyes. Even though he could not see behind the dark lenses, he felt sure her eyes were fading from purple back to blue.

"One wrong decision and the world collapses."

They stood in the sand with ocean breezes surrounding them until the clock moved to seven.

"It's time," she said as she moved around him and up the steps.

Matt walked the ten feet to gather his flip-flops. A frown and an idea formed when he realized his Kathleen had morphed back into the cold woman from the first night.

Before approaching her table, Matt caught Sam's eyes. He pivoted and walked to the bar. "Rosie here?"

Sam's gaze flitted around, nodded toward Rosie taking an order in the back corner. He returned his focus to Matt. "Everything okay?"

Matt chuckled. "I honestly have no clue how to answer that. But I have an idea, a theory to test."

Sam filled a glass and waited.

"Have you met the real Kathleen?" Matt asked as he reached toward the beer Sam extended.

"Not sure what that means. This"—he pointed in Kathleen's direction—"is pretty much what we see."

Matt nodded, taking one large gulp before adding, "Can you and Rosie join us at the table?" He held up his palm when he noticed Sam's confusion and worry. "Do you or Rosie read?"

"Read, as in books?"

"Yeah. Novels. Kathleen reads. A lot. When I asked her about the book she's reading, I got to experience the real her. I think if we—me, you, Rosie—if we talk about books, she might relax." Matt took another drag on his beer, looking at the ceiling. "Of course, it could backfire." He shrugged. Frowning, he waited.

"What are you trying to accomplish?"

Matt twirled the beer around on the bar. "I wonder if we can bring *that* Kathleen back. Can she relax anywhere but at that bungalow?" He pulled in a deep breath as heat moved into his cheeks. "And I want to see if her reaction is my imagination."

"Explain that last one."

Matt forced his eyes to meet Sam's. "When you and Rosie actually sit down, I expect she'll react bodily—shaking, breathing hard. That seems to be how it starts when she's threatened."

Sam's eyes hardened before he interrupted on a snarl. "We aren't a threat."

Matt took a deep breath. "That's just it. Everything is a threat. *Everything.*"

Sam's face softened. He looked over at Kathleen and back to Matt. "Keep going."

"When that starts, if I touch her—hold her—and speak in a confident voice, it fades." He looked at Sam. "Not always instantaneously, but in obvious reaction to my touch."

Sam took a step back, crossed his arms over his chest. "Say that again."

Matt turned around, checked on his Kathleen before he turned back. "I know it sounds bizarre. That's why I want to test the theory. Talk to Rosie. Come to the table if you're willing." Matt looked up at the clock above the bar. "Can I get her tea?"

A few minutes later, Matt placed the tea on the table and tapped Kathleen's shoulder.

She flinched but turned his direction.

"Willing to take out the earphones?" He pulled one out. "Join me for dinner?" He pulled out the chair next to her and sat down.

Kathleen looked at him, at the dangling earphone, back to the sea, back to him. She balled her hands into fists but rose, turned her chair, removed the other earphone, and sat.

Matt reached over and put his hand over hers. Covering her wound, he rested their hands on her thigh. "Thank you. I don't want a salad. What else should I have?"

After swallowing several times, she tipped her head his direction. "I've only had the salad." She pulled her lip into her mouth and chewed.

"Willing to try something different?"

After another round of swallowing, she squeezed his hand and answered, "I think you sitting here with me is enough change for one night."

Matt smiled and nodded but worried inviting Rosie and Sam had been too great a risk.

"Hey. I chose for you," Rosie said as she put Kathleen's salad and a hamburger on the table. She plopped into the chair.

Sam's arms appeared. He put two more hamburgers on the table and moved to take the last chair. "Matt, Kathleen."

Pretending that this was a normal meal on a normal night,

Matt removed his hand from Kathleen's and grabbed the ketchup. His attention on his food, he missed Kathleen's movement. "Hamburger," he said. "Thanks for not forcing more salad in me." He looked from the ketchup to find Rosie's eyes wide and her face losing color. From the corner of his eye, he saw Sam stand and move toward Kathleen. Matt sat back in his seat as Sam reached her.

Sam stooped and carefully took Kathleen's hands in his.

Kathleen exploded out of the chair. "No. Nobody touches me," she hissed as she backed into the railing, her feet racing to find a foothold.

Sam rose, looked at Matt and then back at Kathleen. "Kathleen." He moved closer, kept his voice low and gentle. "Kathleen. It's me. Sam."

Kathleen's face jerked to Matt. Clamping her bottom lip between her teeth she began to shake.

Sam reached to catch her before her legs gave way.

"No, Sam," Matt said as he, too, moved to Kathleen. "Let me get her."

Matt grabbed Kathleen around the waist, held her up and pulled her into him. With his lips pressed into the scarf, he asked, "Where are you?"

Her hands clutched at the back of his shirt but her head continued to shake and a drop of blood appeared where she bit her lip.

"Who's got you?"

Her right leg stopped. Her left leg stopped. Her breathing slowed, but Matt still heard convulsive swallowing. When it stopped, he spoke into her ear. "Let your lip go," he said as his thumb rose to pull her lip free. "Take a second, look around. Rosie's. You *are safe* here. Right decisions—" He paused before trying again. "Right decisions can build new worlds."

Her breathing slowed while he wiped the blood from her chin. "All right, love, Sam and Rosie are joining us for dinner." When she didn't move or respond, he added, "I've got you. You reach for me and I'll be there." When he still received no response, he winked and added, "They read."

It took a while, but soon her face lifted to him and the tiniest smile curved on her lips. "They read," she whispered.

"Let's eat." He dropped his hands from her neck, turned her chair back toward the table, grabbed her hand again. He looked up, relieved to find Sam and Rosie doctoring their burgers as if nothing odd had happened.

Kathleen freed her hand from Matt and created her checkerboard. As she followed her ritual Sam and Rosie filled the silence with chatter.

Matt kept his hand on Kathleen's knee. He responded at the appropriate times, munched on his burger and fries. But his focus remained on Kathleen, ready to intervene.

Kathleen ate her six bites, placed her napkin on her plate, finished six sips of her tea. Her hand found his and she dug her fingernails into his skin.

Rosie jumped in, "Matt tells me you read. What are you reading? I just started the Mitch Rapp series. It's old. Do you know it?"

The fingernails dug deeper as her breath expelled and her shoulders started to fold inward. For several seconds, no one moved, no one spoke. Kathleen's hand jerked in Matt's hand, her fingernails released his skin and her shoulders squared. Leaning forward, she asked, "Has he met Anna yet?"

Matt's attention bounced between Kathleen and Rosie before returning to Sam.

Sam's eyes were huge as he stared at Kathleen.

Matt took another bite, chewed around his grin. *That's my Kathleen.*

"Wow," Sam mouthed at Matt.

Matt's grin turned into a smile as he nodded at Sam.

Matt and Sam finished their meals, sat back and watched the women talk as if these fictional characters lived next door.

After he finished his beer, Sam rose, collected the dishes, and tilted his head to Matt.

Matt stood, gathered the beer glasses and Kathleen's tea glass before following him.

"Holy shit," Sam said as he placed the dishes on the bar. "I don't know what to say."

Matt put the dirty glasses next to the dirty dishes. "Two different people."

Sam put his hands on Matt's shoulders. "Yeah, that was interesting and wonderful. But what I'm asking about, what I'm trying to understand, is her reaction *to you.*"

Matt shrugged as best he could with Sam's pressure on his shoulders. "She's mine." He rolled his eyes and hated the sweat on his upper lip. "Does that sound stupid? I feel like a Neanderthal."

"Any other time—yeah, it would." Sam shook his head. "But are you ready for that? For her?"

Before he could formulate a response, Sam added, "Has

she told you why she's here?"

"Not yet."

"Matt, I'm afraid all you've done—all your mother has done—is open Pandora's box. A box she has kept closed for a reason."

Sam's face fell and his arms dropped to his sides. "Remember, Rosie and I will be here."

Matt's brows furrowed as Sam walked away. He turned and watched his Kathleen leaning close to Rosie, talking and smiling. Moving toward her, he said to Sam's retreating form, "It doesn't matter why she's here. Whatever's in that box, we can handle it together."

Sam replied, "It may not be possible."

"I know how to fight," Matt said so only he could hear. What Matt didn't tell Sam was his own body's reaction to her. How he calmed in answer to her panic. How her presence made him feel complete.

WHO?

"How did you end up going to Rosie's every night?" Matt asked Kathleen as he walked her home, his hand laced with hers, his thumb caressing the bumpy flesh.

After a delay, she answered, "I promised."

"My mother?"

He felt her headshake. "No and yes. I promised someone else first. Your mom just asked me to keep that promise."

"Why?"

"Why Rosie's?" she asked as her bungalow came into view.

"I guess I'm wondering what the promise was."

At the bottom of her steps, still standing in the sand, she dropped his hand and faced him. Between the darkness and the shadows from the deck, he could not interpret her emotions or needs. "After…" She swallowed loudly enough for him to hear in the darkness. "After…" she tried again, moving one step back.

Matt moved forward and reclaimed the step she'd taken backwards. Wrapping his hands around her, he helped her to stay in place. "After?"

She swallowed again and spoke too fast, "When I left

Charlotte, I promised someone I wouldn't hide all the time. She asked me to find a place to eat dinner." After a long pause, she added, "I do the best I can. I live up to the letter of the promise."

Matt squeezed her waist. "After what?"

"Don't let them out," she said. "Please don't make me let them out." Her voice wavered, her breath quickened, and even with his hands on her, she began to tremble.

"Let who out?"

She backed away. Her legs hit the bottom step, causing her to fall. She used her hands to crawl backward up the steps.

Matt lifted her and positioned his body flush with hers, giving her as much contact as he could. "Okay," he started as he moved his hands to her neck. "Okay, love. Tell me something about this Mitch guy you and Rosie were so excited over."

She settled, but instead of talking about the book she tilted her face to his. "I think I'll go in now."

Before he let her go, he kissed her nose. "I'll see you tomorrow." He watched as she dragged her feet up the steps and across the porch. His own breath thickened as he saw her struggle to open the locks. When he heard the door click and the locks re-engage, he closed his eyes and fought the need to be with her. "Let who out?" he whispered.

WAITING

Kathleen didn't bother brushing her teeth, changing her clothes, or climbing into her bed. She went directly to the closet, folded herself deep into the corner, and waited for the doors of her memory to open and the attack to begin.

THE SEVENTH

Matt charged into the kitchen, snatched up the seventh note.

I realize you have lots of questions, and I'm going to give you what I can—let me warn you now, it's not enough. I'm running out of time, so I have to be more blunt. All I can do is hope you've done the work to be ready.

She exists, she does not live. I have some suspicions, but I don't have facts. She's damaged—physically and mentally. She's afraid. But, Matt, the threat is internal, not external. She hides because she believes that her memories won't find her. They will. Memories can't stay locked behind closed doors. She will face these memories alone and perish or someone will face them with her. Maybe that someone is you.

Let me tell you what else I know. You also exist and do not live. You exist inside a career you never chose. A career I'm not sure you would have chosen. You glided into NNJ and never considered if there was something better for you. Your dad and I allowed it. We were relieved to leave our company in your hands. When I met Kathleen, I realized we allowed you to live our dream instead of creating your own.

I wish I could tell you more. It's not my story to tell. But it is yours to hear. Help her open those doors.

~ Mom

Below his mother's handwriting a note was added, a note in his father's hand.

M—consider your strengths—you can use those ~ Dad

Matt bit his lip and stared at the words. He'd read the letter five times and each time his pulse increased and a pain pierced behind his eyes. "You've told me nothing," he said to the page. "Nothing."

His attention bounced around the room as he sought a way to channel the energy building in his body. When his eyes alighted on his laptop he jerked it toward him, found a Wi-Fi connection, and began a search. Thirty fruitless minutes later, he slammed the cover down and lobbed the computer to the couch.

He talked to a mental image of his mother and father while he paced the small space. "I don't believe you told me everything. You're right; she just exists. And you know why. You've given me a five-thousand-piece puzzle but with no fucking picture and no straight edges to get me started." He slowed his walk, went to the deck and planted himself in a chair.

Without having to read it, Matt revisited every word in the letter.

"I'm a fucking tax attorney. None of those strengths matter," he spoke to the clouds drifting over the moon. As the clouds thickened and fog rolled onto the shore, he considered his options. Call his dad. Read the next letter. Seek out Rosie or

Sam. *It's not my story to tell.* His mother's words kept Matt off balance, unsure how to proceed.

As deep night filtered into a darkened morning, Matt shuffled around all the questions he wanted answered. *She will face these memories alone and perish, or someone will face them with her.* Matt placed the seventh letter back in its envelope then changed into workout clothes.

Walking toward Kathleen, he rearranged the questions in his mind, ordering them, prioritizing them. With a grunt of annoyance, he replied to his father's advice, "Well, at least one skill an attorney has is understanding the power of what to ask and when to ask it." Increasing his pace, he chose his first salvo.

INTERROGATION

The planning, the plotting, and the preparing evaporated. His determination wilted. His courage drained to nothingness.

Kathleen moved toward him. Gone was the purposeful stride. Gone were the swinging arms. Gone were the earphones. Her toes dragged through the wet sand, her head hung on her neck as if her feet were lead and needed supervision. Dried blood created lace patterns on her arms. Only the outfit reminded him of the woman he'd chased the day before. Matt moved to block her path.

She stopped when their toes landed six inches apart. Before he could say or do anything, her torso tilted forward and her forehead landed on his chest. Matt wrapped one hand around her neck and the other pulled her fully into him. "Love," he whispered into the top of the ball cap. "Let's get you home."

Her head shook against his breast. "Not finished," she muttered just loud enough for him to hear above the waves roaming at their feet.

"I think you are." He rested his chin on the top of her head, embracing her more tightly.

Her shoulders and head dropped even more. "Got to keep

the promise."

Matt held her against him as a curtain of rain moved toward the shore. Distant flashes of lightning alerted him to the intensity of the coming storm. "Where are your headphones?" he asked at last.

Her heavy hands rose to her ears. Rather than answer, she dropped her hands back to her sides.

"Let's you get home," he said more forcefully. "I'm starved, and we're about to get smacked with a storm." He moved his hands to her waist, gently turning her. He tucked his left arm around her waist, pulled her close and guided her back toward home.

"What book have you been listening to?" he asked, hoping to find his Kathleen again.

"Just a story of a cop trying to undo wrongs and accept a woman's love he doesn't believe he deserves."

Her listless tone frightened Matt. With his free hand, he tugged on the roots of his hair, swiped at his lip and tried again. "What are their names?"

"Chace and Faye."

"Does he deserve her?"

She didn't speak words, but her body changed. She stood more upright, her gait lengthened somewhat, her arms began short swings. After several steps, she tilted her head up to look at him. "Maybe he does." Her voice held a hint of wonder that Matt could not interpret. Her face returned forward and though she never reached her normal pace or posture, she seemed more in control.

When he saw the bungalow, Matt asked, "What are our plans

today?" He felt her back stiffen, but his own courage and determination had returned.

"I, Matt, I—"

With his hand already on her waist, he halted their progress and turned her to face him. Before she could respond and before he would begin, he raised his hands and took off her sunglasses. He caressed the dark caverns under her eyes with his thumbs. He watched as the blue and purple warred. "Kathleen," he started as he continued to trace her cheeks, "I cannot, and I hope you cannot expect me to leave you today. I can sit on the porch, and if you won't allow that I'll sit on the sand just off your steps." He dropped his hands to her shoulders and leaned closer. "Somehow, some way, I will protect you today." He looked back to the rapidly approaching storm. Turning back to Kathleen, he ticked his lips up. "I'd rather stay dry."

Her eyes moved from his to the storm. "No one has ever been inside my house while I'm there." Her hand moved to his waist where she gripped him. "No one," she added as she took in deep gulps of breath. A crash of thunder exploded, forcing both of them to jump and stare as the bright lightning slithered closer.

"Let's head in before we get electrocuted," he said.

Her defeated gait returned, forcing Matt to choke off the desire to pick her up and carry her home.

She dragged herself up the steps and across the porch. At the door, she rested her forehead on the wood. "I'd like to sit on the porch," she said, looking down at the doorknob.

He ran his hand up her spine. "Let's get in, go to the bathroom, get your arms cleaned up, and snag coffee and something to eat. Then we can go back to the porch and Harry." He ended his directive with a tease.

"You're okay sitting on the porch?" She hurried on, "I have drop-down plastic so it's safe even in a storm."

"As long as I'm near you, I'll be fine. Open up, though, because I have to go to the bathroom and I desperately need caffeine." He stepped back a few inches and watched as her shaking hands unlocked six deadbolts.

Before she opened the door, she turned her bright purple eyes at him. "In and out, okay?"

He leaned over and kissed her forehead. He gently squeezed her waist. "Bathroom, arms, coffee, porch. Got it."

MIRRORS

Matt followed her inside and she directed him to the bathroom. He looked around the space. Gray wood floors, a living space on the right, a kitchen with a long bar on the left. In this cursory tour Matt knew something was wrong, but he had no time to understand what.

The bathroom was unremarkable. A large garden tub, a shower, a toilet, a pedestal sink and a small door Matt assumed was a linen closet. Other than a bottle of soap and a gray drying towel there were no decorative items. After washing his hands Matt lifted his head, preparing to fix his wind-mussed hair. He took two steps back on a gasp. Instead of a mirror, he stared at a blank white wall. Spinning around, he searched the walls. Empty. With a hammering heart, he opened the door to the small closet. No mirror.

He tiptoed out of the room and across the hall, hoping to find the master bedroom. A white-walled room filled with only a queen size bed, two nightstands and a six-drawer bureau. Nothing on the walls. He smiled when he saw books littering both nightstands. He gazed around the room once more. No mirrors. With a new question on his roster, he stepped back into the hall and found her in the kitchen.

"Let me help," he said as he grabbed the bowl of strawberries and the plate of bread in her hands.

She blinked up at him. "Coffee?" she asked with a slight tremor in her voice.

"Absolutely," he said as he noticed the purple invading her irises. He put the food back down, gathered her forearms in his hands and inspected the tiny cuts. "What happened?"

Her fingers ran over the marks. Without looking at him she said, "Birds." She pulled her arms away. Her eyes begged him not to ask anything else.

"You get those arms doctored and I'll get those storm screens situated. Can you handle coffee and water or—"

"I can do that," she cut him off as tension left her shoulders. "Give me a few seconds to change and I'll meet you out there."

"Got it." He turned and felt her eyes follow him. Sadness engulfed him when the locks clicked behind him. "I'll make you safe," he said over his shoulder at the door.

Matt's long legs were crossed at the ankles, his arms resting behind his head. The storm screens blocked the wind but did little to minimize the boom of the thunder or crashing of the waves. With his eyes closed he listened to the pit-pat of rain hitting the plastic sheeting. The questions in his mind shuffled, re-organizing themselves until he heard the locks flip. Without changing his posture, he rotated his head toward the door and watched as she balanced two coffee mugs. Under her arms she held water bottles and books. "Here, hand me something." He stood and reached across her chair to take the mugs.

"I didn't ask, so it's just black." Wearing a fresh pair of yoga pants and a white t-shirt, she leaned across the seat, placed the

150

water bottles on the table, threw her leg over the cushion and plopped down.

Once she seemed comfortable, he handed her a mug of coffee and sat in his chair. "Black is perfect. Is that banana bread?"

She looked at the food sitting on the table. "Zucchini." She grabbed a piece of bread, took a sip, and followed that with a bite.

Matt imitated her position and actions. In silence, they ate the bread and the strawberries.

"Is that my Harry Hole book?"

She grabbed one of the books and extended it to him, nodding.

"You still reading about Rachel and her deadbeat husband?"

With small smile, she said, "He's not a deadbeat. He *was* a deadbeat. Now he's just dead. But, to answer your question, no, I finished that yesterday."

Matt blinked and his eyebrows pulled in. "You finished that entire book in one day?"

"I told you I read."

"Yeah, but there's reading and there's *reading*." He took a moment to regard the scarf. Black and red polka dots, wound around her head at least three times, tied in a knot at the nape of her neck.

She shrugged, put her empty mug on the table, turned away, scooched down on the seat, bent her knees, and opened a book.

For several minutes, he tried to screw up the nerve to ask just one of his many questions. Instead, he opened Harry Hole and tried to concentrate on the whodunit.

Glancing her direction several minutes later, he found her studying the storm. "I've always liked storms," he said.

Her body jolted as if she'd forgotten he was here. "Me, too. Lighting is my favorite."

"Lighting?" he asked with a smile in his voice.

She turned her head with a flat mouth. "What?"

"Lighting? You mean lightning?"

Her eyes narrowed, her mouth pinched together. "I didn't say lighting. I said lightning." She raised her left hand to squeeze her lips.

Matt watched her fingers worry at her lips, wondering what caused her left ring finger to be removed. "No," he laughed. "You said lighting."

She continued to twist her lips, but she turned her face away as her left foot bobbed. Within seconds the movement moved up her leg and the right foot joined in. When the book fell to the floor Matt jumped up and went to her.

"Sit up, let me in behind you," he said, even as he used his hands to move her forward. By the time he'd swung his body in behind her, the vibrating had moved into her entire torso and her teeth clanked together as if the air had turned to freezing. He gathered her close and whispered into her scarf-covered ear, "Who's got you?"

Her head shook, but he got no reply.

He tucked his nose into her neck, rubbing at the goosebumps rising on her arms. "Shh, love. Tell me who is sitting here with you."

In a strangled voice, she said, "You."

He snuggled his nose in deeper. "Who? Say my name." Her torso relaxed, but her legs continued their tremors. He wrapped his legs around them, cocooning her. "Who am I?"

She took a deep breath, a tight shiver running through her body into his. "Matt, Matt Nelson, Betty's gift." Her head dropped so that her forehead rested on the arms he'd crossed over her.

Matt's own body stilled at her words. *Betty's gift.* He forced himself to focus solely on Kathleen. "Tell me what happened."

"Lighting," she said. He could hear her swallow and feel the left foot begin its dance.

After tightening his hold, he said, "Explain."

Her hands grabbed his forearms and twisted the skin until it burned. "Courtney called it lighting when she was little." The twist tightened.

Matt bit his lip against the pain.

She added her fingernails to the twist. "It was. I used to correct her all the time. I wish I hadn't done that."

Matt wiggled his arms and her grip loosened. "So why did that cause this reaction? It sounds like a good memory."

She became as rigid as a board. "No memories. I don't want any memories."

She hides because she believes that her memories won't find her. His mother's words forced a thick sheen of sweat to appear on Matt's lip. After taking a few breaths, he felt his courage walk away. "What book are you reading today?"

Within seconds, her body relaxed and the mood on the deck brightened. She brought the book in front of his face. "*Mr. Darcy Gets a Wife.* It's a follow-up to *Pride and Prejudice.* It's not by Jane Austen, but the author does a decent job getting her voice."

"You've read it before?"

"Many times." She shrugged as if to indicate that was a stupid question because it was normal to re-read books.

He planted his chin on her shoulder. "Why re-read when there are so many books to read?"

"Sometimes I have to know there's a happy ending." Again, her response told him the answer was obvious.

Her shoulders flattened and she moved out of his embrace. "I'm fine now. You can go back to Harry." She moved forward, allowing him room to get out from behind her.

Taking the cue, he lifted himself off the chair, planting a kiss on the top of her head before re-settling in his own seat.

She went back to reading and he pretended to read. But all he could think about were Kathleen's words. *Betty's gift.*

The storm blew in and blew out. Matt turned pages he didn't comprehend. *Answers. I have to get answers.* When he turned to ask about lunch and mirrors, he stopped.

His Kathleen had rolled to her side, her hands tucked under her cheek, her legs curled to her stomach. His Kathleen slept.

Matt watched her for a long time and dreamed of a day she could be at peace when awake. He rose, preparing to take in the dishes. His mouth dried and then refilled with bile as he choked on acid. The scarf had shifted and what he saw quickened his breath, forced tears and fists to form.

His Kathleen's ear was gone. Not just gone. Torn off her head. Mottled shades of pink and bright red flesh surrounded the opening like little coral fingers. Craters and mountains of damage surrounded the tentacles, extending inches into her hairline. Slice marks. Burn marks. *What the fuck? Ravaged. My Kathleen has been ravaged.* His eyes dropped to her left hand. He swallowed another bubble of rage and fear. Slamming his eyes shut, he fought for control, he fought the fight instinct, he fought the flight instinct. Opening and closing his fists, he attempted to regulate his breathing. After several deep breaths, he wiped the tears from his eyes and let his face rest in his palms. When at last he felt capable, he opened his eyes.

SEEN ENOUGH?

Kathleen's eyes searched his face, but that was her only movement.

"Kathleen." He fell back into his chair at the same time she rose.

Her movements were calm, deliberate, eerie. Her eyes remained on him as she removed the scarf and gave him a full view of the devastation.

Matt's hands gripped the edges of his chair; he swallowed and searched for what to say.

Her face turned back to him. No blue, no purple. Her complexion had turned gray, and so had her eyes. "Seen enough?" she asked him in a dead voice.

"Kathleen," Matt tried again, although he had no idea how he wanted to finish the sentence.

"No, Matt." She stopped him with a raised hand and that leaden voice. She re-wrapped the scarf around the scars. "I'm sorry to learn about your mother. I wish I could have told her goodbye." She paused but not long enough for him to speak. "As you can see, the storm is over. You can go home now. *All the way home.*" She shifted to her door, opened it, disappeared inside.

Just as he stood to go to her, to open her door and find her, he heard it. Click. Click. Click. Click. Click. Click. Six deadbolts slid into place. His Kathleen had barricaded herself from him.

Shoving his hands in his hair, Matt jerked at the roots. He pounded, pleaded, "Kathleen, don't. Please don't do this." He moved to the right, put his forehead against the window so he could peer through the tinting. What he saw tore through him, creating an agony he'd never known. His Kathleen had sunk to the floor, her back against the island, her body shaking hard enough to rattle the dishes. He pounded on the window. "Kathleen, love, open the door. Please, I'm begging." Nothing about her changed, and he knew in that second she was not here. Memories had swallowed her. Memories he needed to understand.

Helpless, Matt watched, continuing to plead with her to let him in. Long, torturous minutes later, she stilled, wiped her face, rolled to her hands and knees. She crawled to the back of the house. Not once did she glance toward him.

Matt's head fell against the panes of glass as Kathleen dragged herself down the darkened hallway. He waited a few more minutes, silently pleading while his own tears fell and his own trembling began.

When it was obvious she was not coming back, he forced himself to move, to plan. *Answers. I'm getting some fucking answers.* He placed his palm on the tearstained pane. "I'll be back. Hold on."

GIVE ME SOMETHING

As he dried his face, he ran to Rosie's. It was after the lunch crowd and before the dinner crowd, so the place was virtually empty. He found Rosie right away and cut to the chase. "I fucked up and I need your help to make it right."

Matt hadn't seen Sam until after he'd spoken. Sam wasn't as tall as Matt, but he was broad and powerful and he invaded Matt's space. "Is she all right?" he said with recrimination in his voice.

Matt stepped to the side so he could see both Rosie and Sam. "Physically she's fine. But I won't lie. I hurt her. I was stupid. I was unprepared. *I had no idea.* I fucked it up," he said, shuffling his feet and ignoring the lone tear as it dripped from his face.

Rosie shoved beers in both Sam and Matt's hands. "Getting into a pissing contest won't help Kathleen now. Let's sit and listen to what he has to say." Rosie led the way to a booth in the farthest corner. Sam and Matt sat across the table and measured each other while Rosie locked the door and turned the sign to "closed".

Scooting in with Sam, Rosie looked into Matt's face. "So, spill it and leave nothing out."

Without hesitation or embarrassment, he did. He told them everything he could remember until those deadbolts slid into place. He did not tell them about his mother's letters or Kathleen calling him *Betty's gift*. "So, how do I fix this?" Matt finished with eyes pinned on Rosie. He forced his voice to sound professional, even as sweat poured down his face and his beer bottle spun around and around.

"I'm not sure what to tell you," Sam replied honestly. "Kathleen's a beautiful bird with both wings broken. She hobbles around, but she can no longer fly. She may not even want to." Sam sounded as defeated as Kathleen had looked a few minutes earlier.

Both Sam and Matt looked to Rosie, silently begging her for guidance, for solutions. Rosie ignored their stares while she peeled the label off her bottle.

"Rosie, please," Matt urged. "Give me something."

Her shoulders remained slumped, but her eyes leveled to his. "Why, Matt? Why should I do that? You've been here, what, five, six days? You've threatened to leave. You can go back to your snow, your career. Sam and I will be here for Kathleen."

"No." Matt slammed the beer bottle on the table. "That's unacceptable. I fucked this up. I am the one who hurt her. I won't leave here until I make this right."

Rosie touched his arm and lowered her voice. "You didn't hurt her, not really. That happened a long time ago. You saw a tiny glimpse of her real pain. As much as you seem to care and want to help her, I'm afraid the damage is done."

Feeling as if he'd been punched, Matt sucked in a breath, wiped his lip and clutched Rosie's hand. *What happened to my girl?*

Looking at Matt, Sam broke the oppressive silence. "So, Rosie asked why we should help you. I guess the question is, do you still *want* our help?"

Matt understood what Sam was asking. Whatever answer he gave would irrevocably change his life. His attention darted around the bar while his mind reminded him of Kathleen's smile and his desire for her to laugh. Matt raised his eyes to Sam and stared for a long minute. "I'm begging for your help."

Sam nodded once, resignation, relief, and worry warring on his face.

Rosie wasn't as willing to give in. She pulled her hand away from Matt's and insisted, "I asked you why you want our help. I'm asking again."

Matt looked from Sam to Rosie. He let his brain form the words, and the truth he'd been avoiding, flow into the space. "Because I love her. She and I belong to each other. I fought it, but I knew it the instant she walked on the deck wearing that blue dress. I found the life I'm supposed to build." As he spoke, Matt's confidence grew. Kathleen was his to protect, to shelter, to hold. His mother had been right.

"It won't be easy," she challenged. "It might not be possible."

Matt's face brightened the smallest degree. "A worthwhile life is not an easy life." He paused and added, "Someone very important told me that."

Rosie nodded and took charge. "Okay, Sam, call in Mike. You and he will run the show for a while. Kathleen's not usually here until nine. I'll be back before then. If she shows early, text me. And, for god's sake, Sam, act normal. If you tiptoe around her you'll make things worse."

Rosie grabbed Matt by the arm before Sam could even agree. "Let's go. I've got a story to tell you."

"Where are we going? And what did you mean when you said she won't be in until nine?" Matt asked Rosie as she dragged him out of the restaurant.

"To your condo. We need to talk where there are no distractions. And it's Saturday. She comes in later and stays until I close. Then she walks me home." She sighed, laughed a small laugh. "She doesn't talk, but she stays next to me until I lock my door."

CHRISTMAS

They reached his rental before he could process what he'd learned. With water bottles in hand, they made their way to his deck and settled into the wicker chairs. Matt prepared to ask questions, but Rosie stopped him. "Let me tell you this my way. When I'm done, you can dig around and see if I left anything out."

"Fair enough. But please get started. I need to find my way back to her."

Rosie took a long pull on her water and began, "Kathleen showed up here just over two years ago. We knew a lady from Charlotte had bought the old Robbins place—you can't keep stuff like that secret here. We also learned she was planning to make this a full-time residence. That's rare. My Bob was still alive and he often helped Sam with tearing out walls. Bob loved that stuff. He couldn't build a damn thing, but he could sure tear shit apart." Rosie's face saddened as she spoke of Bob with a surprising tenderness.

She looked back at Matt and continued, "Anyway, I was curious about my elusive new neighbor. We all were. Sam would only talk about the remodel and Bob was almost as tight-lipped." She shook her head in remembered annoyance.

"Eventually Bob gave me some tidbits. Kathleen liked books since the second bedroom was filled with bookshelves. She had good taste because the new design made the house appear larger. I would love the bath." She stopped, took a deep breath. "God, Matt, he was telling me about her house. I wanted gossip on the lady, not decorating tips. I thought I'd kill him." She went quiet for a while as she allowed memories to play across her face.

When he could stand it no longer, Matt prodded, "Rosie, keep going, okay?"

Rosie refocused. "One night I was mad at Bob over something silly. When I started to yell at him he winked at me and said, 'Honey, if you'll forgive me, I'll give you information on that new lady.'" She smiled at the memory. "He told me that her name was Kathleen, Kathleen Bridges, and that they hadn't met her. Sam rarely even spoke to her on the phone, and when he did, he couldn't call her directly. He had to go through a switchboard. Matt, she built that space, worked with Sam daily, and never once showed her face. Bob felt sorry for her, even though he'd never met her. I tried to tease Sam, but—Sam was, and still is, solicitous of Kathleen."

Rosie closed her eyes for a long time and then said, "'Thousands of books, lots of locks, dark tinted windows.' That's how Bob described the place."

Another long pause: "It was a long time before she came into Rosie's and sat at the same table she uses now. I didn't know who she was, but Bob thought she must be our new neighbor. Lonely. Lonely defined Kathleen." She closed her eyes, wiped her nose and went on. "A loneliness that's palpable. She came in every night after that—same table, same order. She always left a large tip." Rosie snorted, rolled her eyes. "I think she felt guilty that she used the table for so long. One time she left me a note—or a business letter. It asked me to deliver the same meal whenever she came in. She gave me a credit card number and told me to always include a twenty percent tip. That was her way of keeping conversation to nothing."

Rosie twirled the empty water bottle in her hand and looked at her feet. "Bob died," Rosie spoke softly. "He died without warning, and I understood, for the first time in my life, what lonely meant."

Matt reached out and took Rosie's hand. He'd watched as his dad worked through his loneliness to rebuild a life without his mother. Lonely seemed a terrible place to live.

Rosie gave Matt a sad smile and patted his hand. "I still miss him sometimes. Thirty years is a long time."

"When I came back to Rosie's the loneliness really hit. Bob and I had opened that place together. We spent every night there as a team. Kathleen was at her usual seat. When I delivered her tea, she turned to me and lifted her glasses. It was the first and only time she had ever shown me her eyes. They are so blue. It was such an intimate moment I've never told Sam. It's a blue you cannot describe. After that, I understood the headlines."

"A shocking blue. A Minnesota sky. My favorite color." Her mention of headlines sailed past his conscious experience and settled into his subconscious like a billboard waiting to be turned on.

"She looked at me. I swear she looked *into* my loneliness.

'Go to a fictional world. Life is better there.' That's what she told me." Rosie shrugged. "That was it. She dropped her glasses back on her nose and turned back to the ocean. About three weeks later she left a book at the table. First book I'd read in years. She was right, fictional worlds are better."

Both Matt and Rosie turned to look at a new storm starting over the ocean.

"I read that book in two days and the next night I sat at her table. She never looked at me. She never moved. I didn't even know if she'd hear me with those damn headphones, but I asked anyway." Rosie turned to Matt and her eyes held his. "I asked her who she'd lost." Her chin quivered as tears continued to stream down her cheeks.

Matt tensed, gripped his knees, and licked the salty sweat from his lip. He wanted—needed—the answer, but he knew it would change everything. Again.

He watched Rosie choke back tears before she said in Kathleen's emotionless voice, "'Everybody. Everybody.'"

Matt stood and paced the small space. "But that can't be right. She said she has two kids, two grandkids. She even told me what they do for a living, where they live."

"Think back. What *exactly* did she say? Did she say 'has' or 'had'? Did she give you any hint they are part of her life now?"

"Nine hundred fifty," he whispered so low Rosie didn't hear him.

She paused again, and in what seemed a non-sequitur, she looked at Matt and asked, "Have you ever heard of Marcia Conners or maybe even the Conners family?"

Matt again ran both hands through his hair, pulling hard at the roots. "No, I don't know a Marcia Conners."

"Think, Matt. Christmastime, three years ago. Where were you?"

Matt's eyes hardened and his lips pursed. "What the hell, Rosie? I don't know and I don't care right now. I wasn't with Kathleen, and that's what's important."

"This *is* important. Sit down." Rosie's voice hardened. "Where were you that Christmas? Do you remember anything out-of-the-ordinary that happened?"

Matt closed his eyes, taking in several breaths. He remained standing but tried to trust Rosie. "I would have been in Minnesota, at my parents' house. Christmas Eve would have been Mom, Dad and me. Pizza, beer, and football. Christmas Day, my sister and her family come over for presents and a fancy meal." He opened his eyes and shrugged.

"Go to *that* Christmas, Matt. Three years ago."

Matt closed his eyes again and he filtered back in time. The Christmases ran together. Opening his eyes again, he said, "Give me some help. Our Christmas has been the same for twenty-five years. How can I remember a specific one?"

"Before I answer that, Matt, let me say one more thing. I will not judge you if you decide to go. Neither will Sam. You will not be leaving Kathleen alone, I promise you. We will force ourselves into the gap. We will take care of her."

"Tell me, Rosie."

Rosie slumped back in her chair and gave Matt pieces. "The news would have focused on one story, the story of the Conners family. The news stated they lived in Asheville, but they actually lived forty-five minutes into the mountains. The story ran for days. The *only* news for days." She stared into Matt's eyes and added, "Try again. Everyone was affected by the story."

"Can you not just tell me?" Matt yelled.

Rosie's head shook and a single tear slid down her cheek. "A family. One survivor."

Matt's eyes widened and then closed as the story flashed through his mind. He remembered turning into the kitchen to find his mother crying in his father's arms. The TV was on mute. Matt had halted in the door worried that something had happened to his sister or her family. He remembered his mother's voice as she spoke into his father's shoulder, "I hope she doesn't survive. She's not going to want to live anymore. She'll be haunted."

Matt's eyes flashed open and he folded into the chair. "I remember. A family was killed in their home on Christmas Eve. A neighbor found them. Only the mother was alive, barely. I remember my mother saying that the woman wouldn't want to survive. She used the word haunted." Matt's throat convulsed as his head shook from side to side, trying to avoid the truth. "I didn't remember the name Conners or the Asheville part, but I recall the basic details. Nephew and his friends entered the home and killed everyone. Except the mother. They tortured her."

Rosie's tears dripped off her face like raindrops.

"Rosie," Matt whispered after a few minutes, "I still don't get the point of this. What does that family have to do with Kathleen?"

Rosie's wet face lifted and she said, "Kathleen Bridges' real name is Marcia Conners. Her legal name is Marcia Kathleen Bridges Conners."

Matt's feet took him to the bathroom in time for his breakfast to return.

JUST ONE

He purged. As he brushed his teeth he heard the front door click closed. He refused to think. He cranked up Led Zeppelin and climbed on a treadmill in the fitness center. He jacked the speed to ten miles per hour, ran until his body wanted to collapse. After a shower, he opened Jeff's files and his work email. He worked steadily until 8:30 when hunger forced him into the present.

He walked to the diner down the street, ordered a greasy hamburger and fries. By 9:30, he was in his condo, phone in hand, waiting for someone to answer.

"United Airlines, how can I help you?"

"I need to make a reservation. Next available flight, prefer first class, but I'll take whatever I can get. Raleigh to Minneapolis."

"Yes, sir, how many are flying?"

Matt swallowed, looked at the counter and his mother's notes. He ran his hand across his lip before turning away.

"Sir?"

Forgive me, Mom. You were right. I'm not ready.

"Just one."

STRENGTH

Matt ignored the pile of letters on the counter. He walked straight to the bedroom, pulled his luggage out of the closet and threw in his clothes—no folding, no separating dirty from clean. Shove. Shove. Shove. Stalking to the bathroom, he repeated the process with his toiletries—didn't even close the bottles. Cram. Cram. Cram. He tossed the case towards the front door. A simple plan—pack, get out of this town, find a bar near the airport, lose himself in sports and beer until he needed to be at the airport. *Five hours to kill. I can make it for five hours.*

He ran both hands through his hair and turned to the counter. Pulling the laptop bag close, he tossed in the pen and the pad of paper. Next, the laptop and cords disappeared into the bag. He gathered the opened letters, folded them in half and thrust them into the side pocket. Three envelopes remained unread.

Matt spread these three missives in front of him. The numbers eight through ten condemned him. His mother's disappointment radiated off them.

"I can't, Mom. I'm sorry. It's too much. *She's* too much. I can't help her. How can I help her?" His voice pleaded as he touched each envelope. "Please understand. I get it. *I do*. I'll make sure

Rosie and Sam have whatever resources they need." He picked up the eighth envelope, noting its thickness. "I promise you, I'll make changes. I'll even listen to myself more. But I have to leave here." He stuffed the unopened envelopes into his bag, put the luggage by the door before he walked to his deck.

Watching yet another storm kick up, Matt dialed his father.

"How's the beach?" his father answered.

"Not what I expected. But I'm heading home tonight. Back in the office Monday."

A long silence thickened between the two men.

"Dad, you got something you need to tell me?"

"What letter are you on?"

Matt's mouth watered and his hand braced on the phone. "I've got three more to go."

"Have you met her?"

"Yeah. I saw her my first night here. Before I even opened the first letter. Did you agree with Mom?"

A small laugh preceded his answer. "Not at first. I thought she'd lost it. But as the story unfolded, as she showed me the letters, well—"

Matt's elbows settled on his knees. When it became obvious his dad had nothing more to add, he asked, "Dad, in the last letter, you told me to use my strengths. I'm a tax attorney. What strengths could I possibly have to help her? Do you understand the situation here?"

Matt heard his father suck in a deep breath and exhale. "I've never told anyone about the day I met your mother. Not the truth, anyway."

"You mean in English Lit at U of M?"

"Yeah. You know the basics but not the whole story, because I've always been too embarrassed or too bloated with pride to tell anyone except your mom. And I didn't tell her for years." Another deep breath. "I sat in the sixth row. In those big classes, I always sat in the sixth row. I was leaning forward to talk to Mark about plans for the weekend." He stopped.

After several moments, Matt prodded, "Dad?"

With a thick voice, he went on, "A chill ran up my back. It was like an ice cube traced up my vertebrae. I remember spinning to find the source of the cold."

Matt's dad stopped talking and Matt's heart skipped a beat while he held his breath, waiting on the rest.

"Anyway, your mom had just entered the room, wearing red pants one size too tight and a white shirt tied up at the waist. Shit, Matt, I even remember the little white tennis shoes and the red bow in her ponytail. Her socks were pink. Her face jerked to mine. She held my stare the entire time she walked up the center aisle. Never felt anything like it. Haven't since. And I never let her go."

Matt started to breathe again when his lungs screamed at him. "Dad," he uttered the word as half-plea, half-awe.

"What was she wearing that first night?"

"Fuck. Blue dress, white flip-flops. She carried a striped bag and had earphones in her ears." On a pained whisper, he added, "A blue and pink scarf. Dark sunglasses."

Matt's father didn't answer.

"Help me, Dad. Tell me what to do."

"Oh, Mattie-boy, I can't tell you what to do. Only your heart can do that. I can tell you that no matter what you decide, your mom and I love you, are proud of the man you are. And even though she's not here physically, we will always be in your corner."

"You told me to think of my strengths. What useful strengths does a tax attorney have?" Matt's gaze moved to the churning sea.

"A tax attorney is not who you are. A tax attorney is what you do. Matt, your strength is just that. Strength."

"Strength?" Matt repeated the word as a question. "Do you know who she is? Did Mom?"

"I know. Your mom suspected but never knew for sure. I found out before I agreed to let Jessica give you those letters."

"Do I have that kind of strength? Does any man?" Matt's eyes closed so he wouldn't miss one nuance of his father's response.

"Do you love her?"

Matt sucked in a breath. "I do, but how can that be? I don't—"

"You won't be on your own. I'm here. Jess. Patti. Dave. We'll be here for you, for her."

Matt didn't respond, but mentally he added Sam and Rosie to his father's list.

"The day they told your mother there was no hope for treatment, I was so angry. At the doctors. At medicine. At the world. At your mother for just accepting it. As she labored over those letters, I asked her how she could give up hope." He pulled in a deep breath, let out a strangled sigh. "She gave me that radiant smile and said she had plenty of hope."

Matt gripped the phone as he listened to his father swallow

back tears.

"Hope…" he started. After a loud, wobbly intake of air he continued, "She told me she had all the hope in the world. Mattie, don't you see? She poured her hope into you, into Kathleen. It's up to you to decide what to do with it."

A thick silence settled across the phone line as Matt let his mother's hope filter into his soul.

"If you love her, Mattie, then you have the strength for anything. I learned that in the last several weeks of your mother's illness."

"Dad?"

"I'm here when you need me."

"Dad?" Matt's voice pleaded again.

"Read the next letter." Matt's father disconnected.

LIGHTNING BOLTS

Love can be like a slow spring rain. Or love can be a lightning bolt. Either way, love is frightening. Just like you knew it wasn't love with Sarah, you will know when it is love, too.

We don't know who we are—how strong we can be—until we meet the person we're meant to be with.

However love comes, whenever it comes, DO NOT RUN FROM IT. You fight, Matt. Tooth and nail. Fight.

Matt rubbed his knuckles as a slightly hysterical laughter boiled up and over.

NO MATTER WHAT

Long, purposeful strides carried Matt across Rosie's deck. Letting the door close behind him, he ruffled his hair, sending droplets to the floor. Matt's pace didn't slow. *She's here.*

Rosie blocked his forward progress and grabbed his biceps. "Are you okay?" Her smile was gentle but her grip told him his demeanor worried her, maybe even frightened her.

Matt's shoulders loosened and his face dropped to hers. "Where is she?"

Rosie's head tilted back towards the rear of the restaurant. "Last table, near the register. Her back's to us."

Matt's eyes tracked the location. "Has she said anything? Acted any different?" He asked these questions as he tried to move past Rosie.

She gripped him harder. "The rain drove her inside, but she hasn't taken a bite of the salad. Are you all right?" she asked again as she shook him.

"I will be when I get to that table," he said with a small smile.

Her eyes narrowed. She squeezed once more then turned and led him toward the bar.

By the time they reached the bar, Sam was sliding a Sierra

Nevada and a tea his direction. "I'll be nearby," Sam said.

Matt nodded his thanks at the support being offered.

Kathleen's back stiffened and her hands confirmed the position of her sunglasses, the scarf and the earphones.

She feels me, too.

She wore the same blue dress from the first night.

Without turning, she said, "Go home, please." Her body and her voice mirrored each other. Frigid.

Matt paused just long enough to close his eyes, breathe deeply, and screw up his courage. "I am home." He slid into the seat across from her. "Besides, your ice is melted." He placed the tea before her, set his beer on the table then clutched his thighs so that his shaking hands didn't show.

She pulled out one earphone. Her pursed lips gave away her annoyance. With one hand, she gripped the new glass, with the other she again checked the scarf. "Is this a game to you?" She didn't show signs of thawing.

"Anything but that." He smiled at her and forced his shoulders to relax. "I understand you haven't eaten. Not even six bites?"

As if melting, her shoulders slumped, her chin dropped, her hand slid from the glass. "I can't." She took one more breath then raised her face to him.

Matt clenched his thighs harder, warding off the compulsion to take the sunglasses from her face. "You don't have to do anything. Not right now. Except, please, let me see your eyes. I have something I need to say and I want to see you."

She shook her head. "Matt, I…" Small wrinkles extended past the sunglasses when she closed her eyes. She shook her head a second time and kept her face directed at the table.

They sat in silence for a long time while Matt tried to gauge her level of distress. Kathleen played with the condensation on her glass.

She raised her torso and the dark sunglasses. "What do you want from me, Matt? My life was bearable until five days ago. What are you expecting?" Her voice sounded resigned. "Sex? Will you leave me alone if I go to your condo and fuck your brains out? You think the side of my head is nauseating. You'll be shocked how hideous I am under this dress. But if you keep the lights out I'm sure I can satisfy you." She filled her lungs as each word rose in volume and punched into the air. Her voice fell back to a whisper. "Or is that it…you want to see the hideousness I keep covered? I'm a sideshow. A carnival ride for your vacation."

Even knowing she said those words only to force him to leave, the anger at the accusation rose. Each word smashed into him, making breathing difficult. He no longer wanted to flee; he wanted to fight. As he searched for the right words, he watched as the only person who mattered in his life wilted before his eyes. Her forehead hit the table with a thud, and her arms slipped to hang at her sides.

Warring between hostility and tenderness, he noted Rosie and Sam in his periphery. With a shake of his head, he warned them not to come over yet. After pulling in one more full breath, he exhaled the anger and allowed his hands to drift across the table. With his index finger, he lifted her chin. Slowly he pulled her sunglasses from her face and the other earphone from her ear. He placed a hand on each side of her face. "Open your eyes," he said while his thumbs stroked her cheeks.

When her eyes opened Matt swallowed at the agony aimed at him. Her pupils filled her eyes. No blue. No purple. Only pupils. She clasped her hands around his forearms and squeezed until pain shot up his arms.

"I can't," she begged.

"Shhh. Let me talk for a second. Just listen. Anchor yourself to me. Stay here. We are safe at Rosie's. *You are safe with me.*"

She swallowed and gripped even harder, using those fingernails as weapons. Her wide, harrowed eyes didn't blink.

His left hand continued to caress her cheek. With his right hand, he cupped where her ear should be. "I know those words were your way of pushing me away. But I will answer each one so we have no misunderstanding." Matt lowered his voice. "I don't want anything. Not really. Not like you're thinking. I want to get to know you. I want you to get to know me. I want to spend time together. I want you to laugh because I made you laugh. I want to love what you love. I want to tour your book collection. I want to know what you're reading. I want you to recommend books and then listen as I try to guess whodunit." He took a deep breath, dropped his hand from her cheek, pulled her nails out of his arm. "I want to tell you about my mom. I want to hear about your family," he said with a croak to hide his impending tears. He tilted his mouth in a small smile. Moving one hand to caress her ear, he sat back as her eyes drifted closed and she snuggled into his touch. "And," he continued with a careful tease, "I think having your body under mine sounds like paradise, but that might need to wait."

When her eyes flashed open she rewarded him with the barest tick of her lips. To his relief and exaltation, she leaned her head deeper into his palm.

"Kathleen, I swear to you that if you are ever in my bed, it won't be fucking." He punctuated the final words and wiped away the single tear that moved down her cheek. He leaned across the table, nuzzled her face, and said into her damaged ear, "What *I* want is for you to be safe. What *I* want is for you to never push me away, for you to let me make you safe again." Relaxing back into the bench, he added, "What is it you want, my Kathleen, what do *you* want? I'll move heaven and earth to be what you need."

Her eyes widened and her face jerked out of his hand. Tears streamed down her face. Staring at him, showing him her weariness and her abject terror, her blue irises turned a stormy gray.

"They're gone, Matt." She spoke with an eerily calm voice. "*All* of them. Everyone I've ever loved. *Gone.* I'm so tired, Matt. Do you understand?" She pushed away from the table. Her gray eyes blazed inches from his own. "I want to be gone, too."

Matt's arms thwomped onto the table. He sat immobile as Kathleen raced out the door into the pouring rain. The restaurant door thwacked behind her. Shaking himself, he realized she'd left her sunglasses, her bag, and even her shoes. The impact of the last few seconds held him in his seat. Time seemed to stop. Sound dropped away. The shadow of her danced behind his closed eyes.

Rosie's cold hand touched his and shook him from his stupor.

"Rosie," he whispered in a tormented voice.

Her lips pulled into her mouth as she squeezed his hand. She uttered no words, no advice, no solutions, no guidance.

"Rosie," Sam barked, forcing both Rosie and Matt to jump

and look to him. "Go." He pointed toward the bar with a ramrod straight arm. "Grab your phone, head toward her bungalow. Try to catch up with her." He stood back, extended his hand, and helped her from the booth. "I'll be along in just a second. Let me talk to him first," Sam finished as he tilted his head at Matt.

Sam leaned his hips into the table and pushed until the edge sat against Matt's chest. "You," he said. His right index finger extended to just one inch from Matt's face. "You," he started again, "need to get out of here. Out of this bar. Off this beach. Out of this town."

Matt's fists clenched as he glared at the finger so near his nose. Before he could respond, the table pressed deeper into his chest as Sam repeated his demands.

Matt slapped Sam's hand out of his face, forced the table back and rose. "Back the hell off."

Sam placed his hands on his hips and moved his chest closer to Matt's. "You sit here while your girl runs into the storm and my girl runs after her. Coward," he muttered.

Matt's eyes closed as he sought calm, a semblance of control. His mother's words ran through his mind. His father's assurance of his strength attacked him. The life he wanted formed in his head. He slumped back in the bench, placed his face in his hands. "Help me, Sam," he said into his palms.

Neither of them moved.

"Shit," Sam said as he took Kathleen's vacated seat. "If you have any hope—any hope at all—of helping Kathleen you absolutely cannot fall apart every time she does. Don't you fucking tell us you love her and then sit on your ass while she fights for her life," Sam started with patience and ended with anger. "I heard her, Matt. I heard what she said." Sam knocked Matt's hands away so he was forced to give Sam his attention. He turned his head towards the door and back to Matt. "So, what do you guess she's doing now, huh?" Sam moved out of the booth, paced back and forth. "I should have forced Rosie to keep her goddamn mouth shut. Just run home. Rosie and I will find her."

Sam's words battered into his consciousness. He shook his head, moved the table out of his chest and stood to his full height. "I get it, Sam. I meant it. I will take care of her. We all will."

"Matt." Sam's tone softened. "Take a few minutes. It's not going to get easier. Far from it. You have to be in or out. She can either depend on you *no matter what*, or…" He left the sentence hanging.

Matt placed his palms on the table, crouched so Sam could look into his eyes, see his sincerity, his commitment. "In, Sam. Always. No matter what."

Sam nodded once. "Then go catch her."

FIND HER

Matt raced to the door just as Sam's phone buzzed. "Wait," Sam called across the restaurant. "It's Rosie. She's at Kathleen's. No sign of her and she didn't pass her, either."

Matt closed his eyes. *Mom, give me some of that hope.* Turning to face Sam, he asked, "Where else would she go?"

"I don't know," he said as he typed on his phone. "I'm telling Rosie to hang there and let us know if she arrives." Sam looked up at Matt with fear bracketing his eyes.

Matt's heart rate ratcheted up a few more beats as he paced back and forth with guilt, fear, worry, and dread climbing in his chest. "Do you have a flashlight?"

Sam went behind the bar, pulled out two industrial flashlights. He pushed one across the bar. "I'll contact Roger. The way she left…" He shook his head. Fresh lightning powered through the sky. "This storm…"

"Roger's the sheriff, and he knows who Kathleen is," Sam explained at Matt's confused look before he tapped more keys on his phone.

The need for a sheriff increased Matt's tension but also sharpened his focus. He grabbed the flashlight. "I'll head the direction she walks in the morning." He moved back toward the door, rattling off his phone number. "Send me your number, Rosie's number."

Sam walked from behind the bar and caught up to Matt just as he reached the doors. He pulled Matt in, clasped him across the shoulders, giving him a quick pat on the back. "We'll find her." Sam held Matt's gaze for several seconds. "We *will* find her," he said one more time.

"But what will we find?" Matt voiced the fear neither man wanted to acknowledge.

A large man in a sheriff's uniform pushed in behind Matt and Sam. A young woman with a long thick braid hanging over her shoulder clutched his arm.

"We were on our way here when I got your text. What the hell happened?" Roger started in on Sam.

"It doesn't matter," Matt interrupted, stepping in closer and facing off with Roger. "The whole story can come out later. Right now, what matters is that Kathleen left the restaurant in extreme distress. Our priority has to be finding her. Explanations and recriminations need to wait."

Roger looked at Matt before turning to Sam. "Who the fuck is this guy?"

Sam moved in beside Matt. "Matt Nelson. Roger Wilkinson. Roger, there's a lot to tell, but Matt's been getting close to Kathleen over the last several days." When Roger's eyebrows rose, Sam added, "Closer than anyone else has ever gotten. Yesterday she was laughing and talking. She seemed almost normal. Today…" Sam swallowed, looking to Matt.

"She's in danger. That's what matters right now." Matt

stood taller, squared his shoulders. "I saw her without the scarf," Matt said bluntly, confident that would be enough.

Before Matt's eyes, Roger Wilkinson transformed into a sheriff. He straightened his back, and his left hand rested on his holster. His voice turned authoritarian. "Where's Rosie?"

"She followed after her. She's at Kathleen's bungalow."

"Rosie knows her best so I'd like to get her back here," he said and turned to his wife, "Cheryl, head over to Kathleen's house. Call immediately if she shows up. Do not enter that house. Cheryl—" He pulled her into his space, gripped her upper arms. "I'm serious. Do not enter that house. We have no idea what we may have to handle." He moved his hands to the side of her neck when he saw her begin a protest. "I know you feel sorry for her and want to help. You can help by staying safe." He kissed her forehead, pushed a flashlight into the woman's hand, and turned back to Sam and Matt.

"Sam, get Gary over here. The more people we have helping, the better." He used his radio, calling in deputies.

A man Matt had seen playing pool at Rosie's sauntered over.

"Gary, Kathleen's disappeared. She's out in the weather. Scared and desperate," Roger said. Tossing him the keys, he said, "Go out to my car. Get the flashlights from the back."

While they waited on Gary to return Roger had everyone exchange phone numbers. Roger turned to Sam. "What about him?" He glanced over at Matt. "Just based on the vibe I'm picking up, I'm wondering, is it safe for Kathleen if he finds her?"

Matt straightened to his full height, arms rigid, eyes narrowed.

Roger planted his hand in Matt's chest. "Hold up, Mr.

Nelson. As you said, our first priority is her safety. I don't think you can be objective right this second. I need to hear from Sam."

Sam stepped between the two men. "She was in bad shape when she left," Sam replied. "But…" He paused and looked at Matt. "Unless she needs immediate medical attention, it would be best if Matt is there. I say whoever finds her just keeps an eye on her, intervenes if necessary, but waits until Matt can get to her." Sam looked over as a dripping Rosie came through the door.

"Sam's right. Kathleen might not realize it now, but Matt is her only way back to the living." She leaned toward Matt and squeezed his arm. "It may be mutual," she said directly to him. Turning back to Roger, she finished, "There's something between them we don't understand."

"Okay." Roger dictated more orders, "Gary, Rosie, head north. Matt, Sam, head south. I'll stay here and coordinate a street-by-street search. Look carefully. The storm will make it hard to see anyone." Roger looked over at Matt and added, "Watch for evidence she went into the sea. Her scarf or something."

"I understand," he whispered to Roger. "Let's just find her."

Roger ensured everyone had a high-powered flashlight. "Still no sign at home," he said as he looked at his phone.

Matt flipped on the flashlight, straightened his shoulders, and stalked into the raging storm.

METAL DOOR

Flashlights spread out over the beach. Each man called out Kathleen's name even though the sea and ongoing thunder drowned out their voices. Rain poured in sheets as Matt and Sam searched the sand, the grass, and even the darkened water. Matt's worry and panic increased with each boom. *Mom, please keep her safe until I get there. Please.*

Lightning and thunder reduced in intensity as the storm moved away. Rain slowed to a steady beat instead of a pounding force.

"Have you been in her house?" Sam asked between shouts.

"For twenty seconds. Long enough to go to the bathroom and be shooed out."

"What observations did you make in those twenty seconds?"

"No mirrors. I had planned a list of questions, but then I saw her ear…" Matt stumbled over the words.

"That bad?"

"Worse." He swallowed and then shared with Sam, "It looked like a child learning to use scissors or maybe using them with their wrong hand." He swallowed again, following the light with his eyes. "I think a sharp knife was used. It reminded me of what I pictured as a boy when I heard about

193

scalping." He wiped the rain from his face, chewed on his lip, and gave the last piece, "Sam, someone used cigarettes on the outer edges. They were creating a piece of morbid art." He shivered both from the cold wind and the memory of the look on her face. "I can't imagine what my face showed."

They walked several more paces, shouting her name, before Matt asked, "Has she ever mentioned birds, or do you know if she has ever had birds?"

Sam didn't speak, but Matt felt him grow tense as his strides lengthened and his feet dug more deeply into the sand.

"What?" Matt demanded.

"When I was building the house we were planning the upstairs. It was to be an office or extra space. One large room. So I suggested she not even put on a door. 'Keep it airy' is how I explained it. She insisted. It was the only time she was aggressive. She told me to put in a door. A metal door. Six locks. She wanted an outside door on the inside. When I asked her why—and I shouldn't have asked, but it just blurted out—she said, and I quote, 'maybe the birds can stay locked away'. I have no fucking clue what that meant, but I do know what's in that room and it has nothing to do with birds."

"Sam," Matt whispered, "what's in that room?"

"Everything she's trying to forget."

CATCH HER

They trudged through the surf without talking. Every few minutes, Matt checked his phone, praying for a message. Step after step, as minutes turned into hours Matt's fear tightened his chest. His legs turned to jelly, but he found the strength to keep going.

At 4:03 AM both phones buzzed. Matt closed his eyes. He couldn't breathe. He clutched his phone and looked up at Sam, pleading for a rescue.

Sam glanced at his phone. A small smile appeared in the eerie blue light of the phone. "They found her." He turned the screen to Matt.

Safe. Walking slowly back toward house. Four miles until home. Hasn't seen us. Will wait for Matt as long as we can.

Matt turned north, a renewed energy kicking up the sand.

"Hold up," Sam yelled, "another message came through."

Matt halted and swung around.

"What does it say?" Matt hollered.

"*Scarf gone.*"

Matt spun and his jelly legs turned to sinew and determined muscle. "Thank you, Mom. Keep watch until I get there."

Matt was oblivious to Roger's presence until Roger stepped

in front of him and placed both palms on his chest, sending him flying backwards into the sand.

"What the fuck?" Matt hollered as he picked himself up and wiped off wet sand.

"Listen, man. I understand you want to get to her, and you will. I want you to relax for a second and consider the best approach. I touched base with Rosie and she's over two miles out and moving slow. You've got plenty of time. They are keeping a safe distance behind her and will be there should anything happen."

"I need to be there. Not this Gary guy. Not Rosie. Me." After a few seconds' pause with no comment from Roger, Matt spat, "Just let me get there."

In a calming gesture, Roger put his hands on Matt's shoulders. "I will. Breathe for a second. You need to think this through. How are you going to handle her? I can't in good conscience let you go barreling in."

Matt backed up one step, bent with his hands on his knees, and tried to calm his racing heart. His legs wanted to melt into the sand. Closing his eyes, he realized the rain had stopped. "She must be freezing," he said to his knees. "Her scarf. It's gone. She needs that scarf," he said through tears. "Let me go to her."

"Matt, what will make Kathleen feel safest at this point?" Sam asked. "Her safety. Remember. That's the goal right now."

"Me," he said but shook his head, and admitted, "I have no idea."

"I think it's best if she goes on home without even knowing we followed her. She'll hate this attention. That could send her spiraling even further. You can go see her tomorrow, after we've all rested," Roger suggested.

Stepping into Roger's space, Matt put his chest inches from the uniformed man. "No fucking way. I don't have a speech prepared. I do know I'm going to her." He puffed up his chest and leaned his face one inch closer. "The only way you can stop me is to arrest me." He stormed ahead of Roger, Cheryl, and Sam.

Matt's progress stopped when his phone buzzed. He looked at the screen and back to the three people behind him.

Cheryl gripped Roger's arm while Sam read the message. "*She's moved into the surf but she's just standing there.*" A panicked energy vibrated among them.

Another buzz.

"*She's backed up.*"

Matt stared at the blue light from the phone before he said, "Let him know I'm on my way. I'll get there. I will catch her."

Matt raced off and barely heard Sam say, "He's right, Roger, let him go."

BRICE

The surf swirled around her ankles. Her wet clothes were plastered against her shivering frame. Thick but slow raindrops plopped on her bare head, dripping into the hole that used to be an ear.

"Mom," his voice spoke into her good ear as the memory of his hands rested on her shoulders. His chin perched on the top of her head.

She could smell the cologne he always wore.

"Mom," he said again. "Let's back up a few feet."

Her feet shuffled backwards, stopping in the wet sand with the surf now several feet away.

"Do you remember your rules for crying?"

Kathleen ducked her chin against her neck and gave him one nod. "No crying unless bleeding or puking," she said with a scratchy voice.

"I get why you taught me that. Good advice for a boy who cried every time he bumped into something." His arms came around her waist.

"I wish I'd held you every time, instead," she said into her chest.

"Can you imagine what I would have turned into?" He vibrated with a quiet laugh. "Not a cop, that's for sure. Maybe an inmate."

Neither spoke as the moon peeked around the clouds.

"It's not good advice now. Sometimes crying is the only answer. And"—he pulled her close—"you have arms to hold you. You can cry now, Mom. Okay?"

Rather than answer, she let her legs fold beneath her. His scent did not follow her to the sand.

MORE TO SEE?

When his Kathleen came in to focus, Matt slowed his pace, regulated his breathing. "I'm here now, Mom. I got her." He looked around and saw Rosie and Gary walking toward him from the grass at the back of the beach.

"She hasn't moved in a long time," Rosie said. "She seemed fine and then her legs folded underneath her."

Sam caught up, looked over at Kathleen. "What do you want us to do?"

Gary's voice broke in, "I think—I've already said—we should call an ambulance."

Rosie spun around to face him. "If I thought she was physically hurt, I would have been the first to call. But Gary, this is not physical. Let Matt talk to her. I'm sure he'll get her whatever she needs." She turned back to Matt, searching his face for reassurance.

Matt nodded an unspoken promise and pulled Rosie in for a tight hug. "Thank you. For her. For me. For my mom. Thank you," he said.

Rosie pulled back with tears in her eyes. "How can we help now?"

"Can you get into her house?"

Sam nodded and pulled out a huge key ring. "I still have a key so I can fix things for her from time to time."

"Rosie, go over there, run a hot bath, find pajamas. Prepare whatever she would find comforting. Can you do that?"

Rosie started to nod then halted. "She's never allowed anyone but Sam in her house."

Matt glanced over to ensure his Kathleen was still safe. "Just be gone before we get there. Leave the door unlocked. I doubt she'll even notice, and I'm sure she's too tired to care at this point. If she gets mad it will be at me. I'll cross that bridge when I get to it." He turned back to Rosie. "Okay?"

She nodded and gave Matt one more squeeze. "Please keep us posted. We'll be at the restaurant until we hear from you."

Hoping his father's belief in his strength was well founded, Matt nodded and walked toward his Kathleen.

Kathleen pulled her legs up to her chest and dropped her face into her knees. With her arms hanging at her side, she reminded Matt of a marionette after the puppeteer drops the strings.

Quickening his pace, he soon slid in behind her, using his own body to create a private shelter for her. "Hey, love." He leaned in to kiss the back of her neck. "Good morning," he said into her partial ear.

"Is it?" she asked with a hoarse voice.

"I'm sitting here with my Kathleen. She's safe. So, yeah, it's a good morning." He rested his chin on her shoulder, tightened his four limbs around her. Hoping to transfer his limited body heat into her freezing skin, he touched her everywhere he could. "Are you ready to head inside now? We need to get you warm."

"What does your mother want from me?" she croaked.

Matt ignored the question and nuzzled his nose in her hair. "I've never seen a beach sunrise. Based on those colors, this one might be something to see," he said

No response. No movement. Kathleen didn't seem to notice his touch.

"Kathleen, I want to say the exact right thing. I want to tell you that everything will be okay. But I decided during my search I would never lie to you—not in words, not in intentional omission, not in action. What I can tell you is that you are safe with me. I will carry you—us—as much as I can. I believe—truly believe—that together we can build something new, something that both honors the past and creates a future. Use my strength until we rebuild yours." He nudged her with his legs and chin. "Look."

Both heads turned to watch the sun showing its oranges and pinks. He kissed her shoulder and added, "My mom sent you to me. Maybe someone sent me to you."

Kathleen's head fell to rest against his face. "Oh, Matt…" She let the words trail away.

"Let's get you home, Kathleen. We can start there. A hot bath, some rest." He stood and extended his hand to help her.

She reached to check her scarf.

He placed his palm against the damaged side of her head. "No, Kathleen, there is no need to cover. We're alone. And you *never* have to hide with me."

When her forehead landed in his sternum, Matt scooped

her into his arms. "I've got you now and always."

With every step, her body relaxed into his. By the time he reached her porch, she was sound asleep in his arms. "Thanks, Mom," he whispered into the wind.

Rosie opened Kathleen's door just as Matt took the last step. His eyes widened and he pulled Kathleen tighter, tucking her face into his chest.

"I just finished," she mouthed to him. "Do you want me to stay and help?" she asked as she glanced at Kathleen's decimated ear.

Matt moved his hand to cover the damage from Rosie's gaze.

"Her feet," she said. "Oh shit."

Matt kissed Kathleen's head and looked to her feet. Blood dripped from her toes. Matt closed his eyes, inhaled, held on even tighter. "Miles," he said to Rosie, "she walked miles in the sand. I'll take it from here. She will hate my seeing her, and adding you to the mix could only make things worse."

"Her bath is ready but it might be too hot for those feet. I put pajamas on the bed. I got out a bottle of water. She's got to be dehydrated. So are you."

Rosie stood on her toes and leaned into Matt's ear. "You'll help her, right? Your mother wasn't imagining things?"

"I won't let you down. I won't let her down. We were sent to each other." When he saw her puzzled look, he said, "Someday, I'll explain that to you."

Rosie nodded, wiped her face, and walked away.

Matt pushed the door open and walked toward the bathroom.

The water in the garden tub steamed while candlelight

fluttered around the edges. A vanilla smell wafted from the water's surface. A water bottle stood sweating in the corner.

Matt gently woke Kathleen and lowered her to sit on the bathroom counter. "Kathleen, we need to get these feet doctored and get you in the bath before you're tucked into bed."

In a gesture that surprised and thrilled Matt, Kathleen leaned her forehead into his chest. Her voice wobbled. "I'm so tired. I just want to sleep for a while."

Gathering her hands in his, he placed her arms around his waist. "Hold on to me, Kathleen. Hold on. I've got you. Give me fifteen minutes and you can sleep." He kissed her cheek, pulled back and lifted her chin. "Let me take care of you."

"Fifteen minutes?" she whispered with gray eyes focused on him.

"I promise. You've been walking in the sand and ocean air for a long time. Let's get the sand and salt off, get your skin warm." He stepped back, reached to her feet. His fingers landed on a toe ring he hadn't noticed earlier. "Your toes are bleeding." He ran his fingers on the tops of her feet. "Let's take this in stages. First, let me wipe off these feet and hands to get rid of the sand. Then, take a bath. After that, let's get water in you while I doctor those toes. I'll tuck you in and you can stay there for as long as you need." He paused and added, "I'll be here when you wake up."

"You said fifteen minutes," she said, watching a drop of blood splatter on the floor beneath her feet.

Kissing her nose, he said, "But the fifteen minutes doesn't start until you get into the bath." He reached behind him to the linen closet he'd discovered earlier, grabbed washcloths and a box of first aid supplies. He lifted her foot and winced.

"I don't feel it," she said.

"That's good, but the water will sting and tomorrow you'll be tender. After your bath, we'll coat the toes in antibiotic ointment. Can you sleep in socks?"

"Tonight I could sleep in anything." She tried to pull her foot away but he held on.

"Let me clean this for you. Please."

"This is not your fault." Her gray eyes turned to him. Blue leaked into the irises.

"I won't say I don't feel at least a little responsible. But you're right. It wasn't my fault." He lifted her foot, kissed the top of it. "Now, no more arguing or you'll never get to sleep."

In less than five minutes, Matt had Kathleen's feet and hands clean enough. Thankfully only her big toes had bled. They weren't cut, just worn from the rough sand. "All right, let's get you in the tub."

When her feet touched the tile her entire body flinched. "Shit," she muttered. The pain seemed to wake Kathleen, to bring her fully into the present. Her hands rushed to her head. "The scarf," she said. "I need my scarf." Her voice rose and warbled.

Matt plastered his wet, sandy body to hers. He pulled her hands away from her head, stopping her from snatching at her hair. He pinned her arms to her side. "Shhh, Kathleen. It's just you and me. No scarf, no sunglasses, no earphones. None of those are necessary with me."

Her head rattled side to side. She tugged on her arms, trying to free herself. "No, no, no, can't see." She wailed and fought harder.

Matt's arms tightened and his voice firmed. "Enough. Kathleen. Enough."

Her wailing stopped, but she still struggled to get away.

"First, you're going to stop fighting me," he commanded, clamped his arms tighter over hers and waited until she acquiesced. "Perfect. Now let's take this beautiful, but ruined, dress off and sink you into that warm water."

She shook her head against him. "You can't—I can't—you can't," she sputtered and choked. "No, no, not the rest. So much worse. You can't—"

"Stop," he ordered. "Stop. Give me your eyes." He used his hand to lift her face to his. The eyes she presented were the brightest purple he had ever seen.

"Please just go." Desperation laced the plea in her voice.

Matt hesitated for several seconds, not wanting to leave her and not wanting to cause her more stress. *What could be worse than what he'd already seen?* The purple began to spark. "I will go to the kitchen. Rosie left pajamas on your bed. As soon as you're ready, let me know and I'll help you snuggle into bed."

On a loud burst, Kathleen let out the breath she'd been holding and closed her eyes.

"Look at me. You need to hear this. You need to *get* this." He waited until her eyes, rose to him. "I'm doing this *for you*, not me. Whatever is underneath that dress won't scare me away, won't make me leave you. You are *my* Kathleen." He squeezed her waist with both hands. "This body is perfect to me." With a kiss on what remained of her ear Matt backed away. "Your fifteen minutes start now." He shut the bathroom door behind him.

He remained just outside the door, listening. Something landed on the floor, followed by water sloshing. Matt put his forehead against the bathroom door and took in a few breaths. "Safe," he whispered. "Safety. I promise you that."

LONG ENOUGH

Matt pulled his phone from his back pocket as he walked toward the kitchen. He sent a quick text to the entire search group.

Safe. Tired but fine. Staying here. Will keep you updated. Please don't visit until we talk. Thanks for everything.

Within seconds his phone pinged. Everyone responding with the same theme of support.

Matt pulled up Sam's number and sent a second message:

Could you go to condo and get my stuff? It's packed. Don't want to leave even for a second.

He frowned at the text, embarrassment and regret engulfing him as he thought of how close he'd come to running. Now that he was here, he felt his life was ready to begin.

He remembered Sam's earlier comment and his own sense that something was amiss with Kathleen's home. Matt leaned against the counter and perused the space.

The entire front was one long rectangle. The kitchen was separated from the living area by an island with two bar stools. Black granite, black appliances, grey cabinets. Even without inspecting the cabinetry Matt recognized excellent workmanship. The living room held a gray L-shaped couch, one matching black end table and coffee table. The couch faced a faux fireplace with a black mantle. A small desk with a large Mac sat in the corner.

The bathroom sat on the left directly across from the bedroom at the back of the house. Between the sleeping and living areas stood two additional doors and one set of accordion-style doors. Matt knew one of those rooms was Kathleen's book room. The accordion doors, he assumed, hid a laundry facility. The other door remained a mystery he was too drained to consider.

Shrugging at his inability to take in the details and understand his unease, he checked the time and got busy making Kathleen a hot chocolate.

When the drink finished brewing, he started to the back just in time to see Kathleen walk across the hall to what he knew was her bedroom. He waited a few minutes so she could get dressed without his interference. *What more does she need to hide?* When the overhead light went out and a softer lamplight gleamed down the hall, he pulled himself from his worry.

Taking that as his cue, he walked forward, turned right and found his Kathleen sitting in her bed, the comforter pulled up to her neck.

"Still here?" Kathleen's voice gave no hint of emotion. He was grateful it wasn't the same dead voice he'd suffered at Rosie's, but the weariness still twisted his gut.

The dim light kept him from being able to read her eyes. He checked his watch. "Seventeen minutes, not bad. And, yes, I'm still here. I'll be around for a while." He leaned against the doorjamb. "I made hot chocolate. Thought you could warm up your insides."

She stared into his face for a few beats then looked at the

steaming mug. Her hands extended as she said, "I love hot chocolate. Even in the heat of the summer. Seth—" She paused, blinked several times. "Seth used to make fun of me." Her left foot wiggled under the sheets.

Matt strolled forward and placed the drink in her hands. He sat on the bed next to her knees, using his body to push her and give himself room. He palmed her cheek, caressed her soft skin. "Tonight, we sleep. We don't talk. We don't think. I can guess who Seth is and I can't wait to hear all about him, but not tonight." He dropped his hand and moved so he bracketed her body with his arms. "We have plenty of time—*years*—to talk." He waited for a response, and when it didn't come, he rose. "I'm going to get the antibiotics for your feet."

When he returned, her pajama-clad legs rested on top of the comforter. He positioned himself at the end of the bed and applied ointment to her toes.

"Socks are in the top right hand drawer," she said when he finished.

He dug out a pair and put them on her feet. "There, tuck back in." He lifted her legs and put them back under the covers.

She eyed his movements while she sipped her drink. Her wet hair lay plastered to her head. Where a left ear should be Matt only saw shadow. He smirked, cocked his eyebrows as he tugged on the collar of the long-sleeved flannel, plaid pajama top.

"They were lying on the bed. I forgot I even had them." She took another sip and offered him a tiny, shy smile. "Not attractive, I know, but they are so comfortable and were perfect for North Carolina mountain winter."

Matt tried to hide his laugh. "I suppose I shouldn't tell you that my mother had the same pair." He winked at her.

Kathleen chuckled then took a long gulp. "No, you probably shouldn't."

Matt reached over to the nightstand, snagged the water bottle she'd brought from the bath. "Let's get this water in you. Do you want something to eat? Aspirin?"

She exchanged the empty mug for the bottle. "I need to sleep." She drank the entire bottle in one long pull and handed it back to him.

"Okay, scoot down. Get comfortable."

She lowered her body and rolled to her side. Tucking one hand under her chin and the other between her knees, she let her eyes drift closed.

He tucked the blankets around her. "I'll shower, but I'll be nearby," he whispered as he planted a kiss on her cheek.

"That's not necessary. I've been alone a long time…"

"You've been alone long enough. So have I." He trailed his fingers over her cheeks. "I'll be here when you wake up."

When he switched off the lamp, he heard Kathleen's shaking voice say, "Light. I need the light."

Matt clicked the light back on and waited for her body to relax.

As he made the turn into the hall he heard her say, "Seth, is he right? Did you send him?"

Matt rested his back against the wall and listened. Kathleen spoke no more, and within seconds her breathing settled into a steady rhythm.

SEVEN LAUGHING FACES

Matt's body jerked when he saw a man standing in the kitchen. His laptop case and the bright orange box sat on the bar and his luggage sat next to Sam's leg. "How long have you been here?"

Sam cocked his eyebrows at Matt's aggressive question.

Matt started again, "Sorry. I'm tired and you startled me." He nodded to his stuff. "Thanks. I'm desperate for a shower." He ran his hands through his wet hair. "I hate to ask for more from you, but could you stay here while I do that? I don't want her to wake up and me not hear her."

"Slow down. Of course I can stay. I'll do anything I can to help you help her. But first, how is she? How are you?"

"She's asleep. Drained. Weary. Her toes will be fine. I got a cup of hot chocolate and a bottle of water in her before she fell asleep." He shrugged. "As for me, I'm just taking it one minute at a time. She's safe, so I'm good."

"Go take your shower. I won't go anywhere. I'll make us both a cup of coffee."

Matt nodded, grabbed his bags and turned to head down the hall. Abruptly stopping, he turned back to Sam. "I know this will sound wrong after all you've done tonight. Especially since I'm new here and haven't done a good job proving myself. But"—he paused, straightened taller—"don't touch her. Please don't touch her. Okay?"

Sam lifted his palm. "I understand. I wouldn't want anyone to touch Rosie, either. Take your shower. Nothing will happen to her. If she wakes, I'll knock on the bathroom door."

"Good." He turned to the bathroom. He took a short, scorching shower.

Clean body. Clean hair. Clean clothes. Matt felt reborn. Wearing shorts and another well-worn U of M shirt, Matt walked into the kitchen, looking forward to a quick cup of coffee and sleep.

Sam turned his direction with large, wet eyes. His hands gripped the counter so tightly the white of his knuckles showed.

Matt's body stiffened and his stride lengthened. "Sam?"

Sam closed his eyes, dropped his arms. "This house."

Matt glanced around, still not grasping the problem. "What?"

"No color. Nothing. Nothing says a person actually lives here." Sam opened his eyes and pivoted toward the living area. He pointed at the fireplace.

Matt's eyes followed the finger. "Sam—" he started but he didn't know how to finish.

"She did that."

Matt stared at the mantle and the wall where a fire might be.

"She had me put in a mantle even though there was no fireplace. I thought it was a creative idea." Sam's voice sounded thick and very far away.

Matt walked to the mantle and touched a frame. "Backwards," he said unnecessarily. "Every picture is backwards." His finger moved to the frames that hung under the mantle. Five rows of five. Each one turned the wrong way. Turning back to Sam, he wiped the wet from his cheeks. "What's behind that door?"

Sam walked to the first door in the hallway. He flicked on the light, illuminating a set of stairs that ended in another black door. "Those locks—"

Matt walked up the steps and sighed as his hands touched each of the six locks.

"Look at the wall," Sam said from the bottom of the steps.

Matt's head shifted that direction and his heart clenched. It took a long time, but he counted every single mark. Nine hundred fifty-one. Swallowing the tears, Matt put his head against the wall as his mind made the mental calculation. "I know what this is," he said with a mixture of awe, sadness and desperation. "She's counting the days since her family died." He stopped trying to swallow back the tears. "What's in this room?"

"Come on down. Check on Kathleen and we'll talk."

Matt wiped at his face. "Please tell me something that can help her."

"Go, check on her. I'll give you what I know."

Matt found Kathleen asleep in the same position he'd left her. Even though it was unnecessary, he confirmed the blankets were tucked in close. He pulled the door so it stood open enough to hear her if she called.

When Matt entered the kitchen, Sam asked, "Coffee?"

Matt's head tipped. "I get the feeling I might need coffee."

With silent agreement, they walked around the bar and sat on the stools.

"I knew her story, of course. At least some of it. The media's view. She never mentioned it. She didn't tell me who she was. I only figured it out because legal documents came addressed to Marcia Conners. To me she was simply Kathleen Bridges. This arrived"—he indicated the furniture, the computer, even the items in the kitchen—"a few weeks before she did. I unpacked everything, put it in logical places. I made sure her Internet worked. Four days before she moved in, a woman arrived. She introduced herself as Stephanie Culberson and said she wanted to see the house and had boxes to deliver." Sam paused to take a sip of his coffee. "It was odd, but the entire thing had been so odd. I showed her around, helped her bring in several boxes. After she toured the place she told me, 'These go behind the locked door.' So I hauled them up the steps."

Matt and Sam looked toward the steps to the top floor.

"I asked her what was in them. Before she answered she confirmed I was 'the Sam'—those were her words. When I told her I was, she said, 'These boxes contain her good memories. One day, she'll have to face them. I hope she doesn't try to do it alone.' She gave me a sad smile and told me to call her if Marcia—that's what she called Kathleen—needed her. She slipped me her card and left. Kathleen moved in four days later and you know the rest."

"Did you open the boxes?"

"I opened one. I'm ashamed to admit that. I told myself I was just trying to help her. But I was being a nosy SOB." He smirked, rolled his eyes. "The first thing I saw was a family portrait. Seven laughing faces and a drooling dog." Sam looked away from Matt. "I didn't look at anything else. I couldn't. I can't imagine Kathleen opening those boxes." Sam rose, put a palm on Matt's shoulder while he reached into his pocket. "Here's Ms.

Culberson's card. I've carried it with me everywhere, petrified I'd have to call her." He squeezed Matt's shoulder. "I called you a coward, and I'm sorry for that."

Matt swiped at the tears moving down his face.

"What do you plan to do now?" Sam asked after he returned to his seat. He spun his coffee mug around and around.

Matt shoved the card in his pocket. He ran his palms over his face a few times. He stretched his neck, rolled his shoulders, before finally turning to Sam. "I'm staying. Absolutely staying."

Sam's eyebrows arched but his tone remained curious and supportive. "For how long? You have a job to return to, a life." He looked at Matt's packed luggage. "Rosie and I will take care of her. We won't let her continue this way. We'll force the issue."

"I tried to leave after Rosie told me who she is. What she suffered. I panicked. But one thing my mother showed me is that I don't have a life. I have a job. My life, as it turns out, is asleep down the hall." His mouth started in a firm line but ended with a large smile. "I stay. I take care of her. I'll be asking for help. But my mother gave Kathleen to me. Someone gave me to Kathleen. We will build something together."

"When things settle out I want to hear more about your mom. But, bottom line, at least for now, you are staying here—with Kathleen—here, at her home?"

"Yes. Without a doubt. The only way she can get rid of me is to call Roger."

Sam laughed. "That'll be hard. She doesn't have a phone."

Matt chuckled, too. "Well, that's that, then."

"But seriously Matt, you have a job, responsibilities."

Matt sipped his coffee and looked again at Kathleen's space.

"I don't have all the answers. Not exactly. But what I can promise you is that I'm not leaving her. If I have to buy that condo and spend all day on the sand at the edge of her steps, I will. With each passing second, I understand that better and better. When she wakes up, she and I will make some decisions and face a few things. Whatever she decides, it has to include me. It has to." He checked his watch, noting it was already 9:30 in the morning. "I'm exhausted. I'm sure you are, too. How about we go to bed for a while? I'll contact you tomorrow with an update."

Sam moved to put his mug in the sink. "Rosie and I will be here. Whatever you need, whenever you need it. We're one phone call away. I'll do my best to keep Rosie away until you give us a nod. But she's worried, freaked, feeling guilty. Don't make us wait long." He held open his palm.

Matt looked down and saw Kathleen's house keys. Snatching them, he said, "Thanks, Sam. Seriously. Thanks for everything." Matt wanted to look Sam in the eye, wanted to show him his sincerity. Instead, his face turned toward Kathleen's room.

"Matt, you aren't going to want to hear this." Matt turned to see Sam's hand on the doorknob, his face reflected in the window. "But I need to say it. It may already be too late. She may not be able to come back again. She may not want to."

As the words, the warning, the truth, ricocheted in Matt's brain, the door clicked shut. Fighting tears, he walked to the door, flipped the six bolts in place. *Safe. I'll keep her safe. She'll be able to handle it. I'll be strong enough for both of us.*

He closed his eyes, leaned against the wall, and rubbed his chin. Sam's words pursued him. *It may already be too late. She may not even be able to come back again. She may not want to.* Tipping back his head, he stared at the white ceiling. *I can't accept that. It can't be too late.* His head dropped. *Don't think. Tomorrow. Get dressed for bed. Then sleep.* Pulling himself to his full height, he looked at the couch, briefly considered sleeping there. *She's woken alone enough.* He walked toward the back of the house.

Matt rushed through changing his clothes, brushing his teeth. He flipped off the bathroom light and let the soft light from Kathleen's room guide him to her. Stepping into the room, he stopped. Her bed stood empty. He whirled around the room. Empty.

"Kathleen."

He changed course and headed down the dark hall to the kitchen.

"Kathleen."

Rounding the counter, he looked into the shadows. "Kathleen." His voice sounded strained as the beating of his heart sped up. *Relax. She can't have gotten that far. I was gone for three minutes.* He shot across the room, turned the knob and pulled. Locked. Still, he checked each deadbolt. "Kathleen," he shouted.

Alarmed, he bolted to the darkened stairs and faced another locked door. Stumbling back down, he opened the accordion doors to find the washer and dryer. One door left. Matt grabbed the knob and pulled. Darkness. He searched for a light switch and bright white light blinded him. The book room.

"Kathleen."

No answer. Somewhere in Matt's consciousness he registered the sheer number of books. In this moment, though, all he could do was search. He went behind each shelf. No one. Empty.

Sweating, he clenched his jaw and walked back to the bedroom. No Kathleen. "Kathleen," he yelled again. Nothing. He stood still. *Think, Matt, think. I've checked every room. Where could she be? Stop panicking and think.*

He walked to the other side of the bed, searching the floor between the bed and windows. He crouched and searched under the bed. Nothing. Looking around the room, he saw one more door. He took the five steps. *My Kathleen.*

Matt stared, swallowed, then swallowed again. His legs folded underneath him and he scooted himself to her. His Kathleen. Hiding under the hanging clothes, she'd curved into a tight ball on the hard floor. Old tennis shoes served as a pillow.

"Oh, Kathleen." He traced her cheek with his finger. No response. She was asleep. His Kathleen slept on the floor in a closet. "How often, Kathleen?" he murmured. "How often do you sleep here?" He bowed his head and kissed her temple.

She didn't stir.

Matt slumped back against the wall and watched her sleep. *It may be too late.* Sam's words tormented him. *What do I do, Mom? Do I wake her? Let her stay on this hard floor?* He shook his head, bit his lip and considered his options.

He walked to the bed, pulled off the comforter and grabbed both pillows. Back in the closet, he moved into the small space between Kathleen and the wall. He lowered himself into that eight-inch space, stretched out behind her. Carefully he lifted her head, removed the shoe-pillow and replaced it with the real one. Crumpling the other pillow into a small bundle, he shoved it under his own head. He tossed the comforter over their bodies, curled his body to embrace his Kathleen with his entire length. "Tomorrow, love, tomorrow we find a way to get you out of this closet."

Holding on tight, Matt slept.

GIFTS

Matt's eyes flashed open. Without moving one muscle, he sent his eyes and senses on a search. Dim light. Hard floor. Stiff muscles. Vanilla smell. An irregular cadence of breathing. The soft brush of clothes against his face. He waited. Listening. A song filtered in. His body curled around hers.

With his right hand resting on her hip and his left arm tingling from its position over and around her head, he forced his body to stay still. He waited and listened as she sucked in two gulps of air. When her body quivered, he acted.

His right hand moved over her body. He forced his aching left arm to move underneath her waist so he could pull her closer as he rolled her to face him. "Shhh, love. You're safe."

Her body convulsed as she tried desperately to hold back sobs.

"Let go, Kathleen. You can cry now. I've got you." His right arm continued its soothing course but his left hand wrapped around her neck, tucking her face into his neck. Before he'd fallen asleep he'd put a few pieces together. Blue eyes meant she was here, in the now. The intensity of the blue told him the degree of her panic. Purple appeared if she entered the past. Gray he interpreted as 'no man's land,' a place where she barred access to either the present or the past. He understood the mirrors, the scarf, the locked doors, the tick marks. He did not understand the birds or the closet. As he'd fallen asleep, he pondered how to find out without hurling her into pain. "Love, why the closet?"

She struggled against him for a few beats before she choked on her sobs.

Tears ran down his neck and into his shirt as he held her tight against him.

"Birds can't reach me here," she slurred between gulps of air.

"Can you explain that?"

She slurped in more air, wiped her face on his shirt, pressed her forehead deeper into his neck. "Lisa." Her voice was so soft that he only heard her because her mouth sat near his ear.

Matt thought of the card sitting in his pocket. "Lisa?" he whispered back. Her body tightened, but she refused to answer. "Kathleen, how often do you sleep in the closet?" He moved his hand to run across her mangled ear and through the hair that remained. He found her left hand, ran his thumb across the rough edges where her ring finger used to sit.

"Nine hundred fifty-one."

Matt's heart squeezed until he struggled for breath. He closed his eyes, stroked her head before settling his palm on her neck. "We have a lot to talk through. But, Kathleen, this is the *last night* you spend in a closet. That——" His voice broke on the tears. Struggling for composure, he continued, "That, I can promise you."

For several long moments, silence, stillness and a thickening air descended in the darkened room.

"Matt…" Her words dissolved into incoherence.

"I've got you. If you let me—and I'm begging you to let me   I'll have you tomorrow and the next day."

"Matt," she heaved through choking sounds. "Don't make promises you can't keep. Those promises are the ones that plague you."

Matt squeezed at her neck then pulled her back so she could see his face. "I'm not sure what my mom told you about me." He kissed her nose and wished there was more light in the closet so they could see each other's eyes. "But I can be a tenacious asshole." Enough light filtered in so he could see her big eyes blink up at him. He kissed her nose once more. "No more closets. We will find another way to make it through the night. *We* will find a way to keep the birds away."

"They can't be kept away. I have to let them out," she said with a shaking voice. "I know that. I've always known that."

Before he could form a response, his stomach reminded him of how long they'd been in that closet. Embarrassed, he dropped his hand to cover the sound. His embarrassment waned when her stomach made itself known, too.

"How long have we been asleep?" she asked with a slight smile in her voice.

"I have no idea, but apparently long enough for us to get hungry. Let's find food." He helped her roll over and rise. "You get changed." He smirked at the old-lady pajamas. "I'll meet you in the kitchen."

Before planning food, Matt went to the deck and moved furniture. Back in the kitchen, he prepared two ham sandwiches, tossed a handful of chips onto paper plates.

Finding a bag of Oreos, he stuffed those and two water bottles under his arm. He left the door to the deck open so that Kathleen would know where to find him. He placed the food on the table, tossed a water bottle on her chair and then settled into his own. He drank the entire bottle in one long gulp. Through the open door, he heard her shuffle into the kitchen then open and close a drawer. When she didn't appear, Matt tilted his upper body off the lounger and peered into the bungalow. Not seeing her, he went in pursuit.

She sat on the top step to the locked upstairs room. Her fingers were tracing the tick marks.

Matt moved to the step beneath her, sat, and put his arm around her waist. "Why do you do this?"

"I guess you know my story now."

"Only the basics. No details. That's your story to tell when you're ready. Can you explain this?"

She kept her fingers moving but answered, "It's the safest place for me to remember them."

The cap of the permanent marker popped off. He reached out to stop her hand before she added the next mark. "Can I make a suggestion?"

Her body tensed, and she attempted to pull her hand back. When he wouldn't let go, she nodded.

"Let's turn around and start the other wall. We'll add to the memorial while creating one to honor the days we move forward." Matt grabbed the pen from her shaking hand and slid her into his lap, enveloped her. "Talk to me."

Her body vibrated before she looked back at him. "What if I can't move forward?"

He smiled at her, kissed the edge of her mouth. "I didn't say 'you'—I said 'we'."

She dropped her head into his chest. "What if I don't want to?"

He turned so he spoke into the mauled hole. "You do. If you didn't, you wouldn't have survived this long. You wouldn't keep promises." He took a deep breath, rubbed his cheek against hers. "And your family wants that for you, too."

Tears dampened his shirt.

He found the marker on the step below him. He lifted her right hand from his chest and placed the pen in it. Then he waited.

She turned the pen over and over in her hand. She looked at the wall with the memorial marks. She looked at him. "What if I can't? What if I just can't?"

He ran both hands through her hair and held onto the back of her head. "One minute, one decision at a time. *That* you can do. I'll be there to catch you."

Her eyes got bigger and bigger, but the dimness of the space did not allow him to see the color. He jumped when her hand gripped his wrist. He held his breath as she fit her hand into his palm, turned her body, and with his help put a tick mark on the clean wall.

"One and nine hundred fifty-two." She faced him and gave him a frightened smile.

Hoping to lessen the tension, he rumbled, "Feed me."

"What time is it?" she asked as she descended the stairs.

"Close to sunset."

She hustled. He caught up to her on the deck. The sky

reminded him of those middle school experiments where you mixed several liquids, and then let the liquids separate into layers. In the sky, the top layer was a dark, looming gray. Beneath the gray there was a deep blue streak. Then a fluorescent pink was followed by an eye-piercing yellow. And, as a coup de grâce, a bright orange flattened against the dark water. Matt stood next to her. "I've never seen anything like that," he said with awe.

"Sunset pink," she said on a sigh.

Her left foot tapped, so he pulled her flush against him. "Sunset pink?"

She tilted her chin toward the pink stripe. "Sunset pink. Courtney's favorite color. And it only exists in a sunset after a storm." Her foot increased in speed and the shaking moved up her leg.

"Keep telling me." Now that he could put pieces together, he understood she had memories that needed to become a part of her life. Good memories. Beautiful memories. He encouraged her to bring those memories to the present. Cocooning her, prepared to intervene, he let her struggle through the story.

"Her wedding was set for the February after…"

Matt moved in behind her, clamped his arms around her waist. "You can do this. Bring her alive for me."

"She wanted her wedding to be sunset pink and black. But you can't buy sunset pink. We visited at least twenty bridesmaid stores, florists, even fabric stores. This pink only exists in the beach sunset." She snorted. "She was pissed. If she couldn't have that pink, she'd have no color."

Another snort. "You think you're tenacious. Wait until you meet Court."

Matt's arms flinched around her. *Fuck. Present tense.* "Kathleen?" He placed his chin on her shoulder.

"Everything will be black. She'll be in white and the flowers will be white, but everything else will be black."

Matt's eyes closed, seeking the right words, any words.

"I know, Matt. I know she's not here," she said before she walked down the steps and toward the waves.

The orange ball of sun sank at the same rate as Matt's heart. "Kath," he called, giving her a new name, a name only for him.

She turned toward him. "Give me a few minutes, okay?" She turned away and walked until her feet entered the froth.

Matt kept a protective eye on his Kathleen.

She stooped and collected a handful of sand. As she stood she watched the sand sift through her fingers then bent and collected more. Satisfied with her safety, he collected the chips and sandwiches, walked inside the bungalow, keeping the door open so he could keep her within sight. He found his phone and updated Rosie and Sam, explaining he and Kathleen would not be in tonight, but they could expect them tomorrow.

Kathleen walked back and forth in the shallow water, kicking the foam with what seemed like fury. Matt's shoulders relaxed. "You be as angry as you need to be," he said, even though she couldn't hear him. "Let it out, love. I'll be here." He returned to his seat and debated how the evening should go.

"How are the toes?" he called when she was close enough.

Peeking at one foot then at the other, she nodded. She climbed the steps and planted her head in his chest. "My kids loved the beach," she said to her feet.

"Let's eat and you tell me how you ended up here."

"You moved things," she said as she claimed the lounger in the back corner and took the plate he offered.

"I didn't want the table between us. It's as simple and complex as that," he said before popping several chips into his mouth and straddling his chair.

She placed the plate in her lap, checked her scarf and sunglasses then tilted her head at him. "Thanks for making dinner." She took six bites of sandwich, ate six chips before she placing her napkin over the remaining food and setting the plate on the deck.

Matt took a chip from his plate, extended it toward her. "Have one more."

She took the chip, inspected it as if it were a foreign object. Shifting her face to his, she raised her shoulder in question.

"What's with the six bites?" he asked with fake nonchalance, keeping his eyes fixed and his body ready to move her direction.

Her head tipped. "Six bites?" Her eyebrows furrowed and her lips disappeared between her teeth. "Wha—I—I—" Her voice quavered and her foot rocked side to side.

"Hold on," Matt tossed his plate on the ground, moved behind her, cushioning her between his legs and arms. "Okay, Kathleen, what's…"

"What are you talking about?" Her voice squeaked with panic as the tremors moved up her legs. The chip crushed in her palm, littering crumbs on their laps.

"Every time you eat you only take six bites. Six bites of salad. Six bites of zucchini bread, four strawberries, but that was six bites." He nuzzled her neck, pulled his long legs across hers.

"Lucas," she whispered and the tremors moved into her torso.

"I've got you. Tell me."

"Lucas, Lucas, he——" She dragged in air, punctured his thighs with her nails. "He was a terrible eater. So they had a rule. He had to eat six bites of everything on his plate." The words left her on a rush. "Do I really do that?" Her nails dug deeper even as the tremors lessened.

"Every meal I've seen you eat."

"Matt," she started and stopped.

He waited a few beats, then encouraged, "What, love? What are you thinking?"

"Do I do other weird things?" She hiccupped on each word.

Before he answered he shifted her so her legs hung to the sides and her torso faced him. He removed her sunglasses and put his palms on her neck, using his thumbs to trace her cheeks. "You cut your salad into a checkerboard pattern. Very precise. You wear a toe ring that is lovely but it's not a toe ring. It's a ring, a real ring." Her eyes reminded him of a lava lamp from his youth, undulating between blue and purple.

"Seth used to cut our salads that way. Me, Court, Amanda, and Kiley—all the girls. It was a family joke." A single tear leaked from her eyes and her hands clamped his forearms.

"You eat your salad with a spoon."

"Kiley," she said on a hush. Her eyes widened as she stared

at him. "I don't understand. Why do I do that?"

Matt's thumbs caressed her cheekbones, wiping at the streaming tears. "I think while you've been trying to forget, they've been wanting you to remember."

"The birds," she said. Her eyes burned a brilliant purple and her entire body spasmed.

With a strength and speed he didn't realize he had, Matt collected her against him, rose from the chair, and darted to the closet. He situated himself in the deep corner and lowered himself with her still in his arms and now on his lap. "Kathleen," he asserted. "Where are you?"

She swallowed, gulped in air, swallowed again.

"Look at me." He tilted her head so her eyes aligned with his. "Open your eyes. Tell me where you are."

Her eyes opened, blinked as she struggled to breathe. "Closet," she choked out.

"Who's holding you?"

"You."

Matt smiled. "Who are you with? Who am I?"

Kathleen's head shook. "Matt Nelson, Betty's son. Tenacious asshole." Her head flopped into his neck. "Her gift," she added.

Matt's heart thudded in his chest. Gathering her against him, he kissed the top of her head and whispered, "Thank you, Mom."

Once Kathleen's breathing returned to normal, Matt asked, "Kathleen, what did you do when this happened before I came?"

Still speaking into his neck, she said, "It didn't start

happening until you got here."

Matt's body flinched and his head lay back against the wall where he stared at the clothes above him. *Mom, what have you done?* "Do you have the energy to tell me about the toe ring?"

Her left leg lengthened and her fingers stretched to touch the jeweled ring. "You're right. It's not a toe ring. It's a purity ring. Seth gave it to Court for her fourteenth birthday. She wore it every day until she got engaged." Her leg bent and she twirled the ring on her toe. "After…" Her voice shook but she kept going, "Eli sent it to me. After. He thought I should have it. While I was still in Charlotte, I had the ring sized."

"Eli?"

Her foot dropped and she looked up into his eyes. "Court's fiancé." A fresh tear emerged. "He sent a few other things. They're in boxes." She looked into the dim bedroom. "Upstairs." Her voice trembled and Matt knew it was fear. He knew it was fear, because he felt it, too.

SHE HATES ME

Matt found Kathleen tucked into her bed, reading a book. "Hot chocolate," he said. Handing her the mug, he nudged her with his knee, forcing her to give him 'his' side of the bed. "Still reading about Mr. Darcy?"

After taking a sip, she looked up at him sans sunglasses but with a bright red scarf and those same old-lady pajamas. "No, I finished that one. This is about Henry VIII's last wife."

"Wait, you finished another one? It was, what, four hundred pages?"

She gave him a cute smile and bright blue eyes. "Matt, I read at least a book a day."

He shook his head. "I haven't read five books since college, and on most of those I cheated." He took the book from her hand, marked the page, and dropped it to the floor with a loud thwack. "What are your favorite types of books?"

With a raised eyebrow, she answered, "No horror. No self-help. Few biographies. I prefer happy endings. But I have to have them to read them." She looked pointedly at the book on the floor.

"I was hoping we could talk for a while, then I'll give you your book back."

She huffed but moved herself to sit next to him with both their backs resting against the headboard. His legs reached toward the end of the bed while her knees bent as if ready to prop a book. "I get to go first." She took another sip, laid her head back, and closed her eyes. "What's the Nike box?"

Matt laced their hands together, running his thumb over the back of her hand and the scars from her missing appendage. "Letters. My mom wrote me letters before she died."

Keeping her head against the headboard, she turned away from him. "About me?" Her shoulders dropped as she tried to pull her hand away.

Gripping her hand, he said, "No. Me. There were hints of you, but I didn't recognize that. She wanted me to come here, to find you. She didn't say that until the fifth letter, and even then, it was cryptic. But more than that, she wanted me to…" He took a deep breath. "She wanted me to find me." His voice broke.

"I don't want to be a project," she said with an odd combination of sadness and determination.

With his face remaining forward, he said, "If I had not seen you the first night—*before* I opened the first letter—then I might consider you a project. A rescue mission, I guess. But that first night—" He moved them so their eyes locked. "Seriously, Kathleen, our reaction to each other tells its own tale. We may have things to face together, hard things. Facing *those* is our project. You," he said as he kissed the corner of her eye, "are not a project. You are my gift."

Her eyes blinked at his use of words. "The last night she was here, before she walked away from my table, she told me she had a gift for me. That's when she made me promise I'd go to

Rosie's every night." A tear dripped down her face. "She told me the gift would arrive there."

"Well, she felt the need to give me a few kicks in the ass first," Matt teased.

She smiled, wiping at her face. "Can I have my book now?"

Matt leaned over and snagged the book. Holding it just out of reach, he asked, "Do you normally wear the scarf to bed?"

The arm she'd stretched to grab the book dropped, and she jerked her hand from his. She ran her hands over the scarf. "No." She gripped the scarf with both hands.

Matt put the book in her lap. Maintaining eye contact, he reached up and unwound the scarf.

Her eyes grew, her throat convulsed, but she held still.

With the scarf gone, he ran his hand across her damaged head, into her hair. "No hiding. I get why you wear it. But here"—he looked around the room—"or anytime we're alone, you do not need it."

She stared at him but said nothing.

After a few moments, he winked, smiled, and said, "Now, read."

Her breath left her body as her hands groped for the book. Once she held it, she shifted and buried her head in the pages.

As she read Matt filtered through what he knew and what he didn't know. Falling back on ingrained habits, he searched for the best way to get the information he needed. Lost in thought until she shifted, he looked over to find her settling under the comforter.

With her hands tucked under her pillow, she lay on her side, her bad ear exposed to him. "What are you thinking about?"

Matt moved so he, too, lay on his side. He tucked one hand

under his cheek and moved the other to run through her hair, caressing the bumps and scarred flesh. "Sam met Stephanie. Did you know that?"

Her head pulled back as her eyebrows knitted. "What?"

He put his leg over hers, paying attention to any movement in her body. "Just before you moved here, she brought some boxes."

Her eyes widened, flashed, then narrowed. "It sounds strange, but I never wondered how those boxes got here. I saw them. I locked them away." Her hand moved to grab at her ear. "She hates me."

Matt put his forehead to hers. "No, love. I don't know her. But no one who hates you would come here just to check things out."

She rolled to her back and straightened out. "She has to hate me."

Matt's leg still lay across her legs. He let his hand drop to wrap around her middle. "Explain that."

Kathleen's hands met on her stomach and her fingers danced with each other. After a deep sigh, her voice remote, she gave him more pieces to the puzzle. "She stayed in Charlotte the entire time I was hospitalized. Days, weeks, months. If I was awake she was in that chair. She went with me to physical therapy and every procedure possible. She talked to doctors when I was too drugged to understand. She brought us real food. She read to me when I couldn't hold a book. God, Matt. She learned how to tie a scarf, and we spent hours practicing until I could cover myself in seconds."

She took a break and snuggled into Matt's hand as he caressed her wounds.

"When they moved me to a rehab center, she returned home. Still, she made the drive every Sunday for visiting hours. She always brought a box of books.

"The medical shit was hard. The mental shit was much harder. Twelve hours a day, seven days a week of some type of therapy or homework or a book I had to read. That's when I discovered how to hide behind Brice's iPod and fiction. We weren't allowed to sit in our rooms. 'Isolate', they called it. But I learned I could sit in the common areas with my earphones or a book in my lap and that satisfied them.

"I had been in the rehab center for two months when the prosecuting attorney from Charlotte came to see me. The trial was getting ready to gear up and he, of course, needed my testimony. Lisa, my primary therapist, wasn't thrilled with the idea." Her eyes turned his way and refocused on him with an intensity he'd not seen. "It was something I *had* to do."

He lifted to sit above her with his head resting on his palm. *Pay attention*. The words flashed in his mind and he knew his mother had planted them there.

Kathleen rested for a few minutes.

"His name was Oscar." She snickered, but it wasn't with humor. "Who names their kid Oscar? He was nice, tender with me. He looked to Lisa for guidance every step of the way. Best of all, he was determined that the boys should face the death penalty."

Matt's eyes closed and he flattened his palm on her back. He opened his eyes and met her in the memory.

"The time came for me to face the defense attorney. Oscar had prepared me for my deposition. He explained that the defense attorney was more interested in publicity than winning. It was a no-win case, really. The defense attorney agreed to let Lisa go with me. She sat next to me during the five-hour deposition process. Five fucking hours that felt like days." She shook her head. "Stephanie sat in the lobby."

"Lisa wasn't allowed to proof the questions, but she could tell them when I needed a break. Otherwise, she had to be silent. They asked about facts. He asked the same questions a thousand ways. But I didn't remember." Her voice rose and her breathing increased.

"Lisa tried to tell him, but he cut her off." Kathleen twisted her face up to Matt. "I didn't remember. No matter how many times he asked me, I didn't remember."

Kathleen sucked in a deep breath. She seemed to be gathering strength for what came next. Matt braced himself to listen and to protect her.

Her voice turned robotic, making Matt more anxious. "The trial happened much faster than anyone expected. The night before I testified, Stephanie, Lisa, and some of the other therapists took me to dinner. They were—they are—a great group of people and they wanted the best for me. Stephanie told stories of our misspent youth. That night I actually laughed. My first laugh." Kathleen's energy drained as if a plug had been pulled. Her eyes dropped away. "And my last laugh."

She clamped her hands over his, swallowed several times before looking toward the ceiling. "The best meal I had had in over six months. The only *decent* meal I'd had. We even got a carafe of wine." She smiled up at him, relaxed her hands and nestled closer to his body. "They presented with me with a big box. Wrapped pretty with a fancy bow. Inside, underneath pink tissue paper, were a black skirt, pumps, and a pink top. 'To make you feel confident tomorrow,' the card said. When I left that restaurant, I felt—" She paused. "Strong, ready, supported."

Pausing again, Kathleen shrugged out of Matt's grasp. She rolled to face the wall.

His fingers trailed up and down her spine. When she took in a deep breath, he coaxed her to roll back toward him. "No, love, don't turn away. I've got you. This time I've got you." Full, dark gray eyes met his.

In that automaton voice he hated, she began again, "I had to wait in the lobby until my turn. That was fine by me. Stephanie sat with me, holding my hand and talking about some book she was reading. She chatted like a monkey in a tree. When the bailiff called my name, she hugged me. 'You got this,' she told me. Her fingers were the last time anyone touched me until your mother arrived here."

Matt sucked in a breath and remembered her violent response when Sam tried to touch her.

Kathleen's shoulder slumped and her voice turned resigned. "But we both knew it was a lie. I still didn't remember. I would be no help." Her face fell into his chest.

"Do you want to stop? It doesn't all have to come out tonight," Matt said, unsure whether he was protecting Kathleen or himself.

"Lisa sat behind Oscar," she kept going as she lifted her head and gave him blue and purple eyes. "Lisa had no influence there. The judge was in charge. Lisa was moral support only. Oscar was great. Lisa had explained that my memory hadn't returned. He had an expert planned to explain my condition. I don't know all the details—maybe I should have been focused on justice but—" She touched her ear, her side, her hip.

Matt's eyes followed her hand and again he wondered what more he would have to see. What more she'd endured.

"He asked me about us—who we were, I guess. He asked me what I remembered of that day and seemed satisfied with my inability to answer. By the time it was over, I was exhausted. Proud, too, in a way. I thought…" She choked on the words before gathering control.

Her voice changed from emotionless to aggressive. Each word dripped like acid. "It wasn't over. The defense attorney was not the man I had met earlier. It was some woman. I remember she was tall and she had on super high heels. Even then I wondered why she needed to add six inches to her height." Kathleen's words spat out of her mouth. "That bitch. Even from the podium she wanted to tower over me."

Her hands twisted his shirt into tight balls. Her eyes flared a blazing purple. Redness moved into her cheeks as sweat ran between her eyes.

A chill raced down Matt's back and his own fear sweat formed.

"Before she came to the podium, she leaned into my nephew, placed her arm over his shoulder. Together they laughed at something. I half-expected her to ruffle his hair." Anger rolled off Kathleen in waves as her legs pinwheeled and her breath clogged in her throat.

"Kathleen." Matt sat up, tried to collect her in his embrace, but she fought him. "Kathleen," he tried again. With his hands on her shoulders he shook her. "Kathleen, come back here."

Her purple irises sparked as she kicked at him.

"Love," he said as he clamped her arms against her sides. "You're with me. Come back to me. It's over now." He rocked them until her body settled and her eyes calmed.

On a whisper and with her eyes pinned to his, she said, "She started off nice. 'We're sorry for your loss and your continued struggle.' That's the last thing I heard. As she approached the podium, she held a pad of paper and underneath the pad was a picture. T-bone—" Her voice dropped lower and Matt strained to hear her. "My handprint in T-bone's blood." She broke free from his embrace, rolled to the floor, landing on her hands and knees. She crawled into the closet before Matt finished processing her words.

Racing to her, he gathered her in his arms and tucked them both into the corner of her closet.

Words fired like bullets. "She asked question after question. I have no idea what she asked. I have no idea what I said. Sometime later Lisa collected me from the witness stand. I never spoke to Stephanie again. I sent her a letter, a letter detailing what I wanted done with our stuff in the mountains. I took her name off my approved contacts list. I moved here."

Matt held her as she made herself more comfortable against his body. As she slipped into sleep he slowly lifted them both off the floor. Satisfied she was safe and sound asleep, he went into the kitchen and found his phone.

STEPHANIE

Not caring about the time, Matt pulled Stephanie's card from his pocket and dialed the number.

"Hello," a woman's voice answered.

"I'm looking for Stephanie Culberson," Matt said, watching the bedroom door for signs Kathleen had awakened.

"This is she. Who's this?"

"My name is Matt Nelson. I'm…" He paused, unprepared for how to begin.

"What can I do for you, Mr. Nelson?"

Taking a deep breath, he said the one thing he knew she'd understand. "I'm at Rosamunda Beach."

Stephanie sucked in an audible breath. It took several seconds before she said, "Is Marcia okay?"

"Marcia?" Matt said with question in his voice. "Kathleen, she goes by Kathleen now."

Another long silence.

"Is Kathleen okay?"

"She believes you hate her," Matt said, puzzled by his own choice of openings.

"She's my best friend," the woman said over tears. "Can you tell me what's happening?"

Matt looked down the hall again. "Let me check on her and I'll tell you what I can, are you willing to hold on a few minutes?"

"It's been almost three years. I can wait a few more minutes."

Matt tucked the covers more tightly around Kathleen's body, kissed her head. "Sleep, love." He left the door open in case she needed him.

"Can you tell me about the trial?"

She didn't answer.

"Ms. Culberson," he said when the silence stretched on.

"Maybe you should start first."

Matt fell into one of the barstools and began talking. He talked about Jess, the box, his mother's meeting Kathleen, his mother's losing battle with cancer, the letters, his purchased plane ticket, the race to find her on the beach, Kathleen's version of the trial. He told her everything. Everything.

"You want me to start at the trial?" Stephanie said after several long minutes of silence.

"What does she remember?"

"Before the trial she could get as far as our walk the morning before the attack."

"And after the trial?"

"The attorney—the one with the high heels—either she didn't believe Marcia's amnesia or she was just cruel. She would ask questions in a nice enough voice but she continuously walked from the podium to the pictures on display in the courtroom. She never pointed to the pictures or referenced them. She just hovered near them. Marcia would stare at a picture—"

"What kind of pictures?" Even though he knew the answer, he wanted no confusion or misunderstanding.

"Crime scene photos mostly. I found her, you know." Stephanie hesitated. "I went over for lasagna and stepped in blood. The blood." A sob tore through her. "It was everywhere. But there was no Marcia. Seth, the kids, the babies, even the dog." Her voice rose and Matt squeezed the phone. "But no Marcia. When I found her, she was blessedly unconscious."

After a long silence, she continued.

"Marcia kept saying she didn't remember. Then the lawyer put a new picture in front of her. It was of us at the mall near her rehab center. We were having coffee, looking at cruise brochures for my son's honeymoon. In the photo Marcia was smiling, almost laughing. The attorney simply asked if she remembered the day. She pulled out another one. A group of us having dinner. In the picture Marcia has a glass of wine and a gift bag in her lap. The gift was the outfit she was wearing on the stand. I remember clearly that Marcia just blinked up at her—but Marcia was no longer there. Not really. The attorney politely—and I mean sickeningly politely—asked Marcia how mourning was going. Marcia blinked some more. Next the lawyer asked how much money she made from her family's death. That was how she said it—'How much money did you make?' There were objections. Chaos erupted. I don't know what happened legally. I watched my best friend disappear. Marcia Conners went into that courtroom. She never left."

Matt sat in silent anger, silent anguish, while he listened to Stephanie Culberson, his Kathleen's best friend, cry.

"I spoke with Lisa, Lisa Bartlett, her therapist, once more before Marcia took us off her medical information. Lisa said she hardly spoke, barely ate, refused to try. Marcia believed—believes—she failed her family. She also believes that attorney wanted to destroy her. Lisa told me Marcia had given up. I always wondered if that attorney was satisfied." She took a deep breath. "Everyone got a life sentence, even Marcia."

"I don't know what to say. There is nothing to say."

"Tell me you are going to help her. Just tell me there is hope. Tell me I can have my friend back one day."

Matt thought about his mother's letters and his father's words. "My mother decided to hope, to hope for Kathleen, to hope for me. I can tell you I love her, I will give her all my strength, all my everything. I will also tell you that I'm lost. I don't know how to help her."

"I got a letter from her, four weeks after the trial. Four weeks of her refusing to see me, refusing to take my calls. Enough of Marcia's personality was in the letter that I knew she'd written it. But the letter was clinical. Maybe I mean professional. She told me how she wanted the house and its contents handled. She enclosed a check. A large check. She basically paid me to close the Conners family away."

Matt spoke over the pain clogging his throat, "What did she want you to do?"

Stephanie responded with a professional tone, as if reading a letter from a bank. "Donate anything I wanted to Goodwill or whatever organization would benefit the most." Her voice shifted back to the sadness of earlier. "If there were items she needed to have, I was to box them and ship them to Rosamunda Beach in care of Sam Crowley. I shipped most, but I kept a few boxes—the most special items—and hand-delivered them to Mr. Crowley. Did she believe I would ship boxes and not go see this new home, this Sam?"

"I don't think she knows you were here, or at least she didn't until I mentioned it. Sam never told her."

"That's more proof that Marcia Conners is gone. She knew me better than that."

"What about the house, the property?"

A harsh laugh erupted through the phone. "According to the letter, after the home was released from the police and court people, I was to have it torn down. Put the property on the market. Sell it for whatever I could. I could give it away. I could do whatever I wanted with the proceeds. She had the proper forms—all the legal documents—allowing me to do this."

Even though she was many miles away, Matt felt the air thicken. He sat straight in the chair, tightened his stomach, and waited on a coming blow.

"The house is gone. I bought the property above fair market value because I couldn't imagine anyone else living there. I donated her proceeds to the police station where Brice and Amanda worked."

With each word her voice hardened and Matt stiffened.

"Her last line—before she signed her *full name*—was 'Do whatever you want, Stephanie. Apparently I've made enough money off my family.'" Tears choked the woman's voice, but she continued, "I understood then those pictures had registered, she'd heard every word that wicked woman said to her. That lawyer took away any strength Marcia—Kathleen—had. She took away her courage."

For the first time in his life he wanted to hurt someone, several someones. He wanted to start with the defense lawyer and move out from there.

"I'm not sure why I told you that. I guess I wanted you to understand that I'm not sure I know this new person, this Kathleen Bridges. I know Marcia Conners."

"I've seen glimpses of Marcia. She's still in there. Kathleen has to find a way to reconcile both. I have to figure out how to help her do that."

"I met with Lisa several times, and she had me read several books. Funnily enough, from time to time she still sends me one. We were assuming Marcia would come back to live here, next to me. Lisa won't talk to you—she's careful about patient confidentiality. But I can try to answer some questions." Stephanie's voice filled with hope and determination. "I've always said love would bring her back."

"Birds," Matt said. "Can you explain the birds?"

"Birds?" Stephanie whispered. "Yeah, I can tell you about the birds."

"Let me check on her again." Matt put the phone on the counter, leaned his forehead into his hands and tried to settle his own heart. Pulling himself together, he walked down the hall, ensured she was sound asleep and safe in the bed. He sat next to her, stroked her head, and told her how much he loved her. "My Kathleen," he whispered into his kiss. "Hold on a bit longer. We're going to find a way."

BIRDS

Matt put the phone to his ear as he prepared a cup of coffee. "I'm back. She's still asleep."

"Okay, I found my notes on PTSD. Lisa sent us to classes and one of the professors used birds as an analogy. I remember it because Marcia—Kathleen—is deathly afraid of birds. She won't even go in a butterfly house. It struck me then how apt his example was. Let me read from my notes." He heard paper rustling.

"Hold up, let me get situated." Matt pulled out his yellow notepad and his pen. It seemed that both he and Stephanie felt calmer with a plan, a partner in Kathleen's recovery. "Go," he said when he was ready.

"There are as many ways someone handles trauma as there are people. Some decide to close off from everything. It doesn't work forever." She took in a large breath, then plowed on, speaking so rapidly Matt struggled to follow.

"Imagine a room, and in the room, are three doors. The first door is painted a simple neutral color. Hanging from the doorknob is a sign that reads 'Before'. The second door is a deep red with a sign that reads 'The Event'. The third door is gray, a dark gray, like a storm cloud. Its sign says 'After'.

"Each door has locks. The first door, 'Before', has one lock. Relatively easy to open. The third door, 'After', only has one lock because it's mostly empty anyway. The middle door, 'The Event', has locks from top to bottom. Let's say fifteen or twenty. All different types of locks. There are even bars across the door. Entry seems impossible. Yet the door bulges and cracks. If you listen closely you can hear something, lots of somethings, pounding, begging for release. Behind each door you would find birds. Are you with me?" She paused, either to gather her own thoughts or to let Matt gather his.

Matt gave a guttural response. Not a word, not an agreement, only an acknowledgement he was listening. His forehead pressed into the counter and the phone painfully pushed into his ear. His right hand fisted around a sheet of paper.

"Each room has several different types of birds, you see. The first room has a variety of birds—pretty ones, dull ones, mean and ugly ones. Probably the same type of birds we'd all have if our lives were represented by birds. The third room, 'After', doesn't have many birds and those that are there are gray and boring. But in 'The Event' there are thousands of birds. All the birds that scary movies use. Ravens, crows, vultures." She stopped.

"Go on," he choked out. "Finish."

"Each bird represents a memory, an experience or set of experiences, or even beliefs about herself."

"Stephanie," Matt said, frustrated, "I'm a tax attorney. I work with numbers and tax codes all day. I have no artistic ability. I don't even know good art when I see it. I'm sure there is a point to this picture you've painted, but can you please tell me in words, rather than pictures? Can you please just spit it out?"

She took a deep breath. "If a PTSD patient wants to build something out of the tragedy, well, she has to open those doors, all three of them. In order to live, not just exist, we have to let all the birds of our lives have their place."

Matt's eyes widened, his chest constricted. "Let me make sure I understand. She has literally closed off all her memories."

"I think before the trial, she had opened the first door. Lisa was helping her pull the birds out in a way she could handle. She and I could look at photos and laugh at our kids' antics. But the trial, those pictures, that woman. Her accusations were too much, too fast, so graphic. Marcia reinforced the doors, stuffed the birds back in, and ran. She understands that to enjoy the good memories of Before, she will also have to endure the memories of The Event."

"But she does remember some things. We've talked about sunset pink and toe rings, lightning."

"I'm not sure. I know Lisa was being really cautious about it. We were hoping she would stay in rehab until she'd processed everything."

"How do I help her do that?"

"Would she go back to Lisa?"

"What if she won't? What do I do? Those birds *are* getting out. I'm watching it happen." His voice was laced with despair, hopelessness.

"Help her to open the good memories slowly, very slowly. Watch her carefully. If—"

"If?" Matt pressed.

"You've already described her panicked reactions to the good memories. Imagine if those doors were to be thrust open and she were to be swarmed. No matter what, Matt, she's going to need help, *professional help.*"

Matt gripped the counter and phone until his fingers hurt. "I'll get that for her," he said.

"As much as I want that, please remember that she must decide. I wanted to force her to stay last time. But we can't make that decision. Not you. Not me. You can kidnap her, force her on a plane and into Lisa's office. But unless she wants to confront the past, she will lock us out. You'll become another bird behind a locked door." A long sigh came through the line. "I know that from experience."

"And if I can't get her there?"

"I'm talking as if I'm an expert. I'm not. All I can do is tell you what I understood. As much as we'd like to let one bird out at a time, it doesn't work that way. When that middle door opens—and it will one day—those birds might pummel her. The swarm. I used the word 'pummel' quite intentionally. Those birds are clamoring to get out. Picture them pecking at the door, seething with fury at their entrapment. I honestly can't believe she made it this long. She was making great progress until that damn trial," she said with equal parts disgust and anger. "Something could happen, a trigger. Then the door will open—probably without any real warning—and she'll be overtaken, buried in birds."

Matt closed his eyes and took deep breaths. "That's what happens when she panics?"

"I don't know. I'm not there and I'm an armchair therapist. But I'm guessing a bird gets out and she tries to fight it back into the closet. She runs or tries to run to get away." Stephanie's voice sounded strained, tired, worried. "Is this helping or making it worse?"

Matt walked toward the front windows. "Both. What do I do now? In the meantime? Before I can convince her to get help? How can I help her?"

"I suppose my advice is to pay attention. Constant attention. Until you build the support system she needs, try to keep her focused on good memories. When the doors open, those birds could come fast and furious. Protect her when they arrive."

Matt opened the door and stepped to the railing. "I'm so out of my depth," he said, not actually speaking to Stephanie.

"I think you probably are. I was. But right now, it also seems you're all she's got, the only one she's been willing to let past the locks."

Matt's body shot straight, his excitement leaked over. "What if you came to visit?"

"No." He heard her take in a deep breath. "I think anything directly out of her past could open that door too fast. That's why I've stayed away. I don't want to cause her any more pain. You've seen despair and hopelessness. What's inside her, though, is anger. Extraordinary rage."

Matt stuffed his hand into his hair and collapsed back against the chair.

"Attention. Constant attention. I can do that," he said. "Anything else?"

"Does she still read?"

Matt chuckled. "Oh yeah. You should see the book room." He glanced down the hall to the first door on the right, where a veritable library sat.

"Use the characters to get her talking. She reveals a lot—a whole lot—about herself, where she's at, what she needs, through the characters. We often used characters to tell each other how we felt when words wouldn't come."

Matt tried to remember the specifics of what she'd said about people in the books. All he could conjure was her excitement. He'd not paid enough attention. "Pay attention," he said into the phone.

A long, uncomfortable silence greeted him. He gnawed on his lip and waited it out.

"Just before the trial, Lisa and I discussed a trip for Marcia and me. We thought getting her away from the routine might help her relax more. She spent every hour of every day either at that rehab center or at a doctor's office. Maybe you can get her away from the beach. Give her a taste of something different."

Matt's face relaxed into something of a grin as a new picture emerged. *I'm taking my girl home. To the safety of my town, my father and my mother's garden.* "I'm taking her home." The silence stretched and what little relief Matt had found evaporated.

"Good luck, Matt. Be careful. She's strong. But she's also fragile. Please keep me posted."

"Here's how I see it. Kathleen has a team. Me, Sam and Rosie, my family, and you. I think together, with all our hope surrounding her, we can hold her while she fights. You have my number now. Feel free to use it."

Neither he nor Stephanie said anything for a long time.

"There's one more thing."

After a long pause, Matt prompted, "Yes?"

"If those birds get out, if they attack—"

"Go on."

"They could take you down, too."

Matt looked down the hall and then at the counter. He closed his eyes and tried to picture his life without Kathleen. All he saw was her laughing, wrapped in a U of M scarf. "I'll fight them with her if it comes to that."

"Okay," she said softly. "I hope we meet soon."

The phone disconnected before he could respond.

Checking the clock, Matt cleaned up his mess. He prioritized. He created mental to-do-lists. He found strength and confidence. When he felt satisfied with his plan, he climbed in next to Kathleen, curled his body around hers. As his mind shut down and his body forced him to sleep, he prayed for the first time since he was a small boy. He prayed his mother and her Seth were watching over them. He prayed his Kathleen would forgive him for breaking open her past.

FREAK

A cold and lonely bed made Matt bolt up. He rushed to the closet. When he found it empty, his heart rate settled, but soon lurched again. With long, quick strides, he checked the bath and the kitchen. Empty. Looking to the door that led upstairs, his heart kaboomed. He twisted the knob. The stairwell was dark, the door above closed tight. *Relax. Relax.* He placed his hands on his knees, gaining control. He walked to the front door, turned the knob, and found it locked.

Circling around, he hustled back to the bedroom for his shoes. There, on the nightstand, a paper fluttered.

Walking. Back by 9. K

Relief caused his heart to turn over again. He plopped onto the bed and allowed himself a few minutes to settle. The clock read 8:20.

Matt brewed two cups of coffee and went back to the deck. Leaning against a column, sipping his coffee, he watched his Kathleen approach, her gait steady, her head up, her headphones in place. Not carefree. Far from carefree. But not beaten down. *That's my Kathleen. We'll face this.*

His phone buzzed, pulling him from guard duty. The name

on the screen had him wanting to crush the device in his palm. *Helping rich people keep their money out of the hands of the IRS*, his mother's words registered.

"Everything all right?" she asked a few feet from the steps.

Grateful he could explain the turmoil in his gut with a half-truth, he said, "Remember when I said I was a tenacious asshole? Well, this guy—" He held up his phone. "He makes me look like a pushover." He extended his hand, hoping she'd take it.

With her white scarf fluttering in the wind and her sunglasses in place, she stopped at the bottom step and tilted her face to his.

"Take my hand, Kathleen. Get used to taking my hand."

With sweat running in rivulets down her neck, she looked at his hand and then at his face. She put her hand in his and accepted his help up the steps.

"How are the feet today?"

"No problems. But it's steamy after those storms and now this bright sun."

Hand in hand they walked into the bungalow.

"You shower, I'll rustle up something for breakfast. Meet on the deck?"

"Sounds fine, except I need coffee and water first." She pulled out water, took several gulps. "I assume you're going to work today?"

Matt settled on a stool, sipping his coffee, watching the sweat run between her shoulder blades. "I have some things to accomplish. I see the Mac. Do you have internet access here?"

She leaned against the counter, finished the water and took a sip of coffee. "Yeah. The network is 'Sam was here' all as one word."

Matt chuckled. "'Sam was here'?"

"He left me notes on how to change it. But why bother? I use it once a month."

"Let me guess. The password is 'samwashere'."

"Yep. Easy."

"Got it," he said behind smiling lips. "Move out of the kitchen so I can get us some food," he said as he prowled around the bar. Just before she moved away, he wrapped his arm around her waist and pulled her into him. Smelling her salty skin, he said, "Gotta change that network name and password, love. We want you secure in everything."

She turned in his arms so she plastered her wet shirt to his dry one. "All I do is transfer money to my accountant and buy books."

He pulled her sunglasses off and smiled at the bright blue facing him. "You buy books?" he teased. "We're going to change it anyway. Go take that shower and think of something new." He nipped at her nose. "If you don't come up with something we'll go with '01?!mattisherenow0523$'."

A loud bark of laughter burst from Kathleen as she dropped her forehead into his shoulder. "Shower. New password. Got it." She twisted from his arms.

Watching her walk away, he relived that laugh. "More laughing," he promised her after she closed the door behind her. "More laughing." Smiling, he prepared breakfast and planned how to get her home.

<<<>>>

"Thanks for making breakfast," she said, sitting next to him on her lounger.

"We're almost out of food."

"I'll go to the store. You need to work. Do you want anything specific?" The conversation was casual, comfortable, as she nibbled and watched people come to the sand.

Relieved at her acceptance of his presence, he rested his hand on the chair and grinned. "I'm more meat and potatoes than salad, but I can take care of that at Rosie's, so just get whatever you want."

The air on the deck cooled. Her face was directed away from him. "Hey," he said as he put his plate on the table and moved to her. "What just happened?"

"Rosie's," she whispered as she adjusted her scarf and sunglasses.

Matt remained in his own seat but watched her closely, ready to act. "Yeah. Thought we'd go there for dinner."

She nodded, but her fingers clenched into fists and she kept her face turned away from him.

Matt reached across the space and covered her fists. "Tell me what's happening."

"I'm embarrassed." A tear slipped beneath the glasses.

Matt left his seat, shifted her forward and moved in behind her. "I get that. I hope you trust me when I tell you it's unnecessary. Kathleen, Rosie and Sam just want you to be healthy and happy. What happened the other night is one step in that direction."

She nodded again.

"Where do you shop? Do you want me to go with you?"

"Two miles into town. I go every Monday. If you want to go, that's fine. But don't you need to work?"

"I do, but…"

"I'll be fine." She sighed on the words. "It's part of my routine. The only difference is that I have to buy more."

"Okay. Let's go make the list, get these tasks done so I can get back to Harry and you can get back to Henry VIII."

Kathleen didn't respond or move so he prodded her with his body. When she still didn't move, he asked, "Kathleen?"

"I need to mark the wall," she said with a slight tremble in her voice.

"Well, let's get that done."

Together they collected the trash and dishes, set them on the bar and walked up the steps with marker in hand.

"What did Seth do?" he asked.

"He was in IT," she said as she ran her fingers over the marks.

"How did you meet?" He put his arm around her so he could detect any reaction she might have.

"High school."

"High school?"

"We met in middle school. But we didn't start dating until our junior year." Her voice seemed conversational and he sensed no stress in her body.

"Damn. I don't even remember who I dated in high school." He moved his hand to join hers as she continued to count each mark. "How long were you together?"

"Thirty-six years." Her voice hiccupped, but her body stayed loose. "We got married when I was nineteen."

"How would you describe him?"

"Patient," she blurted the word as if she'd said it many times. "So patient." Her face came to his with a sad smile. "I used to tell him he was too patient."

He lifted a shoulder. "Maybe he was."

Her eyebrows rose as her eyes looked into the distance. When she turned back to him she had a sweet grin. "Yeah, maybe he was." She shifted herself so she faced the new marks. She raised her hand, looked at him, and only after his hand joined hers did she add a new mark.

Matt stood, waiting for her to stand before walking down the steps. When he reached the bottom, he turned to see her still at the top. Her palms rested on the door.

"Seth, Brice, Courtney, Kiley, Lucas, Amanda, T-bone." Her words floated in the air. Before he could go to her, she pushed off the door and ran to him, flattening herself into his chest. His arms sheltered her in his embrace as he waited on her reaction. She nuzzled into him for a few minutes then pushed away. "Groceries."

He saw only blue irises. Relieved, he kissed her temple. "Groceries."

After making a list, she collected her straw bag, sunglasses, and iPod. "I'll be back in a couple hours."

"Hours? You said it was two miles away."

"I walk."

"Kathleen, turn around for a second." He waited until she turned away from the door. She put her hands on her hips, tilted her head, raised her shoulders, and waited. Matt scratched his ear and smiled at her posture. "Tell me where this store is. And tell me at what time I should start to worry."

Her lips pursed, and he knew she rolled her eyes at him.

"Humor me, okay?"

"Fine," she flounced at him. "It's that way." She flung her arm out. "You can't miss it. It's the only grocery in town. It's 10:15. You can worry at 12:30. Can I go now?"

Matt fought back a laugh. "Go."

The door clicked shut behind her. Matt dug out his laptop, got settled onto the counter. Frowning when he had to use 'samwashere', he made a quick note on his legal pad to change that later today.

"Hello, little brother," his sister called across the Skype connection.

"Hey."

"I hope you called me to settle this Jeff shit. He's driving us crazy and won't listen to anyone but you. It's like the rest of us are idiots." She settled back into her executive chair, holding her mug between her palms.

"He's such an asshole. And, yeah, I called to talk about him." Matt's eyes looked past the screen. "Sort of."

"Sort of." Patti's face filled the screen as if she were trying to enter Kathleen's kitchen.

"Patti, are you still coming to Minnesota this weekend? I've got things to talk to you and Dad about. And"—he smiled—"I'm bringing someone home."

Typical of his sister, she heard only one thing. "What do you mean 'sort of'?"

"Look, I plan to call Jeff today. But I'm also calling Alex and having him take over Jeff's case."

"Jeff's not going to agree to that. According to him, he's so important that only the first name on the letterhead is good enough. Look, I get you're on vacation. I get you have some mysterious project for Mom. But, NNJ—you can't just ignore the firm." Her arms flew around as she mounted an argument. "If you'd planned this vacation I could see it. You just bolted."

Matt deflated in his seat as he considered his sister's words. "I'll do right by NNJ, but I've got other things on my plate right now. Alex can handle Jeff or Jeff can take his business somewhere else."

"What *other things?*" She sneered at him. "Mom's little project?"

"Patti," he warned.

"I talked to Dad. All he'll tell me is you've got some woman you need to *handle.*"

"Patti," he warned again.

"Don't start, little brother. You disappear without a word, leave us to handle your work, give me some bullshit about letters from Mom. You call and say you're focused then disappear again. And now you tell me you will 'sort of' be doing your damn job."

"You have no clue what you're talking about."

"You're absolutely fucking right. I haven't a clue. Last time I checked, I'm not first on the letterhead, but I am partner in this firm and a member of this family."

"Patti," Matt's tone softened when he heard the hurt in his sister's voice. "I promise to tell you everything this weekend. I need this week. My focus has to be here." He settled back, closed his eyes, and enjoyed the idea of a week with his Kathleen.

"Matthew, open your damn eyes and tell me what the fuck is going on."

He ignored his sister and thought of Kathleen's laugh, of her waiting for his hand to mark the wall, of her burrowing into him as he helped her let the birds out. The picture his mother wanted him to create filled his mind. "I've got her," he said to his mother.

"What? What did you say? Matt, open your eyes. I need—no, I fucking deserve—some answers."

He opened his eyes and grinned at his sister. "I'm not a tax attorney anymore. I'll make sure my cases are properly passed off and I'll make sure the Minnesota office is settled. But, Patti, I am not coming back to NNJ. I have something else now." The rightness of the words settled in his body.

"That woman," Patti shrieked. "This is about some woman you've known for, what, six days? A project for Mom. Is that what you think Mom wanted? This is unacceptable. Do you hear yourself? You're giving up your life for a stranger. You're fifty years old and you are acting like a damn child."

Matt's nostrils flared and heat moved through him. "Look, I won't let NNJ suffer. I'll do what it takes—with your and Dave's help—for a smooth transition. But…"

"Who is this woman? What is she after? What's her game? How did she suck Mom in? Better yet, how did she suck you in?" Each sentence punched into the air.

"As usual," Matt punched back, his shoulders shooting up, "you are opening your damn mouth without engaging your brain."

"Yeah, let's talk about that," she spat. "I talked to Dad and he's just as cagey as you are. What's wrong with this woman? What's the damn mystery?"

Feeling his face heat and rage beating in his chest, he leveled his head, moved close to the screen. "Patricia, be careful what you say next."

With her index finger, she pounded into the screen. "She's either a master manipulator or a freak."

"Fuck you, Patricia. Just fuck you." He disconnected. Matt crumpled back into the seat. He flexed his fingers, trying to stop the trembling. "Fuck," he said again.

"She's right. I'm not playing any games. I don't want anything. But I didn't ask you to come here or stay here. I'm more a freak than you know. Go back to NNJ, to your family." The sweet voice from just a few minutes ago was again that monotonous tone he despised.

Matt spun the seat and bolted to Kathleen. He ripped the sunglasses from her face to find dark gray staring up at him. With his palms settled on her cheeks, he pulled her face to his. When she gasped, he consumed her mouth. A kiss of fear, of desperation, of promises not yet made. A kiss of possession. He gave the pieces of himself he'd never given another soul.

Her arms came around his waist where she gripped his shirt. Wrapping her leg around his calf, she clutched him closer. Her body plastered to his as her mouth encouraged his passion. Accepted his strength.

Teeth clanged, hands roamed, her nails dug into his back as he pushed the scarf from her head, shoving his hands in her hair, controlling the kiss.

When they pulled apart, breathless, he put his forehead against hers. "Kathleen, I have so much to say to you, things I haven't even figured out yet. But let me say this now. Please never tell me to go again. I've got you today, tomorrow and the next day. So let's not waste your time or mine debating the issue." With that, he closed his mouth on hers again, allowing his hand to travel down her back, cup her behind, and pull her deeper into him.

He knew the second she realized what was happening. She went from being with him, giving herself over to him, to a being struggling, fighting tiger.

"Don't, Kathleen," Matt pleaded. "Don't pull away from me. Let me take care of you."

Her hands came to his chest and she thrust him backwards. Large eyes raged at him, dared him to come closer. The purple, the blue, the gray warred for control. She breathed in large gulps of air as sweat bloomed on her forehead.

He closed the gap, reached for her. His hands landed on her waist. "Kathleen."

She jolted away, slamming her back into the door. "No, no, no," she started to chant. "No, no," she screamed, shaking her head in violent jerks. Saliva flew from her mouth. "Don't touch me, don't ever touch me."

Her struggle increased, but he refused to let go. He stepped deeper into her space, moved his hands to her shoulders. "Kathleen, where are you?"

Her fists rose in the small space between their chests. She punched him over and over. Matt stood still.

Her arms rose higher, a wild keening started as her palms slapped at his face. He stood still.

She kicked him. She pulled at his hair. He stood still.

Her right hand found his left ear. She pulled and twisted, she dug her fingernails into his scalp, leaving a trail of bleeding scratch marks. He stood still.

"Let me go. Let me go," she wailed. She slammed her head on the door. One strike. A second strike. A third. Matt moved.

Taking two large steps back, he pulled her away from the door.

Her hands flew into her hair where she began to snatch out clumps. Her fingernails clawed through the damaged flesh, leaving streaks of blood. Blazing wild eyes searched the room behind him as she tore at the pieces surrounding her ear. "Why couldn't they kill me too?" she howled.

When a small line of blood dripped from her cheek and landed on the floor. Matt pulled her hands away from her head and pinned them to her sides. Her head flew back and forth, sending mucous and tears flying into his face. He stood still.

She banged her forehead into his sternum. He shifted so she hit the soft part of his chest. Thump. Thump. Thump. Her feet began to dance, to run in place. He held on.

He held on until her legs collapsed beneath her. He followed her to the floor, scooping her into his lap.

"Seth, Brice, Courtney, Lucas, Kiley, Amanda, T-bone," she repeated a continuous loop until both her voice and her body gave out.

He sat with her gathered in close and listened as her breathing settled. He rocked her, ran his hand up her back, and waited.

"She's right, I am a freak," she said with her face planted against his shirt.

Matt closed his eyes against the pain of her words, the anger at his sister, the fear in his heart. "Love, you are not a freak. Please don't say that again. I can't explain Patti right now except to say she often speaks before she thinks."

"I used to be so normal. I was the funny one." She pulled back and looked into his face. "What if I can't be normal again?"

He wiped at her face with his thumbs. "You won't be that

person again. Together, we'll help you find a new normal."

She looked at his torn, bloody shirt. She inspected the claw marks on his head. "Oh my God, Matt, what have I done?" She shook her head. "I'm so scared. I'm so sorry, I…" she wept into his chest.

Before she could finish, he placed a chaste kiss on her lips. "No. No apologies. We won't be apologizing to each other. You needed that. And I want to be everything you need." He leaned away, pulled the ruined t-shirt off his body. He wiped her tears, her sweat. He wiped her nose and around her mouth. He kissed each eye, her nose, her forehead. Gently he turned her head so he could dab at the bloody scratches. "You use my body however you need. If you need to hide, burrow in me. If you need to rail against the world, let me be your punching bag. If you need to yell, scream, cry—whatever you need, I will hold on."

She sagged into him. "Did I hurt you?"

"No, love. I've had many more formidable opponents than a five-foot pixie," he teased, hoping to lighten the mood.

"I wanted to hurt you."

"No, you didn't want to hurt me. You wanted to hurt yourself." He leaned his back against the door, pulled her deeper into him. "What are you scared of?"

She didn't respond for so long Matt wondered if she'd fallen asleep.

"Remembering. Not remembering. Feeling. Not feeling. You."

Skype rang. Matt's phone rang. They stayed on the floor.

After the third round of rings she sniffled. "You need to talk to her. She didn't do anything wrong."

Matt cupped her jaw and stroked the welts. "She did do

something wrong. She followed her normal pattern. Either way, Patricia can wait. You are the focus now. Can you explain why you're scared of me?"

She shrugged, but words spilled out. "I don't feel. Ever. It's how I stay alive." She looked into his eyes. "Until you arrived. You make me feel. You're opening the doors."

They sat as the ringing phone continued to echo through the small space.

"Do you think it's time to open the doors?"

"It seems I have no choice."

He lowered his mouth to hers, trying to give her his strength, his resolve. She met him in that space, accepting his promise and offering her own. His kisses trailed up her neck over to her eyes, across her nose and back to her mouth. He deepened the kiss. He moved his lips to the missing ear and bloody flesh. He showered kisses over every scar. Her breath quickened, but she allowed him to give her his love. As he returned to her mouth, she clutched at his forearms.

"Thank you," she whispered against his mouth.

He pulled back, kissed her forehead. "My Kathleen." He ran his nose up her cheek and into her hair. "Groceries?"

"I forgot my wallet."

After one more long kiss, Matt helped her gain her footing before raising himself up. "Let me get a new shirt while you clean your head. We'll go to the store together. Maybe..." He arched an eyebrow at her. "Have lunch in town?"

Her eyes widened and a deep breath passed between them. "Don't you need to work?"

Matt glanced at the computer, at his laptop bag, at his to-do list. "Nope. I do not." He smiled up at her. "What I need is to feed my Kathleen and get beer in this house."

"Lunch in town?"

"If you're willing." He moved closer, gathered her to him. "We can decide when we're there."

"I can try." Blue eyes pierced him. "I can try."

"Fair enough." He turned her away, swatted her butt. "Hurry, woman. Hungry man."

She disappeared into the bathroom.

"I'm scared, too. Scared out of my mind," he said to the empty hallway.

MORE MESSAGES

Almost strutting, Matt held the groceries in one hand and his Kathleen's hand in the other, thrilled that she'd agreed to lunch in town. She'd sat paralyzed when the waitress approached their table. But by the end of the meal she'd relaxed enough to talk to him about her Henry VIII novel. Since she limited her intake to six bites, he worried she didn't eat enough, so he ordered dish after dish. With a wide smile, he pictured his Kathleen eating her six bites of eight different items.

"I'm not going to want my salad at Rosie's," she said as they walked toward home.

"I haven't had her wings yet."

"Do you plan to work this afternoon?" She flexed her hand in his. "Or call your sister back?"

"Work, yes. Patti, no. Not yet. But you don't need to worry about it. Patti doesn't just like to be in the loop. She likes to *hold* the loop, preferably a loop she created. Usually I don't care. I think that's what has her the most flustered. This is how it sometimes goes for us. She opens that mouth, pisses me off, pisses herself off. We have a standoff for a few days. Been that way since I was a kid. You going to curl up and read?"

"I'm going to take a nap."

"Perfect. If I get my tasks done in time I'll join you." After walking several steps in silence, Matt asked, "Did you ever work?"

"Yeah. I was a high school teacher for twenty-three years."

"Let me guess. You taught Lit."

"You are a smart guy."

"What was your favorite book to teach?"

"*Pride and Prejudice*," her answer popped out.

"Okay, that was definitive. What was your least favorite?"

"I didn't like the dystopian stuff," she said after a few minutes.

"*1984*? That type of book?"

"Yeah. But I particularly hated *The Handmaid's Tale*."

"I bet you were an excellent teacher."

"Why do you say that?"

"Because you're so enthusiastic when you talk about stories," he said as Stephanie's words filtered through his mind.

"Stories say things we often can't. They give us a chance to explore emotions we aren't supposed to admit."

"Can you give me an example?"

Changing her voice to sound like a man, she quoted, "*'What haunted people even, perhaps especially, on their deathbed? What chased them, tortured them and brought some to their knees? Regret. Regret for things said, for things done, and not done. Regret for the people they might have been.'*" She slowed her pace and looked over at him. "That's a line from a detective novel. Do you see what I mean? The author uses words to convey something we all experience but rarely express." She faced forward and resumed her normal gait.

As they made the turn onto the sand near her home, she stopped, took off her glasses, and showed him blaring blue eyes.

"You can only regret things you can control. You know what I regret? I regret I let an awful attorney destroy my life a second time." She forced her sunglasses back in place and pounded up the steps.

Matt watched her disappear into the darkened house. He listened as cabinet doors slammed, wondering if anger or despair consumed her more. He searched for a way to help her deal with emotions he could never understand. *Get her off this beach. Make her feel safe. Then Lisa.* When no more sound filtered from inside, he shook the sand from his feet and went to find her.

He dropped his grocery bags on the counter and stalked in her direction. In the book room, Matt took a few minutes to look over the space. A ten by ten room, its four walls were covered with floor-to-ceiling bookshelves. Three additional sets of double-sided shelves extended into the room. Estimating and calculating, Matt guessed the room held over six hundred feet of shelving. And every inch was covered in books. More books stood in stacks around the space. Thousands of books. Kathleen stood in the back of the room, her fingers trailing spines with her sunglasses dangling from her hand.

"Looking for something specific?" he asked.

"No, not really. Our conversation reminded me of what these books say. I'm just touching them." A serene face shifted his way. "I've loved books since I was a teenager."

"You said you loved teaching *Pride and Prejudice*," he said as he moved in behind her. "Do you have an all-time favorite read?"

Her bottom lip pushed out and she turned around in the space. "No. I have some standouts, some I like to re-read, but I like too many to choose just one." She chose a book and flipped through the pages. When she found a highlighted section, she held it out for him.

Matt read aloud, "*The emotion is real. It's gripping his whole body, ready to lift him off the chair by the scruff of the neck and slam him against the wall.*" He flipped through the book and found two more highlighted sections. "Did you choose these quotes for a reason?"

"No." She shook her head. "I wanted you to see that every book I've ever read has something special."

Matt slid the book back in its slot. "Do you mind if I look through here more later?"

"Of course not. Take anything you want. Just give it back when you're done." She walked to the next section, pulled out a book, and left the room.

Matt chose a book at random, shuffled through the pages until he found a marked passage. "*A single moment that had split reality into two distinct alternatives.*" He closed his eyes against the truth of the statement. After returning the book to its spot, he left the room, looking forward to spending time in Kathleen's thoughts.

Finding her on the lounge chair, he said, "Okay if I work for a while? You good here?"

Lost in her fictional world, she didn't look up. She turned a page and nodded.

Matt leaned against the doorpost and watched her. *I want her this relaxed in the real world.* He placed an arm on each side of her hips and planted a kiss on her head. She tilted her head back, smiling.

Matt took the mouth she offered him. She stiffened, but instead of pulling back, he pressed in closer. As before, she retreated, then relaxed and joined him in the moment. Her hands wrapped around his biceps, her mouth pressed deeper. Hearing his phone ring, he felt her withdraw. "Kathleen, love, they can wait. You will always be the priority." He ran his nose over her jawbone, up to the mangled flesh. "Never pull back from me, okay?" He found her mouth again.

Only when he was ready did he draw back. "I'll want to hear about them." He tilted his head at her book.

Before he stepped over the threshold, she spoke. "No one except doctors has touched me in so long. No one has been allowed."

Matt froze, spun to face her. "Let me see," he said, mimicking taking off sunglasses. When he had her eyes, he said, "Last week, I sat in my office, miserable. I didn't even know I was miserable. I looked at the Minnesota sky and thought it was the prettiest blue I'd ever see. Who knew I'd find that same blue staring at me from such a beautiful face."

A pretty pink blush formed on her cheek. "I don't understand what's happening."

"I don't either, and I don't give a shit. It's happening, and we're going to let it. Okay?"

She blinked at him a few times but didn't respond.

"One more thing," he said, "and, yes, I know this makes me sound like a caveman, but I'd like to keep it that way."

Her head tilted and her eyebrows drew in. "What?"

"I don't like that you've been alone for so long. But I do like that I'm the only one allowed to touch you. Let's keep it that way." He winked and walked into the house to the sound of her snicker and his damn ringing phone.

Realizing it was Patti calling, Matt ignored the phone. When he shut off his computer several hours later, he marveled at the calm he felt with such life-changing decisions. Satisfaction with his decision remained, but the calm evaporated when his phone rang again. Before completing his last and most important task, Matt headed for the deck to check on Kathleen.

She lay on her side, curled into a ball, sleeping. Her sunglasses sat on his chair and her hands rested under her cheek. Her scarf had shifted and the entire wound was exposed. From the doorway Matt watched her steady intake of breath. "Sleep, love," he whispered. "I'm here." Turning back to the kitchen, he found his phone and called his dad.

"Patti's screaming my head off," his father said instead of hello.

"She got my email, I presume."

"Oh yeah. She's twisting my arm for information I don't have."

"Have you read the email?"

"It's coming up now, but she read it to me several times. Each time she got louder and more frantic."

"All it says is I want a meeting with the executive team on Monday."

"Your sister is reading between the lines. As I'm sure Alex, Dave, and Nick are, as well."

"And you?"

"Mattie," he whispered, "you do what you need to do. I didn't give you those letters expecting the world to go on as it always has."

"I'm bringing her home." The words tumbled out.

"She's agreed to that? Don't misunderstand. I'd much rather you come here than me have to drag my ass there. But—"

"She'll agree. I've got to get her off this beach, out of her box.

280

She'll have more support there. Me, you, Jess, Mom's garden, even Patti. And it's a stopover. I'm thinking of it as a stepping stone to where she needs to be."

"Matt—"

"We can come back here or go wherever she wants. But first we have things to face. We need help for that," Matt continued to think out loud.

"Matt—"

"I want her to see your house. Mom's garden. And there are a few things I can only finish from Minnesota. I can't leave her here. I won't leave her here. Never alone."

"Matt—"

"She'll get that. She'll be willing. She's—"

"Matt. Stop. I'm with you. I get it. What I'm asking is what are your plans if she doesn't agree?"

Matt shook his head, frowned. "She will. She has to."

"When will you talk to her?"

"Tonight for sure. I want us home Thursday night or Friday morning at the latest. That was my main reason for calling. I can't handle Patti right now. She called my girl a freak, and if that wasn't bad enough, Kathleen heard her. If she says the wrong thing again I might lose my mind, but I'd like us all to have dinner Friday night. Dave can help keep her contained. Can you make that happen?"

"Of course. But what are you going to tell your sister about Kathleen?"

Matt planted his elbows on the granite and shoved his hand into his hair. "Nothing. It's not my story to tell. She hasn't told me much yet. I'm letting her tell me at her own pace like Mom said. I will follow Kathleen's lead all the way. Her safety and comfort are my priority."

"I'm not sure Patti will sit still for that."

"No. I can't violate Kathleen's confidence. I'll talk to her about how much she's comfortable with my sharing. This is not about Patti." Matt's voice dropped to a pained whisper. "Dad, she doesn't remember much. She's shoved it deep in a vault, and when happy memories come, she reacts violently. Can you imagine what it will happen when the memories aren't good ones?" Matt swallowed back the lump and added, "She can barely say their names, and when she does she frequently uses present tense."

"Mattie—"

"Do you see? She has so much to confront. I'm going to get her the help she needs, but forcing her to open up to my sister is not something I'm willing to do. And you know Patti. If you tell her, her mouth will open and she'll insert both feet."

After several long minutes of silence, his father said, "Do we want to do dinner here at the house or in town?"

"Go ahead and make reservations, but let me think. If we end up at the house, we can order pizza or something. Go ahead and invite Jess, too."

"I'll call Patricia now. I'll avoid her interrogation."

Matt snorted and rolled his eyes. "That'll be fun. I'll make it even worse. Tell her I've already packed my laptop away and as soon as we're done, I'm turning off my phone. Jess knows how to reach me for a family emergency, but I do not want to talk about NNJ. *At all*."

"She'll be a banty rooster."

"You raised her."

"Touché. Do you need anything else before Friday?"

"Just time with her. But thanks."

"Love you, Mattie-boy, and I can't wait to meet her."

Matt blinked through the sting in his eyes. "You'll love her, too."

"I've loved her longer than you have. She gave your mom a reason to hang on as long as she did." After a deep sigh, he added, "Before you talk to her, open the next letter." He disconnected without waiting on a response.

Matt's head whipped around and his eyes settled on the bright orange box sitting on Kathleen's desk. Shaking his head, he opened the box to stare at the two remaining envelopes. The ninth letter was thicker than the others. Secure in his plans and not wanting any interference even from his mother, he chewed on his lower lip as he considered whether to open the letter or not. He folded the envelope and stuffed it into his pocket. He had thirty minutes before he needed to wake Kathleen for their dinner at Rosie's. *Mom, I'll read this soon. I want to spend time in that book room.* After confirming Kathleen still slept, he went in search of more information.

His eyes roamed over the shelves. Not knowing much about books, it was difficult for him to tell if they were arranged in any particular way. Deciding to pull three books from three different locations, he strolled from shelf to shelf and grabbed at random. Sliding to the floor, he began to turn the pages.

The first book, *Dragonfly in Amber*, had over seven hundred pages and yet he found only one marked quote: "*There aren't any answers, only choices.*" In *Half Broke Horses*, several places were marked, but two struck Matt as pertinent to his Kathleen: "*I stopped crying because there just wasn't any cry left in me by then,"* and *"There was no such thing as reality because the world was as you chose to see it."* The third book had so many places marked the pages were more yellow highlighter than not. He moved around the room, replacing the books and reading titles. The top shelf in the back held twenty identical books. Dark blue spines, about a foot tall, various thicknesses. Matt plucked the fifth one off the shelf. A small box tumbled off and landed at his feet.

Eight inches long, two inches wide, faded wrapping paper showed pale Christmas snowmen. Matt sucked in a painful breath when he saw the label. *To: Our Marcia From: Love you, Seth.* Stumbling backwards, he slid back to the floor. Matt was certain she did not know this gift existed. Placing the gift next to him, he opened the blue book and discovered he could feel even more sadness, even more pain for his Kathleen.

The Conners Family 1994 was emblazoned on the first page. In the center was a picture of his Kathleen, a man he assumed was Seth, and two kids. He assumed Courtney was about four and Brice about twelve. All four faces laughed at something in the distance. Matt traced her face with his fingers before turning the page. It seemed that every event in their lives was recorded in photos, mementos, and Kathleen's words. Few pictures of her existed, forcing Matt to assume she held the camera. Fascinated, he looked at every photo, read every word. Amazed that she didn't just record fun memories, he read about broken hearts and angry arguments at soccer matches. One photo showed a clearly angry Seth yelling at a defiant Brice. A large black and white photo showed a crying Courtney. Near the end of the book, he found one page devoted to Kathleen. She smiled over a birthday cake with her shoulder-length hair curled behind her ears. Holding his teeth between his lips, Matt traced the perfect left ear. The captions told him that Kathleen's birthday was this Friday. Blindly he reached down and put his hand on the gift Seth wanted her to have. *Seth, if you can hear me—I'll take care of her.* He put the book back, took the gift and stuffed it in the bottom of his suitcase.

Nuzzling his face into her neck, he said, "Kathleen, time to feed me."

She stirred and grumbled but didn't wake.

Nipping at her jaw, he tried again. "We need to leave for Rosie's in fifteen minutes."

She rolled to her back and blinked up at him. "Not hungry."

"Wings, beer." He dropped his mouth to hers, giving into the growing passion. "Now, up. Feed me," he said against her lips. With both hands, he collected her and pulled her to her feet. With his hands on her hips, he encouraged her forward.

Her hands went to the scarf. Finding it out of place, she began a frantic backpedal. Even when the back of her knees hit the lounger and she fell into it, her feet continued to move.

Matt moved in behind her, tucked her face into his neck. "Shh. Relax and fix it."

After several deep breaths Matt felt her adjust the scarf. When she put her arms back down, he tilted her face to his. Blue warred with purple. "Stay with me," he said, keeping his eyes pinned to hers. "You do not have to cover with me. Until you're ready, I promise I'll help you keep covered. *Out there.* But not with me." After kissing the tip of her nose, he continued, "You're gorgeous. These scars"—he placed his fingers over the scarf—"show me what a survivor you are. In some ways, they add to your beauty." Her large eyes watched him and slowly they returned to his favorite color blue. "Feed me," he said as he again helped her to stand.

HEADLINES

"Grab our table. I'll go get a beer and see if Rosie and Sam have a few minutes to sit with us," he said when they hit the deck. With his hand on her lower back, he felt her falter. He guided her to her normal table, watched her settle before he went to solicit Sam's help.

"Sam," he said when he got close to the bar, "got a second?"

"Everything okay?"

"Yeah. We had a good day. Progress. But I need to ask you a couple of things and I don't want to do it at the table."

Sam filled a glass then pushed it toward Matt before settling against the back bar.

"Did you help unpack the book room?"

"Yeah. Probably six boxes of books and three boxes of photo albums."

"Did you look at the photo albums?"

"I opened one to see what it was, but, no, I didn't look through them."

Matt's body relaxed, relieved that Sam had not seen such personal images. Just like he wanted no one else to touch her, he wanted to be the first one to share her memories. "Did you unpack a gift?"

Sam looked around the room before his eyes came back to Matt. "Yes. Seeing that made it all seem real, you know? I struggled with what to do with it." He shrugged and frowned. "In the end, I just tucked it on top. Did she show it to you?"

"No, I was looking through her books—and by the way, she has over a thousand books in there now—and it fell. I'm trying to figure out if she knows it exists."

"I doubt it. Those boxes all came directly from her home in the mountains. A neighbor—that Stephanie person—packed up her personal stuff and sent it all directly here. I wanted life to be easy for her, so I unpacked."

"But you didn't unpack the boxes Stephanie brought?"

"I planned to but when I saw that family picture—I convinced myself that I was invading her privacy. Truthfully, though, I couldn't face it. I didn't want to see all that she'd lost."

Matt nodded, took a drink. "I'm planning to take her with me to Minnesota."

Sam exploded off the bar. "What? You can't take her from here. She's safe here."

Matt's palms came up. "Not permanently. Just for a few days together out of this rigid routine. I talked to Stephanie last night and she thinks the best way to help Kathleen is to get her back to the same therapist she had in Charlotte. I thought Minnesota—meeting my dad, seeing my mom's garden—would be a stepping stone." He paused and took another drink as Sam settled back against the bar. "And I have to go back and close out some things. I can't leave her here alone."

"Rosie and I can take care of her," Sam said.

Matt shook his head, turned to look at Kathleen staring at her ocean. "I know. You've been taking care of her for a while. But she needs a change and I, well honestly, I'm not ready to be away from her." Turning back, he added, "But I was hoping you two could join us for dinner."

Sam's head tilted as he stared at Matt for a long moment. "Sam?"

"Rosie's taking her salad over now. What do you want?"

"Wings." He turned to go but looked back. "Thanks, Sam."

Sam's chin came up. "Be careful with her."

"Yeah, I know."

Matt walked to the deck, bent to kiss Kathleen's neck and pull out the earphones. "Your salad is here. Turn around and join us, okay?" She gave him a small smile, turned her chair, and began to create her checkerboard.

A few minutes later, Rosie and Sam appeared with enough wings and fries to feed an army. Grinning, Matt pulled over a plate, pulled off six wings and six fries and put them in front of Kathleen. She blinked up at him. "Six," he mouthed. Her lips pursed together, but Matt was almost positive it was to hold back a giggle.

"Kathleen," Rosie almost squealed, "I think I'm in love with Jamie."

Sam joked on a bite. "Excuse me?"

Matt actually heard Kathleen stifle the giggle this time.

"Oh, my," Rosie said, "he's this Scottish Highlander that I swear…" She gulped and her eyes sparkled. "I swear he can come home with me any damn time."

Kathleen's laugh burst across the table, stunning all of them.

"Have they gotten married yet?" She leaned closer to Rosie.

"The best sex scene I've ever read."

As they ate their wings Sam and Matt watched the two women smile and talk. His Kathleen, his lovely gift, lit the table with her enthusiasm and bright smile. When Sam caught Matt's eyes, he smiled.

"When do you head back?" Rosie's question startled Matt and forced him back to the moment.

"I need to be in Minneapolis Friday night, so either Thursday night or Friday morning." He felt Kathleen stiffen. "Kathleen's going with me, she just doesn't know it yet," Matt said with a wink at Rosie.

With a wing halfway to her mouth, Kathleen froze.

"Kathleen? Look at me."

It took several long seconds, but finally her head ticked toward him. "I can't—"

"Yes, you can. It's only for a few days. I want you to meet my dad. See my mom's garden." He placed his hand on her neck and began to knead. "You can. You need to."

The wing landed with a loud plop and her head dropped into her neck.

"Look at me, please." He used his hand to move her face to him.

"My family is here," she said with a whimper.

"No, love, they aren't. They're here." He tapped her head and her heart. "Your family is always with you. I want us to find a way to get them out of that locked room."

Her body jerked as her chin tucked lower.

"When I talked to Stephanie she thought that maybe your

routine—"

Kathleen's body shot backward, and her head flew up. "Stephanie? You talked to her?" Her voice rose on each word. "Stephanie?" She stood, moved away from him, sheltering herself behind Sam.

Slowly Matt also stood. "Kathleen, I—"

"No," she hissed. Her hands flew to her scarf, her sunglasses. Her face darted around as her hand squeezed into Sam's shoulder.

Matt's eyes dropped to her hand at Sam's shoulder. As his heart began to pound, he forced himself to re-focus on Kathleen. "Kathleen, she loves you."

"But you called her," she shrilled and moved her body more into Sam's back.

"I did." He began to move around the table. "Listen," he said firmly, "I need you to hear me." He moved a step closer, extended his hand to her. "She wants you back in her life." Matt felt Sam and Rosie's eyes on him, but he kept his focus on Kathleen, keenly aware that he might need to catch her.

"I can't go, I can't leave, I can't—" Her feet began to scuttle and spittle began to ooze from her mouth. "You shouldn't have, you, you—" Her breath came faster than the words.

Matt moved one step closer, but Kathleen moved further away while keeping her hand on Sam.

"Take off your sunglasses," he commanded.

Her head shook violently and her nails dug into Sam's shoulders. "Doors need to stay locked," she whispered as her body began to jerk.

"Sam," Matt barked.

Sam turned and caught Kathleen in his lap.

"Rosie, move," Matt said when he reached their side of the table. He grabbed Kathleen's trembling body from Sam and settled them in Rosie's chair. He jerked her sunglasses from her face and saw nothing but purple. "Fuck." He tucked her body in tighter but kept her eyes looking at him. "Kathleen, tell me where you are." The purple brightened. "Rosie, take Sam's seat. Start telling me about this Jamie person."

Her eyes, huge and filled with tears, Rosie sat and started talking about a dress and a ring and an evil uncle.

Matt's hands settled on Kathleen's neck and around her waist. "Kathleen," he spoke over Rosie, "Rosie needs to know if Jamie and Claire stay together. Can you tell her?"

Rosie kept talking. Sam settled in near them, protecting them from prying eyes. Matt watched Kathleen's eyes. He saw blue begin to filter in. "Keep talking, Rosie. She hears you."

The shaking in Kathleen's body began to slow. Her hands moved to clutch at Matt's arm. "There's my girl," he said. "Now, can you tell Rosie if Claire and Jamie stay together?"

Kathleen swallowed and blinked. "I can't tell her that," she said. She planted her head in his chest, took several deep breaths and then gave him blue eyes. "I'm sorry."

He put his fingertips on her lips. "You're apologizing. That's my role right now. But no apologies, remember?" He winked, left a swift kiss on her lips. "Do Jamie and Claire stay together?"

Shaking her head, she said, "It's a series. I can't tell her the ending. That would ruin it."

Matt snorted and dropped his forehead back to hers. "Rosie, it seems my Kathleen is unwilling to ruin the ending for you."

Rosie and Sam both chuckled with obvious relief. "Well, can

she at least tell me if Jamie survives the battle?"

Kathleen's bright blue eyes turned to Rosie. "Of course, it's only the first book. You can't kill off the main love interest that early." She turned back to Matt. "I've only eaten two wings. I need to finish the other four."

Kathleen retrieved her sunglasses and put them on. They all returned to their seats and began to eat as if the last few minutes never happened.

"Kathleen," Sam said after all the wings were devoured. He waited until she lifted her face to his. "I think you should consider a trip with Matt. Your home, your things will be safe here. Rosie and I will keep an eye."

"My room," she said.

"I know," Sam said. "I know it's important to you. How can I take care of it so you feel okay taking a few days away?"

Her throat worked and her hand tightened on her tea. "Marks."

"I saw them," Sam said carefully while Matt reached over and pulled Kathleen flush to his side. "Would you like me to keep the count for you?"

Her face moved from Sam, past Rosie and over to Matt. "I can't leave them." She pulled her sunglasses down, showing Matt only blue. "Forgive me." She stood and walked away.

Matt watched her go before turning to Sam. "Thanks."

"Don't you need to go after her?" Rosie said. "Shouldn't one of us go?"

"No." He turned to Rosie. "She showed me her eyes. That was her way of letting me know she's in control. I'll give her a few minutes." He placed his hand on Rosie's arm and squeezed.

"Trust me. I won't let her be alone for long. She's angry. She's afraid, understandably, but she's here."

"Is that how you meant to spring a trip on her?" Sam asked with a mixture of accusation and curiosity.

"No. That was a clusterfuck. I was planning to discuss it with her on the porch later tonight. I wasn't planning to mention Stephanie at all. Not yet. But when Rosie mentioned it—well, I did exactly what I shouldn't." He rolled his eyes at himself. "I did exactly what my sister does all the damn time. I opened my mouth and choked on both feet."

Rosie huffed and her eyes narrowed, but she let it go. "Explain the eye thing."

Matt sat straighter in his chair, placed his elbows on the table, propping his chin on his fingers. "What color did you see?"

"Blue." She frowned at him. "We talked about how blue her eyes are."

"Did you see any other color?"

She shrugged, looked over at Sam then shrugged a second time. "Have you seen anything other than blue?"

"Nope. But I haven't seen them very often. You sure she's okay?"

"I'll catch up with her in a few minutes. We've made some headway. I promise I'd be out there now if I thought she needed me. What she needs is to feel angry, even if it's directed at me right now."

Sam relaxed back into his chair and took a long pull on his beer. "You asked about her eyes. What is it that you see?"

"Well, I see purple," Matt said to their startled faces. "When she's present her eyes are blue. A few different shades of blue based on her emotions, but blue. When she begins to remember someone from the past, her eyes turn purple. The more the memory invades, the more purple I see."

"Holy shit," Sam said. "That explains the sunglasses."

"No," Rosie said. "We only see blue. That purple is more of their weird-ass connection. Those sunglasses have another meaning."

Sam and Matt raised puzzled eyebrows.

"The headlines," she said to Sam. "I think she hates her eyes now." She turned to Matt. "Did you go online and read about it?"

Matt shook his head. "I haven't. My mom said in one of her letters that it was Kathleen's story to tell. I'm honoring that. But—"

"That's probably for the best." She twirled her beer on the table.

"Rosie, is there something I need to know? That I shouldn't wait for? You mentioned headlines earlier. Do I need to understand that?"

She twirled her bottle and Sam pulled in closer. "That trial," she said before looking directly at him. "The media, god." Shaking her head, she took in a deep breath and sighed. "*Greed Turns Blue. It's in Her Eyes. The Eyes Have It. Blameworthy Blues.*" She sighed again and let one tear fall. "For days they speculated how Marcia Conners—" She stopped. "She bought that house, sight unseen, four days after the trial. By the time she arrived here, Marcia Conners was buried."

Sam moved his chair closer to Rosie, pushed her face into his neck. "Cry, Rosie. Just cry for her."

As Rosie cried, Sam said to Matt, "Go. Try to get her to Minnesota."

Matt nodded and stood. He gave Rosie a kiss on the top of her head and squeezed Sam's shoulder. Shoving his hands into his pockets, he felt the envelope from his mother. Pulling it out, he walked down the steps and then opened it.

SETH

His hand landed on the small of her back, just as it had for thirty-six years.

"Honey," he said. "Slow down a bit."

Kathleen slowed but would not look to her left, where Seth always stood. She wanted him to stay. She wanted him to go. She wanted to yell at him. She wanted to hold onto him.

"Do you remember our map?"

Kathleen's feet tripped over each other, but she did not fall. She slowed her pace even more, shuffling through the sand so she could keep her eyes firmly closed.

"Map, Honey? Do you know where it is?"

"No." She shrugged. "I guess it's upstairs."

"Damn those locked doors. Do you remember which states we never visited?"

Kathleen pulled the US map into her mind. Forty-seven states and Puerto Rico were colored with a yellow highlighter. She pictured Seth's blocky handwriting. "States We've Seen. States Still to See."

"North Dakota, Rhode Island and—" She stopped walking. With her image of Seth, she sat down in the sand.

"And?" he asked.

"Minnesota," she whispered.

"We never made it to Minnesota. I think it's time you finished coloring that map. Don't you?"

"I don't want to leave here."

"Why not? What's here?"

"Seth." She swallowed. "You are. You all are."

"You once said that I was too patient. Do you remember that fight? I was letting Courtney get away with something. I have no idea what, but you got all pissed. Told me I was too lenient, too patient. You told me I was creating a princess nightmare. Do you remember?"

Kathleen smiled at the memory. "Yes, I do. She'd left my car on empty yet again. Rather than make her use her money and her time, you were planning to go to the gas station. I was furious."

"Marce, how many times did I go to the gas station for you simply because I wanted to take care of you?"

Kathleen rolled her eyes and shrugged, knowing he was right and hating it all over again.

"We did good, Marce. Really good. Brice, Courtney. We did good."

Kathleen dropped her chin into her neck and nodded. "I know you have a point. You always work around to some point."

"My patience is running out. This is not what you and I agreed to. We promised each other several times that we would live full lives, even when one of us died. Remember? You are not taking care of you. I don't want to be locked in that room. None of us do. We are wherever you allow us to be. And I still want to go to Minnesota."

"Seth," she started to answer, but she felt his kiss on top of her head and knew that he was gone. "You always got the last word. And you were always right. It's always been annoying."

KATHLEEN'S LETTER

Matt pulled out three items. Two folded sheets of paper and another envelope. As he trudged through the sand he stared at Kathleen's name on the envelope. Quickening his pace, he soon leaped onto the deck of her home. She sat in her chair, a book on her lap, but her head faced the ocean.

"Hey," he said as he took his chair. "I've got something for you." He put the envelope on her lap.

Her face turned to him and then to the envelope.

Shrugging, he said, "It's from my mother." He held up his two pieces of paper and the empty envelope. "It was in here."

She pulled herself into a cross-legged position and turned the letter over and over in her hands. "I'm scared to open it."

Matt laughed. "Join the club. This is my ninth letter. I've felt the same way each time." When she simply continued to toy with the letter, he said, "Want me to read mine first?"

She nodded without turning in his direction.

Opening one of the letters, he began to read.

Mattie—
If you decided I'm crazy, then I assume you are back in Minnesota.

301

Alone. If that's the case, know that I love you and I trust your judgment. Please let your dad and Jessica know. They know what to do. Jessica will get through to her. I love you always,

Mom

PS—You likely need to start searching for a new assistant.

He faced Kathleen and pushed the sheet toward her. "That's all it says."

She took the sheet, read it, and handed it back. "What does that mean?"

"I think it means that if I didn't find you, my dad and Jessica were heading to the beach. I get my tenacious asshole from my mother." He smiled at her. "Good thing I found you. Jessica can be quite a force."

She gave him a sad smile and then looked toward his second sheet.

Opening it, he began.

Mattie—

I'm so relieved you've found her. The instant I saw her, I knew she was yours. I knew you were hers. Now the work has to begin. She's strong. She's courageous. But she needs your strong arms to hold her, to guide her, to keep her moving forward when all she wants to do is go back into hiding.

She needs you. And you know what, so does her family. Those beautiful people she lost need to be found, brought into focus. Our family—you, your dad, Patti—we can love her and love who she loves.

Take her home, Mattie. Show her my garden. I've got something special there for her. Just for her. She'll know it when she sees it.

Open my last letter when she finds it.
My love to you both—always—Mom

The letter fluttered to Matt's lap as he chewed on his lower lip. Without turning in her direction, he said, "Open that. Please." He swallowed the tears threatening to overtake him.

He heard the paper tear, heard her gasp. He stared at the darkening sky and waited. When she began to whisper, he gripped his thighs and listened.

"Kathleen—

"I have to assume that if you are reading this, then my Matt is sitting near you. What can I tell you about him? He's a tiger. He's a kitten. He's so loyal. So strong. I've never seen him in love, but I can imagine his ferocity, his protectiveness, his steadfastness when he finds you.

"I know you have so much hurt inside you. Take his hand. He can help you hold it all. Your family, my darling girl—"

She stopped and began to sob.

Matt went to her, scooted in behind her, wrapped his body around hers and finished reading through his own tears.

"Your family, my darling girl, don't want you to hide on that beach. They want you to live. They want you to remember their smiling faces, their laughter, the good times and the hard ones. They want you to be proud of them, to show them off to the world. Let them out— enjoy them—share them.

"I know this is so, because as my death gets closer, I think of what I want for Joe, Matt, and Patricia. Life. I want them to live full lives. I want them to carry my memory with them to every new experience. Somehow,

303

somewhere, I'll be living it with them. I know that's so.

"Kathleen—let Matt take you to my garden. I have a gift for you. You've been a gift to me and I know you'll be the greatest gift I could ever give my boy.

"Lean on him. He's brave...he'll catch you, he'll hold you. If you let him, he will love you and yours.

"I expect to meet your family very soon. Together, we'll be watching you come back to the living. Take us on adventures.

"All my love, Betty."

Kathleen continued to sob and Matt let his own tears join hers. After a long time, he traced the date at the top and said, "My mom died four days after writing this."

"Do you think she found Seth?"

He stuck his wet face into her neck. "Oh yeah. My guess is she's getting Lucas to eat more than six bites."

She snorted, but Matt wasn't sure whether it was with a heavy or light heart until she said, "Do you think she can get him to eat something green?"

"Yeah, love. I'm sure she can."

"What do you think is in her garden?"

"I have no idea, but I hope you have the courage to find out."

She pulled the letter from his hand and re-read it. "Can I think about it overnight?"

He pulled the letter from her hand, dropped it on his chair and turned her so she faced him. Kissing her mouth, her jaw, her neck, into her damaged ear, he murmured his love. When her lips came to his neck and trailed upward, he stood and lifted her. He walked them to her room.

A PRACTICE FIELD

Without letting go of her mouth, he gently laid her on the bed and stretched out beside her. With one hand, he loosened her scarf and combed his fingers across her scars and through her hair. His other hand roamed down her body. When he reached her thigh, he pulled her leg up and around him. His hand trailed under her shirt while his mouth moved across her neck. Kathleen's hands stayed in his hair, pulling at the roots as she tried to burrow deeper.

Pulling back, he moved his hand to the buttons on her shirt. He froze when her body went rigid. Her hands dropped to her sides where she twisted at the comforter. Looking at her face, he found her eyes forced shut and her bottom lip trembling as her teeth worked on the flesh.

"Whoa, Kathleen." He brought his hand to her neck. "Open your eyes. Let me see."

She shook her head, refusing to open her eyes, but she said, "I'm here." She swallowed and tightened even more.

"Tell me what's happening."

"They didn't stop at the ear." One tear slipped to the pillow. "No one—"

Matt closed his eyes, remembering her reaction when he wanted to help her into the bath. Opening his eyes, he stroked her face. "Am I hurting you physically?"

She shook her head.

"Can I hurt you physically?"

She shook her head and clamped her teeth on her lip.

With his thumb, he pulled the lip free and kissed the teeth marks left behind. *He's brave. He's strong.* He recalled his mother's letter to Kathleen and held onto her belief in him.

Matt rolled so Kathleen was pinned beneath him. He leaned over her body. Beginning with her damaged ear, he rained kisses on her. Across her forehead to the other ear. Across her face to her eyes, her nose, her cheeks.

He lingered on her mouth for a while. Then he kissed down to her collarbones and across her neck to the hollow in her throat.

She trembled, she sobbed, she whimpered. Her hands gripped the sheets, but she did not try to stop him. He unbuttoned the first button, kissing her deeply as his fingers unbuttoned the next button. He finally had all the buttons open. He kissed a straight line from her head to her navel. Her shirt covered her breasts. He was ready and willing, but he needed her to be *here*.

Back to her mouth he moved. She was shivering. "Kathleen, you can do this. I want to see you. I've never wanted anything more. I will love every piece of your skin, scarred or not."

She went perfectly still except for the tight grip on the sheets. Her eyes squeezed shut while tears oozed down her face.

"Tell me where you are."

"Here," she murmured, "with you."

Slowly he moved the top away from her right side. Her breast was beautiful. Her waist curved in delicately above womanly hips.

He kissed her, every exposed inch. He handled her breast and kissed her nipple until her body responded. He moved back to her lips and devoured her. She kissed him back, but she kept the rest of her body utterly still.

Matt bared her left side. Bile rose in his throat. It wasn't the scars, not exactly. It was the brutality. The frenzied madness on her skin overwhelmed him. Some monster had hacked at his Kathleen. Butchered. For the third time in two days, he had to close his eyes against a building roar.

Matt immediately began to kiss each scar, each tender wound. He traced each one with his fingertips. He wanted to kiss away the horror. He wanted Kathleen to have a new feeling to associate with her body. He kissed and stroked every pink piece of flesh. He saw the beautiful breast, but the scarred skin held his attention. The scars spoke of unendurable pain that had been endured. They spoke of heartache, of the strength to survive.

As he caressed her skin, wanting to love her in the way she needed, he noted each scar. There were a few on her shoulder. *A practice field.* The rest started just below her left armpit. Lowering the waist of her shorts just enough to give attention to each one, he saw that they extended to about an inch below her hipbone. Surprisingly, just the barest bit of breast tissue was involved. He stroked the small scars on the underside of her breast.

"I've always wondered why they left my breasts alone," she barely whispered. "I was old enough to be their mother, maybe that's why." Her voice sounded shallow but was filled with menace.

Matt didn't say anything. He just kept loving her and letting her say whatever might help her. He concentrated. He paid attention to every word, every movement.

A boundary had been set on her skin. A perfect three-inch-wide path. Some seemed like burn marks, others like a really sharp knife. And, most horrific all, some looked as if a dull serrated knife had been sawed into her skin, leaving behind bumps and grooves. Some were light pink, some darker, and some a dark purple, like a bruise that never healed. Bile rushed him for a second time.

"According to the doctors, at first they burned me with cigarettes but soon they moved to a lighter," she whispered. "They would heat the knife and lay it on my skin. I have fought not to remember, but I can never forget that smell." She wasn't quoting a doctor. Her mechanical voice sounded as if she was watching it all and simply reciting the clinical details. "Then one of them produced one of those pocket knives that hunters carry around. He really enjoyed himself."

Matt squeezed his eyes shut, fighting hard to focus just on her.

"The others happened when one of them lost control. He grabbed the bread knife we had sitting on the counter to cut the French bread."

Matt finally made his way back to her face. He wiped the tears away. She still had her eyes squeezed shut. Her hands were coiled into tight fists, so tight the skin looked ready to crack. Otherwise, she was perfectly still.

He kissed her deeply then. "Oh, love. I don't know what to say. There is no way for me to make this better." Slowly, tenderly, hoping he conveyed how much he loved her, even or especially with the scars, he said, "I love you, Kathleen. Just as you are."

Before the final word finished, Kathleen threw Matt off her, pinning him beneath her thighs, straddling his midsection. With an aggressiveness that grew from rage, passion, and loneliness, Kathleen captured Matt's body. Beginning with his lips, she kissed, nibbled. Then she bit, used her teeth to pull on his flesh. She declared war on his body. His cheeks, his eyebrows, chin, jaw, right ear. Moving to his left ear she grabbed his earlobe with her teeth and tugged viciously. She clawed and scratched.

Matt's hands gripped her waist, anchoring her to his body. "Do it, Kathleen. Do whatever you need."

Using her hands, her fingers, her nails, she tore the shirt from his body and scraped over his torso. As she pinched and scratched one of his nipples, she chewed on the other.

"Whatever you need, love."

She moved down his body, attacking his abdominal muscles, biting, scratching, pinching, twisting. She jerked the last of his clothes off his body.

Matt tensed and writhed, hissed and moaned when Kathleen used both hands on his penis, his testicles. He bucked, but he held on to her hips and allowed the assault. "Take your power back, love. Take it back."

Mouth, teeth, hands, nails were everywhere, leaving welts, bruises, abrasions. Matt continued his encouraging words, but now they were said between moans and growls and even curses. Unconsciously his body moved, his hands roamed. As she grew more out of control he ripped her clothes from her and watched as her body moved.

Rising above and over him, she slammed herself down on him, taking him into her body in one savage movement.

Lost in the passion and frenzy, Matt forced himself into her. The sounds in the room were primal, animalistic. Their bodies rocked together over and over again. Kathleen bent to Matt's mouth and clamped his bottom lip with her teeth.

"Holy fuck," Matt shouted as blood ran from his opened lip, triggering both of them to release everything.

Covered in sweat, Kathleen collapsed on top of Matt and buried her head into his neck. Her hands gripped his biceps. Shaking from both exertion and confusion, she gulped in air. "Matt, I'm so——" she began.

Before she could continue the sentence, Matt rolled her under him and shushed her with a tender kiss to her lips.

"Kathleen," Matt whispered as he stroked down her damaged body, encouraging her to make eye contact. "I know you have things to say, emotions to process, but let me make one thing perfectly clear."

"Matt, I'm so——" she tried again as tears began to fall down the sides of her face.

"Shh, love. Listen to me first and then you can say whatever you need. Okay? Can you do that for me?" Matt waited until he saw a slight nod.

"You are never to apologize to me. I never want to hear the words 'I'm sorry' for what just happened in this room. Never. If I had wanted you to stop, I could have made you stop."

"But, but——" She choked on the words. "I hurt you. I've never hurt someone before. I don't understand what happened to me," she said through her clogged throat.

Matt lifted his body off her so that she could see his torso. "Love, you didn't hurt me. Look. You didn't break the skin. I know you think you were rough with me. Every mark you see will be gone before the sun comes up. And even if you had hurt me, I would still not want you to apologize."

She traced a few scratch marks, a few small nibble marks. "I don't understand. I thought I was biting you. I know I tasted blood." She licked her lip. "I still taste it."

Matt laughed lightly. "Yes, you did taste blood. But that was because I bit my bottom lip to keep from screaming so loudly the police would be called." They lay in silence, Matt gently stroking Kathleen while her tears stopped.

Finally, she spoke, "Matt, what happened to me just now?" A palpable fear entered the room.

Matt carefully rolled Kathleen so they lay face to face. He wrapped his leg around hers and pulled their lower bodies together. His palms held her face. He placed his face next to her damaged ear. "I think we just survived the first bird."

Kathleen sucked in a breath and her entire body tensed. Matt saw the unmasked fear in her eyes. He kept his eyes pinned to hers, touching her every way he could.

When she buried her face in his neck, he rolled to his back, encasing Kathleen safely in his arms and legs, protecting her.

"Matt, what do I do now?" she whispered so quietly he almost didn't hear her.

"You hold onto me and I hold onto you."

He could feel her eyelashes on his neck as she blinked several times before she nodded. He waited and held her until he felt her entire body relax into his side. Turning out the light, he snuggled down into her.

"I need the light," she muttered as she cuddled deeper.

"No, you don't. I'm here. I've got you. If you wake up, find me. I'll be right here." He squeezed her into him.

"I guess we're taking you to Minnesota," she said as she slipped into sleep.

SUNDAY, 2 TO 4

Matt felt Kathleen as she tried to move away from him. As soon as she moved her leg, he grabbed it and put it back. "Not yet, love, not yet. Let's enjoy the sun shining on the bed for a few minutes." He moved her hair off her face and kissed her cheek before moving to her mouth.

"I need to get some clothes on," Kathleen said as she clutched the sheets around her naked body.

"Please don't retreat from me. I want to do to you what you did to me last night. One slow inch at a time." Matt grinned and nipped at her cheek.

"I can't, Matt. It's daylight. You saw it all last night, but the daylight—I can't do the daylight."

Matt crawled on her, capturing her face between his palms. "You can. I'll start on your shoulder. I'll go slow, I promise. I'll move the sheet down one tiny piece at a time. I'll prove to you that you can handle it and so can I."

She made no response.

"Look at me."

She still didn't respond.

"Kathleen, I need your eyes. I can't see what you are feeling with your eyes closed. Just give me your eyes and we'll take it from there." He waited and waited. Eventually, she looked at him. Her eyes were glittering with tears. All three colors showed. It was if she couldn't decide which emotion to let through, couldn't decide where safety lay. He kissed her eyelids and forced the tears to fall down her cheeks. He kissed the tears off her cheeks. "Okay, here is what I see," Matt began. "You are so scared. I'm not sure exactly what of. There is no way for me to ever be in your shoes, so I won't pretend to be. But let me give you some things to consider. One, I am not going anywhere. Two, I find your body beautiful. Do your scars hurt me? Of course they do. Do I wish you didn't have them? Yes, desperately, I wish this had never happened to you."

Kathleen's eyes searched his face, letting more blue leak in.

"Three, I want to see you in the daylight. I want to show you that it's you I want, Kathleen, *all* of you." Matt didn't wait for the response. He started on the left side of her head. Then he moved to the shoulder and he kissed his way down, inch by inch. He used his hands, his fingers, his mouth to delve into every corner of her body. He missed not one square inch. Her fingers, her toes, behind her knees. He touched Kathleen in places and ways he'd never considered before. As he explored he noted what caused her to squirm, what caused her to gasp, to cry out, to beg. He made damn sure she stayed in this moment, with him.

With his mouth on the small scars under her breast and his finger inside her, Matt watched as she climaxed. When his mouth worked its way back to hers, she kissed him sweetly, tenderly, exhaustedly.

With a wicked tone, he said, "My turn, love." Her body

responded immediately as her legs fell open and her hips lifted. She invited him in. As he slowly entered her, she grabbed his buttocks and pushed, begging him. He obliged with force and barely controlled emotion.

"Look at me. Give me your eyes, Kathleen. When I make love to you, I want your eyes." In less than a minute, with Minnesota blue staring at him, they tumbled into the abyss.

"Sated," Matt said into the top of Kathleen's head as she sprawled on top of him, her leg thrown across his. "I've never used that word. But that's the only word for right now."

She didn't stop tracing Matt's nipples when she snickered and said, "Well, let's see. There's satisfied, satiated, gratified, gorged, fulfilled, slaked, quenched." Her fingers played with his chest hair. "Are you sure about this trip?"

"Go ahead, give me all your objections. You can put my lawyer skills to the test."

She folded her palms on his chest, rested her chin on top. "I don't even own a piece of luggage. I certainly don't have clothes for Minnesota chill. I don't have a passport."

"Whoa. Stop. We're going to Minnesota. You don't need a passport." He laughed as he toyed with her sweaty hair. "Luggage we can buy. Why don't we just go shopping once we get to Minnesota?"

"What are the plans?"

"Well, Friday we apparently have to go shopping, but then I'd like to take you on a tour of my town. Friday night, I was thinking dinner with my dad, Patti, and Jess."

She stilled and he heard her deep breath.

"Patti will be fine. She's mad at me, anyway. Not you. She's going to be focused on my plans for NNJ over anything else."

"What?"

"Saturday, I guess I was thinking we'd spend the day with my dad in Mom's garden. Both Saturday and Sunday are football. Monday, I have to be at NNJ and I thought you'd either go with me or hang with my dad."

"Wait, Matt. What about NNJ?" She pulled up to look down at his face.

Wearing a small smile, he put her hair behind her good ear and massaged the damaged one. "I'm not going back to NNJ."

She reared back and started to speak but he put his fingers on her mouth. "Let me talk. I told you I was miserable there and didn't know it. Now that I know it, I cannot imagine sitting in that office dealing with asshole clients and the idiotic IRS." When she tried to speak around his fingers, he pressed more firmly. "Look, you can call Roger and have me kicked out of here, but I'm not going back to NNJ. I figure we just take it one day at a time and build something together." He dropped his fingers and raised an eyebrow. "Your turn."

"Your career," she said.

"No, my job. My dad said something interesting the other day. He told me that being a tax attorney is what I do, it's not who I am. I'm lucky. I don't have to work again for the rest of my life. So why would I work at something that doesn't enthrall me?" He swiftly twisted them so he was on top. He bit at her shoulder. "And since this enthralls me—" He began to kiss her.

"What if I have an episode while we're traveling or with your family?" She gulped but didn't look at him.

"Then we deal. Every time, no matter what issues arise, we deal." He responded as if the answer was obvious. "I would never take you somewhere you aren't safe, you know that, right?"

"I know." She rolled him off, pressing her side against his.

Shifting to his side, Matt's fingers outlined the scars on her hip. "They offered to fix it."

Blinking, he looked from her body to her face. "What?"

She stared at the ceiling and let another bird free. "I was in the hospital for four months. Every day, all day, somebody would be touching me, looking at me, poking me, prodding me. I was a specimen. I didn't talk, I didn't agree or disagree. I felt unable to help myself. Keep doing that." She moved her hand to touch his, encouraging him to start his caress again. "It was as if I was a monkey they could experiment on. And I know, I know that some enjoyed it when it hurt." After exhaling a long breath, she quirked her lips. "One morning I woke up with yet another strange face peeling off my bandages. He didn't introduce himself, he didn't say hello or ask me how I was. He examined." She shook her head. "He mashed on the side of my head like I used to do with melons. He held a flashlight to my ear." She sighed then rolled so she faced him.

Matt ran his fingers up her spine and waited.

"'I can fix that. I can fix that right up and get you back to normal.'" She used a man's nasal voice. She closed her eyes tight then opened them wide. "He actually thought fixing my ear would get me back to normal." Blowing a loud breath from her nose, she finished, "I never want to see a doctor again. I don't ever want anyone else to touch me."

Matt pulled their bodies flush against each other. "As long as

I can touch you, we'll work out anything else."

She wiggled underneath him. "I need to get my walk in."

Understanding her need for routine, especially with so much change coming her way, he moved off her. "Would you rather go alone?"

She scooted to the edge of the bed and wrapped herself in a sheet. "I'm okay either way. I'll be listening to Jules and Nate fight, anyway."

Matt's eyebrows quirked up as he put on his shorts.

"My book. The two lovers fight all the time, trying to ignore how they feel about each other."

"Ahh. You go. I'll get a few things done and make some breakfast. You okay with me using your laundry?"

She tilted her head at the laundry basket in the corner. "Feel free to do mine, too." She walked past him, receiving a smack on the ass.

<<<>>>

Assuming he had about ninety minutes, Matt got busy. He smiled as he sorted their laundry. Twirling a pair of her panties with his finger, he tried to remember a time he'd ever done a woman's laundry. When he came up empty, his smile broadened.

He booted up his computer, purchased two first-class tickets to Minnesota for Thursday afternoon. He quickly read through Jessica's message assuring him all the partners were planning to attend the meeting Monday. She also promised all the files would be ready for transfer. Smiling, he sent Jess a new message with a very special favor. He deleted all the messages from Patti unread.

By the time he rotated the laundry and made two cups of

coffee, Kathleen was opening the door and he was feeling more confident in his plan.

She took the offered water bottle but otherwise gave him no acknowledgement. Matt tensed when she walked past him and to the top of the stairs to the locked door. He stood at the bottom and watched her count the marks. "Sam will keep these up-to-date for you."

She turned his way, but the shadows prevented him from seeing her face. "No, I think this will be my last mark."

Taking the steps in two long strides, he sat in front of her, used his hands to shift her face so he could see her eyes. "Are you sure?"

"Yeah. They aren't marks on a wall."

Still holding her face, he asked, "Would you be willing to go to Charlotte and see Lisa again?"

Her head shook slowly.

Surprised, Matt searched her face. "Why?"

"She would require me to live at the Center."

"What?"

"I love her, I do. But she works at an inpatient center. *Inpatient.* I lived there for most of a year. I cannot go back." She squeezed his arm.

"I know this sounds like a stupid question, but what does inpatient mean, exactly?"

"I would have to live there, sleep there, eat there. I'd be in some sort of therapy from eight am to eight pm. I'd only be allowed a visitor one day a week. Sunday, two to four." She tightened her hands on his arms. "Please don't ask me to do that."

Matt's own head shook and his chest deflated. "Never. I had no idea. I didn't even think of that, to be honest." His palms began to sweat at the thought of her away from him like that. "We'll talk more. Let's focus on Minnesota, for now. One thing at a time, right?"

"Are you sure about this trip?"

"For you or for me?"

"Both, either."

"Yes and yes. I've got you, love. I promise you that."

Her eyes closed and she leaned her forehead into his.

"Do you want me to sit with you?" He looked at the wall.

"No, I'm all right. It's time. It's past time. They are angry at what I've become." She pulled back and shrugged, giving him a sad smile.

Watching her eyes for several seconds, he finally rose. "Okay, the dryer is squawking. The coffee is cold. I'll leave you to it, but just call me if you need me." Kissing her forehead, he moved back to the kitchen.

Turning the coffeemaker back on, frustration at his own naïveté built in his chest. "Please help us find another way," he said to his mother, to Seth, to the universe. Closing his eyes, he pictured locked birds. As the hair on his arms rose, he imagined the cacophony of flapping wings, pecking beaks, scratching and cawing. *So out of my depth. Mom, I need your help here.*

MIRRORS REVISITED

Finally, she started to relax. From the second he'd put her in the car, every one of her muscles remained tense. She'd stared at the check-in people, unable to process their request for identification. When she'd approached the security gate and realized she'd have to remove the sunglasses, she'd backed up, trembling. He'd spoken to the security people and they'd allowed her to enter through a separate gate. She still had to remove her sunglasses, but she was able to keep her eyes closed through the machine and the agent stood ready to give her the glasses back.

At the gate, she'd placed earphones in her ears and sat rigid, immobile. He'd spoken to the flight attendants, who allowed her to board before anyone else. He had her settled in the seat, facing the window, a blanket on her knees before anyone else boarded. She remained just as rigid and immobile. She spoke not one word. She refused to let him see her eyes. She refused to eat, go to the bathroom or take a sip of water.

The ride to his condo was much the same and he'd begun to worry about this trip. He was ready to call Stephanie, get Lisa Bartlett's number, and beg her to break confidentiality and help him.

"It's not what I expected," she said as she traced her fingers along his granite countertop. "I've been here before," she added when she reached his floor-to-ceiling windows overlooking the Minneapolis skyline.

"What?" he asked with relief and confusion flooding his system as she seemed to settle and come back to him.

"This place—it's in just about every romance novel that takes place in a city. The hero," she spoke to his reflection, "is always wealthy with a condo in the sky. You even have the black granite and subzero refrigerator." She smiled at him behind her glasses.

Matt looked around his condo. The kitchen, dining and living rooms were all open to each other and wrapped in windows. His dining room furniture was glass and chrome. The center of his dining table held a large silver bowl filled with yellow, blue and silver balls. A leather couch, two leather chairs with footstools, glass and chrome accent tables matched the dining room pieces. A gas fireplace opened to both the kitchen and living area. "Patricia did all this. She loves that kind of thing and I didn't care. I've never sat at the table. I only sit in the living room if I have company. I use the kitchen for coffee, beer, and breakfast and I usually stand at the counter with my laptop open." He moved to place his chin on her forehead. "But I do love my view."

"I wasn't being critical. It just doesn't fit with the Matt Nelson I know and the Mattie your mother talked about."

"Come here." He put his hand out to her. "Let me show you what's me." He pulled her to the first door on the left. Before he opened it, he kissed her forehead and said, "This is your space too." He lifted the sunglasses from her face and grinned when she pulled in her eyebrows. Opening the door, he escorted her inside.

"Matt," she said on an exhaled breath. "How did you—" She stopped and walked deep into the room.

"I had Jess go on a shopping trip for me. It turns out she's a reader, too. Did she do all right?"

Her bright eyes came to him and she presented him with a huge smile. "Perfect." She tapped each book on the shelves. Without turning away from her new library, she said, "What did you have on these shelves before?"

"Tax codes and law books."

She turned and looked at the rest of the space. Picking up one of several U of M blankets, she said, "This room does seem more like you."

"Everything in here I chose—well, except your books." Pointing to an old, well-worn recliner, he added, "I've had that chair for over twenty years." Moving his finger to the desk in front of the large window he said, "That was my dad's when I was growing up. The desk and the chair."

"How big is that TV?"

"As big as the wall could handle."

She snagged a book off the shelf, bounced on the large leather sofa and wrapped her legs in the blanket. "Seth always wanted a huge TV. He would have loved all this. Except he'd want Blue Devils, not Gophers."

"He can't be perfect." Matt moved closer so he could see her eyes in the dim light. Relieved to find a smiling bright blue, he sat down next to her. "Do you know that book?"

She turned the book his direction. "No. I know the author but this one is new-ish."

"Can we talk before you settle in?" He ran his fingers over her cheek, slowly unwound her scarf. His thumbs ran across the dark circles under her eyes before he took her hands in his. "First, this is just as much your home as the beach house is. So, no sunglasses, no scarf." He waited for a nod. "You seem very tired."

She took back the scarf and wound it back around her head. "Give me a bit of time to get used to this. You made me accomplish a lot over the last few days," she said.

"Is there anything I can do to help you settle down? You've had your shoulders up to your ears since we left this morning."

"I'm scared," she whispered.

"Can you explain why?"

She looked around the room. "I don't know how to behave. I don't feel safe." Her fingers began to twist around the blanket. "Not physically. But—" She looked up at him through drooping eyelids. "My locks, my room, my closet."

"How about this. I'll start a fire in here and then order us some food. You just get comfortable, read. After we eat, we'll put you in the monstrous tub I have." He pulled her legs straight on the couch, tucked the blanket around her, and walked toward the door. "Want anything special to eat?"

She looked up from the book, lifted her eyebrows as if the question confused her. "I've eaten salad every night."

"What was your favorite food? Your go-to meal when you didn't want to cook?"

She wiggled a bit then smiled a huge smile. "Pizza.

Pepperoni, mushroom, extra cheese. Could we do that?"

Matt's smile matched hers. "Thick or thin crust?"

"Thick, always, and that garlic butter to dip the crust in." She wiggled again, deeper into the cushions. "Kiley and Courtney would feast on the crusts and butter for days. Pigs. They'd giggle as butter ran down their chins, down their necks and into their shirts. Just like pigs."

"Hey, look up at me," Matt said when her head dropped down.

She gave him bright blue eyes and an even larger smile. "Pigs."

"Pigs we'll be. Do you want beer, water? Those might be my only choices."

"Pizza and beer," she said as if the answer were obvious. She pulled the book in front of her and disappeared into her fictional world.

Matt strolled to the kitchen, found the menu, and ordered. He spent a few minutes tossing junk mail and sorting the other into stacks based on topic. He gathered two beers, paper plates, and napkins. "Pizza man said thirty minutes," he said as he turned in to the room. He halted when he found the couch, the entire room, empty. The blanket was tossed on the floor. The book lay on top. "Kath." After placing the supplies on his desk, he went in search.

Placing his foot inside his bedroom, he stopped and held his breath. Kathleen stood before his dresser mirror. She was leaning close to the surface and tracing the dark circles under her eyes. She pulled back and ran her finger on the mirror, outlining the scarf around her head. Matt took one step back. He stayed closed enough to watch over her but far enough away to give her this time.

Slowly she unwrapped the scarf and let it fall to the floor. She turned her head and looked sideways at her wounds. Lifting her index finger, she traced each bump, ridge, and scar. She pulled on the hair that grew in tufts between scar tissue. "I never looked," she said, finding his profile in the mirror. "Not once. I had Stephanie cover the mirrors in the hospital. And psych rehab centers don't have mirrors because they're glass and suicide instruments. We had something that was like looking into a hubcap. I never bothered. I couldn't avoid my body. But this—I never wanted to know." She shifted her eyes back to her scars. "I can't decide if they're worse than I thought or better." After a long time, she added, "It hurt. I remember that." Once again she found his face in the mirrored glass. "It hurt."

With those two words, Matt moved into her space, pulled her body tightly into his, and just held on.

She watched him in the mirror. He watched her. He paid attention—to her body's signs, to her eye color, to the tears that started to form. "Tell me how to be here for you right now."

"How can you stand to look at it?" Her gaze had shifted from his eyes back to the side of her head, to the hair that stuck out all over.

Matt shrugged. Not in nonchalance but because to him the answer was simple. "You're my Kathleen. I love everything about you."

They stared at each other in the glass for a long time.

Then, quite suddenly, Kathleen burst out laughing. "Brice would have his finger down his throat right now, gagging on what you just said."

Matt remained quiet long enough to ensure his Kathleen was there, in the space with him. Once he was sure he, too, laughed. "You'll love Joey. He hates any kind of romantic stuff. He says that makes men look like pussies."

Kathleen pulled back and looked sternly at him.

Matt threw his hands up. "His word, not mine. He's what, twenty-two or something?" When the doorbell rang, he added, "Saved by the bell. Pizza, beer, ballgame."

ABOUT SARAH

"Ready for a bath? You have butter on your neck and cheese hanging off your chin," he teased. "After that we can climb in bed and you can tell me about one of your favorite books."

She ran her fingers through the cheese and butter. "At least I kept it off my shirt," she said as she wiped her greasy fingers on his shirt.

He grabbed at her fingers and sucked them clean. "Bath, bed, book."

She pulled her fingers out of his hands and hugged the book to her chest.

Laughing at her look, he said, "You can take the book with you to the bath. Stay in there as long as you like."

She pulled away, took his cheeks in both palms. Staring at him, she said, "Thank you." For the first time, she initiated a kiss.

"Okay, change of plans," he said as he pulled her to her feet. "Bed, bath, book."

Her feet tangled in the blanket, causing her to stumble into him. "How about a bath together?"

"What?" he asked as he helped her find her footing.

A red bloom filled her cheeks. "Never mind," she said as she dropped her face to her chest.

Lifting her chin with his index finger, he said, "I haven't taken a bath since I was a boy. Unless you count ice baths after a game."

Her eyebrows jerked up and she began to laugh. "You have had girlfriends, right?"

"Well, I've had women spend the night. But, no, I haven't had a girlfriend since Sarah." He pulled her next to him and walked them down the hall, through his master bedroom and into the huge bath.

She went around him and then around the space. "Patti?"

"Yep. I use the sink, the toilet and the shower."

"Are you telling me that tub has never been used?" she asked, standing at the bottom of the three-step entry to his Jacuzzi tub.

"I suppose Patti might have used it, but I doubt it. She usually rents a room closer to the office or stays with Dad." He strolled behind her and fiddled with the faucets.

As the tub filled she leaned over, searching through the basket of bubble bath, bath oil and salts. "Do you think these are still good?"

"I think," he said as he checked and adjusted the water temperature, "that those are brand new. I'm sure they weren't here last week. My guess is Jess put those in here."

"Vanilla? Lavender? Jasmine? Peach?" She held up each one for him to inspect.

"You decide."

As they both undressed and sank across from each other

in the hot peachy water, Matt thought of how far she'd come in the last few days. No longer did she wear sunglasses with him or Rosie and Sam. She didn't wear a scarf at the beach house, and she no longer flinched when he touched her scars. From time to time she would talk about her family and her life before the tragedy. Relaxing into the bubbles, he said, "Okay, this is nice." He wrapped his hands around her thighs, slid her toward him, sloshing water all over the floor.

Giggling, she plastered her chest to his. "I can't believe you've never done this. Not even with Sarah?"

"I've never bathed with a woman before." Sliding his hands up her inner thighs, he said, "I think I've missed out on something quite nice."

She squirmed, wrapped her arms around his shoulders. "Do you remember when you went caveman on me?"

He murmured into her breast.

"Well," she slid her hands down his back. "I'm glad this experience is all mine."

He moved his mouth to her damaged shoulder. "Everything is yours. Everything." He lifted her and placed her exactly where he wanted her.

As their passions and the water cooled, Kathleen sat between his legs, her toes turning the hot water on and off. "Tell me about Sarah."

Laying his head against the tub, using a sponge to drip warm water down her back, he said, "How about we meet in bed and I'll tell you anything you want to know." Rising from the water, he stepped out. He dropped the sponge into the tub and kissed the top of her head.

Matt went to the den, grabbed a book off the shelf that he hoped was a mystery. Returning to find her already reading, he whipped the comforter from her legs. He paused, his breath hitching in his throat. No woman had ever worn his clothes. Not even Sarah. Seeing Kathleen now, Matt was punched with an overwhelming feeling of protectiveness, of ownership. He fought not to growl or beat his chest. It was as if his old t-shirt stamped her as his. And, more profoundly, *more satisfying*, it stamped *him as hers*. "God," he whispered as he tried to shake off the primal need to claim her.

She looked at him and then followed his eyes to his shirt on her body. "I'm sorry. I didn't think you'd mind." Obviously flustered and embarrassed, she started to stand.

He lifted his long legs and gently pushed her back in the bed with his toes. Realizing he was frowning, he shook himself. "Oh, no." He put his hands on either side of her legs, leaned down, and nibbled on her lips. Pulling back so their noses touched, he said, "My reaction was not what you think. My reaction frightened me, because it was out of character. Powerful. Visceral." He planted his forehead into hers.

"It's soft and smells like you," she said shyly.

Matt snuggled his nose into her neck. "For the first time in my life, I felt—" he chuckled. "I felt Herculean." He nipped her neck. "Seeing you in my shirt…" Another nip. He used his nose to move the shirt from her shoulder. "I want to use the word possessive. But I know there are more accurate words than that." He licked at the scar on her shoulder.

"Proprietorial, overprotective, dominating," she offered him while keeping her hands gripped around the book.

"Covetous. That's the word. It looks better on you than me, that's for damn sure." He kissed her cheek then nudged her so he could take his place beside her.

She harrumphed, scooting around until she was comfortable. "Sarah?" she prompted.

He repositioned her so that her head lay in his lap. As he stroked his fingers through her hair, he started, "I met her in my first year of law school. I was twenty-three years old and thought it was time to grow up. You know, stop the partying and woman-chasing, finish law school, find the wife, have the kids. The American dream." He paused to adjust the pillows behind his back. "We had been dating a little over a year and I thought it was time to buy the ring. I was planning to ask her between Thanksgiving and Christmas. But, as usual, my annoying sister mucked things up." He rolled his eyes.

"We were at my parents' for Thanksgiving. Me, Sarah, Patricia and her husband Dave. Sarah had gone to bed early and Patti, Dave, and I were watching some game on the big TV in the basement, drinking beers and whining about law school. Patricia, as she likes to do, abruptly changed the subject. 'So, Mattie, you going to marry Sarah?'" Matt said with a mocking woman's voice.

"I said, 'Yeah, I suppose so.' Patricia snorted at me. I mean truly snorted at me, just like the pigs on my grandpa's farm. 'Suppose so,' she mocked me. 'That doesn't sound like love.' In my usual way, I told her to mind her own damn business and that ended the discussion, or so I thought."

He looked out the window but continued when Kathleen knocked him with her elbow. "The day after Thanksgiving

Mom asked me to take her to the mall. I should have known something was up. My mom never needed anyone to take her anywhere. On the way to the mall she persuaded me to stop for coffee. That should have been my second warning. My mom liked to get to the mall the minute they opened on Black Friday. We sat down with our coffees and she started right in, 'So, Patricia, tells me you *suppose* you're ready to marry Sarah.'"

"'Yeah, I was thinking of it. Don't you like her?' I asked her."

"'Of course I do, Sarah's a wonderful person and she'll make a great wife and mother and lawyer.' When she paused, I knew a bomb was about to drop."

"The bomb," Kathleen said with impatience.

Matt smiled. "'And, well, I'm just wondering if she will be a great wife to *you* and a great mother to *your* kids.'" Matt mimicked a bomb exploding. "Anyway, she finished with this statement: 'Mattie, I'll love whomever you marry and if Sarah's the right one then good for you. But remember that marriage is the hardest thing you'll ever do and in order to succeed it has to be an overwhelming kind of love.'" He stopped talking and looked out the window at the darkening sky.

"You broke it off with Sarah, I assume."

He looked back at her. "No, not yet. I went ahead with my plans. I bought the ring, I planned a nice dinner at our local Italian eatery. I had the little speech all memorized." He paused to play with her hair and trace over her scars.

"Can you please get to the punch line?" She pushed at him again.

"Okay, okay." Matt leaned down to kiss her cheek. "Hold

your horses. So the Friday night before I was planning to execute my proposal, we were watching a chick flick. At the end of the movie, as she always did, Sarah was crying. While we cleaned up the popcorn and beer bottles I asked her why she cried. I can picture her clearly. She leaned against the kitchen counter and looked at me like I was crazy. 'Matt, don't you know? All girls want that—the man who can't take his eyes off her, who can't enter a room without touching her somehow, can't breathe without her.' I was floored. I saw my parents. Patricia and I were often embarrassed because they made mushy eyes at each other. We complained because my dad was always patting my mom on the rear. We'd begged my parents not to make sexual innuendos around us. Sarah was right. That was what she wanted, what she deserved." He shrugged, grinning. "And, well, I wasn't that person for her. Rather than propose, I told her I couldn't be what she needed. I think she understood at the same time I did. All's well that ends well. She's married now to an attorney near Boston with two kids. Her husband, Nick, manages our Boston office. We're still friends. She and Patti actually became best friends over the years." Pinching Kathleen's knee, he smiled. "I'm glad I listened to my mother then. I'm more glad I listened to her now."

Kathleen's gaze shifted from his face to the wall above him. Her hands sank to her lap and her eyes started to shift from blue to purple.

"Kath, can you look at me?"

Her shoulders drooped so slightly that under any other circumstance Matt might not have noticed. "Patricia," she breathed. "What does she know about me other than that I'm a freak?"

Wanting to slide down next to her but choosing to stay relaxed in his position, he said, "She knows your name— Kathleen Bridges, not Marcia Conners. She knows my mom wanted me to find you. She knows you are important. Very important. Beyond that, nothing. I haven't spoken to her and my dad promised he would not share anything about you. We tell her whatever you want, when you're ready. No sooner."

Kathleen's hand moved from her lap to touch her mutilated ear. "We have to tell her something."

Hoping his posture projected confidence and a carefree attitude, he said, "Not really. We have several options. We can tell her some version of the truth—whatever feels okay to you. We can say nothing and let her think what she will. We can even tell her it's none of her damn business." Now he shifted so they lay face to face, their legs tangled together under the sheets. "All she cares about is that I'm happy. She's pissed right now because I've been ignoring her. She's also worried about my plans for NNJ because I've kept her out of that loop, too. Hopefully she's embarrassed at her own behavior. But, seriously, she's got to learn to think before she speaks." He wrapped his hands around her neck, pulled her in for a soft kiss. "Can you tell me what really has you worried?"

"Your dad, what does he know?"

"My dad is your champion. He's convinced he had more time with my mother because of you."

"Does he know who I am?"

"Yes. Before he would give me the letters he researched

you. He actually knows more than I do."

Her eyebrows quirked up.

"I only know the barest details that Rosie gave me and the bits you've given me. My mom told me in one of her letters that it was your story to tell. I agree. When you are ready, and only when you are ready, you'll tell me." He squeezed her neck, "And, love, when you're ready, I will be here to catch you."

"I don't want to remember. I don't want to face it."

"I know. Let's get through this weekend, enjoy Minneapolis and football and beer. No worries. No stress. After I get through with NNJ on Monday we can talk through what our next step will be. Deal?"

"Matt, I *am* a freak," she whispered. "There's no real way for me to hide that. And it's not just your sister. There's your father and your colleagues and strangers. I stayed hidden for a lot of reasons. I wear dark sunglasses, but I can see how people look at me." Her fingers moved back to the missing ear.

Gathering her hands in his, he said, "Kathleen, you are *not* a freak. But even if you were, then you are *my* freak. I love you exactly how you are. Exactly. I want us to work through your sadness, your anger. I want to see that brilliant smile and those glorious blue eyes every day, all day. I want to hear all your stories, look through all those photo albums. And"—he kissed her nose—"we will take *baby* steps in that direction, beginning next week." He retrieved the book from the end table where'd she placed it. "You can update me on who's who in this book."

"What are the plans for tomorrow?"

"I was thinking we could do a morning walk, but you don't have warm enough clothes yet. So first we shop. Then I thought a tour of U of M—that can count as a walk. Lunch. Visit Dad. See Mom's garden. Nap." He wiggled his eyebrows suggestively. "Dinner with Patti, Dave, Dad, and Jessica. Cool?"

"Jessica, who is she exactly?"

"A second mother to me and Patti. She was the first person my Mom and Dad hired at NNJ forty-two years ago. She's the one who forced me to the beach." He winked. "I owe her a huge raise, which I will be sure happens first thing Monday."

A grin lit her face. "And she's a reader."

"More importantly, she's your champion, too. Sit next to her at dinner tomorrow night. You can talk books, and if my sister decides to open that mouth of hers, you'll enjoy watching Jess slam it shut."

"Are you sure I can do this?"

After staring at her for a long time, he finally said, "Love, we have a lot of hard things to face. But tomorrow is not something we *face*. It's something we do. Together. I will be there. I will not let anything happen to you. And if it gets to be too much—well, I'll know it because I'll be paying attention and we'll get out of there." He continued to make eye contact until he saw her nod. As she began to tell him the plot, he listened and hoped his sister would behave.

DO YOU THINK?

"**W**ell, that was an interesting experience," Matt said to Kathleen when they climbed back into the car. "I've always been told that shopping with a woman is torture."

She buckled her seatbelt then turned to face him. "I've always hated shopping. I knew if we didn't get in and get out some salesperson would start asking me to try things on. I didn't do that before. I damn sure don't do it now." She checked her scarf and her sunglasses.

Backing his Mercedes out of the spot, he said, "Well, the weather will keep us from walking the campus. Why don't we just drive through, grab some lunch, and head on out to Dad's place? Okay?"

"Did you bring the letter?"

"In my pocket." The tenth letter, the last letter. The old saying about a thing burning a hole in your pocket never felt more true than right now. He reached across the console and found her hand. "Okay?"

"Afraid."

"Of?" He chanced a quick look in her direction before entering the highway toward U of M. She faced forward, her body rigid, her hand squeezing his.

"Want to take a detour? Visit a bookstore?" He couldn't see her face, but he felt her turn his direction and the tension in the car dissipated.

"Really?" she asked with wonder in her voice.

"We can do the tour another time."

As they pulled into the parking lot of the huge bookstore Matt asked, "How long do you want to hang here? I'll call my dad with an ETA."

"Two hours. No less." She slammed his car door and almost ran to the double doors.

"Two hours. In a bookstore?" he asked as he caught the door for her.

"I'd prefer more. But I can make do with two. The one near me used to have a coffee shop and delicious scones. You can always get some sports magazine or whichever paper you like." Kathleen's body began to bounce, but this time it was excitement, not horror, filling her with so much energy.

He patted her behind. "I'll grab coffee and scones and find you."

Carrying coffee and two scones, one blueberry and one cranberry-orange, he found her at the front display. She'd only made it five feet into the store and was mesmerized by the new releases. He handed her the coffee, kissed her cheek, thrust the blueberry treat her way. "You okay here if I walk around and see what's so special about this place?"

She didn't glance up from the book she was flipping through. "Of course. Why wouldn't I be?" She turned a complete circle, her arms outstretched with coffee and food acting as compass points. "I'm surrounded by other people's stories." She smiled at him, took a huge bite of the scone, set her coffee down on a shelf and picked the book back up.

Two and a half hours later he set off in search of his Kathleen. It took him a while to find her, both because the store was large and because she was sitting on the floor, cradling a few books, lost to everything around her. Lowering himself to sit across from her, he said, "What are those?"

Startled, she looked up. "A series of books I read."

"Remove your sunglasses and tell me what's so special about them," he said, recalling Stephanie's advice and sensing that there was something that required his attention.

Her eyes flicked to the books in her lap and then back to him. "I've read these many times."

"Hold up," he said. Reaching over, he removed the sunglasses to discover bright blue staring at him.

She held up one with a blue cover and shook it at him. "This is the book I was listening to when you found me. The one with Chace and Faye?"

Goosebumps ran up his arms. *Come back here. Please, Kathleen, come back here.* "And?"

"I know every word in every book." Her hands roamed the spines in her lap. "These are my friends."

Gathering himself before he responded, he maintained eye contact, took a sip of his fresh coffee, and asked, "Can you tell me what's so special? What you liked so much?"

She tilted her head and furrowed her eyebrows. She looked at him quizzically, obviously not knowing the answer.

"Okay," he said. "Which one of those was your favorite?"

Quickly her hands landed on one of the books and she held it up to him. "This one," she said with excitement.

"Tell me," he encouraged.

She began to prattle on. Something about Ty getting out of prison for a crime he didn't commit. Lexi agreeing to marry him for $50,000. "Oh, Matt, the break-up scene was one of the best—or worst—I've ever read. The words he said. The *way* he said them. And then when he eventually went after her she was dead inside." Her voice sounded pained.

"What do you mean, 'dead inside'?" he asked.

"Well, her life had been hard. And his words, his meanness." She shivered. "She ran from Colorado to the beach. She spent every day just sitting on the beach, living in a fleabag hotel. When he arrived to apologize and take her home, she refused. She was done. Done trying. Dead but breathing." She looked away from him, frowning. She turned back his way with her hands trembling.

He reached across the aisle and took the book from her hand. Holding her hands between his, he asked, "Kathleen, if these stories cause you such anguish, why do you read them?"

She looked at him like he'd spoken a foreign language. Pulling her hands free, she rose to her knees. Leaning a bit closer, she flipped the last fifty pages near his face. Her voice was loud, oblivious to their surroundings, thoroughly intent on holding his attention. "Matt, the author creates these tragic scenes. Horrible words spoken. Physical horrors, too. In this book, the heroine has a scar right here." She indicated a place through her eyebrow. "And in this one," she continued, picking up a different book in the stack, "she has a scar on her stomach. And that doesn't include the words spoken—mean words, words meant to hurt, circumstances never fully put in the past. And yet—" She held the book to her cheek. "The author gives them their happily ever after. Scarred, wounded, tragic. But eventually—" Tear-filled bright blue smiling eyes bored into him as she clutched all six books to her chest. "Eventually they get their happily ever after." She walked on her knees, still clutching the books, until her nose almost touched his. "Do you think I can get a happily ever after? Are you my happily ever after?"

Neither blinked, neither moved except to breathe.

Matt's mind churned the words over and over. *Do you think I can get a happily ever after? Are you my happily ever after?*

He thought about the last fifty years. He thought of his idyllic childhood, his parents and their love for each other, his sister. He thought of Sarah and the other women he'd known. He thought of cases won and lost, money and friends accumulated. He remembered in minute detail the last week. The first night at Rosie's. The horrible night searching. The time spent protecting Kathleen from herself. He thought of Stephanie, of birds, of memories and tick marks. He thought of his t-shirt on her body. He thought of how their lovemaking made him feel. He thought of her scars, both physical and emotional. He thought of a quote he'd read in her book room. *"It's strange, I think, the way our lives turn out. Moments of circumstance, when later combined with conscious decisions and actions and a boatload of hope, can eventually forge a future that seems predestined."*

Matt dropped his forehead to hers. "You're mine. Kathleen, don't you see? I'm saving you and you're saving me. We will build a happily ever after. We'll open those doors together."

Right there in the middle of books and coffee cups and people, she crawled into his lap and buried her face in his shoulder.

Wrapping around her, he held on. His legs fell asleep, his arms tingled. He held on. People stepped around them. He held on. His back ached. His neck stiffened. He held on.

"I think we have to leave. My two hours are up," she said into his neck, even though she didn't loosen her arms or try to stand.

"A few more minutes. Just, just—" He paused and swallowed painfully. "Just let me hold you for a few more minutes."

Several minutes later she wiggled out of his lap. Gathering the six books, she smiled. "Let me pay for these and then see that garden."

THE GARDEN MESSAGES

"Is this what you expected?" Matt asked as he turned in to the driveway. On the short drive, she'd regaled him with all the details of Nina and Max, Laurie and Tate. It was as if by having those books, those people, sitting in a bag on her lap, she could relax. As he walked around to open her door he promised himself he would read every one of those books.

"Um. Yeah, actually. It's beautiful but homey." She stared at the redbrick ranch house with its large trees.

Taking her hand, he led her toward the front door. As soon as their feet hit the bottom step, the door flew open and his father stood with arms open wide. "Come to me, my girl," he said, but he didn't wait on her to climb up. He rushed and engulfed her in an embrace. "Thank you," he said so that Matt could just barely hear. "Thank you for coming. She's smiling on us." Pulling back, he turned to hug Matt. "Come in. Show your girl around and I'll meet you in the greenhouse."

Kathleen looked over at Matt. "A greenhouse?"

"Yeah," Joe answered. "We have a somewhat short season with all the cold and snow. Several years ago, when I realized she was serious about this, I had a greenhouse built."

"Dad," Matt laughed, "allow me to introduce Kathleen. Kathleen Bridges, this is my Dad, Joe Nelson."

"Smartass," Joe said. "Go. Give her the nickel-tour. The good stuff is in the garden." He disappeared into the house with Matt and Kathleen trailing behind him.

"Can we go to the garden first?" she asked Matt.

"Absolutely."

"Did you bring it?"

"It's still in my pocket." He patted his pocket and grinned. "Safe and sound. I'll give it to you when you're ready."

She grinned and put her sunglasses on top of her head. "I have to find the surprise first." Taking his hand, she pulled him in the direction Joe had gone.

With her mouth gaping, Kathleen walked around the greenhouse. She touched the leaves of several plants, put her fingers in the dirt of still others. "Who maintains this?"

"Mostly I do. But Jess does have to rescue me sometimes," Joe answered with pride. "Before Betty passed she made me make a few promises. One was to be sure Matt found you and another was to keep these plants thriving. The first promise was easy. The second—well, let's just say, a few of these have suffered under my tutelage. But I'm learning." He turned to Matt. "Let's leave Kathleen to find all my mistakes. We'll make some hot chocolate and come back."

Matt looked from Kathleen to his father and back to Kathleen. Her sunglasses were still perched on her head and her eyes a bright blue. "Hey, love," he said and waited until she gave him her full attention. "You okay in here for a few minutes?"

She looked around the space. Glancing up at him, she nodded

toward his pocket.

He pulled the letter out and handed it to her. "I'll be back in a just a few minutes. Do you want to wait?"

She twirled the envelope in her hands. "Maybe. But I want to have it with me when I find it."

Bending toward her, he kissed her forehead. "Hot chocolate coming up."

When the door of the greenhouse closed, Matt asked, "Do you know what the last letter says?"

"Yes." Joe strolled toward the house.

"Dad? Is it safe for her to open it alone?"

Joe opened the back door and ushered Matt through it. "I wouldn't have suggested we leave her alone if it wasn't. But I doubt she'll open it without you. I wanted to talk to you about Patricia. Alone."

Matt's back straightened and his nostrils flared. "Dad," he asked, "is she going to be a problem tonight?"

"Let me just fill you in," he replied as he turned in to the kitchen. "She did some digging—"

Before he could finish the thought, Kathleen came barreling in. "It's a message. Or a series of messages." She squealed as her body plowed into Matt's. "Come," she sputtered through her laughter, tugging on his shirt.

"Okay. Can you tell me more?"

She bounced around him. Ignoring his questioning look, she asked, "Can we open the letter now?" She thrust it his direction.

"Go," Joe said, "I'll make the hot chocolate. Show it to him."

Kathleen pulled at Matt's shirt, dragging him back to the greenhouse.

On the back wall a sign dropped from the ceiling. *Kathleen's Garden*, it read in a fancy script with vines decorating the border. Plants adorned the space.

Her fingers reached to touch the leaves of the first offering. "This is a dogwood sapling."

Matt placed his finger on hers and traced the edges of the trunk. "And?"

"It means 'love undiminished by adversity'."

Matt's heart skipped a beat. An energy moved into the space that made him both excited and afraid.

She moved their fingers to the next plant. "Pink carnations." She pointed at the card stuck in the dirt. "Never forget you." Her voice softened with each word as if something sacred was happening. She handed him the letter. "Read it. Please."

He opened the envelope and took out the paper. Before he began he pulled Kathleen into his embrace.

Matt & Kathleen,

You've found it. You've found each other. I started growing this special garden the minute I returned from North Carolina. Remember, Kathleen, what we talked about?

Matt paused and looked to Kathleen for explanation.

"Flowers and plants, they have words of their own," she said before touching one of the blooms.

Tell Matt what each one means. Some of them are for you. Some of them are for him. Some are for what you two will be together.

Matt pulled her in closer, swallowing back the lump choking him. "Keep going."

"The next one." She extended her hand to the third plant, rubbing it between her fingers. She sniffed her fingers and then put her fingers to his nose. "Rosemary," she said, as she smelled it again. "Remembrance." She shivered in his arms but kept going. Using her other hand, she rubbed the next plant, smelled, and then pushed her fingers in his face. "Eucalyptus. Protection."

Matt put his hand on the plant. "I think that one's for me." He let a tear fall.

"Fennel. It has a strong smell and it means strength." She snickered as she touched a large pink bloom surrounded by red leaves. "Sugarbush."

"Soft," he said. "Does it having a meaning?"

"Courage. Is that for you or me, I wonder?" She nestled her body closer to his and forced them both to take a step nearer to the blooms.

"Both."

She twirled the pot around and touched each bloom.

"What are the last two?"

"That's celandine. A type of poppy. It represents joys to come." She turned in to his chest, wrapped her arms around his waist and cried.

Matt dropped his face into her neck, pulled her tighter, and let his own tears gather.

"The last one," Joe said from behind them. "Do you know that one?"

Kathleen pulled back, wiped her eyes, and turned to look at the last pot, which held the smallest plant of all. "It's still such a baby. I don't recognize it."

Joe moved in next to them. "She researched a while before she settled on this one." He rotated it. "Lily of the Valley."

Kathleen's breath sucked in and her body shuddered.

"What?" Matt asked his dad.

"It means—" Kathleen stopped and turned to Joe. "It means 'return of happiness.'"

Choking back tears, Matt said, "That one is for both of us."

"Finish the letter, please," she said.

It's time, Kathleen, to begin again. You can move forward and still remember. Take Matt's hand. Tell him your story. Tell him everything. Use his strength to rebuild yours.

This garden is now yours. Together, I expect you to come visit enough to take special care of it. And you are to take special care of each other.

Kathleen, thank you for loving my boy.

Mattie, I love you always.

~Mom

When they turned to each other they were alone with his mother's final, and most important, message.

LET ME INTRODUCE

Kathleen's high energy since leaving the garden began to disappear when they left for dinner. Dressed in a navy-blue dress and a jeweled scarf, she'd checked her scarf and her sunglasses over and over again as they'd driven the few miles to the hotel restaurant. Matt had tried to engage her in conversation about books or plants. Just like she had on the trip to Minnesota, she sat perfectly rigid the entire time. After making it through the revolving door, she reached back, found Matt's hand.

"I've got you." He dropped her hand but pulled her into his side, holding her close around the waist. He steered her towards the steakhouse at the rear of the space. The maître d' showed them to a table tucked in the back of the restaurant.

His father beamed at them when he rose and greeted Kathleen with a kiss on the cheek.

"I'm scared," Matt heard her whisper to his dad.

Matt looked to the table, found his sister's eyes and held them.

Her eyes were narrowed on him and her hand gripped the wine glass too tightly. "Little brother," she said with enough sarcasm to irk Matt.

"Patricia," he said as he pulled Kathleen away from his

dad and into his embrace. "Kathleen Bridges, this is my sister, Patricia. And next to her is my brother-in-law, Dave." Dave stood, shook first Matt's hand and then Kathleen's.

"Nice to meet you both," Kathleen said with a voice that to anyone but Matt sounded totally gracious. To Matt it sounded as strained as her body felt in his arms.

Keeping his eyes on Patti, he noted how his sister tracked Kathleen's movement to adjust her scarf. Frowning, he started to move in front of Kathleen when Patti rose, extended her hand, and said, "Kathleen. It's very nice to meet you."

"You, too," she said before looking up at Matt.

Guiding her to a seat next to his dad, he said, "When is Jess expected?"

"Now," an excited voice said behind him. "Sorry I'm late. Friday afternoon at the office." She hugged Matt and then pulled Kathleen in for an embrace. "I'm Jessica. And it's about time I got to meet you." Jessica pulled back, reached up, and clasped Kathleen's head in her hands before kissing her on both cheeks.

Matt stiffened, flattening his hand against Kathleen's back to gauge her response.

Jessica moved out almost as fast as she moved in. "Move over one," she said to Joe. "Let me sit next to her. You've had her all day."

As seats were adjusted, Matt noted the two extra places at the table. He also noted the look on Patti's face. Alarm bells began to ring and a cold warning moved up his spine. "Patti," he started but didn't get to finish.

Relief forced the breath from Matt when Nick and Sarah

moved toward their table. Shaking Nick's hand and kissing Sarah's cheek, he shifted to introduce Kathleen.

Kathleen stood next to him, but before he could say anything, Sarah said, "Marcia Conners."

Matt's head jerked to Sarah. Then it jerked to Patricia, who sat there with a sick grin. Before everything processed in his mind, his dad barked, "Matt."

Matt spun around, instinctively reaching for Kathleen only to have her slip out of his grasp. Slowed by the confusion, Matt stood helpless as Kathleen ran through the restaurant and into the lobby. Looking at his dad's harrowed face, he said, "Dad?"

"Go, Matt. Find her."

Rooted to the spot, Matt just stared at his father.

Joe's face reddened and his finger shook when he pointed it at Patricia. "How could you?"

Matt's head rotated to see Patricia wilt in her seat. "Dad?" he asked again with his eyes on Patricia.

"Matt," his father barked again. "Go. Find her. Now." Joe moved around the table and placed his hands on Matt's shoulders. "Mattie, we'll explain later. Right now, you need to find her. Look at me." He shook Matt's body.

"What's happening?"

"Go, Mattie. We'll join you in a second."

Nodding, Matt searched his father's face and then darted to the lobby with Jessica and Dave on his heels.

The three of them dispersed in the lobby.

"She's not here," he said when they met in the middle. "She's—" Matt shook his head, having no idea how to finish the sentence.

"Fragile," Jessica finished for him.

Matt cocked his head at Jessica and tried to determine what was wrong with her statement. "Strong," he corrected, running his hand through his hair, "and fragile."

"I'm sure we can find her. What the hell happened, anyway?" Dave added but didn't wait for an answer. "Go talk to the doorman. Jess and I will look around here more carefully."

"Call my cell if you find her. Don't approach her." Matt's eyes filled. "She—" He swallowed and wiped at his eyes. "I told her I'd keep her safe." His eyes held Jessica's.

"We'll find her," Jessica said. "Let's not worry about anything else until after we find her. Yes?"

Twenty minutes later they'd searched everywhere. The doorman had not seen her; the front desk had not seen her. The concierge had not seen her. The only place she could be was up. Twenty floors to hide.

"What the fuck did you do?" Matt roared and charged his sister when she and her father entered the lobby.

Joe stepped between his children and put his hands on Matt's chest. "Later, Matt. We'll deal with this later. Let's keep our focus on finding Kathleen."

Matt took a step back, glared at his sister before looking back to his father. "Dad, I promised her. I told her she'd be safe. I don't understand—"

"Where have you looked?"

"Everywhere."

"Dave, do two things for me. Get Patti to your room and

see that she stays there. Then call taxi companies. Maybe she slipped past the valet."

With an angry and confused expression, Dave grabbed Patti by the elbow and steered her toward the elevators.

"I want to help," Matt heard Patti say, but Dave kept her moving away from him.

"Jessica," Joe began, "I assume you checked the ladies' room. What about the men's?"

"I checked there," Matt said as his body began to fold in on him.

"Okay. Jess, go to all the floors that have public bathrooms. Check both the men's and women's."

When Jess rushed away, Joe turned back to Matt. "You need to buck up. I get you're scared, angry, confused. But right now, you have to find her. So stand up straight. Be the strength that woman needs."

Matt put his hands on his knees and stared at the floor for several long seconds. Then he stood to his full height, threw his shoulders back. "Find my girl." He looked at his father. "We've got this floor covered. Jess has bathrooms. Dave has taxi companies. Let's find out from the manager where all the public spaces are. Ballrooms, fitness center, everything. We can split those."

Joe hurried off just as Matt's phoned buzzed. "Yeah."

"Where are you?" Dave asked.

"Near the elevators. Did you find—"

Dave came spinning around the corner. "No luck with the taxis. They have a stand here. She would have had to use one of those. What do you want me to do next?"

"Check with Dad. See how far he's gotten. I'm going to check out the car and the garage." Matt's pulse picked up, his breathing accelerated.

"Okay, Matt, you're freaking out. And, seriously, if you don't calm down we have no hope of finding her, and when we do find her you can't help her like this."

"Right. She's fine. She's just sitting somewhere we haven't discovered. Waiting for me to take her home." He took several deep breaths. He closed his eyes then opened them. "Right."

"You're the only person here that knows her. You need to think, where would she go? Did she have money with her, a cell phone, did she know anybody here?"

"She brought nothing with her. She bought that outfit today and she didn't have or want to buy a purse. She said she didn't need it. She doesn't even own a cell phone. Her wallet is on my counter. Fuck, Dave, she doesn't even know my address." He sniffed in tears, rubbed his nose and cheeks. Forcing himself again to stand tall, he asked, "What else? Keep thinking."

"All right. Did you have a room booked here?"

"No. Fuck. No, we were going to spend the night at my place with a movie." He gave Dave a pained look. "I promised her a chick flick."

Dave's phone rang, causing them both to jump. He dug it out of his pocket. "Jess," he said, looking at Matt, "Hey. You find her?"

Matt paced in front of the elevators while Dave talked. When he hung up, Matt looked to him.

"No, they've searched everywhere. Even behind curtains.

She's not up there. She must have left the hotel."

They both glanced out the window at the end of the hall. "She didn't have a coat. Nothing." Matt walked to the window, placed his palm on the glass and looked out. "It's forty-five degrees and my Kathleen is in a strange city without money or any way to contact me." He forced a deep breath out. He turned wet eyes to Dave.

"We can look in the ballrooms that have parties. Maybe she just slipped in one of those and has blended in."

Matt's eyes closed again. The cold running up his back caused him to shiver. "Yeah, that makes sense. Do that." He didn't open his eyes. He just swayed from left to right.

Using a calm voice, Dave interrupted Matt's worry and dread. "Matt, go home. See if she's there. We'll start making calls, finish looking in all the ballrooms. If we can't find her then we'll call the police."

Matt's eyes tightened. One tear leaked down his face.

"Just go home. There's nothing you can do here and hopefully you'll find her waiting for you."

With his eyes still closed, Matt said, "Dave, we have to find her. She—she—fuck. She's all I've ever wanted. I promised I'd protect her. I can't do that if I can't find her. She's supposed to be *safe* with me."

"Take some deep breaths," Dave said as he began pulling him to the garage. He forced Matt into his car. "Call me when you get there. I'll call you if I learn anything new. Start thinking of where else we could look."

By the time Matt arrived at his condo, he had talked himself into believing Kathleen would be waiting for him.

Maybe she'd paid attention when they drove around and she did know his address. Maybe she'd convinced a cab to take her for free. His brain tried to tell him why those weren't reasonable predictions, but Matt forced himself to believe. With long steps, head held high, he strode into the elevator.

The hallway was empty. His condo was empty. His soul was screaming at him.

With forced self-control, Matt focused on finding Kathleen in a methodical, logical manner. He did everything he could think to do. He called the police. That was a waste of fucking time. He called his dad, Dave, and Jessica over and over again. He called the night manager at the hotel. Dave had already talked to him. Hospitals reported no patient matching her description.

Standing in his empty kitchen, his heart pounding and sweat pooling on his upper lip, he looked at his phone then at the ceiling "Fuck," he said before he dialed.

"Sam. It's Matt."

"Everything all right?"

"No. Kathleen. She…something happened. I'm not even sure what. She was there one minute and then she—"

"What, Matt? Talk to me."

Matt shook his head, trying to remember exactly what happened. All he remembered was Nick and Sarah arriving at their table and that look on his sister's face. As the memory began to coalesce, a knock on his condo door interrupted his thoughts. "She's here," he said to Sam as he hung up the phone. "Kath—" Shaking his head, he refocused. "Dave." His shoulders dropped with weariness. "Please tell me you found her. Please tell me you've come to get me to take me to her. Please, Dave, don't tell me she's still missing."

Dave pushed his way in. "Matt, let's go sit on the couch. Your dad and Jess are still looking, but I need to fill you in."

"No," Matt yelled, "just tell me. You obviously haven't found her or you'd be telling me."

Dave walked toward the leather couch in the magazine-worthy room. "I talked to Patti and I do have some news. Come sit down." Dave's hands shook, ratcheting up Matt's fear. "Matt, I just need you to sit down," Dave commanded. "I'll get us some water."

Matt slid onto the corner stool. "Just fucking tell me. Whatever it is. Just. Tell. Me." He scrubbed his hands through his hair, placed them on his knees, glared at Dave.

"Calm down, Matt." He handed him a glass of water.

He flung the water glass across the room, smashing it on the wall. Watching the water drip down, he said, "Sorry." Turning to look at Dave he said. "I'm all right. I just needed to get that out. Tell me."

Dave began to pace and his hands shook so badly he had to put the glass on the counter. "Do you remember what Sarah said when she came to the table?"

"No." He pulled on the roots of his hair, trying to remember. "Can you just get to the point?"

"Think, Matt. What did Sarah say to Kathleen?" Dave asked.

Matt cocked his head. "I shook Nick's hand, kissed Sarah. I was about to introduce them." Matt's body reared up, his eyes bulged, his nostrils flared. "Sarah called her Marcia Conners." His head spun to face Dave. His breath left him in a rush. "Oh, my god." He shook his head, trying to find his bearings. "How—I don't—"

"I didn't know," Dave said. "Patti, she was angry, worried. She took it upon herself to do some digging. You can find anything on the Internet. One thing led to another and she discovered the connection between Sarah and—Why didn't you tell us?"

"Because it's her story to tell," he yelled. His bottom lip trembled. Tears poured down his face. "Her family. Her entire family was slaughtered. Is that what you need to know?"

"What else did she tell you?" Dave asked calmly.

More confused than before, Matt wiped his nose with the back of his sleeve. With his palms, he wiped the tears away. Sitting at the counter, he answered, "A lot, Dave. She's told me a lot. What the fuck do you want?" Matt's voice rose, his words shook. "Do you want me to tell you she's missing an ear? That she's horribly scarred from her shoulder to her hip? That those monsters cut her and burned and sawed into her? What is it you want to know, Dave?" Matt, totally out of control, pushed himself out of the seat, paced up and down, swallowing past the lump, past the fear.

"Matt, think about something for me, okay?" Dave continued calmly. "What did she tell you about the *trial*? Did she ever talk about the trial?"

Matt rubbed his temples. "Is this going to help me find her?"

"I know this is hard. But I need you to think about this. What did she tell you?"

Matt thought back. Oscar, pictures, blood. The defense attorney he wanted to strangle. The defense attorney who had almost put the final nails in his Kathleen's coffin.

"Oh, my god. Please don't tell me," Matt whimpered as it all came together. He fell against one of the stools. "Sarah. Sarah was the defense attorney, wasn't she?" Matt's sobs shook his body.

"Yeah, she was."

Matt's eyes looked into Dave's. He grabbed Dave by the shoulders, shaking him. "We opened the door. The door, Dave. The birds, oh my fucking god." He dropped his hands. "God, Dave, what do I do? I don't know where to look." Matt's hands clutched Dave's arms. "I don't know what to do."

"Here is what we're going to do." Dave pealed Matt's fingers from his biceps. "You're going to eat something and you're going to think about where we should look."

"My Kathleen is out there somewhere hungry and you expect me to consider food?" Filled with rage, he pushed himself to his feet.

"Matt," he commanded. "When she sees you, she doesn't need to see what I'm seeing now. It would scare her even more. If you're supposed to be there for her, then you *fucking need to be there for her*. As far as food, if you don't eat you'll be totally useless. I didn't ask you to order in a five-course meal. But I'm telling you to put some food in your system. You've lost focus and you have to have focus to help us."

By the time Matt finished shoving soup into his mouth it was 12:20. His girl had been missing almost four hours. While he ate, Dave re-called the hospitals. Jess, he knew, was keeping in contact with the police, who at this point were unwilling to offer assistance. They worked with hotel management to search nooks and crannies. Reluctantly, the security staff was reviewing the video feeds.

"I think I'll head back to the hotel," Matt's dead voice spoke. He didn't move from the stool. He pushed the bowl away, lowered his head on folded arms. "Mom, help me."

"I don't think that's what you should do."

Matt didn't lift his head. "I can't just sit here. When this happened last time—"

"What do you mean 'happened last time'?" Dave interrupted.

"At the beach. I pushed too hard. She ran. It took us a while but we found her. On the beach, sitting in the sand." Matt's head lifted and settled into his palms. He looked at Dave through the reflection of the refrigerator. He shook his head, lost focus.

"What was she doing while you were looking for her?"

"Walking. She walks everywhere. Dave," Matt shifted his chair so he could look at him. "Her toes were bleeding. She'd walked in the sand for hours."

Dave said nothing for a while. "I think that gives us good information. It might simply be that she's walking the streets."

"It's forty-five degrees or colder. Downtown Minneapolis has some rough areas. She has no idea where she is." He snorted. "Yeah, good information."

Dave pulled his phone out. "This is Dave Johnson. You've been speaking with Jessica Sanders about the missing woman. It may be that she's walking the streets. Something like this happened before and she just walked." He listened. "Great. I'll have my phone."

"Who was that?"

"The police officer I spoke with earlier. Jess has told her a bit more of the story. She agreed they needed to get involved. She's going tell the officers near the hotel to spread out more on the streets."

Matt let his eyes drift to the ceiling. He pulled his own phone out, scrolled to the number he needed. "Sam. We haven't found her. Has she called you? You are the one number I know she knows." Matt's lip started to tremble again. "Sam, you can yell at me all you want later. Just call me if you hear anything." With gentle fingers Matt hit 'end'. Looking at Dave, he explained. "That was Kathleen's friend— one of only two. He built the interior of her beach house. If she knows how to reach anyone, it will be him."

Matt looked at his phone. 1:33. He rose from his chair and started to clean broken glass. "We had such a great day and she looked so pretty tonight," he said to the shards. "Just one second. I let go for one second."

"We'll find her." Dave sounded confident, reassuring.

Matt walked to his bedroom. On the dresser sat Kathleen's iPod and her current book. He ran his fingers over them. He sat on her side of the bed. "I never thought I'd have a side," he said to the pillow. "I need you to come back. I won't let go again. I won't lose focus." Looking around the room, a new memory found him. Matt popped off the bed, ran back to the kitchen. "Closets," Matt yelled as he came into the kitchen. "Tell everyone to start checking closets. That's where she'll be." Matt snatched up his keys.

Before Matt could explain more, his phone rang. The noise

echoed off the windows and granite.

Matt and Dave stared at the phone as it skittered across the counter.

Dave's eyes lifted to Matt and he grabbed for the phone. "This is Dave Johnson."

Matt's eyes widened as he tried to decipher what was being said and by whom.

"He's right here." Dave extended the phone. "It's Jessica."

Matt snatched the phone and turned to face the windows. "Jessica?"

"We found her."

Matt's head hit the window. "Thank God." Matt started to pace. "Where is she? Is she all right? Is she hurt?" Matt couldn't get the words out fast enough.

"Matt, I need you to collect yourself."

He took a deep breath but failed to collect himself. "Jessica, just talk."

"The housekeeper found her asleep in the supply closet on the sixth floor. She doesn't seem to be hurt. I think she's just asleep. She's obviously been crying—mascara is all over her face. We've put a blanket over her and the hotel manager is calling an ambulance. Your dad and I are just a few feet from the door which we've left open about an inch."

"You said she was fine. What's the ambulance for? You said she was fine. Is she fine—" Dave pulled the phone from his hand.

"Jessica, it's Dave. Hold on a second."

Matt placed his chest against Dave's, shoved him back a foot. "What do you think—"

"You were throwing questions at her. Not even listening to answers." Dave put the phone back to his ear. "All right, Jessica. I think I got enough from listening to Matt. *Do* not compromise her health. We will be there in ten minutes. If the paramedics get there before we do, see if they can wait on us. I truly think it would be best if Matt could be there first, but Jessica, you need to do what's right for her."

Dave clicked off and chased Matt running down the hallway.

DEATH SENTENCE

Eight minutes later Matt stood outside the supply closet. His Kathleen lay curled into a ball, surrounded by mops, buckets and cleaning supplies. No scarf. Her bare feet stuck out of the hotel blanket, her only mattress a cold, dirty, concrete floor.

"Mr. Gubbins, right?" Matt asked the hotel manager.

"Yes, sir." The bespectacled man twisted his hands together and clucked either his worry or his annoyance.

"Here's what I want to do." Matt's tone allowed for no argument. "When the ambulance team arrives, have them ready and waiting down by the elevator. My father will give them an update." He nodded at Joe standing two feet away.

"Dad." He looked at the tired man. "Tell them the situation. But she's had some pretty bad experiences with medical people. They need to give me a chance to coax her. I need you to handle that." Without waiting for a reply, he turned back to the manager. "Once they're in position, I'll wake her. I want *no one* near us. *No one.* I don't want her eyes to land on anyone but me. Can you do that?"

"Yes sir. I'll get the nearby rooms vacated."

"I want her off that floor in less than twenty minutes."

Matt pointed to the radio on the man's belt. "Have someone bring me more blankets. She has to be freezing, and that is unacceptable."

"I'll get you the blankets and get started on moving guests. I think the ambulance will be here any second." The manager walked away, speaking into his radio.

While everyone else got to work, Matt entered Kathleen's closet. She hadn't moved. Lying down next to her, he bit down on his forefinger, fighting the urge to touch her. He felt desperate to see her eyes, check her for injury, hear her voice, kiss her. But he couldn't risk waking her until everything was in place.

Twenty-two minutes later Dave opened the door slightly and whispered, "Everything's ready, Matt. What do you want us to do?"

Matt stood and followed Dave to the hallway. "First, ask the manager if there's a way to dim the lights in this hallway. Then, ask the paramedics to stay near the elevator until I call for them." Matt looked down the hallway. His father, Jessica, the manager, and two paramedics all stared his direction. "Once I wake her...depending on how that goes..." Matt shook his head, swallowed. "Let me just wake her and we'll go from there." Dave nodded and turned to walk away when Matt grabbed him. "Listen. I have no idea what state she's going to be in. Do not let anyone come down here until I tell you."

Dave's eyes widened.

"No matter what you hear, Dave."

"Matt—"

"Trust me, Dave. I've got her. I won't let anything happen." Matt pushed Dave down the hall.

A few seconds later, the hallway lights dimmed and Matt re-entered the closet. He sat down and carefully lifted her head into his lap. "Kathleen, love," Matt said softly as he allowed his fingers to trace her cheek. "I need you to wake up."

Her eyes didn't even flutter.

"Kathleen." Matt raised his voice and applied a bit more pressure. "We need to get you off this floor. Wake up for me?"

Still she didn't respond

Matt rubbed his forehead, trying to decide how to proceed.

"Kathleen," Matt said with the authority she'd responded to many times before. "I need you to wake up now. Open your eyes, love. I'm the only one here."

She didn't open her eyes. Instead she shut them more tightly.

Matt let his breath go. "Good girl." He palmed her cheek. "Now that I know you hear me, you need to open your eyes."

She didn't respond.

"I need to see your eyes. I *need* to see them. Please love, *look* at me."

Tears began to spill down her face from under her closed lids. Matt stroked her cheek and leaned down to kiss her mouth. "Kathleen, I've got you," he murmured. "Open your eyes and let's go home."

Her eyes clamped tighter. "I don't want to see anymore." She choked on her tears. "I had the doors locked. I had put the images away," she hissed as her hand moved to claw at her ear.

Matt grabbed her hand, pinned it to his chest.

Her eyes flared open, and even in the dim light, Matt could see the dark gray.

Her eyes drifted closed again. "*Your* Sarah, she loved making me look at every picture. She started with the dog." Her voice stopped on a sob. "She loved it."

Matt fought back a combination of anger and nausea. He kept his palm on her cheek and her hand away from her face.

"Listen to me. I want you to open your eyes, *right now*."

Angry, gray beams shot at him.

"Okay, love, that's a beginning. Now, let me tell you the plan. I'm going to walk with you every step of the way. There will be no surprises. But, Kathleen, there will also be no arguments. We are leaving this closet in the next minute. Do you understand?"

She didn't respond, but her eyes flared at him. He didn't, couldn't, care right now. He was getting her out of this damn closet.

"First, I'm going to run my hands over you and check for injuries. You let me know if anything hurts."

She just stared into his face as his hands roamed over her.

"Do you feel any pain?"

Kathleen shook her head, but she did not blink or otherwise move.

"Okay, step two. I'm going to get off this floor and then I'm going to pick you up. If I hurt you in any way, you tell me immediately and we'll figure out another way. Do you understand?"

She nodded but otherwise remained motionless.

Matt laid her hand on her chest, raised himself and then struggled to pull the dead weight into his arms.

Her head fell back over his arm, her eyes wide and still unblinking.

"Put your head in my neck. Tuck yourself in."

When she nuzzled into his collar he finally took a deep breath. He kissed the top of her head. "Wrap your arms around me."

Matt pushed the closet door open all the way. "The lights are dimmed, but keep your head tucked in." He made his way into the hall and turned toward the elevators.

Heading that way, he bent to Kathleen's face and gave her several kisses before he told her what to expect. "Okay, love, I have paramedics waiting."

A feral response hit Kathleen. Her legs kicked out. Like a cat dropped in a scalding pot, her back bowed as she tried to get out of his arms.

He clutched her to him, stumbled and stopped walking.

An inhuman wail emanated. Her pupils dilated so that no color showed. Screeching, she clawed at his cheeks, went for his eyes.

He tipped his face up, pulled her even tighter. "Kathleen, please stop."

She clawed at his neck, her body thrashing as the wail increased in volume.

Matt saw the paramedics and Dave rushing down the hall. "Stop," he said. "I've got her." The men stopped. "Dave, I'm asking you to keep them back," he spoke over Kathleen's rant. Still twenty yards away from help, he put his back to the wall and slid down.

"No hospital, no doctors, no ambulance. No one touches me," her wails turned to words. Words wild with fear and fury.

"Matt," his dad said frantically from behind the paramedics. "We have…"

Clamping both of her hands in one of his, he yelled down the hall. "Back them up, Dad. Do whatever it takes, but all of you back way the hell up." He wrapped his free hand around her neck and pulled her flailing body into him.

"Shhh, Kathleen, shhh," Matt crooned to her. "Shhh, I've got you. Let's just sit here for a few minutes."

Her energy gave out as quickly as it had come. One second she was fighting, the next she'd curled into stillness. "No hospital, Matt, no hospital," she begged over and over.

"Shh, love. Shh." Matt's head nuzzled into the back of her neck. "Kathleen, listen, I can't—I have to be sure you're okay." He turned his body so that she was tucked between the wall on one side and him on the other, completely blocked from the audience.

When she finally settled enough for his words to penetrate he said, "Kathleen, we need to make a deal, okay?"

"I tried, Matt, I really did," she barely spoke.

He nuzzled deeper and spoke loudly enough for the first responders to hear him. "Here's what we need to do. I can't take you home without knowing you are uninjured. I *can't* do that. So I'm going to have *one* paramedic, just one, meet us right here on the floor."

Her head began to thrash.

"Kathleen, hear me out. I'll hold you the entire time. He'll tell you everything he's going to do before he does it."

"He'll see me. He'll have to look. I don't want him to see me, Matt. Only you."

Matt looked up to see one paramedic had gotten closer. "I think he can check you out just fine through your dress." Matt looked at the man for confirmation.

The paramedic pursed his lips, but he nodded.

"Oh, Matt, I'm so sorry. I thought I was ready. I wanted to be ready," she cried into his chest.

"You are ready. This is one of those setbacks. Tomorrow we move forward, just like we've done before. We get through today and then the sun comes up tomorrow and we face it together." Matt nodded for the paramedic to come closer.

"I think this is a death sentence," she said as her eyes drifted closed and her body stilled.

Alarmed at the words and at the look on the paramedic's face, Matt silently pleaded for him to be careful, to be gentle, to let him take his Kathleen home. Keeping his eyes trained on the man, Matt said, "Love, I'm going to shift you around and then settle you back in my lap. He can't see you like we are now," Matt said as he made the necessary adjustments.

The paramedic moved closer.

Kathleen's body began to tremble.

"Keep your eyes closed. I'm right here." He squeezed her. "Take a second to feel my arms and legs around you. Can you feel them? I'm not going to leave, and he won't be doing anything to you that I can't see and monitor. Feel me, just focus on that. We will keep you tucked into me as tight as we can. When he wants to check your arm, we'll give him only that."

"Mrs. Bridges," the paramedic began.

"Kathleen, call her Kathleen," Matt told him when he felt her body jolt.

"Kathleen, my name is Evan. I'm just going to check you out and then we'll get you out of here. I'm going to check your blood pressure, and while that does its thing, I'm going shine a light in your eyes. Okay?"

Kathleen didn't respond, but she didn't fight him, either.

Matt pulled Kathleen's arm out and watched as the paramedic applied the machine. Matt tilted her head back gently as Evan carefully peeled open one eye, then the other.

She slammed them closed so fast Matt could not see the color.

"Now, I'm going to feel your head. I want to be sure there are no bumps or cuts that may have caused a concussion."

"No, Matt, don't let him do that, please." She tucked into a tighter ball.

"Let him just get it done. He'll do it quickly."

Kathleen's death grip tightened and the shaking returned.

Matt saw the man wince at the ear. Evan tilted his head, indicating to Matt that he needed to look. Matt shifted Kathleen so he could see.

Blood pooled into the open hole. The raw skin was scratched deep in many places. Chunks of hair had been ripped from the roots. Matt closed his eyes, trying to calm his racing heart.

"I'm just going to go over your body. You'll feel me squeeze in different areas. If that causes any discomfort, let me know.

I'm checking mainly for broken bones. I'll start at your neck and work my way down. Do you understand?"

"No, please," she begged him.

"Kathleen, love, he's not going to remove your clothes. He's just going to use his hands. He won't see anything, I promise."

Evan nodded his understanding again. Sadness replaced Evan's frustration. When he got to her hands, he nodded again for Matt to look. Steeling himself this time, Matt glanced down. Kath's fingernails were broken off. Some of her nail beds bled. Where her ring finger used to be, the flesh oozed fresh blood.

Turning her hands over, both Matt and Evan saw more claw marks and fingernail indentations so deep that blood had congealed.

Evan's hands briefly touched up and down Kathleen's torso, testing for broken or bruised ribs or other painful areas. Finding none, he quickly moved to her legs where he showed Matt scraped and bloody knees. "Crawling," the paramedic mouthed at him.

Matt swallowed hard.

Evan removed the blood pressure monitor but remained kneeling. "Okay, Kathleen, I'm done." His gaze moved from Kathleen to Matt. "Let me go talk to my partner and I'll be right back."

Kathleen curled into a tighter ball and twisted Matt's shirt in her hands. Matt bent his knees, confining her more tightly. Rubbing her cheeks and placing his forehead against hers, he whispered how proud he was, how tomorrow would be here soon, how much he loved her. Soon her hold on his shirt opened, her head lolled back, and she slept. Focusing exclusively on her, Matt jumped when a strong hand landed on his shoulder. Turning his head, he faced his father's sad face.

Stooping down to Matt's eye level and keeping his hand on his shoulder, Joe said, "The good news is that physically she seems fine. Blood pressure's up but they felt that was to be expected. She does have a lot of cuts that need attending."

Matt saw his father's lips move but he didn't actually register the words.

"Matt." He shook him, "I need you to listen. We do have one issue that needs to be handled."

Matt blinked, took in a deep breath and focused.

"Because of her situation, her history, and"—Joe swallowed, tightened his hold on Matt's shoulder—"because of what she said, we are going to have to take her to the hospital."

As the words penetrated, Matt tried to scoot away, but Joe pressed in harder, preventing any movement. "Dad—"

"They've given us no option." Joe looked over his shoulder at the small group.

Matt's eyes followed Joe's, landing on the police officer standing between them and the paramedics.

"Dad?" Matt's voice quivered as his body folded around Kathleen.

"Listen, Mattie, we don't have a choice. But I did get them to agree to let you ride in the ambulance."

Tears dropped from Matt's eyes onto her neck. "Dad, please don't let them take her from me."

"Matt." Joe's voiced changed from tender to one that expected obedience, the same voice he had used with

Kathleen. "That option is no longer available to us. If we fight them on that, then we risk being barred from being with her at all. Now, focus. Find that strength, lean on my strength. Tell me what we *can do* right now to help you help her."

Matt blinked at his father, tried to think, tried to create a plan.

"They are not going to wait much longer."

Matt's eyes darted to the cluster of people to see Evan, flanked by the officer, begin to steer the gurney in his direction.

He looked to his father. "First, when I stand up, get the phone out of my pocket. Find the number for Stephanie Culberson in my contacts. Call her. Tell her everything. Ask her to give you the contact information for Lisa Bartlett. Call her as soon as it's reasonable. Somehow get her on the phone. Tell her whatever you need to get her to help us." He winced as the gurney got closer. "Evan, please give me a couple of minutes to get things organized." He glanced at Kathleen's sleeping face.

Evan halted, staring at Matt for a long second. "Two minutes, then we have to get moving."

Matt nodded both his thanks and his comprehension. "Jessica," he called down the hall.

Jessica shoved the officer out of her way.

"I need you to go to my house. There's a bag of books we bought from Barnes and Noble today. There's a small Christmas package in the outer pocket of my luggage. Grab that, too."

"I'll leave right now." She turned but stopped when Matt called her name again.

"Get her some scarves, Jess." He swallowed back tears, forced his shoulders up. "Get several of my t-shirts." He closed his eyes as he tried to think of anything else. Opening his eyes, he said, "Go. Just get anything, anything at all, you think will bring her comfort."

The gurney rolled closer. "Mr. Nelson, it's time. Greg is going to come down here and help me get her settled on the gurney. I've spoken to the doctors at the ER. They've authorized a sedative. As quickly as we can we'll get an IV going and give her a sedative. She's asleep right now. If she wakes, we'll have her back to sleep in just a few minutes. I've also told them who you are, your relationship with Mrs. Bridges based on a conversation with your father and Mrs. Sanders. They'll treat you like family until she tells them otherwise."

"Thank you." Matt tried to control his rattled breath. "I'll put her on the gurney," he said as he used every ounce of energy he had left to stand. "Kathleen," he whispered into her ear. "Love, we're going to get some medicine in you. Fluids. You just stay asleep. This will all be over soon." Kissing her cheek, he moved to the gurney.

She moaned when he released her but did not open her eyes.

Leaning close to her face, Matt held her cheeks with both hands as Evan and Greg secured her with straps and placed the blood pressure cuff back on her arm.

"Pressure's better. I'm about to stick her," Evan said.

Matt swallowed the lump and put his nose against hers.

Blue eyes blazed open and Kathleen's body rocked up

against the restraints.

"Kathleen," Matt stayed as close as he could, "I've got you."

"Kathleen," Evan said. "Can you count backwards from ten for me?"

Her body increased its speed and her eyes faded to gray. Matt knew she was not in that hallway with him.

"Mr. Nelson, count for her."

"Ten, nine, eight, seven—" With his thumb he wiped the tear he'd dripped on her face. "Six, five."

Her eyes fluttered closed, her body stilled.

"She's out," Evan said. "Let's move."

The gurney rushed down the hall with Matt holding on.

PROMISES I COULDN'T KEEP

Like a caged animal, Matt paced the emergency waiting room. When they'd taken her away, Kathleen had still been sedated, but that had been over twenty minutes ago.

"Matt," Joe said as he stepped in front of his pacing son.

"If she wakes up—Dad, if she wakes up surrounded by all of this—" Matt shook his father.

"They will come and get you as soon as they can. I was able to reach Stephanie and Dr. Bartlett. I'm not sure but I believe they'd talked recently because she seemed to be pretty updated. Can you pay attention and hear what she said?"

Matt dropped his arms and took a few deep breaths. "Tell me."

"She's coming here. But she's not licensed in Minnesota and she does not have privileges at this hospital. Today she's pretty sure they will get her wounds treated, keep her pretty sedated until they get a psych consult. She's already sent up some information for the consulting doctor to see. She's hoping they'll hold off any decisions until she gets here. But remember she can't control that."

Matt nodded and then looked to the ceiling.

"Matt, what can I—"

Matt pushed off the walls, nostrils flaring, fists forming. "Why is she here?" he asked the question to Dave, but he kept his eyes pinned to his sister. "Why would you?" Matt roared as he met his sister in the middle of the space. "I knew. I've always known—I just never wanted to see it. Did you want to destroy her or me?"

"I, I—"

"That's a yes or no question. Did you get what you wanted, Patricia? Do you finally have all the control? Are you happy now that my life is hard, too?" Red-faced, screaming, Matt fought for breath.

"Matt," Dave said as he tried to step between the siblings. "Settle down some or that cop will force you out of here."

Clenching his teeth, Matt took one step backwards and turned his narrowed eyes on his dad. "Tell her to answer me."

"Lower your voice. You don't want to give them reason not to let you see Kathleen."

"Dad," Matt's voice lowered but the menace increased.

"I knew," Patricia said. "I didn't realize—"

Matt swirled and only Dave's body prevented him from crashing into the object of his rage. Lifting his finger, he pointed over Dave's shoulder and into his sister's face. "Get out of here. Never fucking come near me or mine again."

"Matt, let me expla—" she began with a quivering voice.

"Dave, you want to help me? Then get her the fuck out of this hospital. Keep her away from me." Matt shoved his finger into Dave's chest. "Get that bitch. Out. Of. Here."

On some distant plane of Matt's consciousness, he heard

Joe's intake of breath, Patricia's whimper and Dave's attempts to convince her to leave. "Just get her out of here. Please," Matt said as he slumped into a chair, folded his arms on his knees, and rested his head.

Before he could restrain the rage, a nurse said, "Matt Nelson. I'm looking for Matt Nelson."

Darting up, Matt met her at the door of the emergency room. "Kathleen? How is she?"

"I'm Jackie, her nurse. She's asleep. She woke up for only a few seconds and we gave her another sedative. She should sleep for a while, but we'll be keeping a close eye on her."

"Can I go to her?"

"Follow me." She looked behind Matt at the people gathered around him. "But let's keep it to just you. We're trying to keep her in a calm environment."

"We'll be here, Matt. Keep us posted," Joe said.

Matt didn't turn, didn't acknowledge his father's words. He carried his relief and worry as he followed the nurse.

Just outside the door to room 7, Jackie stopped. "She has a lot of bandages. Especially around her ear and fingers. But don't let that make you anxious." She smiled at him. "We have a tendency to overdo things like that. She didn't require any stitches, so she'll be healed in just a day or two if we keep it all clean and coated with ointment." She reached a hand out and clasped his arm. "If you need me, just push the button." She pointed down the hall. "I'll be right there for the next ten hours. You can stay as long as you like."

Nodding, he said, "I'm not leaving." He stepped around her and pushed through the door.

Standing inside, Matt's knees began to buckle. Bandages created a gauze helmet around Kathleen's head. Tubes ran into her arms and under her blankets. Red lights, green lights, blue lights blinked in a pulsating rhythm. Closing his eyes, Matt forced the bile down, breathing to the rhythm of the maddening beeps.

His Kathleen lay so still, so pale in the dim light. Her left hand rested outside the blanket. Where her ring finger should be, mounds of gauze sat. Each fingertip was wrapped.

Ignoring the beeps, buzzes, and drips, Matt moved to the bed. Leaning over to kiss her cheeks, her eyelids, her mouth, he muttered his apologies, his love, his commitment, his promises.

"Hey," a voice whispered from the door.

Without moving his face away from hers, he turned his crying eyes toward Jess. "Jess," he pleaded.

She moved into the room. "Let me in for a second." She bent to kiss Kathleen's forehead. "Betty's looking out for you," she whispered. Standing, she looked at Matt. "I brought all the stuff. It's just inside the door. I'm going to sit with her while you change, wash your face, clean up a bit."

"No, Jess. I'm not leaving this room."

"Look down, Matt."

He looked at his chest. His white shirt was ripped and had small blood stains from Kathleen's episode. Touching the spots, he frowned.

"She does not need to see that. You have your own cuts to doctor. When she wakes up she needs to see a man she can trust and depend on to help her make the next step."

Matt raised his eyes to Jess. Sliding his hand down Kathleen's arm, he tried to pull her hand into his. Blinking at the resistance, Matt stared down and then felt a new rage build. "Holy fuck," he said through clamped teeth as he held Kathleen's arm so Jess could see. "They have her strapped down in this bed." Carefully he replaced her arm under the blanket, leaned across to her left arm. Lifting it, he found another strap. "Holy fuck." His head began to shake. "No way, no way. Jess, go get the nurse. I want these off her." He started searching for a way to remove them.

"Matt," Jess said from behind him. "They aren't going to take them off." She used her hands to stop his search. "They can't. Not yet."

Matt looked over his shoulder at Jess. "What? Why? I'm here. I won't let anything happen to her."

Jess held Matt's face just like he'd held Kathleen's earlier. "Mattie, they can't. You understand that. It's just for a few hours and she'll sleep through most of it." She patted his cheek and dropped her hands. "Now, go change." She moved in front of him, settled in the chair, found Kathleen's hand under the blankets and began talking to her.

Matt backed away, swiped at his face. He found the bag Jess had left, ducked into the en suite bath and made himself presentable.

"I'm back. Go home. Sleep." He helped Jess stand. He hugged her tight and then settled into the chair, found his Kathleen's hand.

"I'll be here. Your dad is here. Dave is here. We'll be here at least until we know what's next." She kissed the top of his head.

Turning back to his Kathleen he tucked one of his t-shirts behind her neck. With one hand, he held her, and with the other, he propped open one of the books she'd bought that day. "Okay, love, you listening?" He began reading to her.

<<<>>>

"Here," his father said, startling Matt from the book he'd been reading. "Food, coffee. And I'm guessing you could use a bathroom break."

"That's okay. I'm fine," he said wearily.

"Go. You need to be good, not fine. I'll be right here. You'll be gone sixty seconds and only ten feet away." Joe moved next to Kathleen's bed. "Has she woken up?"

"No. She hasn't moved." He showed his father the harnesses holding her to the bed. "I actually hope she doesn't until I can persuade someone to get these off her."

Joe reached down, touched the harness and then looked at Matt. "I'm sorry this happened."

"The one thing I was warned about was her getting triggered and it all exploding open." Matt swallowed, looked first at Kathleen and then at his father. "I thought of all places she'd be safe here. I thought my family," he choked back the sob, "would be safe for her."

"We'll make her safe, Mattie. I promise you."

Matt caressed her cheek. "She told me just after I met her not to make promises I couldn't keep."

Without waiting for a response, Matt went to the bathroom and washed his face. Returning to Kathleen's side, he found his father reading to his girl. With an aching chest, Matt

386

leaned against the wall, ate the bagel and drained the coffee.

"Take a nap," his father said after Matt had thrown the trash away.

"No. Not that. I can't do that."

"Matt—"

"Go home, Dad. You sleep for both of us. When her eyes open, I want her to see mine."

Joe moved out of the chair and Matt moved back in.

"Sam called."

Puzzled, Matt looked at Joe.

"I still have your phone." He pulled it out of his pocket. "I filled him in. He said to tell you that both he and Rosie can be on the next plane. I told them to wait and I'd call them after you meet with the doctor."

"Right. I hope we're not here long enough to need that."

Joe said from the door, "Dave is getting Dr. Bartlett from the airport in about an hour. He's bringing her straight here. Jess got her a room at the Marriott."

Looking at his father, Matt said, "Thanks." He took a deep breath and added, "Dave needs to tell her exactly what happened and why it happened."

Joe winced but nodded in agreement. "Love you, Mattie-boy."

Matt closed his eyes. "I know, Dad. I love you, too." When he opened his eyes, he was alone again with his Kathleen.

Caressing her arm, he said, "Lisa's on her way, love. She'll be here before you wake up. She's going to help us." He lowered his head to rest on her bandaged fingers.

<<<>>>

"Matt," Dave whispered and shook Matt awake.

Jerking up, Matt looked around and blinked the sleep from his eyes. "Shit," he said as he turned to Kathleen. Finding her still asleep, he let out a long breath. "How long have I been asleep?"

"No idea. I just got here with Dr. Bartlett. But she's fine. I spoke with the nurse. She checked in about thirty minutes ago and all was okay. She thought it best to let you sleep. You want to take a few minutes to freshen up? Dr. Bartlett—Lisa—is meeting with the attending physician right now."

Matt bent to Kathleen's face. "Love, you need to get ready to wake up. Lisa's here and we've got work to do." He nuzzled his nose against hers. "It's time for you to come back to me. Dave's here. I'll be back but you won't be alone." He kissed her lips. Turning to Dave, he said, "I won't be far—in that hallway. If she wakes up, if she even stirs, call me."

After Dave nodded Matt splashed water on his face and prepared to find the hospital doctor and Dr. Bartlett. Just before he opened the door he said, "Dave, I know it sounds crazy, but don't touch her." Without waiting for a reply, he charged out.

I DID IT

Finding Dr. Bartlett was easy. Standing just outside Kathleen's door, Matt stumbled into two people with their heads together.

"Lisa? Dr. Bartlett?"

The woman blinked up at him. "Lisa's fine. I assume you're Matt Nelson?"

Shaking his hand and tilting her head toward the man in the white coat, she said, "This is Dr. Vickery. He's the attending physician. He assures me Kathleen's physical injuries are minor."

Matt shook the man's hand and muttered some sort of thanks, but he kept his attention on Lisa. "They have her tied down."

With a sad smile, she said, "I know. I'll speak with the on-call psychiatrist. There's not much we can do about that for now. And Matt, she needs to wake up so we can assess where she is."

Matt started to speak, but Lisa stopped him with a touch on his forearm. "I've already got a call in to him. We are fast-tracking this as best we can. Please don't get agitated and impatient. That will just make everything more difficult."

He nodded but bit his lip in frustration.

"I'll be making my rounds in a few minutes," Dr. Vickery said. "In the meantime, you two can talk in a conference room." He pointed down the hall before walking away.

Matt stopped Lisa before she headed the direction indicated. "I don't want to be that far away. Can we just talk here?"

She stared at him for a few seconds and then pressed her back against the opposite wall. "Your brother-in-law gave me an update," she said. "I also heard from Stephanie. I know this is exactly what you didn't want to happen. But now that it has, we simply deal with it."

Matt mirrored her posture. He clenched his fists and asked, "How do we deal with it?"

"Let's talk about that in a second. Tell me how you're doing."

He flattened his palms against the wall and took a deep breath before replying. "Fine. I'm fine."

"Let's start over. One of the most important aspects of this process—of helping Kathleen—is honesty. When I ask you a question, I need you to be as open and honest as you can." She stared at him, waiting.

Matt closed his eyes for several seconds as he took in more air. After wiping his lip, he opened his eyes. "I'm scared out of my mind. Scared for her. Scared for me. Scared because I just don't know what to do and I *always* know what to do."

"You should be scared. If you stood before me all calm, cool and collected I'd be worried. What I need to know is if you are up to whatever we might face."

Matt didn't look at her. He didn't lift his head. "That's the third time I've been asked something like that. Do not ask me that again. I'm here. I'm staying here. Talk to me about what we do for her."

"That's up to her."

Matt's eyebrows drew together and his fists flexed open and shut. "What? What does that mean?"

"Kathleen is the only one who can decide if she wants to face this. It's an uphill climb that she knows well. She may not—"

Lurching from the wall, Matt shoved his hands in his hair. "And if she doesn't want to get well?"

Lisa didn't change her posture. Her voice remained calm. "Then she doesn't. She could go back to that beach or…"

"No, don't say it. Do not say that." Matt collapsed against the wall, bent in half and moaned. Keeping his head between his knees, he said, "If she wants to go back to that beach, then we go back there. If we're twenty steps back, then we inch forward." He lifted his head and stared up at her.

"Look, let's not jump to any conclusions. The doctor says she hasn't awakened. Once she does we'll see where we are. Why don't we head back in there? I'd like to see her for myself, and I know you want to be there and not here."

Before she opened Kathleen's door, Matt clasped his hand on her bicep. "Do not give up on her."

"Never. I've never given up on her." She squeezed his hand and then entered the room.

"She hasn't moved," Dave whispered. "I'll be in the lobby if you need anything."

Matt took his seat as Lisa approached the bed.

"Crawled?" she mouthed when she saw the knee jutting from under the blanket.

Matt tucked her more securely under the covering. "We think so. Can you explain why she goes to a closet?"

She adjusted the tubes and sat on Kathleen's bedside. "That's where she was found."

Continuing to caress his Kathleen's arm, he looked at Lisa and braced.

"Somehow she managed to crawl to the closet. Stephanie found the carnage. According to her, Kathleen was bleeding profusely and unconscious in a small kitchen closet." She smoothed the blankets and held his gaze. "I was there when she woke up in the hospital. I've never seen anything like it. One minute she'd be catatonic. The next she'd be raging." She picked up Kathleen's arm, pointing at the restraints. "We'd think we had her sedated but she'd fly out of her bed. We had to keep those on her for weeks. Before the trial we had gotten her to talk about her family. She was up to December 23rd. The day before the attack, she and Stephanie went on a long hike where they talked and laughed about nothing and everything." Lisa stood and paced. "Then the trial." She looked at Matt. "It's important you understand that until that trial she had never, not once, talked about that day. We were working that way slowly. That attorney—"

Matt winced and dug his fingers into his thighs.

"She never came back after that. She never tried. She wouldn't go to group. She'd sit with me for our sessions and answer only yes or no questions. She wouldn't see her family or her friends."

"Wait," Matt said, "what family?"

"Seth has a brother and sister. It was the brother who found my name and the Center. He persuaded me to go visit her. She's the only person I've ever tried to treat while she was still in a hospital. They stayed in Charlotte for weeks. And once we had her at the Center, the brother, sister, and Stephanie rotated. Someone was there every Sunday for visitation. They'd bring pictures and talk. They kept her supplied with new books. They were helping her heal."

Flustered at this news, Matt cocked his head. "What happened? Why did they stop coming?"

"They didn't stop coming. Kathleen just refused to see them. She took them off the approved contacts list. And then she moved. Only I knew where she went, but I couldn't tell them because of patient confidentiality. She refused to see or talk to anyone..." Lisa paused until he made eye contact. "Until your mother. Until you."

Swallowing, Matt stared into the woman's brown eyes. "I'm still here. She'll come back again. I know she will." After several long minutes of silence, Matt commented, "I'm surprised you're being so open."

She lifted then dropped her shoulders, giving him a small smile. "Well, most of what I've told you is part of public record and media coverage." She shrugged again, moved to take Kathleen's hand. "I spoke to the nurses. I know what happened last night. I figure if she decides to try again she'll need you. And"—she looked at Matt with a penetrating stare—"if she doesn't want to try none of this will matter. Matt, she may not. You need to come to terms with that."

She moved back to the wall. Her cheeks bloomed red. Her voice no longer maintained calm. "The lawyer started with a picture of the dog. Her handprint was in the dog's blood. Poor Kathleen froze. I don't think she actually heard what that woman said. She stared at that picture, and then she traced the dog's face. 'T-bone,' she whispered from the stand."

Tears dripped down Matt's face, but he forced himself to hear the details.

"Next came the babies. Shot, one bullet to each head." She began to pace. "I'll never forget it. The boy's eyes were the same color as Kathleen's."

"Enough," Matt blurted. "Enough." He shook his head and gnawed on his lips while he squeezed Kathleen's hand.

"Yeah, enough. I just need you to grasp where she might be." She stopped in front of Matt's chair. "If that's where she went..." She stood, not needing to complete the thought. "I'm going to check on the psychiatrist. I'll be in the hallway somewhere if anything changes." She checked her watch. "I expect the sedative will wear off soon. But," she said when Matt's eyes sparked, "that might not be why she's out. She may be choosing to stay hidden for a while."

After the door closed Matt turned to face the bed. He sat in silence for a long time, trying to find the right words to bring her back to him. "Love, we've got a garden to take care of. You need to wake up, because I need your help to do that." He jostled her arm. "Come on, love. Wake up." Matt kept his hand on her arm and began again to read about Max and Nina.

Doctors, nurses, Lisa, Joe, Jess, and Dave all came and went.

Wounds were cleaned. Bandages replaced. Nurses checked her vitals and drew blood. No more sedative remained in her system, but Kathleen refused to join him.

<<<>>>

"You've been reading to her all day. You need to get some sleep," Joe said as the sun lowered in the sky.

"I will. The nurses are bringing me a pillow and blanket. I'm going to curl up in this chair." His voice came out scratchy.

"I can't persuade you to go home and get real sleep?"

"Would you leave?" He looked across the bed at his father.

"No, I wouldn't." Joe sat in the extra chair the hospital had provided earlier that day. "Jess took Lisa to dinner, and now they're in the waiting room. Dave is on his way with food."

"Okay." He started reading again.

"Matt," Joe said after he'd read several more pages.

Matt tipped his head to look at his dad.

Joe nodded at Kathleen.

Matt turned his head to see Kathleen staring at him. Jumping up, dropping the book, Matt found her face with his hands. "Love." He kissed her. "Are you with me?" He tried to read her eyes, but the dim light prevented it.

She answered with a question of her own, "Is she here?"

Matt ran his hand over her cheeks. "Who? Lisa?"

Using her elbows, she lifted up as much as the restraints would allow. "Your friend, *Your Sarah*. Is she here? Is she done yet?" It was then that she noted her restraints. Jerking at them, she crashed her forehead into his, violently pulling at her arms.

Matt clamped his hands over straining arms. "Stop. If you keep that up, we won't be able to persuade anyone to take them off. Dad, get help," he barked over his shoulder. "Kathleen, look at me. See me." He put his face right in front of hers.

She stopped struggling and collapsed back in the bed. She looked around the room, pausing at the IV pole, then at her bandaged hand. Her eyes trailed around the bed until she found him again. "Did you do this on purpose?"

"What? No. God, Kathleen." With wide eyes and a sweating lip, he moved into her space. "I would never—"

"She was right."

Matt pulled his face back as his eyebrows drew together. Still holding onto her arms, he asked, "Who?"

"It was my fault."

Neither Kathleen nor Matt moved. Neither blinked. Matt didn't breathe. He felt the heat rising in his body. Thoughts crashed and ricocheted in his brain.

"I did it," she barely whispered the words, but they seemed to echo and bounce around the four walls. Closing her eyes, she shrank into the bed and rolled her head away from his gaze.

Matt's hands dropped from her arms. He blinked several times but could not bring her into focus. Twisting his hands into the blanket, a living rage moved through him. Closing his eyes, praying he could contain himself until he found the proper outlet, he listened to his heart pound.

"Matt." His father's hand landed on his shoulder. "You need to leave for a few minutes."

Matt shrugged his father's hand off but otherwise did not respond.

"The energy rolling off you needs to get out of this room. Lisa is waiting in the hall."

Matt twisted the blanket tighter. He took deep breaths. He swallowed and bit his tongue. Still his body refused to calm. Shaking his head, he looked down at the form in the bed. Abruptly he dropped the blanket, turned on his heels and stomped out of the room.

Still unable to focus his vision, he plowed into Lisa.

"Matt, what happened? Your dad said she was awake."

His body vibrating with rage, he turned bloodshot eyes to her. Staring into her face, he pulled his right arm back and shoved his fist through the wall.

Lisa took one step backwards. "Better?"

Matt shook his fist. "No." He plowed his fist into the wall a second time. He looked down at his knuckles, disappointed they were not more bloody. "I've never been afraid of myself before." He settled against the wall and slid to the floor.

"He's calm now," Lisa said as she waved off security when they headed toward Matt. "In one word, what are you feeling?"

Matt's head bounced off the wall several times before he answered. "Fury." He dropped his forehead to his knees. "She said that it was her fault."

"Mr. Nelson," Lisa started with a strong and angry voice.

"Don't—" Matt bit out as he looked at her and rose.

"Do you believe—"

"Stop." His voice shook, his body shook. His face dripped

sweat. After shaking his head a few times, he said, "I know she did not do this. That's not what has me so angry. What has me angry is that *she* believes it. That someone I know, someone I used to respect, has convinced my Kathleen she helped hurt her own family. That *I* put her back in that hospital room." With painfully clenched fists, he began to pace in the small hallway, ignoring the stares and worried glances from the nurses. "I don't know what to do with these feelings. I'm angry at her. I'm angry at Sarah. I seriously think I could hurt Patricia. I'm just fucking angry."

"Be angry. Angry is good. Angry is normal. But don't take that anger into her room. Trust me, she has enough anger for all of us."

Matt walked to the far end of the hall, spun, then walked back to Kathleen's door. After he'd completed this circuit six times, he settled against her door and looked to Lisa. "Why would she believe that?"

Lisa took a deep breath and reclaimed her position across from him. "Her nephew called her three times asking for money. It started the summer before. The first time she told Seth, and they agreed not to help him. He had a history of violence and drug use. He called two more times, and again she turned him away. She didn't even tell Seth about the calls." She took one more deep breath before continuing. "The last time he called she threatened to take out a restraining order. Just before Courtney came home for the holiday he contacted her. Apparently he found her through some sort of social media."

Matt's head tilted as his chest tightened. "What did he

say to her?"

"It seems he started off nice. He asked her for money. But Courtney laughed and told him that she barely knew him and didn't have any money, anyway. Eli, her fiancé, testified that he stayed nice but in hindsight he ended their conversation with a threat. According to Eli, he told Courtney to tell her mother how pretty her engagement ring was and that he couldn't wait to see it in person. Kathleen never told Seth. She wanted to get through the holidays without the drama. In her own mind, she believes if she'd told Seth or given the nephew the money this would not have happened."

Matt looked at his left hand, touching the area where a wedding ring would rest.

"Yes," Lisa seemed to read his thoughts. "They took all the rings. Courtney's, Amanda's, and Kathleen's."

Rather than look at Lisa, Matt watched his tears drip onto his hand. "Did they take all—"

"Yes, they took all their fingers. "

The noise in the hallway seemed to fade into silence. The bright overhead lights seemed to dim. Matt's rage melted, leaving him exhausted and bewildered. "I should have guessed. In some part of my mind I just didn't want to see. I didn't want to face it." He raised his wet face to Lisa with a silent plea for rescue, direction. Something. Anything.

"Do you still want to—"

"Don't ask. Don't. I will not have that conversation ever again."

"Okay." Her hand came up. "Don't get angry again. I had to ask. You know that."

"Lisa, what I need from you right now is direction. How do I help her? What do I do *right this minute*?"

"First, go wash your face and your knuckles. Then go back inside. Go back to her side. She's going to try to push you away. She's going to try to climb back in that closet."

"If she goes back in the closet I go, too." He walked toward the restroom. Before entering, he looked at Lisa. "Don't go in without me. I'll be back in two minutes. My dad's with her now. Please just wait for me."

EXPECTATIONS

Kathleen looked over Joe's shoulder, not listening to his words.

"I don't understand," she whispered toward the window, not expecting or wanting an answer.

"Understand what?" Joe asked.

"What I did to deserve this."

Joe moved to sit next to her on the bed. "You didn't do anything. Tragedy lands where it lands."

A tear slipped down her face onto the pillow. "When I first met Betty I found some hope. She reminded me of my best friend, Stephanie. We could be together, with all the ugliness sitting between us, and still find something to hold onto. Betty was like that." She rolled her head so she could look at Joe. "When she didn't come back, I wondered if I'd imagined her."

Joe clasped her hand and moved back to the chair. "Betty could be a force. She came back home with all these plans for you and Matt. I told Matt, and now I'll tell you, her hope for you and for him kept her going, kept her hopeful and happy until the very last."

"Do you think I killed my family like Patricia and Sarah do?"

"No. Patti doesn't think that, either. She didn't understand the situation. She was trying to throw Matt off his game. His confidence has always been a problem for her. I know that doesn't make it right or better. But it was about Matt, not you."

For a long time, the passing traffic, the pumping of the machines, and the quiet voices in the hall were the only sounds in the room.

"What will happen to me now?" Her hand squeezed his and her eyes pleaded with him.

"You have decisions to make. Decisions only you can make."

"I don't know how to make decisions anymore."

"I always told my kids and my employees the same thing. Define the goal. Then all you can do is make one choice at a time to move toward that goal."

Kathleen looked at the darkened sky. "A goal?"

"You had a goal to move to the beach. You did that. Now it's time to define the next goal."

"What if my goal is to have no goal?"

"Then life happens *to* you."

Her eyes came back to his and she dropped her hand from his. "What if life is not my goal?"

Joe collected her hand back in his. He lowered his face closer to hers. "That's not a goal. That's —"

"I miss them."

"I miss Betty, too. Sometimes more than I think I can stand. But that's part of survival. I keep reminding myself what she would want for me. What she would expect."

Her eyes moved back to the window, but she kept her hand in his. "I want to be with them."

Joe gave no response. After several minutes, he started talking about the garden Betty expected them to maintain.

CHOICES

As if walking into a meeting with the IRS, Matt took long, confident strides into the room. He oozed confidence that was not real.

Kathleen's lovely face was turned toward the windows. One hand rested in his father's palm. The other wound through the restraints, pulling the straps taut. If she heard Joe talking to her about flowers, she didn't show it. She gave no indication she heard Matt and Lisa enter the room.

Lisa paused and quietly asked Joe to go find the doctor.

Matt's feet didn't falter as he rounded the bed and placed his palm on her neck. "Kathleen, look at me. Please, look at me." He dropped his face into her neck. "Love, stay with me. Talk to me. Say anything. Just show me you're here." He pulled away, sat in the chair his father vacated. "Lisa's here." He caressed her cheek. "Can you come back to me and let her see your beautiful eyes?"

"Lisa?" she whispered but she did not look in his direction.

Matt stooped so that his face rested in front of her dead gray eyes. "She came in early this morning, or maybe it was yesterday. I've lost a bit of time." He half-smiled, half-teased, before touching his nose to hers. "You are so beautiful."

Her eyes flicked to him before settling back on the window. "Can we get these off?" She pulled on the restraints, sounding as dead as her eyes looked.

After kissing her lips, he pulled back. "We'll have you out of those as quickly as we can." He bent low and picked up the book. Holding the book so she could see it, he said, "Can I see those eyes now?"

Slowly, so slowly, dark gray orbs turned to him. Before she could say anything, his dad and Dr. Vickery walked in.

"Ms. Bridges, good to see you." He moved closer to the bed and Matt felt Kathleen stiffen.

Moving his face closer to hers, he said, "Kathleen, you look at me. Only at me. He's going to do a quick check of everything. You. Keep. Your. Eyes. On. Me."

As shivers began to rock her body and whimpers left her mouth, she tucked her face deep into her neck and pulled herself into the tightest possible ball.

The doctor held up his hands and waited. Joe and Lisa both stepped into the hall.

Matt leaned so that his torso hovered above her, protecting her. Using his palms, he shifted her face toward him. "Kathleen, love. Let's get this done. He'll be quick." Matt turned his head to pointedly look at the doctor before returning his eyes to her.

She blinked, looked at Matt then at the stranger. Her eyes came back to Matt and she started to retreat again.

"Ms. Bridges, allow me to check under the bandages," the doctor said as he moved closer to Kathleen's side.

As if his voice brought her back to the room, she jerked, searched for Matt's face and then clutched at him. "Don't let me go."

Matt let out the breath he'd been holding. As much as he hated the reason she was clinging to him, he was relieved she wanted him, relieved she was back in the present. Pulling back, he said, "I'm going to climb in next to you. You bury your head in my neck and we'll get this done." He forced his body into the small space between her and the bedrails and wrapped her in his arms.

Her bottom lip trembled as she tracked his every move. Once he settled she clutched his forearms as if to keep from drowning.

The doctor inched closer, but when he tried to take her bandaged hand from Matt her body jerked, and her fingers dug into his skin.

"Let him check your hand." Matt peeled her fingers out of his flesh and used his own hand to extend her arm to the doctor.

She buried her face under her arm but she allowed the doctor to remove the bandages from both hands and look at her knees.

"Almost all healed up," the doctor said as he moved his hands toward her head.

"Give me a second." Matt stopped him. "Kathleen, point your eyes at me." He waited until she looked up at him. "He's going to take these bandages off your head. You let him do that and this will all be over." He stared into Kathleen's eyes and then gave the doctor a slow nod.

Her feet began to hop around, but the doctor was quick and thorough. "Good news," he said as he moved away. "I think we can leave all these off. I'm going to send a nurse in to get that catheter out. Then we'll see about getting you out of here."

Kathleen's eyes moved from Matt to the blankets over her legs. "Get it out," she croaked as her bound hands tried to reach the catheter tube.

Taking her hands again, he said, "He's getting someone now. Talk to me. Tell me if Nina ever stops hearing from Charlie."

Her attention remained between her legs and her fingers punctured his arms, but she began to tell him about Charlie and Anna and Brody. When the nurse came in she was so into her fictional world that the catheter was removed without reaction. Afterward, she rested her back against his chest and fell asleep nestled into his embrace.

Ignoring his fear, Matt rested his head on the lumpy pillow, and pulled her more tightly against him, stroking her face until he, too, fell asleep.

<<<>>>

His eyes popped open when he heard the door creak.

"Hey," his father whispered.

Kathleen turned her face to Joe but otherwise didn't respond.

"I brought Chinese food." He lifted the bags and smiled at Kathleen. "Matt told me you like that." He plopped the bag onto the tray. "And the gift shop had the perfect thing." He pulled a scarf out of the bag on the floor. With the flourish of a game show host, Joe displayed a U of M Gopher's scarf. "When in Minnesota," he said. He walked to Kathleen's side, kissed her cheek and helped her cover her head.

"Thank you," Matt mouthed to his father before climbing out of the bed and adjusting Kathleen's bed so she sat straight. He sat on the bed next to her and took a plate from his dad. Finding blue eyes staring at him, he shoved a bite into her mouth. "You look good in maroon and gold."

She tried to touch the scarf but her restraints stopped her.

She looked from the ties to Matt. "Can we get these off?"

"Not yet. Soon, I hope."

Joe jumped in with a running commentary on all the sports news of the day.

After the eighth bite, she said, "You've found a way to get me to eat more than six bites."

Matt grinned then kissed her nose. "Maybe I'll feed you every meal." He placed another bite in her mouth and then ate a few bites of his own. By the time dinner was consumed and the mess cleaned away, Lisa walked into the room.

She nodded at Matt and Joe but went straight to Kathleen. "Welcome back. While I appreciate getting to see Minneapolis, I'd rather do it another way." She winked and gave Kathleen a hug. "It smells funny in here," Lisa said with a wrinkled nose.

"Ginger." Kathleen's eyes focused on her lap. "Chinese."

"You feel up to talking with me for a few minutes?"

Kathleen swallowed and looked from Lisa to Joe and finally to Matt.

"Give us a second," Matt spoke to both Lisa and his father, but he kept his eyes with Kathleen. When he heard the door close, he said, "Talk."

"Lisa," was all she'd say.

"Love, we need help. I don't know if Lisa is the only answer but I do know she can guide us in the right direction." He ran his hand over the scarf. "We *get* to make the decisions. Just talk to her, see what she says. Then you and I can decide what's best for us."

"I can't live there. I can't." A tear leaked down her face.

Matt bit on his lip, desperately wanting to tell her that wouldn't happen but not knowing if he could keep that promise.

"You, you—"

"Shh. I'll be here."

Dr. Vickery strode in before she responded. "Good news, those restraints are coming off." He moved to the bed and with a practiced hand, he made the restraints disappear. "IV comes out next."

Matt immediately climbed back in the bed and tucked his Kathleen between his legs. "I've got you." She nestled down as he wrapped his legs around her body. "Can you tell Dr. Bartlett we're ready?" Into Kathleen's ear he said, "We *are* ready." He kissed her damaged flesh, rested his cheek on hers.

Lisa walked in carrying a plant. "Joe sent this in. He said you'd know what it meant." She took the plant to the windowsill before sitting in the chair. "Kathleen, I'd like us to talk privately. Would that be all right?"

Kathleen's hand came to Matt's arms and held on tight. "Can he stay? I'd rather he be here." If Kathleen noticed the plant, she gave no indication. Instead, she hurried to say, "I can't live there again."

Lisa looked between them, registering Kathleen's tight grip on his arms. "Slow down. Let's start with how you feel right this minute."

"Defeated. Doomed. Half-alive."

Matt closed his eyes against the pain those words caused. He tightened his hold and forced himself to remain silent.

"I won't consider living at that place again."

"I know. Are you willing to come to Charlotte at all?" She looked from Kathleen to Matt.

"Matt—" Kathleen broke off and looked out the window.

"If that's where she needs to be and she's willing to let me be there, then yes," Matt broke in. "We go wherever she needs to be." He shifted around her so they could see into each other's eyes. "I go where you need to be. If you let me."

She swallowed, looking over his features.

"I can find you someone here. The reason I think coming to Charlotte is best is because I already have the history, know the story. If you start with someone new, you have to start all over."

"Start over?" Kathleen asked with a trembling voice.

Matt jumped in before Kathleen became overwhelmed. "We go to Charlotte."

Lisa looked from Matt to Kathleen. "Kathleen?"

Kathleen's eyes were glued to the plant.

"Do you know what that plant is?" Lisa asked.

Kathleen bit at her bottom lip and stared at the blooms.

Matt followed her eyes to see several tall, bright pink flowers that looked like sea anemones. Even taller flowers with yellow and white star-shaped blooms extended above the pink.

"Your mom pays attention. Those are blazing stars and daffodils," her voice whispered.

"What do they mean?" Matt asked into her neck, bracing himself for the answer.

"Seth gave them to me when I first started gardening. He didn't really care about the garden but he'd listen and ooh and ahh. He went on a business trip. The hotel had these in the lobby. He stole them." She emitted a short laugh. "He wouldn't take a pen from the office but he stole this huge, fancy dish garden."

"Do they have a meaning?" Matt asked again.

"The blazing star means 'I will try again.'" Her voice broke, but she continued, "The daffodils represent new beginnings." She tucked her face into his neck and blinked against his skin. A cold tear moved from her face down his chest.

For several long minutes Matt held his Kathleen, rubbing her back as he sent thanks to his mother.

Lisa cleared her throat and said, "I spoke with the director. We can work with you on an outpatient basis. That means you'd spend every day, Monday through Friday, all day at the Center. You'd start at eight and not leave until five."

Matt turned back to Kathleen and watched as her eyes moistened and her lip trembled.

Lisa shifted her attention to Matt. "I'd also like you to be in counseling independently and within a couples setting. There are some classes I'd like you to take."

"Matt," Kathleen whispered, "I can't ask—"

"I go where you go." He tilted her head so she could see his eyes and he could see hers. "If Charlotte is where you need to be and you are willing to go, then we go."

She clasped his hand. "Do I have to decide right now?"

"About coming to Charlotte, no. But, Kathleen, look at me." Lisa waited until both Matt and Kathleen looked at her. "You don't have to decide *how* to move forward. It is time for you to decide *if* you move forward. Do you understand what I'm saying to you?"

Kathleen nodded but did not speak.

Matt's gut clenched as he waited on an answer that did not come. "When could we start?" Matt asked Lisa but kept looking at Kathleen. He squeezed her neck, kissed her forehead. "We *are* ready. My mom made sure of that."

"If Kathleen wants to—and remember, it has to be her choice." Lisa's chair scraped back, forcing Matt and Kathleen out of their bubble. "It's Monday now. Call me in the next day or two. If you decide to come to Charlotte, how about we start two weeks from today?"

"And if I don't come to Charlotte?" Kathleen asked.

"Your choice," Lisa said. "If you want other options, call me. I'll do some research based on your plans."

"And if I don't want other options?" Kathleen's voice sounded like she was negotiating a contract, and that scared Matt more than her dead voice.

"Choices, Kathleen. Life is about choices." Lisa came closer and looked more closely at Kathleen. "In the meantime, will you listen to Matt, lean on him? And"—she turned to look at him—"I need to know you'll watch over her. Until we build her strength, physical and mental, I do not want her to be alone."

"She's my world," he said. "I've got her. I promise."

"Obviously I've already met with the on-call psychiatrist. I'll get you checked out of here. Call me when you know what you want to do. If you come to Charlotte, have Jessica call me. We can work together on a schedule and housing. She told me she wanted to help, and you're both going to have to learn to lean on others for support. Kathleen, stay in a fictional world as much as you need to." She let the door close quietly behind her.

Kathleen pulled back into her ball, but this time she snuggled into him. "What if I can't?"

"It's not a matter of can't. It's not you. It's we. But she's right. You have to decide where hope begins and ends." Matt pinched his lips closed. "No matter what, I love you." He kissed the top of her head.

"I'm scared."

After snuggling her into his body, he said, "Me, too. But we take this one day, one minute at a time. We have Dad and Jess. We have Rosie and Sam, Stephanie and Lisa. I have you. You have me." He held her until the room completely darkened and a new nurse introduced herself.

Matt moved out of the bed and into the chair, keeping a protective hold on Kathleen's arm.

"You'll be discharged first thing in the morning. Let me get this IV out. Unless you need something, we'll be able to leave you alone all night. I've shooed all your visitors home for the night."

After the nurse left, Kathleen settled into the bed and linked her fingers with his. "You don't have to stay here."

"Yes, I do. I wouldn't be anywhere else." He leaned in for a tender kiss. "I want to be here. With you. Wherever that is." He rested his forehead on hers, trying to give her some of his strength.

"Do you think you could get Max and Nina off the floor?"

Matt's stress, exhaustion, and fear burst out of him. He put his face in her neck and laughed. "Yes, love. I'll get Max and Nina off the floor." He wiped the sweat from his lip, settled into the chair and read until he heard her steady breathing.

"Mom, I need your help," he said to the rising moon.

PINKIE SWEAR

"You want to update me?" his father asked as he scraped the bar stool across the floor and sat at the kitchen island.

Matt spun away from the coffee machine. "Dad? You didn't leave her out there alone?"

"She's fine. All good. I showed her where all the fertilizer and tools are. She's listening to a book and putzing around. We've got time. Can we talk about Patti?"

"No, we can't. I get that this is not completely her fault. But I'm too angry, too…" He paused, trying to find the right word. "Hurt. She is so far down my priority list right now."

"She's called me every day."

"I am asking you not to keep her in the loop. I do not trust her right now. Can you do that?"

Joe bit his upper lip and leaned over the granite, getting closer to his son. "Matt—."

"Dad, I am asking you to protect us right now. Even from her. Especially from her."

Joe's shoulders dropped. Sighing heavily, he nodded. "Just promise me you'll make her a priority when you can."

"When I can. But Dad, I need you to know that I'll never

fully trust her with my Kathleen again."

"I understand. I just don't want to lose my family. She is truly sorry."

"She should be."

Joe nodded. He looked out the window towards the greenhouse. "Can you give me a better feel for what's been happening?"

Matt turned back to the hot chocolate and coffee preparation and recited his to-do list. "My condo will become a corporate apartment for NNJ. Rosie and Sam offered to close up her bungalow. If it's okay with you, I'll store my Mercedes here. I was thinking we would drive down in the Escalade. I think we'd enjoy the trip and then I'd have a car for us." The cabinets opened and closed.

Matt's attention shifted between the greenhouse and his task. "I've reserved a suite at the Marriott closest to the Center. I'll find a real estate agent once we're in town."

"Matt, stop. That's not what I meant. Are you—is she—doing okay?"

"It's getting rougher the closer we get to leaving."

"You both look tired."

"We've had two nights in the closet." He stared at the stream of coffee, refusing to look at this father.

"You don't have to be tough for me. Just talk. Let it out."

Matt worked the machine and started Kathleen's hot chocolate. His shoulders slumped and then, as if a pressure valve was released, he began to talk. "We've had some amazing times this week. We've walked miles of the city. We saw parts of the campus I've never seen. I taught her how to Skype and she's enjoyed talking to Rosie about a book they're both reading." He turned, resting his hips against the counter. "It's so fun seeing her when she talks about fictional people or plotlines or whatever." He dropped his head into his chest and stared at the floor.

"And?"

"We've enjoyed watching football. She actually knows a lot about the game. She might yet become a Gophers fan." The words were light and fun; his tone was not.

"That's good. We need fans."

Matt nodded but kept talking as if the words needed to escape. "Shopping was an interesting experience." Matt watched his toe trace the tile pattern on the floor. "She hated it. I hated it. The poor saleslady was confused." He raised his eyes to his father's. "She hasn't mentioned her family again. Not one word. She's back to eating only six bites."

"She looks like she's lost some weight in the last few days."

"I'm sure she has. Those two nights—I couldn't get her to leave the closet until the sun rose. Dad, I promised her there would be no more closets."

Joe walked to his son and placed his hands on his shoulders. "Try not to make promises you can't keep. Only make promises where you have control." He moved around Matt and began making his own cup of coffee. "How did she react to the Christmas package you found?"

"I haven't given it to her. I'm waiting until I can talk to Lisa. After her reaction to Sarah, I'm afraid to drop another bomb on her, especially since I don't know what's in that box."

"That makes sense."

Matt sipped on his coffee, looking again toward the greenhouse.

"She was very excited to get back to the garden. She's planning to leave you quite the detailed list on how to take care of her plants." This time the tone was light and a small smile appeared on his face.

"What is she saying about the move to Charlotte?"

"Nothing. She does beautifully when I give her a to-do list. She's super efficient. I've just been operating as if she's agreed to go. But no discussion. We've gone to the bookstore every day, which seems to settle her. But the boxes and suitcases are like snakes. Every time she walks around one I see her fold into herself before she rallies again."

Both men settled into the seats at the island.

"How can I help?"

Matt rotated his cup around on the granite and let thoughts collide in his brain. He held his dad's eyes. "I never understood how hard it must have been on you to watch Mom suffer." Both men's eyes filled with tears, but Matt kept talking. "Yesterday we were watching one of the games and I felt like Mom was there arguing over a bad call. I felt surrounded by all of them. It was as if I could hear Mom, Seth, and Brice screaming at the referee. As if the girls giggled around me."

Matt relaxed back into the seat, closed his eyes, and allowed images to join his thoughts. "In one of her letters—I don't remember which one—Mom asked me to picture what I wanted in life." He kept his eyes closed as the smile grew on his lips. "She *is* the picture. My family. Her family. You all circle us. But she is the picture. Mom asked me if I've ever fought for anything. I hadn't. But I will now." His eyes opened and he stared directly at his father. "I *am* the luckiest man alive. Privileged to be with this woman. Privileged to be part of her family. Privileged to love her with all that I am."

Matt clasped his father's arm as his smile broadened. "Seriously, Dad, she's the strongest person I've ever known. She's holding those birds back with brute strength and willpower."

"Do you really believe that?"

Her soft, choked voice startled both men. She stood at the entry to the kitchen, her arms wrapped around her stomach.

Joe rose, but Matt halted him with a raised palm. Matt turned her direction, held her gaze but stayed in his seat. "Which part?"

"Do you think Betty and Seth…that they…were with us yesterday?"

"Can you take off your sunglasses, please?" Matt wanted to go to her, to remove the glasses, to collect her in his arms. But he understood the time for choices had arrived.

She removed her sunglasses then resumed her protective position. The dark circles under her bright blue eyes were prominent in her pale face.

He looked into those beautiful eyes, but he still didn't go to her. "Yes, love, I believe we were all together yesterday. I think they're with us every day. I see them in your eyes, in your smile, your laugh." His eyes traced around her scarf, down the left side of her body and back to her eyes. "Your bravery."

Kathleen took two steps into the kitchen and stopped. "Do you think I'm ready? That I can do this?"

"No." The word left his mouth with a bluntness that took them all by surprise.

Kathleen's arms tightened across her waist, her eyes widened and filled with tears. Her left leg started to dance.

"Mattie," Joe whispered.

"You can't do it. I couldn't do it. *You* aren't expected to do it. But *we* can. Together." Matt extended his hand toward her. "Take my hand, Kathleen. We can do this together. You, me, Mom, Seth, my dad. All of us. Let me be your safety zone."

Kathleen looked at his hand then to his face. The refrigerator hummed, the coffeepot gurgled, the thick silence stretched.

"I love you, Kathleen. I'm asking you to choose hope. To take my hand. To introduce me to your family."

Matt's voice faded as Kathleen stood staring but not seeing him. She was afraid to take his hand and equally afraid not to take his hand.

"Take the steps, Marcia," Seth whispered into her consciousness.

Kathleen looked at Matt's hand then to his face. Seconds turned to minutes.

"Mom," Brice's voice joined Seth's. "It's time to move forward."

Kathleen's eyes focused on Matt's hand still extended her direction.

"Please, Mom," Courtney said. "We want this for you. Take his hand. We've got you. I pinkie swear."

A tear slipped down Kathleen's face. She focused on and into Matt's eyes. "Pinkie swear," she whispered before she ran those four steps and landed in his arms. She buried her face in his neck, felt his arms wrap around her, felt his lips grace her damaged body.

"Hold on, love," Matt said. "I've got you. We've all got you now."

EPILOGUE

Seven months later.

"Your dad wanted me to give this to you," Dave said to Patricia as he pushed an envelope her direction.

Sliding the envelope closer, she asked, "When did you see Dad?"

"Open it."

She cocked her head, looked at her husband, and felt dread creep into her gut. Turning the linen envelope over, she saw it was the type of envelope that didn't seal. She looked again at Dave.

"Open it."

Slowly, she moved the flap, removed the card and read the embossed print.

Please join me in celebrating the marriage of my son, Matthew Wayne Nelson, to the beautiful Marcia Kathleen Bridges Conners.

She sucked in a deep breath as tears leaked down her face. Her finger trailed over the celebration details.

"This was two weeks ago." She lifted her eyes to Dave and tried to stop the shaking.

"Yes."

"That's why you and the boys went to Minnesota? Not for a game?" She held the card up. "You went for this," she sobbed.

"We were asked not to tell you."

She nodded with resigned understanding. "He's married." She smiled through tears. "How were they?" she asked, staring at the announcement.

"Happy," he said as he came around the island and hugged her to him. "Happy, Patti. She was beautiful. Seth's family attended. Stephanie stood with her. Everyone's working hard on happy."

With her face stuffed into his collar, she said, "Why didn't you tell me?"

"They asked us not to. He's not ready for you yet."

She pulled back and looked into his sad face. "How do I fix this?"

He ran his hands through her hair, tucked her back in. "She asked about you. She wanted me to tell you she forgives you. It's not her, Pat. It's him. He's still angry and he's not ready to trust you with something so precious." He held her while she sobbed.

After her tears subsided, Dave said, "There's something else. It's on your desk."

Pushing off him, she ran down the hall.

In the center of her desk sat a bright orange Nike box.

Walk with Kathleen and Matt through her healing process in
Journey to Change

Patricia's transformation is uncovered in part three,
Decide to Change

Coming Fall 2018

KATHLEEN'S BOOK ROOM

Kathleen's library is too voluminous to catalog here. But she wanted you to know the names of the books referenced in her story. She and Matt stay busy traveling, gardening, and laughing. Together they are filling new photo albums. She still manages to read about two books a week and in every one she finds messages that help her open up more and more. You can contact her at the author's webpage (www.juneconverse.com) for recommendations and to see what they are reading right now. Happy reading ~

The Mountain Man series by Kristen Ashley:

Nina and Max are featured in *The Gamble*.
Laurie and Tate are in *Sweet Dreams*.
Lexie and Ty's story is found in *Lady Luck*.
Faye and Chace find happiness in *Breathe*.
The other books in the series (*Jagged, Kaleidoscope, and Bounty*) are also wonderful.

Rachel and Gabe are part of Susan Elizabeth Phillips' Chicago Stars series. Specifically they are featured in *Dream a Little Dream* but Kathleen loves anything written by SEP.

The Bat is part of Jo Nesbø's Harry Hole series. Kathleen still reads each new novel featuring the somewhat broken detective.

Of course, *Pride and Prejudice*'s author is the unmatched Jane Austen.

Mr. Darcy Takes a Wife is by Linda Berdoll.

Half-Broke Horses is by Jeanette Walls.

The Henry VIII novel mentioned was likely by Philippa Gregory as Kathleen has all her books on a shelf.

Dragonfly in Amber is the second book in the Outlander series by Diana Gabaldon. This is Kathleen's favorite historical fiction series.

Rosie mentioned the Vince Flynn series starring Mitch Rapp. The first book is *American Assassin*.

1984 by George Orwell and *The Handmaid's Tale* by Margaret Atwood are also mentioned.

Last, but not least, several quotes are from Louise Penny's Armand Gamache series. In Matt's discovery of Kathleen's quotes, he has found Louise Penny's books are often covered in yellow highlighter. Because of that, and because the people of Three Pines make Matt smile, he has read every book in this series and anxiously awaits the next installment.

Matt's also reading several books that Lisa recommends. Those are listed on the website.

ACKNOWLEDGEMENTS

They say writing is done in isolation. That may be true but this novel would never have been accomplished were it not for the following people – all of whom I cannot thank enough for helping me bring Matt and Kathleen alive.

Beta readers took their precious time to read my initial draft and provide comments that helped me to create deeper characters and a better story. Thank you Deborah Anderson, Kari Converse, De Culver, Misty Harper, Mary Eve Iwicki, Joan Pressman, K.D. Proctor, and Lisa Vincent. And, of course, a special thanks to my husband Dave who helped me understand Matt's mind and behavior.

My Pathfinder's Group who kept me going with encouragement and challenges that reframed my fears. (www.meredithwalters.com)

Eliza Kirby, editor extraordinaire (www.reedsy.com)
Vanessa Mendozzi, cover design (www.vanessamendozzidesign.com)
Sandra Girouard, website developer and social media expert, (www.pecanmediaservices.com)
Photographer Mary Claire Stewart, www.maryclairephoto.com

It's impossible to name and thank all of the therapists and mental health professionals who have helped me understand my own trauma and supported me as I developed strategies to create a wonderful life. But, I'd like to particularly thank Pegah

Moghaddam, Psy.D., for her ongoing support and her willingness to push me to accept myself as I am.

An extra special thanks to my family who unknowingly contributed their personalities, their quirks and their experiences to this novel. You are my world!

ABOUT JUNE

June happily resides in Sandy Springs, Georgia, with her husband, Dave, and their dog, Sodapop. They have two wonderful adult children and two grandchildren. She is an enthusiastic exerciser and an accomplished cook. She and her husband enjoy hiking with Sodapop, traveling, scuba diving, trying new restaurants, concerts, and whatever other adventures they can find. Reading and a constant desire to learn keeps her busy too.

A trauma survivor who struggles with mental illness, June is continuously reaching for hope like the characters in her books. She openly discusses her personal struggles on her blog, **JuneConverse.com**

Decide to Hope is her first novel and relies a great deal on her own experience with trauma, choices, recovery and hope. If you'd like to discuss trauma, coping and recovery, contact her at **JuneConverse.com** or **DecideToHope.com**